Karl has a unique story.

From being the most awarded advertising creative in Australasia, to professional wrestling heavyweight champion of New Zealand, to completing a Masters in Creative Writing, to writing the first three books in his thriller series, The Truth Files.

Karl is 'the body-slamming adman-turned-author.'

**Become a Truth Seeker today
and discover more of the Truth.**

Sign up to become a Truth Seeker and receive bonus short stories set within the world of Justin Truth, as well as behind the scenes snippets, audiobook chapters (complete with author's commentary), plus loads more exciting stuff—all exclusive to Truth Seekers.

Truth Seekers are the first to hear about Karl's new books, scripts, and publications. And you never know, your name could appear within the pages of the Truth Files one day.
Truth File enthusiasts have been known to make appearances within the pages of his books...

See the back of the book for details on how to sign up today.

Also by Karl William Fleet:

Novels
The Truth Files series:
01: Corporate Truth
02: Criminal Truth
03: Fractured Truth

Coming soon
Emily and the Missing Mansion, a young adult fantasy novel.

Short Films
Signs
Jet Black
Consequences
Finders Keepers

For Cathy.
You make me a better person.

CORPORATE TRUTH

BY
KARL WILLIAM FLEET

Chaos 360

COVER DESIGN: COTTONWOOD STUDIO

FILE ONE:
CLIMBING THE LADDER

CHAPTER ONE

THE SUN FORCED its waves of sticky heat between the mighty buildings of New York City. The air was alive with clanking construction, blaring horns, and the swirl of voices. The masses escaped their skyscraper catacombs and flooded the labyrinth-like streets. Feet walking, bouncing, dodging, stepping, running, in all directions. Kelly Elliott's were among them.

For this lunchtime trek, she'd traded her work heels for a trusty pair of Adidas trainers. To give her legs slightly longer strides, she'd hitched up her black hemline skirt. She had thirty minutes to get from work to the bank and back.

"Babe, I'm leaving now," she said, cupping her phone to her ear, fending off oncoming commuters with one shoulder.

"You sure you don't want me to do it?" Derrick asked.

"I'll be fine." Kelly rolled her eyes.

"I heard your eyes," he teased.

She laughed. "Babe, it'll only take me twenty minutes, tops." Last night she'd canceled their joint credit card after seeing extravagant purchases made in Germany on their statement. Neither she nor Derrick had been to Germany, ever.

"Are you sure? I don't mind."

"It's closer for me. I got this. Look, babe, coming to the subway now. My phone will cut out—call me later?"

"You know it!" Derrick slipped in his new catchphrase.

"Love you ... you know it," she replied.

"Love you more than you know it!" The phone cut out.

She hated to ride the subway, that's why he'd phoned her, to take her mind off it. He was always thinking about her. It was one of the things she loved about him.

For the last five years, she'd worked in reception at the Benjamin Hotel. She loved the job, the people, and the company. Her only problem: the wandering eyes of married men. Part of her job was to be cute, bubbly, and inviting to all guests. She was good at it. Maybe too good. At least once a day, a transient Romeo would flash her a smile with a hopeful glint in his eye. They would flirt, and tell her how cute she was, and invite her to join them for a drink once she finished work. Some were more direct and would ask if she wanted to fuck. She'd learned to act a little timid, excited, and flattered, as if they were the first to have ever propositioned her. Then with a quirky smile and a subtle tap on her wedding ring, she would send them on their way with their egos still intact. Derrick was the man in her life, and all the man she needed.

Kelly put in her earphones to drown out the surrounding noise, cranking up the music to relax. She bounded down the subway entrance stairs with her Metrocard at the ready and checked her watch as she passed through the gate. She was making good time. The less time spent in the subway, the better.

Ahead, she noticed an elderly lady chatting away at a black pug in her arms. The old dear was resting in the middle of the walkway, slightly hunched, and dolled up with what looked like a year's worth of make-up. Another commuter looking at his phone, and not where he was going, knocked into the old woman, causing her to drop her precious pup. As soon as the pug's paws touched the ground, it was off, its rainbow-colored lead trailing behind it. The dog whipped between Kelly's legs, its slobbery tongue hanging out the side of its mouth. Kelly spun and leapt. Her foot stomped down on the lead. The pug grunted as it came to a sudden halt. She picked up the wayward dog and received a multitude of licks for her trouble.

"Here you go," she said to the old lady.

"That's not my dog," the lady replied. "I did have a cat once, it was ginger. I have always wanted a dog. If I got one, I think I would get one like your dog. I'd call him Sparky."

Kelly checked the pug's name tag. It read SPARKY. She gave it back to the confused lady.

As she descended down the downtown escalator, she could feel the air getting thicker, denser, and warmer. Soon she was engulfed by the New York subway's unique sickly, stale smell of stagnant human sweat. It made her want to vomit. It wasn't so much the smell as the idea that she was breathing in other people's dirty secondhand air that freaked her out.

As she reached the platform, she saw the back of her train pulling away—she had missed it by mere seconds. A man in tweed coughed as he bumped past her. She imagined that she could see his phlegmy bacteria particles float into the air, to be inhaled by those around him. She covered her mouth and stumbled away.

A helpful LED sign informed her that the next train was six minutes away. Six very long minutes. The crowd grew thicker, like the air. Knowing she couldn't miss this train, she was determined to get to the front of the platform, thinking the air would be better there. Any vacant spot she saw, she slipped into. Any space that opened, she squeezed through, skillfully making it to the front. She stood tall, defending her spot, like an Amazonian warrior.

A whoosh of air signaled the imminent arrival of the next train, prompting people to jam closer together. Kelly held her prime position, using her elbows to keep people from closing in on her. She leaned ahead and looked down the track, willing the train to appear. A light emerged from the mouth of the tunnel, causing the corners of her mouth to curl up. Not long now.

She felt two hands on her lower back. Not gentle, not tender, not timid, not friendly, and definitely not welcomed. She shimmied to lose them. The hands remained. She pulled away from them. The hands found her again. She swiped at them. The hands held on.

Kelly had had enough. This creep picked the wrong girl, on the wrong day, at the wrong time, to fuck with. She applied her patented angry-bitch face, the one Derrick had nicknamed Medusa. In full Medusa mode, she spun to verbally assault Mr. Creepy Hands. She didn't see him at first, as he was squatting, making himself lower than the crowd around him. He looked up at her from beneath his trucker cap, grinning like a naughty schoolboy. Then he winked and shoved her. Hard. She reached out to grab at anything to save herself. She felt nothing but the incoming thundering train. The force of the impact exploded Kelly's body like an iron anvil dropping on a balloon full of red paint.

The train's brakes hissed as the screeching steel rumbled to a halt. The cabin doors slid open automatically. A disembarking businessman stopped in his tracks—a screaming woman covered in Kelly's blood was blocking his way.

CHAPTER TWO

JUSTIN TRUTH HAD ARRIVED.

He stood in his new office surrounded by his new toys, staring out over his new Manhattan view. On a clear day like today he could see as far as Liberty Island. He breathed it all in. It was exactly what he believed he deserved. He caught his reflection in the glass. His newly imported StrongFit shirt emphasized his gym-hardened physique. He tensed his bicep to stretch the fabric.

He strolled around the expansive room. It was perfect, just as he had requested. He had worked with the designer personally to get it just right: the couch, the carpet, the lamps, even the pantone of tint on the panoramic windows.

He now worked for Soda-Cola International. An American icon, a soft drink company people had grown up with. Once the largest soda company in America, it had slipped over the last decade into the bottom of the top five. Justin was going to get Soda-Cola back to number one.

Waiting for him on his custom-built KBH desk were fifty-two folders, one for every brand he was now responsible for. He would go through them one by one, line by line until he had a strategic plan on how to make each brand more profitable.

He made himself comfortable in his De Sede chair, then removed the top file from the stack: OrangeFizz. He placed it in front of him, unopened. He stared at the '80s-inspired orange logo and gently stroked the faded scar on the right side of his face. The scar ran from his temple to just above his cheekbone, a remnant of an incident from his late teens. A memory that had often returned to taunt him and remind him to think smarter. Massaging the blemish was an unconscious habit he'd acquired while deep in thought.

Justin opened the OrangeFizz file. It was the biggest of his new brands and a good place to start. He spread out the paperwork and inserted the accompanying flash drive into his MacBook Pro. As he waited for it to open, he felt something wasn't right. He lifted the laptop, checked it out from different angles. There was a faint fingerprint on the W button. In his contract, he had specified that his equipment was to be out-of-the-box new, without exception.

He checked the preferences and found no obvious traces of activity. Yet that feeling of something being wrong persisted. He accessed the internal coding and discovered the laptop had been reformatted three days ago, at 4:56 p.m. That confirmed it for Justin. The only reason to strip the hard drive would have been to erase evidence of previous use. He stared at the W. Then it clicked. He knew why the laptop had been reformatted: William Munroe. Carlton had hired the contractor to cover while Soda-Cola waited for Justin to start. It would have been during that time that William's grubby little fingers had desecrated Justin's computer.

Justin called Guy Chambers, the head of Soda-Cola IT.

"*Hello,*" a voice greeted him. "*We are really busy, so if you tell me your problem after the beep, I'll get back to you as soon as humanly possible. . . Beep.*"

It wasn't voicemail, just a monotone voice.

"Hi, this is Justin Truth. I have a question about my computer."

"Turn it off and on again, and that should fix it. Next time, could you dial the IT helpline number."

"I haven't even told you my problem!" Justin shot back.

"I'm sorry, that is usually the answer. Let's start from the beginning. Is your computer on?" the voice asked sarcastically.

"Is this Guy Chambers?" Justin said.

"This is Guy Chambers at your service, princess. What's your problem? Is your computer not working, or can you not find the printer? Look, Justin. Can I call you Justin? You are new here, and all National Marketing and stuff, but I'm the head of Soda-Cola IT services. My team services thousands of computers. I'm not your personal IT man. So, it would be super nice of you if you could phone the helpline, log your problem, and we'll process your request as soon as we can."

Justin took a deep breath.

"Look, Guy. Part of my contract specified that all my computer equipment was to be brand-new. My computer is not."

"I'm sure it is. Look, I have other problems at the moment, like trying to stop the server from crashing. I'll look into it soon-ish." With that, Guy hung up.

Justin held the phone for a few seconds, listening to the dead dial tone. He rubbed his scar, then made another call.

Debbie, his PA, answered. "Hi, Mr. Truth, how can I help?"

"Debbie," Justin instructed, "Go down to IT, and get Guy Chambers for me. Bring him to my office right away."

"So, you have spoken to Guy, yeah? He doesn't leave his office, Mr. Truth. Can I get someone else?"

"No, it has to be Guy. And if you can't convince him, you're fired."

Debbie giggled. "Nice one."

"That wasn't a joke. If you don't get him into my office in ten minutes, the very first thing I'll do as national marketing manager for Soda-Cola North America will be to fire you. Hope that is clear." Justin hung up. He was going to sort out this IT prick, then OrangeFizz, and then the entire company.

CHAPTER THREE

EIGHT MINUTES LATER Justin's office door swung open. A man Justin assumed to be Guy Chambers stormed in with a frustrated expression, his cheeks puffing in and out under his scruffy beard. The man adjusted his Black Flag T-shirt over his portly belly as he penguin-marched to the computer in question. Guy spun the laptop around so he could see the back of the machine. He looked at a sticker and spoke.

"Just as I thought, this is brand-new. The little sticker confirms it." He turned his head to the door and his body followed.

Justin stood. "Guy! Don't touch that fucking door. And sit the fuck down."

Guy stopped. This wasn't the first IT tyrant Justin had dealt with. He scanned Guy up and down, reading his entire life story by his dress sense, grooming, and job title. Justin knew Guy wouldn't be used to people talking to him in this manner. Normally it would be he who sneered at people and dictated terms to them as to when and how things would get done. When it came to computers at Soda-Cola, Guy would see himself as the master of the universe. But he had never encountered someone like Justin before, someone who was a true master of his universe. And within Justin's universe, Guy was nothing but a pathetic atom.

Then Guy did what Justin knew he would, something he wouldn't have done in a long time. He did what he was told and sat down.

"This is not new," Justin said.

"Yes, it is."

"Don't lie to me."

"I'm not lying."

"So, William Munroe never touched this computer?"

Guy's eyes flicked to the MacBook and back to Justin. This told Justin he was right, that William had used this computer for the three weeks before his arrival. And it was likely Guy who'd given it a factory reboot.

"Now, Guy. You don't know me," Justin continued. "But you are about to learn some valuable life lessons. Let's call this Lesson One: Don't fuck with me.

"Lesson Two: Know your role. I have worked with a lot of people like you, Guy. Jumped-up geeks who have no power in real life. Inside a corporation like Soda-Cola, you get a taste of power, you like it. You get a little more, it's even better. All of a sudden, people need you, they kiss your ass to stay on your good side. This is your turn to bully people, just like you were bullied at school. It works most of the time because the average person will put up with your bullshit as long as they can open emails, print files, and look at their Facebook page. I am not your average person, Guy. I am not one to be disrespected, and you will do as you're told."

Justin picked up the laptop, opened it, then snapped it in two over his knee, ripping the keyboard away from the screen. He casually dropped the two bits onto Guy's lap.

Guy opened his mouth to speak. Justin slapped him hard across the face.

"Fuck!" Guy squealed. "You slapped me!"

"No, I didn't," Justin said. He continued. "Lesson Three: Do what you are told. Now, you will have a brand-new laptop on my desk in sixty minutes. You will answer my calls to IT personally. You will tell people I'm the best thing to happen to Soda-Cola. You will do all this because you want your life to be easy. You want your life to be comfortable. And the easiest way for that to happen is for you do to everything I tell you. You mess with me, you lose everything. Do you understand?"

Guy nodded reflexively.

Justin changed his tone to sound soothing and empathetic. "Good. Lesson Four: Get rewarded. Now I see you are wearing a wedding band. Do you have kids?"

"T-t-two," Guy stuttered, now looking totally frazzled.

"When was the last time you took your wife to a five-star restaurant?"

"Never." Guy stammered, confused.

"There is an amazing restaurant downtown called The Red Plate.

You can't reserve a table, but the owner knows me."

Justin pulled out a few hundred-dollar bills from his wallet. He placed them in Guy's hand, and closed it for him.

"Now, you go buy your wife the biggest bunch of flowers you can find, hire a babysitter, shave, maybe even buy yourself a shirt and tie, and take her to The Red Plate tonight. Tell the maître d' you're friends of mine. The entire meal is on me."

Justin returned to his desk and the file, focusing on the pages in front of him. Guy got the message that he was to leave. He meekly made his way toward the door. As his hand touched the handle, Justin spoke.

"Now, Guy, what have we just learned from our lessons?"

"Don't-don't fuck with you?" Guy replied, hoping it was the right answer.

"Yes, and it's better to be on my good side, and to not be a little bitch. Because Guy, bitches get fucked. And the last thing you want is for me to fuck you."

CHAPTER FOUR

JUSTIN Justin added the final touches to an email on his brand-new MacBook Pro that Guy had personally dropped off.

To: Carlton, Curtis
From: justin.truth@sodacola.com
Subject: Day One!

Morning Carlton,
Once again, thank you for the opportunity. This is an amazing company and I can only but try and make you proud. You made the right decision in giving me the job. I have a thousand ideas running through my head about how to take my brands to the next level. I am here 24/7 for you and the company.

PS: In six months, OrangeFizz will outsell LemonGreat. Just don't tell Steve.

Justin.

He read it twice, then hit Send.

Justin rubbed his scar, thinking. He had a theory about starting with new companies. It wasn't about him starting a new relationship, it was about everyone else ending an old one. He had to be clear up front that his way of doing things was now the only way, and he'd get rid of anybody who disagreed. Justin had sorted out Guy. Now it was Debbie's turn. He picked up his phone and hit Debbie's extension. It rang six times before she picked up, three too many.

"Hi, Mr. Truth," Debbie said, with a flat tone.

"Debbie, can you join me, please."

Sixty seconds later, forty-five seconds too many, Debbie waddled in, a fake smile plastered across her face. Justin read each step she took and could already tell that she was going to be spiteful and bureaucratic because of his earlier actions.

"Sit down, please." Justin gestured toward the couch opposite the windows.

When Debbie sat, her feet just reached the floor. She flipped open her notepad, pen at the ready, and grinned extra hard to show she would take notes. She clicked the pen eight times, seven times too many.

"Now, Debbie," Justin started. "I think we need to get a few things straight. I think—"

"Yes, sir." Debbie's tone was sarcastic.

"Never interrupt me while I'm talking."

"Yes, sir. Should I write that down?" Debbie clicked her pen. "Do… not… interrupt."

"The smartest thing you can do right now is listen. Any more smartass comments, and you're fired. Try me."

Debbie shifted her weight on the couch, her lips trembling.

"I didn't hire you," Justin continued. "I know you've been here for thirteen years, working your way from reception and into a prime PA position. Soda-Cola likes to keep people. Debbie, I need someone I can trust. Can I trust you?"

She nodded.

"By getting Guy here in the time you did, you proved to me that you know how to get things done. I like that. Which means I'm going to like you. Do you want me to like you, Debbie?"

She nodded.

"Did you see Guy's face when he left? Have you ever seen him run away like that with his tail firmly between his legs before? Don't think so. I am like no one you have ever met, Debbie, and I'm giving you the opportunity of a lifetime. Are you ready for your life to change for the better?"

Debbie nodded even more.

"Do you like to gossip?"

Debbie paused her nodding. Her eyes flicked to the floor and back to Justin.

"I want you to," Justin nodded, encouraging Debbie to start nodding again. "I can't be everywhere. You'll be my eyes and ears. If people are talking bad about me, you bring me a list of their names with the details of what they've said. I want info. If you find out anything, whether it's juicy truths or just vague rumors, I want you to log it into a file for me. I want to know the dirt on everyone—who cheats on their partners, who leaves work early, who takes home stationery, who is fucking who, which little power groups are hatching secret plans behind closed doors. Anything they don't want other people to know, I want to know."

Justin paused. He'd been using his body language to subtly manipulate her. Making her nod was a simple technique to open her up to suggestions. Now it was time to close the deal.

"I know how much you get paid, Debbie, and if you were to lose your job, it'll be tough for you to get another one right now. If you do everything I ask of you, I'll double your salary."

Debbie's eyes opened wide and her body flinched as if she'd just received a small electric shock. It was the reaction Justin had expected. She was hooked.

"How can you do that?" Debbie asked. "Finance would never approve a salary increase like that."

"I will pay you out of my own salary, Debbie. That's right, I will give you money directly from my own funds. You won't be taxed. It'll be a monthly bonus that will just appear in your account."

Debbie's eyes glowed; she looked skyward. Justin could tell by the dreamy look in her eye that she was already spending the extra money in her head. She was his.

"Do we have a deal, Debbie?"

She nodded like a bobblehead, revealing several chins.

"That's great." Justin grinned. "Now go to your desk and get to work. By the end of the week I want a list of everyone who works here, and any dirt you can gather on them. Now I'm sure I don't have to tell you that what we have just talked about stays between us. If I hear so much as a whisper, I will rain a living hell down upon you like nothing before. You won't just be fired, you will never work again. I will take personal pleasure in making sure you end up destitute and living under a bridge, giving blowjobs for pocket change. Do we have an understanding?"

The woman nodded greedily. "I'll start right away. I know a few things already to start the list with." She got up, and practically skipped back to her desk.

Justin returned his attention to the OrangeFizz file. In the eighties, the drink had enjoyed massive success, but over the last fifteen years, sales had slowly declined. Its main competitor, SummerCrush, had made large inroads, taking half of its growth directly from OrangeFizz.

Justin searched the OrangeFizz list of employees for the advertising agency assigned to look after the OrangeFizz account. Their number was on his speed dial.

"Hello, R and R Advertising," a voice purred. "You're talking to Sophie."

"Hello, Sophie. This is Justin Truth from Soda-Cola. Can you please ask Donna Southland to call me immediately?"

"I'll make sure to pass on your message, Justin."

He hung up. Getting OrangeFizz back on track was going to require a bit of work. From the notes left behind, they were quite far down the track in developing a new campaign with R and R. The campaign was big, and Justin was surprised at how much of the OrangeFizz advertising budget had been allocated toward it.

Justin opened a webpage for Mother's Milk, an independent advertising shop working out of Las Vegas. Justin liked the work they were producing, and their reputation of disliking large, multinational, award-hungry agencies. Agencies like R and R.

"Hello, Mother's Milk. How can I help you?" a voice asked on the other end of the line.

"Yes, can you ask your GM to call Justin Truth at Soda-Cola?"

"Will do, what is the number, please?" the voice inquired.

"If he can't find it, he's not worth me talking to," Justin hung up.

It was only 10:12 a.m., and his day was just getting started.

CHAPTER FIVE

CASUAL LEATHER LACE-UPS aren't the best for running, yet Detective Ross Smith was flying in them. His eyes darted around Brownsville and the buildings he knew so well. This trip to Brooklyn was initially to follow up on a case; he wasn't expecting to be sprinting through the alleyways, chasing down a fourteen-year-old punk in LA Lakers gear.

The skinny kid ran quickly, but not as quickly as he could have because his basketball shoes, like the rest of his clothing, were a few sizes too big. His long legs powered him around a tight corner and toward the main road. With the skill of a linebacker, he ducked and weaved around people, holding the stolen handbag under his right arm. He knocked over some overfilled trash cans behind him to create an obstacle course for his pursuer.

Ross rounded the corner seconds later, jumping over the fallen trash cans. He yelled at the kid to stop, knowing it was a waste of time. His nicotine-stained lungs heaved in pain with each and every gasp of air. The taste of last night's whiskey returned to his throat. His leg muscles screamed at him to stop; he told them to shut up and move faster. Ross thought about discarding his three-quarter leather jacket, to stop him from overheating, but the thought of not ever finding it again made him keep it on. He loved that jacket.

The kid took a hard right toward Betsy Head Park. Even though it was the middle of the day, the park was busy. The kid glanced over his shoulder at Ross. The grizzled detective was keeping up. The kid leapt a fence encircling the outdoor exercise area. His foot clipped the top and he tumbled through the air, crashing onto his front, skinning his knees and knocking the wind out of him. He groggily pulled himself up and ran again, with a slight limp.

The teenager's clumsy fall helped Ross gain some ground, just not enough to grab the kid. Dashing across the road, the kid forced a passing car to skid to a halt. The driver honked furiously and yelled as Ross slid across the hood.

The kid ducked down another alleyway. Ross overshot the entrance and kept running straight. He knew that particular alley looped back to the main road. If he got to the other end first, he could cut the kid off. Each step sent anguish reverberating around his body as he pushed himself harder.

Ross reached the second entrance and turned into it. He was right. The kid skidded to a stop as he saw Ross barreling toward him. The kid was breathing hard. His darting eyes stopped on a tall wooden fence separating the alleyway from a back lot. He jumped onto a large trash can, leapt to a nearby dumpster, and sprang toward the top of the fence. His fingers grasped the railing, pulling himself up in one swift motion. Within seconds he was over the edge and scrambling down the other side.

Knowing he wouldn't be able to climb as nimbly as his prey, Ross threw himself at the fence, twisting in midair so that his back would connect with the long wooden boards. He hoped he wouldn't bounce off and land in a heap on the wrong side of the fence. He didn't. His body crashed through. Chunks of wood went flying. Ross slammed into the kid. Both went down. Ross recovered first and yanked the purse thief up by his basketball jersey.

"You little punk!" Ross panted.

"Fuck you, old man!" the teen snarled. "Eat a dick!"

"No, fuck you, and fuck you for making me run, and fuck you for making me have to deal with you. Do you know how much paperwork I'll have to do after I drag your ass into the station, and for what?" Ross snatched the handbag, and hit the kid on the forehead with it. "For a handbag worth twenty bucks. Fuck, you're dumb."

"Watch your mouth, Grandpa."

"Shut up! Mrs. Anderson's eighty, you little punk."

"That your girlfriend? That's gross. You into granny porn?"

Ross grabbed the kid by the ear and twisted it. The kid squealed.

"Come with me," Ross ordered.

The first stop was Mrs. Anderson's. The kid reluctantly apologized, so Ross twisted his ear a few more times until the apology sounded more sincere. Once Ross was happy, they continued walking in silence until they reached their next destination.

"This ain't no cop shop," the kid said, his eyes widening.

They stood at the mouth of one of the toughest streets in Brooklyn.

"Yes, you're right. No cop shop here, and you aren't going to find many cops walking this street." Ross pushed the kid in front of him. "A friend of mine runs a business of sorts here. He loves this city and is on a mission. See that wall over there, covered in dirt and graffiti? Here's what you're going to do. You're going to clean and paint that entire wall. And once you're done, you will paint it again. Each day you will come back, and if someone's tagged it, you will repaint it. If you decide that you don't want to paint that wall, well, see that guy sitting over there, the one with gold teeth and Just Fucking Die tattooed on his chest? That's Rocko. This is his street and he is that friend I was telling you about. You will report to him until he's happy that you've learned your lesson. If you don't do it, I'm not going to come down and drag you to the station. That massive fuck is just gonna beat the living shit out of you."

The kid froze on the spot, unwilling to take another step.

"You know Rocko?" Ross smiled. "Yeah, of course you know Rocko, everyone knows Rocko. Then you know that you don't want to be on his bad side. Hell, being on his good side is scary enough. Lucky for most, he's found God and wants to do good in his community. That doesn't mean he's a squeaky-clean Christian. Nah, he's more your Old Testament type."

Ross shoved the kid toward Rocko and his crew.

The kid slowly approached them, shooting quick glances back at Ross.

"Have fun." Ross waved.

CHAPTER SIX

JUSTIN SAT ACROSS FROM STEVE BARKER and ordered two porterhouse steaks, medium, with a salad, no dressing, and no fries. Double the protein and none of the carbs. Steve took his time, rubbed his hand over his clean-shaven face, and made a clicking noise in his mouth as he flicked through the menu a few times before deciding on the tomato soup. The young waiter smiled, commended their choices, and disappeared just as their drinks arrived.

"So, buddy, how long have you been with Soda-Cola?" Justin asked as he raised his glass to a toast. "Any tips you can give me would be great."

"Let me think, I started six months ago." Steve laughed. "That's how it feels anyway." Justin joined him with a fake laugh to create a bond between them.

Steve was the brand president of Soda-Cola North America. He was going to be Justin's main competition when Carlton stepped down as CEO in a few years, or at least that was the rumor. Steve was respected and well-liked within the industry.

Steve took a sip of his diet Soda-Cola with a splash of whiskey. He had a strong jawline, and his face was deeply tanned from weekends at his Hamptons beach house with the family, which made his pale blue eyes appear even bluer. A few wrinkles were becoming prominent, and his light brown hair had a sprinkle of gray at his temples. It looked good on him, made him look distinguished.

"It's such a great place to work," Steve continued. "They really look after their own. I just kept my head down, worked hard, and slowly got moved up the ranks. I worked with a lot of great people. It's really like a family, and once you embrace that, you'll love it as much as I do."

"Sounds perfect to me," Justin nodded.

"It is. People love Soda-Cola, Justin. When they hold one, it brings them wonderful memories. They can see we're a family company, with family values. In my time at Soda-Cola I have—"

Justin's phone started to vibrate. It was a number from out of state.

"Sorry, Steve," Justin interrupted. "My mother isn't well, and her caregiver calls me at all times of the day. I have to take this."

"That's fine, Justin. Family is important, and should always come first."

Justin left the table to find a quiet spot.

"Hello?"

"Justin Truth?" a deep voice asked. "This is Sandy Miller from Mother's Milk."

"Glad you could get back to me, Sandy." Justin was impressed by how fast Sandy had responded, faster than Donna from R and R. "Do you know why I called Mother's Milk?"

"This is your first day at Soda-Cola, so you're figuring out who will help you make a difference. You've gone through your roster of advertising agencies, and have worked out that they're not Mother's Milk."

"R and R Advertising are highly awarded, Sandy," Justin replied. "One of the best in the world."

"The best at what? Blowing smoke up their own ass? Sure, they won some awards for a charity TV spot, and a print ad for a washing powder that they paid to run themselves. They don't care about moving product, they care about paperweights for their shelves. You are a smart man, Justin. Someone your age doesn't get the job you have by being stupid."

Justin liked what he was hearing. Sandy sounded like a bulldog, and a bulldog in the right hands was a lethal weapon.

"I think we need to get together," Sandy continued. "See how Mother's Milk can be the solution to all your problems."

"Sounds good," Justin replied. "When are you in New York next?"

"I'm at the airport now, waiting to board a flight to come see you. How about I take you out for a few drinks tonight, and we can chat some more."

Justin knew Sandy wasn't at the airport, but having the balls to say that he was impressed him.

"Done. See you tonight. Text me when you arrive, and I'll let you know where to meet me."

"Deal," Sandy said. "Talk soon."

Justin ended the call, spotted the waiter who had taken his lunch order, and waved him over.

"Hi, chief," Justin said. "How far off is lunch?"

"I think it's just ready now, sir," the young man replied.

"Look." Justin placed a fifty in the waiter's shirt pocket. "This guy I'm having lunch with is someone I want to impress. I think he would get a real kick if I brought out our meals."

"Of course." The waiter winked. Moments later, he returned with their lunch on a tray. As soon as Justin was alone, he ducked into a restroom cubicle with the soup, pulled out his cock and dribbled a small stream of piss into the thick red goo. He gave it a few stirs with the head of the toilet brush, then returned the bowl to the tray.

Justin approached the table, balancing, on the palm of his hand, a tray holding their lunches, as a waiter would, to amuse Steve. The way his face lit up, Justin succeeded.

"Just something I prepared earlier." Justin grinned as he served Steve his tomato soup. Steve dipped his spoon into the red fusion and fetched up a warm sample. He gave it a gentle blow before tasting it. He licked his lips to show Justin it tasted mighty good. He devoured the rest from his spoon with a hearty slurp.

"You are one amazing cook," Steve said with a wink.

"It contains a special ingredient." Justin winked back. "Soda-Cola love."

CHAPTER SEVEN

THE GIANT GLASS DOORS of Soda-Cola automatically opened for Steve and Justin as they returned from lunch. They showed their identity cards to the security guard and made their way to the executive elevators. A woman caught Justin's eye at reception. The first thing he was drawn to were her Kardashian curves, and then when she turned toward them, her dark eyes made his jaw clench and his cock harden. He didn't know her name, but this goddess was going to be his. He could already picture her bent over reception as he fucked her from behind, pulling her long dark hair as she moaned with pleasure.

Steve pushed the button for the elevator, and Justin willed the dark-eyed beauty to join them. She approached the men and stood next to Steve as the doors opened. Justin moved to the back of the elevator so he could take in her body in more detail. Her Christian Louboutin heels made her calves pop, highlighting her toned legs. Justin's eyes traveled higher, to the fitted red dress that started halfway up her tanned thighs, hugging the rest of her body. The neckline, what Justin was really interested in, showed just a peek of her healthy cleavage.

The goddess pushed the button to the fortieth floor. Justin saw no wedding ring. He made a mental note to himself: find out what the people on that floor did. As the doors closed, Justin checked himself out in the elevator's mirrored walls to adjust his pout. He had worked on it over the years, perfecting the natural movie-star look of a certain Mr. Pitt.

"Hi, Steve," she purred, flashing a smile and ignoring Justin.

Steve smiled back. "Hi, Montana. Hope you're having a great day."

Justin raised an eyebrow. *Oh Montana, it'll be a nicer day with those lips wrapped around my cock.* He waited for her to turn and check him out, but she didn't, and continued talking to Steve.

"We need to catch up later and talk about the activation idea for

LemonGreat."

"Sure…" Steve was about to continue but suddenly stopped and grabbed his stomach.

"You OK?" Montana asked, placing a hand on his shoulder.

"I feel a bit queasy," Steve replied with a pained expression on his face. The elevator stopped at the twenty-third floor and a man got in. He pressed twenty-four. Steve looked exasperated at the impending one floor stop-off. It amused Justin how the short twenty seconds between floors pained Steve so much. He would be, no doubt, clenching his sphincter to stop himself from shitting his pants. The elevator door opened and the man got out. Steve hit the Close button multiple times and the elevator continued.

At level forty, the doors opened again. Montana carefully looked at Steve.

"I'm fine—let's talk soon." He stood tall, ignoring the gurgling gremlin in his stomach.

"OK, take care," Montana said hesitantly as she left.

"Have a good one," Steve replied through gritted teeth.

Justin stole a last glance at Montana as she disappeared out of sight. When the doors closed, Steve doubled over. "Man! Are you OK?" Justin said, faking concern. Steve didn't respond. He seemed to be concentrating way too hard on not shitting his pants.

The doors couldn't open fast enough for Steve as he bolted to the bathroom. Justin strolled to his office with a smirk.

As soon as Justin was behind his desk, he opened the staff directory and looked up Montana. There was only one person by that name: Montana Cruz. He found her on Facebook. Her timeline was restricted to her 434 friends, but lucky for Justin she hadn't made the photos she was tagged in "private." He hungrily scrolled through them, took a few screenshots of his favorites, and placed them into a separate folder.

He gave her a quick Google search, too. Then he got Debbie on the phone. "Debbie, what do you know about Montana Cruz? Any info you can get."

"Sure thing, Mr. Truth. Will get right onto it."

CHAPTER EIGHT

"TWO BEERS," Ross gestured to the bartender. "And a shot of house whiskey. The real stuff, not that watered-down dishwater you give students."

"It's always the real stuff!" the bartender barked back.

"Tell that to the judge."

"Hey, Judge! How's your drink?"

An old guy at the end of the bar looked up and smiled, oblivious. His faded blue eyes were warm and welcoming. He nodded, unaware of what was actually asked of him, his days as an actual judge long forgotten at the bottom of a glass.

"Never gets old, that one." Ross smiled and hit back the shot, warming the back of his throat before sliding the empty glass back along the bar for a refill.

Sugar Bar was the regular watering hole for the cops from Ross's precinct. It was dark, smelled of decades of spilled beer, and played '80s rock. The mixture of assorted furniture represented fights that had broken out over the years. *If you break it, you replace it* was a rule everyone followed. A tightly wound collection of alpha males meant fists, and the occasional body, were often thrown. Which led to the next rule of Sugar Bar: *Anything that happens in Sugar Bar, stays in Sugar Bar.*

Tonight, patrons were in good spirits to wish Detective Lucas Donald all the best on his promotion to Amityville. He'd been partnered with Ross for just over a year. In that time, Lucas made sure he received the credit for all the cases they'd solved. Yet, for all the drive Lucas had, doing the hard yards to actually put the pieces together wasn't his strong point. He was a numbers person, whereas Ross was a gut person.

Ross hit back the second shot, grabbed his two beers, and headed for his regular table, exchanging a few grunts and nods with fellow law enforcers along the way. He plonked himself on a stool and dropped his beers on the table; six coasters sat under one of the table's crooked legs to balance it. He knew it was going to be a big night. He downed half a beer as Lucas slid into the seat across from him.

"Ross, glad you could make it, means a lot."

"Wouldn't miss it for the world, kid."

"This could've been your promotion. All those cases we worked, we did it as a team. I told everyone how good you are. You're the yin to my yang, man. You would make a great sergeant."

"No, I wouldn't. Can't see me being nice to people up there in their ivory towers. Can you see me on a golf course, drinking ice tea and eating cucumber sandwiches?" Both men laughed. "Those people give me the shits."

"Well, I'll put in a good word for you, if you like, once I get to my new precinct."

"Not for me. I'm happy for you, Lucas. I want to be promoted as much as I want an apple tree growing out my ass. You have the drive, the fortitude and the determination. I'm happy where I am. I help where I can and make a difference to people who may not get it otherwise."

"You really are old-school."

"I was old-school before old-school was a thing. Now don't make me bitch-slap you in front of everyone. Go get drunk, make a stupid speech, and get home in one piece. Go make me proud."

CHAPTER NINE

JUSTIN SHUT HIS LAPTOP. His Patek Philippe showed him it was 8:33 p.m. His mind raced over what he had achieved on his first day. Not bad, he thought. He'd put some cogs into motion, with a few more planned. His phone vibrated as he received a text.

> Hey Justin. Sandy here.
> Just landed.
> Where do you want to meet?

Justin replied.

> De:Tour on 34th Street.
> 10pm. Tell them you're meeting
> me, or you won't get in.

Justin put away his phone and pushed himself away from his desk, the chair gliding along the floor. It was time to leave. His position gave him unlimited access to Soda-Cola's own corporate drivers. He'd decided to use them sparingly, as he didn't like the idea of having some low-level Soda-Cola accountant keeping tabs on all his comings and goings.

Outside the front of the building, he waved down a cab. As one indicated to pull in, another cab cut it off to get to Justin first. Justin jumped into the aggressive driver's cab, and the original cab tooted its horn in protest.

"Where to, my friend?" the cabbie asked in a thick Indian accent.

"Six-sixty Third Avenue."

"The Luxor Apartments! Ohhh, nice. I have never been inside, but from what I hear it's a total fuckin' pussy pad." The driver stroked his salted mustache. "You, my friend, must be making serious fuckin' cash to be living there. Maybe you could be giving me some tips."

He handed Justin his business card, while pulling back into the busy traffic. It read DAN THE CAB-MAN, with his cell phone number in bold. The card felt cheap in Justin's hand.

"Call me twenty-four-fuckin-seven, my friend. Best cab driver in all of New York City. On the clock, or off the clock, as long as I can make as much as you, yeah buddy!"

"You don't look like a Dan," Justin remarked as he put the card in his wallet.

"I changed it, my friend. Reyansh the Cab-Man didn't sound as good." Dan laughed. "Also very good it make me more American, and America is now my home. Love America, my friend. Home of the brave." Dan adjusted his rearview mirror so he could look Justin in the eye, his head nodding from side to side as he talked.

"You like the pussy, my friend? Of course you do. Man like you, I bet you eat heaps of the pussy. You look like that very handsome man in the movies. What's his name, Brad Pitt? Very sexy man. Not that I like men. I like women. Women's pussy. Me, I'm married to a beautiful woman. Given me three beautiful children, my friend. I love her, but I get bored of her pussy. It's a nice pussy, just a man needs new pussy. And not just the pussy, isn't that right my friend? You know what I am talking about. You like to put it in the asshole? I have done that a few times. Not my wife, not the mother of my kids, you know. But a man has needs, my friend, and sometimes a man got to go and get what he wants. Not tell the wife. Ha ha ha. I can tell you know what I mean, my friend."

"All I can tell you is that I get what I want, and if you can name it, I've had it," Justin said off-handedly.

"Shit, my friend, you are one bad motherfucker!" Dan the Cab-Man grinned.

During the rest of the trip, Justin enjoyed listening to Dan recount all the females he'd paid to have sex with, and what he'd asked them to do. The Luxor Apartments came into view. Dan drove onto the sidewalk, beeping at pedestrians to get out of his way so he could get right outside the front door.

"Not sure this is a parking lot?" Justin remarked.

"Please, mister sir, anything for man like you. You is very good, good special."

Justin smirked. He was entertained by the shabbily dressed cabbie. He pulled out his wad of notes, snapped out a Benjamin, and dropped it on the passenger seat like a candy wrapper. Dan's smile widened, revealing a missing top front tooth.

"Very, very special. Call me any time, my friend!"

Justin strutted up the steps leading to the exclusive Luxor Apartments. In 2005, billionaire property mogul Donald Luxor had the 1920s fabric factories converted into high-end apartments. There were a hundred and twenty apartments split over ten floors. A story later surfaced that Luxor had kept a number of apartments for himself to house his extramarital girlfriends. At one stage, all five of them lived here on different floors. Whoever he felt like, he got off on that floor. It was one of the reasons Justin had paid heavily to secure a penthouse apartment here. The building was designed for security and secrecy.

There were three entrances, two that everyone knew about. One of these was through the double glass doors out front, and the other one was through the underground parking garage. The lesser-known entrance, nicknamed the Donald Door, was only whispered about. It was an old service entry that looked welded shut and had to be accessed down a side alley. It was usable if you had the iron key. Donald was rumored to have used it when visiting his harem.

On the top floor were four penthouse apartments, three too many for Justin's liking. Each was state-of-the-art with keyless entry. You could enter with a thumb scan on the door handle, or by keycard. On the elevator ride up to his apartment, Justin pulled out the cheap business card.

"Dan the fucking Cab-Man." He laughed.

He went to tear up the card, then decided to keep it instead. The elevator doors opened, and three steps in, a neighbor's dog started yapping. It was a sound he'd heard every day since he took up residency. He grabbed his apartment's door handle, but before his thumbprint granted him entry, he was assaulted with a sound even worse than the yapping. His neighbor had flung open his door.

"Ohhh! Hello, Jussst-in. Busy day? I had such a wonderful day myself. Mmm."

The voice belonged to Bill Hampton. He wore a loud yellow shirt with matching pants and held his prized miniature poodle, Mr. Noodles. Bill had never worked a day in his life, and years of indulgence had made his small frame portly. His thinning hair was bleached blond, short, and spiky. Bill had lived in the building since it opened and was now the president of the Luxor's Homeowner's association. Nothing happened here without him knowing about it.

Justin forced a smile. "Yes, very busy. Now I must rush, Bill. I have an important business meeting I'm very late for."

"Ohhh, business. I love me a bit of 'businesss.' Mmm."

Justin tried to open his door, it was still locked. He adjusted his thumb.

"If you ever need me to, oh I don't know, help you put on your shirt, you just call out and I'll be right over. I'm an expert at dressing, and undressing men. I have great tassste. Don't I, Mr. Noodles?" Bill pursed his lips, and Mr. Noodles started to lick them.

"No, I'm fine. You have fun with Mr. Noodles, and we'll talk soon." Justin smiled as he escaped into his apartment and shut the door behind him.

CHAPTER TEN

JUSTIN ARRIVED AT DE:TOUR at 9:43 p.m. The line was already fifty people long. De:Tour was one of the newest, hottest clubs in town. The only way to get in was through Block, a six foot seven Tongan who worked at the door. Justin walked to the front of the line, ignoring those already waiting.

"If it ain't da Truth, da whole Truth, and nothing but da Truth!" Block greeted Justin.

"My man! How's tricks?" Justin stepped in for a bro-hug, slipping Block two folded hundred-dollar bills. Justin never waited, no matter what club he went to; he always made sure he got on the doorman's good side through the use of cold, hard cash.

"Mr. Truth, tricks be keeping me on my toes. Waiting on da call from Dana White any day now."

Justin slapped Block on the arm. There was nothing but solid muscle under his skintight black T-shirt.

"You are the main event," Justin winked. "I've got a business partner coming soon. Can you let him in? He's a bald-headed-looking bastard."

"You know it!" Block grinned, pocketing the cash while opening the door.

Justin soaked in the jealous stares from those waiting, then a tall, leggy blonde with a slightly shorter male companion caught his attention. He slipped Block another crisp Benjamin.

"Blonde in the blue dress, VIP room. Let them both in and after thirty minutes, kick the dickhead out. I'll keep her company."

"And ain't dat the truth," Block showed a mouth full of large gold-capped teeth.

Justin made his way to a premium booth in the VIP area, nodding to a few regulars. As soon as he was seated, a hostess appeared.

"The usual?" she asked with a sultry smile.

"When are you going to throw this in and run away with me, Brooke?" Justin asked.

"Oh honey, maybe this weekend," she crooned. Justin flirted with all the women at De:Tour but never followed up. This was too good a hunting ground to muddy the waters by screwing one of the workers. He'd made that mistake before.

"Then I may need to drown my sorrows," he teased, turning on his best puppy dog eyes.

"Whiskey sour on its way," Brooke blew him an air kiss. Justin leaned back in the booth and scanned the scene. He always sat in this booth, as it was highly visible to people outside the VIP area. Justin enjoyed the stares from people who longed to be where he was.

He checked out his fellow VIPs. In one corner booth was the guy with the famous sisters who had their own reality TV shows. Justin couldn't remember his name, but he did want to fuck two of the man's sisters, especially the eldest. Montana reminded him of her a little.

Brooke delivered his drink. It was perfectly presented, just the way he liked it. Out of the corner of his eye, he spotted Sandy arriving. He'd seen his picture in a few advertising magazines, and it was hard not to notice his closely shaved, round, bulldog head. Sandy moved his head with quick sniffing movements as he scanned the club for Justin.

Justin turned slightly so that Sandy was out of his line of sight. Sandy was going to have to search for him, work a little to be allowed into his distinguished company. Moments later, the bulldog sat across from him, unbuttoning his suit jacket and adjusting his tie.

"Mr. Truth!" Sandy Miller exclaimed with an outstretched hand.

"Mr. Miller," Justin replied. "But please, call me Justin."

"Now, what are you drinking and how many would you like?" Sandy asked.

"Sandy, you have flown a long way to buy me a drink. Why are you here?"

"You know why I'm here," Sandy replied bluntly. "I'm here to do business. And I'll do what it takes to not go home empty-handed."

Justin grinned. This guy was a shark, and was proud to show it.

"Mother's Milk is one of the fastest growing agencies in the world," Sandy continued. "It's not because we win more awards than anyone else. It's because we are hungrier than most. It's because we make shit happen. We sell product. We don't live in a creative bubble. You won't read it on our website, but at the core of our business we believe that consumers are fucking idiots. They don't know what they want. They're millions of fucking dollars in debt, so what do they do? They go and buy a big-screen TV on twenty-percent interest so they can save themselves money by not going to the movies. Does that sound like someone who isn't an idiot?"

Justin nodded. He let Sandy rabbit on with his sales pitch as his eyes kept wandering over to the blonde in the blue dress taking a seat at a high, round table. She was holding hands with the guy Justin saw her in line with. She was visually excited. Her boyfriend was acting all cool, like it was because of him. Justin liked how she smiled. He liked her.

The blonde's eyes lit up even more as Brooke placed a bottle of champagne on their table along with two glasses. The blonde held up the bottle and took a selfie with it. Her boyfriend claimed the bottle, inspected the label, and poured them each a drink. They clinked glasses and she kissed him on the cheek. Justin glared at her boyfriend, she could do so much better.

"—that's why we should work for you!" Sandy finished his sales pitch. He looked happy with his delivery. Justin took a sip of his drink, pondered his answer.

"What do you think of the word 'cunt'?" Justin eventually asked.

"It's powerful."

"I took this Australian model home last week, in my room, got her naked, was about to fuck her. The norm. She pushed me off her, slid up the bed, rested her back on my headboard, looked between her spread-open legs, then told me to 'get that wet cunt.' Now I like the word 'cunt,' just not when I'm fucking. I see a cunt as an insult. Where when I fuck, that's a gift. So, you know what I did?"

"What?" Sandy asked, lacing his fingers together, rubbing his sweaty palms.

"I flipped her over, lubed her up, and fucked her in the ass. Left that wet cunt alone. No one tells me what to do."

"Teaches that cunt for being an asshole."

"I like you, Sandy." Justin grinned. "When you get back to Vegas, I want you to brief your creative guys to do a campaign for OrangeFizz, with a focus on family values. I know that's not new, but I want you to talk safety; the motto being that giving OrangeFizz to your kids is looking out for their safety. There is so much bad shit out there that parents can't control. What you can control is your child, and your child is safe while drinking OrangeFizz.

"That's your brief. You were never here. This conversation never happened. When the time is right, you will fly out and present this campaign. It will feel like a cold call. That presentation will be the first time I officially meet you, and see the work.

"Soda-Cola spends a ridiculous amount of money on advertising," Justin continued. "Getting to be a rostered agency is like winning the lottery, and I'm giving you a loaded ticket. If you play your cards right, you will make a lot of money, but to get this money you will have to invest time and energy, without billing me for it."

Sandy gave Justin a wink and smiled. "So, are we going to get fucked up?" he said, dropping a small plastic bag of cocaine on the table.

"You see that blonde over there?" Justin motioned. Sandy swiveled his large head toward the couple getting cozy over a bottle of champagne.

"Yeah, what about her?"

"I'm going to fuck her tonight. You can catch the next flight home, and get to work."

CHAPTER ELEVEN

IT WAS GAME TIME.

Justin sat sipping his whiskey sour, monitoring the blonde in the blue dress. He made sure he was always in her line of sight. On the odd occasion their eyes did meet, Justin returned a friendly smile. He was known in the club for dropping large amounts of cash, which made him popular with the regulars. As usual, they stopped by his booth to chat, hoping Justin would buy one of his famous rounds. The revolving circus around him was exactly what he wanted the blonde to see: he was important, people wanted to be with him.

Finally, Justin saw what he was waiting for; the blonde's boyfriend left her side and headed toward the bathrooms. Justin gave Block the signal. Block nodded, then turned to follow the young man, grabbed him by the scruff of the neck, and lifted him up. The young man's toes danced along the floor as Block headed to a back door.

"What?... Who?... Stop!" were all the words he could get out as Block pulled the young man's phone and wallet from his back pockets, and threw him down onto the cold, dirty concrete in the back alley.

"Listen up real good, boy!" Block growled. "You be banned. If I so much as smell you, you be dead!"

"Wha, what?" the young guy stammered.

"Be dead, niggah." Block took the cash from the wallet and pulled the battery from the phone. He threw the cellphone at the guy. It made a light *donk*! sound as it bounced off his skull. His wallet quickly followed and skimmed past him like a UFO. Block slammed the door with a bang.

Block swung behind the blonde giving Justin the thumbs up. Justin waited ten minutes, then chose his moment and approached her while she was sending a text. She was frowning.

"Something the matter?" Justin asked.

"I'm fine," she replied.

"You don't look fine. One thing my mother always told me is that you can never leave a damsel in distress. And you seem a little…"

"Stressed?"

"You do. I'm good friends with the people who own this place. I could help."

"Um, it's my boyfriend. He went to the bathroom a while ago, and hasn't come back."

"Have you phoned him? Sent him a text?" He sat across from her.

"Yeah, no answer," she said with concern in her voice.

"That's strange. I know I wouldn't leave someone as stunning as you alone for too long."

She went a slight shade of red, his compliment had the desired result.

"What's his name?"

"Louie."

"Wait here, I'll go and ask around. Shouldn't take long." Justin stood up and gave her his best smoldering look. "What's your name?"

"Jennifer." She smiled.

"Jennifer." Justin found her even more attractive than before. She was the type of girl who didn't know how hot she really was. "That really is a beautiful name. It suits you."

Justin moved next to Block, watching Jennifer as she played with her drink while checking her cellphone. She glanced around nervously. When it appeared that she might go look for Louie, Justin made his return, placing his hand on her shoulder, sitting next to her.

"Jennifer, I wish I had good news. You see that mass of hulk over there?" Justin pointed at Block. "He kicked Louie out. Your boyfriend was caught getting a blowjob in the restroom from some nasty… hooker. She's been caught before sneaking into the men's room to do favors. From what I'm told, he was balls-deep down her throat. What a jerk! I'm sorry. Why would someone do that when they have someone as beautiful as you on their arm?"

Jennifer's face angered.

"He did what?" She went to stand but Justin placed his hand on her shoulder and guided her back to a sitting position.

"Take a big breath, Jennifer." Justin's hand firmly held her shoulder. His eyes firmly held her gaze. "You don't deserve that shit in your life. He's the one that's fucked in the head." He topped up her glass. "Don't let him make you the crazy one. He's crazy."

"I want to… punch him right in the dick!" she sneered.

"That's a good start. But don't leave here angry. Can you please do me a favor? Would you make my night by having one drink with me?"

"One drink." She picked up her glass. "And then I'll have to go."

"And punch him in the dick," Justin said, and got a laugh for his joke. He lifted his own glass. "At least I can now say I had a drink with the prettiest girl here."

During the night, Justin made sure the drinks kept coming, and the compliments kept flowing. It seemed Jennifer was having such a great time that she forgot all about going to look for Louie. If she even peeped at her phone, Justin swept her to another part of the club to introduce her to more fabulous people.

One was Justin's personal trainer, Angus Diaz, who told him about a smaller club called the Bull Bar where the judges of *American Idol* were going to be. If they wanted to go, he was leaving in three minutes and could get them free entry. Justin looked at Jennifer with a raised eyebrow as an invitation for her to join them. She nodded enthusiastically.

Soon they were sitting one table away from the *American Idol* judges, drinking and hanging out in Justin's world, a world he knew Jennifer had only seen on TV. One of the judges had eight girls surrounding him, all half his age, and was encouraging them to kiss each other for his entertainment. Justin kept a close eye on Jennifer while reading the subtle changes in her face. She wasn't as open as she was earlier in the night to his hand on her leg. Her troubled face told him she was remembering that she was still in a relationship and would be thinking she needed to sort things out with Louie first. Justin was right, she switched to water in an apparent effort to sober up.

Jennifer excused herself from the table. Justin watched her leave, then looked at his watch; it was about to hit one a.m. He knew it was time to go. He had another full-on day in seven hours. It was time to speed things up. He reached into his pocket, took out a small capsule, pulled it apart, and tapped its contents into Jennifer's water.

In college, Justin had spent much of his free time researching and teaching himself basic chemistry. In fact, he'd been the go-to guy for the best-quality pills on campus. He didn't want to be a dealer, but if he was going to get high, he wanted to trust that what he was taking was quality. Also, being the guy with access to 'quality' drugs made sure he was invited to the right parties. He swirled Jennifer's water until it was clear, placed it back on the table, and called Dan the Cab-Man.

"Dan, it's Justin. Yes, from earlier tonight—the Luxor Apartments. I need you to pick me up. There's an easy hundred in it for you. I'm with a lady friend. It doesn't matter where she tells you to go, just take us back to my place, the long way. I'm at Bull Bar, see you in ten minutes." He hung up as Jennifer returned and he watched her down her water.

"Hey, I think it's time to go," Justin said. Jennifer gratefully nodded.

* * *

Fifteen minutes later they were both sitting in the back of Dan's cab. Jennifer slouched on the backseat. She forgot for a second where she was and how she got from the club to the cab.

"Drop this beautiful young lady off at her place first, my good man," Justin said with a smile as he looked at her. She smiled back. He made her feel so special.

"Ok, pretty lady, where would you like me to take you?" Dan asked Jennifer in his thick accent, as his head bobbled from side to side.

"Do you know where. . . West is? West 136th and Jackson Street is?" she asked.

"Very good," Dan replied. He adjusted his rear-view mirror, and winked at Justin.

Jennifer went to say thanks but found she didn't have the words. The world was starting to blur around the edges. Justin leaned over and gave her a kiss. She kissed him back a little reluctantly. She liked him, but was still in a relationship with Louie.

She was tired. Her head light. Where was Louie?

Lights moving window. Justin was nice.

She and Louie. Boyfriend. Home was good. Bed soon. Sleep. Talk. Louie.

Home. Where? Jackson Street. Bed.

Jennifer closed her eyes.

CHAPTER TWELVE

JENNIFER OPENED HER EYES.

She was in bed, but not her bed. Her eyes swam around the room, taking it all in. Her head was sore. She ran a hand through her hair. She felt her body—it was naked under the sheets. *What did I do?* She asked herself.

"Morning, sexy," a man said as he walked into the room wearing a suit and tie. He sat on the bed and kissed her cheek. "I have to head into work. There's some coffee, fresh fruit, and muesli in the kitchen if you want some. Stay as long as you want. My place is your place. When you want to go home, give this guy a call, and he'll pick you up, and charge it back to my company." He wrote a number on the back of his business card. Jennifer took the card and gave him a weak smile.

When she heard the front door close, she jumped out of the strange bed and gathered her clothes. She never did this, she had to get home, where was she? Jennifer peeked out into the rest of the apartment. It was like a show home she'd seen in design magazines. Everything was white with highlights of black. All the appliances were stainless steel and looked hardly used. The floor was polished concrete. It felt cool under her naked feet as she wandered about. She stopped in front of a giant oil painting. It was taller than her, and as wide as her arms spread out; the background was a gradient of gray with red handprints on it. She placed her hand over one of the red handprints, wondering what it all meant. Like his other belongings, she thought, this painting was probably worth a fortune.

Jennifer poured herself coffee and put a few pieces of sliced fresh fruit on a plate. She sat on the white leather couch and gazed out at the city, admiring the stunning view of Central Park. Her head was still sore from the drinks she had last night, and she felt ashamed about going home with this guy she'd only just met. She and Louie were still an item, and she wasn't quite sure what to tell him. She checked her phone. No calls, no texts from him. Maybe something had happened to him? Maybe he went home with that hooker-blowjob-slut.

Jennifer checked the phone number on the card Justin had given her, but then put it back in her clutch purse and decided to catch the subway home. She slipped her shoes on, then caught her reflection in a mirror; her blue evening dress wasn't exactly train-travel attire. On second thought, she pulled out the card again and called the number. Fifteen minutes later a cab was waiting for her at the front of the Luxor Apartments.

"Good morning, Miss Jennifer!" Dan smiled as she got in.

"Hi," Jennifer replied, slightly taken aback by the cab driver's personal approach. "Do you know where West 136th and Jackson Street is?"

"Yes, of course. We were on our way there last night, until you changed your mind." Jennifer's mind then clicked; this was the same cabbie from last night. "You are one very lucky lady, Miss Jennifer. Justin is such a wonderful man."

Jennifer placed one hand on her aching head. "I can't remember much of our ride home last night."

"Then it's lucky that I am here. I remember it very, very well, beautiful lady. We were on the way to your place, and you keep going on about a guy called Blue-wee."

"Louie?" Jennifer interrupted.

"Ohhh yes. A Lou-ie. You were very mad at him. Say a lot of things, some I could not repeat back to you. Halfway there you demanded I must turn cab around, and go to Justin's place instead. He told me to keep driving to your place. Then you opened the door, and said you would jump. He couldn't argue, so he gave in to what you wanted."

Jennifer couldn't remember any of this, or how she had gotten herself into such a state.

Dan continued. "Justin is top man, you are very lucky. Lots of ladies want him, but he is looking for someone special. He told me that you were something very special."

The cab driver pulled up outside Jennifer's apartment building where she shared a two-bedroom unit with a girl she worked with. She got out and thanked Dan for the lift. As the cab drove off she saw Louie sitting on the steps of her apartment. He looked angry.

"You're OK!" Jennifer said in surprise as she approached him. Louie got up and stared at her coldly.

"Look, I just want to get my stuff and fuck off," he muttered, sounding upset. "I never want to look at you, or hear from you again!"

Jennifer was confused. "What did I do? You're the one who got kicked out of the club for paying some hooker for a blow job!"

"What?" Louie yelled. "I got kicked out for no reason. The fucking bouncer pulled my phone apart, and ripped out the battery, then took all the cash I had! I couldn't get back in or contact you. So, I waited outside but you never came out. I had to hitch all the way back to my place. I was lucky I had a spare phone battery at home."

"So why didn't you call me to tell me you were OK?" Jennifer pleaded. She could see that he was fighting back tears now.

"Well, when I turned it on, I had a load of texts from you asking where I was. But it was the last few that I couldn't understand, and the video you... you sent." He handed his phone to Jennifer. There was a video of her, sent from her phone.

"Louie, you fuck!" she slurred in the video. "You wanted your cock sucked by that whore, this is how you suck a cock." Jennifer placed her hand over her shocked face as she watched footage of her giving Justin a blow job.

A tear rolled down her cheek. She was so mortified, lost for words. All she could do was to run inside and cry.

CHAPTER THIRTEEN

ROSS ROLLED OUT OF BED.

Before his feet touched the floor, he had a cigarette in his mouth and a lighter ready to go. He took a deep drag, then opened his eyes and his world came into focus.

Ross was the first to admit that his life hadn't turned out the way he'd expected, but shit happens and he'd gotten used to his pile of it. His tiny hovel was your typical one-bedroom shoebox, with worn patches of carpet and a sink full of every single dish he owned. The whole building had seen better days. He'd seen better days. They were a perfect match.

Ross turned on the sink tap and was greeted with the friendly sound of rattling pipes coughing out rusty brown liquid. He let the brown water run freely and turned to the most loved item he owned, an industrial Elektra coffee machine that he'd picked up from a police auction a few years ago. It was large, cumbersome, and bulky, but the dented, polished machine made the best coffee he'd ever tasted.

He ground some coffee beans in a grinder to extract the exotic flavor. The building's water pipes stopped rattling and started clanking, and clear water spluttered from the tap. He collected the water in a rounded glass jug. When he heard a deep 'clank,' he withdrew the jug as the rusty brown liquid spurted out again. He had timed the building's crappy plumbing down to a fine art.

He poured the clean water into the machine, tightened the portafilter, hit a button, steamed some slightly outdated milk, combined the two liquids, and moments later he was savoring a steaming brew out of a classic metal travel coffee cup.

Ross headed back into his room and threw on some clothes. Black pants, white shirt, and gray tie—same as yesterday, same as the day before, and same he'd be wearing again tomorrow. He inspected his face in the bathroom mirror, deciding that he could go another day without a shave, maybe two. He downed the rest of his coffee in a single gulp before returning to the mirror. His hair was more gray than brown these days. Better gray than nay.

He had another cup, then put on his trusty three-quarter jacket. Time to go to work.

Ross was fifty-two and had been a cop for twenty-eight years. He had seen a lot of changes in that time, but the one thing that hadn't changed was the cruelty that people inflicted on each other. He'd seen it grow, which made him sad for humanity as a whole.

Ross was good at what he did, except for the politics, which he found pointless. Politics was a game for younger men. Men who craved power, men like Lucas. As long as his paycheck cleared each week, Ross didn't care who he reported to; he didn't have the fortitude to put up with the bullshit.

"Bullshit" was a word he often heard from his daughter. She was in her early twenties, lived close by, but they weren't close. Not as close as Ross would have liked. He couldn't blame her mother for how she acted, though he would like to. She had grown up without him around, and she often reminded him that was his "bullshit decision." That he'd put other people's bullshit before them.

He'd never cheated on her mother. Sure, they never got married. But he was loyal in that way. He loved her. He loved them both. He may not have been the best partner, but he wasn't abusive. He just wasn't around to show he loved them. One day they moved out, he wasn't sure what day. He just remembered it was a dark day.

Ross's biggest problem was that he found it hard to say no to people, and he'd often forgo his own responsibilities to fix others' problems. If someone wanted a drink, he would say yes. If they wanted to stay out till five a.m., he would say yes. If they asked if he could drive them to Canada to visit their long-lost cousin, he would say yes. He liked to help and liked to be needed. He would've had a happier home life if he knew when to say no. It was this habit of always saying yes that made Whiskey such a close friend during the hard times. Whiskey liked Ross, and he liked Whiskey. Their friendship had cost him countless days of foggy memories. Those days increased the longer he was alone.

On the way to work, Ross stopped at Joey's, a small vendor who sold a bit of everything, and for Ross, that was breakfast. He was a regular, and Joey was expecting him. Before he even asked, Joey had two packets of Marlboros, a cream-cheese bagel with ham, and a packet of jelly beans ready to go.

"Joey!" Ross bellowed as he walked closer. "Keeping your nose clean?"

"The cleanest nose in all of New York. Yous gonna stop the crime today?"

"Why would I want to do that? I'd be out of a job."

Ross placed one pack of smokes in the inside left jacket pocket, and the other in the right. The jelly beans went into the outside lower bottom right pocket, landing on some empty jelly bean bags he always forgot to throw out.

He took a big bite out of the bagel. "This covered?" Ross asked with his mouthful. Every few weeks Ross would give Joey all the money he had in his wallet and trusted Joey to keep track of it. It was a good system.

"Yous all good man. Yous good until next Thursday, I'm thinking."

"Great, same time tomorrow? Thinking bacon," Ross smiled.

"I'm thinkin' yous have whateva I make yous."

A short train ride, and even shorter walk later, Ross was sitting at his desk. It was covered in piles of paper and case files. For the last ten years, Ross had a revolving door on partners, as he wasn't the easiest to get along with. He knew he was stubborn, but most of the guys they sent him were so wet behind the ears they needed towels around their shoulders. Most of the cases he worked on were the open-and-shut kind. It was normally the most obvious suspect. People were stupid. It was the paperwork that was a killer.

Ross was a classic two-finger typist; he pecked away at the keys slowly, and it took him a painfully long time to fill out the most basic forms. Learning to type faster wasn't on his list of things to learn. Walking the streets and busting bad guys, he had all the time in the world for that. That was his world.

CHAPTER FOURTEEN

IT WAS 10:38 A.M. as Justin and two members of his OrangeFizz marketing department, Craig Conway (brand manager) and Clare Davidson (assistant brand manager), arrived at the office of R and R Advertising. The building was ultra-modern in a cool part of Tribeca. The front of the ten-story building was a digital interactive game of Snakes and Ladders.

Justin pushed open the door and entered the building first. Craig grabbed the closing door, holding it open for Clare. Justin's pace slowed as he noticed the blonde sitting behind reception. His eyes zoomed in on her and her healthy-sized chest, which was very much on display thanks to her low-cut shirt. She stood and welcomed each of them.

"Afternoon, Mr. Truth, Mr. Conway, and Ms. Davidson," she smiled. "Donna Southland is expecting you. I'll let her know that you've arrived. Would you take a seat, please?"

Justin couldn't help but take in the sight that was the receptionist. Her long blonde hair was pulled back in a bun, and she wore bright red lipstick. He just had to get to know her better. Could she be the one? He visualized those full red lips wrapped around his cock as her bright blue eyes looked up at him lovingly.

"Hi, I'm sorry I don't know your name, and I can't call you the 'Goddess of R and R,' now can I?" he said with a seductive grin.

"My name's Sophie," she said, blushing slightly.

"Thank you, Sophie." Justin joined the rest of his team on the reception couches. He pulled out his iPhone and clicked on Flowerbox, a simple app for sending flowers in New York. He selected a large, three-hundred-dollar bouquet of roses and included a small note: YOUR BEAUTY SHINES BRIGHTER THAN ALL OF THESE COMBINED.

Justin hungrily watched Sophie as she answered phone calls. *Yes, she could be the one.* Within minutes, a thin woman with broad shoulders emerged from the elevator. Her gray jacket and pants were tailored to her swimmer's build. She walked over to Justin first, with an outstretched hand. Justin gave her a firm handshake.

"Great to meet you at last, Justin," Donna said with a broad smile.

"Thanks, Donna. I can't wait to start working with you guys. R and R has a fantastic reputation."

"Having great clients gives us that reputation," Donna said. "Let's get you all upstairs."

Donna led them into a spacious boardroom on the seventh floor where five members of the agency account team waited. They all stood when Justin entered, and smiled warmly. Five handshakes later, they were all seated around the quirky, oblong-shaped table. The main wall featured a giant touch screen with the Soda-Cola and OrangeFizz logos.

The boardroom doors flung open and a scruffy, short man in faded jeans and a black T-shirt bopped in. He had a large forehead with a bird's nest of brown hair.

Donna stood. "Here he is—Dusty Maine," she announced. "The Executive Creative Director on the OrangeFizz account. Now I don't want his head to get any bigger, but just last month he picked up two Lions at Cannes. A Silver and a Bronze, if I remember correctly." Dusty sat and smiled as some of his team applauded.

"Thanks," Dusty mumbled.

"That's awesome news, Dusty," Craig said.

Donna continued. "All right, we know why we are here. We started on this journey nine months ago with Jacquie, and we're in a great place. She loved the direction, and Craig and Clare have played a massive part in getting us to where we currently are. We've already spoken to a few production companies to test the idea, and they are just as excited as we are."

Justin maintained a poker face, but he didn't like how Donna was trying to make out that the work had already been approved. She was treating this like a courtesy meeting. Justin hadn't signed off anything, and this would be the first major decision he would make for Soda-Cola. It was his account now, and he would be the sole person to decide if this idea was any good. He didn't give a fuck what Jacquie had liked and helped develop.

"I'll hand you over to Dusty and he'll take you through the work," Donna said.

"People." Dusty ran his hands through his Dylan-inspired hair. "We are going on a journey of creative divinity." He swiped the large touch screen in Tai Chi-inspired movements, bringing up images to go with his words. "OrangeFizz is the number-one orange carbonated drink and number fourteen in all carbonated drinks. We want to get it up to number eight. The last time it cracked the top ten was twenty years ago when the market was smaller and there were fewer competitors. Kids love OrangeFizz, and as they get older, they move onto Soda-Cola and energy drinks. Red Bull has had major growth in the last ten years. They don't just advertise to their target audience, they engage them. They become a part of their lives and their identity.

"Now this entire campaign tells teens to 'Capture your Fizz.' We let teenagers make our ads for us. They explain what their Fizz is and capture it on film. They then post their FizzFilm onto the OrangeFizz website, the target audience picks the top five, and we create documentaries about these kids. We play the documentaries as content on MTV and, with the guidance of a director, help the teens create the ultimate expression of their Fizz, which becomes our TV and cinema ads." Dusty looked as if he was expecting a round of applause. His team clapped.

"That is so awesome," Craig commented.

"Thanks, bud," Dusty replied, brushing a strand of wild hair from his face.

"I love the consumer integration," Clare added.

The room went silent; everyone's attention now focused on Justin. He let the silence hang in the air. He liked that they had to wait for him, so he made them wait.

"What an amazing idea," Justin finally began, and the room smiled. "That's what I would have said if you'd presented this work to me five years ago. What's new here? I can count at least twenty brands that get their consumers to make ads for them. Not really sure it has the 'Fizz' I think OrangeFizz needs moving forward. Kids consume sixty-five percent of OrangeFizz, and only ten percent are teenagers. Why would we want to spend our entire budget on ten percent of our consumers?"

"To grow them," Donna replied. "Yes, we have the kids' market covered, and I'm not sure we can grow that anymore. But what if we were to make it more relevant to teenagers, and get them to become brand ambassadors? The kids will continue to love it, even more so because the cool 'big kids' drink it."

"It's Mom who buys it for kids," Justin countered. "She's not a teenager. This form of communication will turn her off. I see us spending millions of dollars to lose sales."

The room dropped back into an awkward silence.

"I understand where you're coming from," Dusty said. "But in today's society the average mom is on Facebook. They are surfing online. They aren't your stay-at-home mom who just cooks three meals a day. They are more edgy than we give them credit for. When their kids ask for OrangeFizz, she will feel like the cool mom because she's in the know."

"I'm sorry, but you're wrong." Justin said. "That would be only three percent of moms. But they won't buy OrangeFizz to start with. We're talking to your average mom, the fat ones, who like to eat donuts, watch TV, and sit on their ass all day. They don't want to cook. They're addicted to sugar. They want to do what's best for their kids, but are just too lazy to do it. OrangeFizz has the word 'orange' in it so they think it's the healthiest soda. And they buy it because of this."

The temperature in the room chilled.

"What do you think, Craig and Clare?" Donna asked. They were trapped; they liked the idea but didn't want to go against what their new boss had just said. Donna was hoping they could pull the conversation back to approving the current idea. Before Craig or Clare could say anything, Justin chipped in.

"They want what is best for the brand. They also know this is not what is best for the brand."

"This answered the brief and Jacquie loved it," Donna said. "She worked on the brand for seven years."

"Yes, seven years of no growth," Justin said. "If this was your answer to the brief, then the brief was wrong. I will go over the old one, and send a new one through. I'm sorry but this is a restart."

The entire R and R team looked deflated. No matter what they were going to present to him, Justin would have killed it. He didn't want someone else's hand-me-down work. Besides, he had plans, and those plans required the money that would otherwise be spent on this campaign. Justin looked Dusty directly in the eye; he could see that the words had hit a nerve. All the months and months of work, gone just like that.

"Now, I can't wait to see what you Cannes-winning creative types will come up with on a real brief," Justin grinned. He glanced at Craig and Clare, who seemed uncomfortable. He had dropped a massive bomb by kicking out all the work. Justin stood up. This meeting was over.

As he walked through the reception area, Justin noticed Sophie holding the generous bunch of roses he'd ordered. A gaggle of fellow office females crowded around her. They were all impressed with the bouquet and were guessing as to who had sent them. Sophie had a big smile on her face. Justin caught her eye, giving her a knowing grin.

CHAPTER FIFTEEN

DEBBIE BRIEFLY ENTERED Justin's office to remind him that the all-staff drink event was about to start. He closed his laptop, and rubbed his eyes. It was the end of the first week, and he had already racked up eighty hours. He didn't mind working long hours, as the money and power made up for it. The Manhattan skyline shined while he checked out his reflection in the window. He looked good, but then he always thought he looked good. Tonight, the staff drinks were to welcome him to the company. The alcohol would be flowing, and his plan was simple: to charm the pants off everyone.

The Soda-Cola company bar was an impressive sight, rivaling many of the top bars in the city. It was recently renovated by a top New York fashion elitist who had designed it in reds and blues, the brand colors of Soda-Cola. Its main feature was sliding doors that opened onto a south-facing deck. The lights and sounds of New York wafted into the room.

Two large Soda-Cola branded fridges, stocked with alcoholic and non-alcoholic beverages, sat behind a well-polished, curved oak bar. On the wall between the fridges, three shelves proudly displayed a large collection of spirits from around the world. It was an open bar, meaning that staff could take anything they wanted. On special occasions like this, a bartender was hired to open people's drinks and mix cocktails, while servers circled the staff with a collection of fine finger foods. A popular DJ played subdued background music. After the speeches, he would amp up the tempo and volume to get the party started.

Justin entered the crowded bar area. He stopped to survey the social landscape, working out whom he should grace his presence with. After all, tonight was all about him. Within minutes he'd categorized the entire room. He picked out the married people who were politely having one drink while watching the clock so they could get home to their families. There were groups of women Justin called Shelfers—in their mid-thirties, stuck on a shelf waiting for Mr. Right, but who'd get drunk and settle for a Mr. Right Now. There were the young ones who were out for a good time, and for whom this was just the first stop to load up on free drinks before their night really started. Hovering close to them were the creepy older men who used any excuse not to go home to their wives in a vain hope that one of the young female interns would get drunk and talk to them. There were also the Roaming Hyenas, the guys seeking out the people above them in order to laugh at their jokes and play the corporate game. Justin was focused on the Bling Girls, who sparkled sexuality.

Justin clocked six Bling Girls he knew he could seduce easily and screw in his office before the end of the night. He acknowledged them, but he had someone more special in mind. His eyes searched for Montana, and he soon spotted her. She was in a far corner talking to a small group of interns, making them feel special. He was confident that after the glowing speeches, she would gravitate to him. He was the best-looking guy here, no contest.

Justin saw Guy Chambers hanging with his IT staff. He'd shaved and looked more presentable than when they'd first met. Guy's eyes lit up when he saw Justin, and he bolted over to him.

"Guy," Justin nodded.

"Hi, Justin." Guy beamed.

"Having a good night?"

"Yeah, these are normally boring as batshit," Guy replied as he scanned the room. Justin could tell by the contemptuous way Guy looked at his co-workers that he disliked people in general. "Knowing you were going to be here is the main reason it's so packed. You're big news. The *man* is here!"

"I am the man." Justin stuck out his chest. "Everything all set for the weekend?" He had learned that Guy was a massive Harley Davidson fan and had arranged for him to go on a two-day Harley tour. Justin had paid for it, of course.

"Yes, I'm so excited. Thanks, Justin."

"My pleasure." Justin amicably put his hand on Guy's shoulder. "And that email thing I asked you to hook up?"

"All on track. Monday morning, and it'll be all go."

"Good."

The room quieted as Soda-Cola's beloved CEO took to the stage. Carlton carried himself with such confidence that it gave those around him confidence. He had a classic swagger that would fit in with the original Rat Pack. He was in his late fifties, his gray hair always immaculately groomed, his shirts crisp, and his tie worn in a double Windsor knot.

"Ladies and gentlemen and... Steve," Carlton started. The entire room cracked up. Steve raised his glass to Carlton with a wry smile.

Carlton smiled back and continued. "Soda-Cola is more than a company to me. It's a family, and family is paramount. Just like a family, we need to look after each other. I take any appointments within Soda-Cola very seriously. And it's no secret that I like to promote from within. I like to foster talent. Looking around this room we have an unfair amount of talent, world-class talent at every level.

"Now, we all know why we're here. It's to welcome a new member to our family. When Jacquie Wentworth left after eleven years to move all the way to Australia, we needed a replacement, and anyone who knew Jacquie knew that wasn't going to be an easy task. We were well aware that we couldn't replace her, so what we needed was to find someone different, someone who would help lift us up to the next level.

"There were some internal staff that could've easily taken her place, which once again speaks volumes for the great talent we have here. But there was one person who really wanted this position, who wanted to be a part of this family, and help us reach new heights. That person is Justin Truth, a young man with an incredible track record. A young man with vision. A man who believes, as much as I do, in strong family values.

"Justin's track record in growing brands is unrivalled. But what many people don't know about is his love for family. He may be a bit embarrassed by this, but let me tell you something about this man. Justin lost his father when he was fifteen, and his mother, let's just say, took the loss of her beloved husband extremely hard. She could no longer take care of herself, let alone her young son. But as they say, through great tragedy comes great triumph. Justin rose to the challenge. He held his family's estate together, and personally cared for his mother. When it became apparent that she might never recover, he made sure she had the best care that money could buy—all paid for by him, her loving son. Now that is a true man! What impressed me the most is that Justin, for the past ten years, has been visiting his mother every single Saturday without fail. If he treats us half as well as actual family, we'll be in great hands. Please give him a Soda-Cola family welcome. I present to you, Justin Truth."

The crowd applauded as Justin made his way onto the stage.

CHAPTER SIXTEEN

"I LOVE WHAT I DO," Justin began. "I love that we can build brands that people will love. I love that we put our personal touch into everything we do. I love working with passionate people. I love having an extended family at work. I love waking up in the morning knowing that today is going to be different from yesterday, and the following day is going to be different yet again. I love that we get paid." Everyone laughed.

"Okay, so we laugh about it but we need to get paid for what we do. One of my key drivers will be to make sure everyone in this room, whether you work within my team or Steve's, will receive the biggest Christmas bonus ever. All I ask is that you give me your trust and your time. Together, we will make greatness happen."

The assembled staff clapped again. Justin could have spoken for hours about how great he was, but judging by the audience, they were ready to drink.

"And as a special present from me to you..." Justin snapped his fingers, and in came ten runway models dressed as silver-service waitresses, each holding a bottle of Krug Grande Cuvée. A redhead with killer curves handed Justin a chilled flute, bubbles streaming up the inside of the glass. He raised it to the group as each person received a glass of the effervescent elixir.

"May this be the first of many," Justin emptied the flute in a single swig.

The others drank their Champagne and applauded. Justin signaled for the DJ to get the music pumping. As he surveyed the room, he watched Debbie doing as he had instructed her to. She was telling everyone how wonderful he was, and that he'd paid for all of this amazing liquor himself.

Justin joined Carlton near the bar and thanked him for the introduction while scanning the room for Montana. She should have flirted with him by now. Someone must be annoying her. Justin continued his conversation with Carlton, who introduced a long line of people to him, all hungry to make a good impression.

After thirty minutes, Justin decided to hunt down Montana and introduce himself. If she liked to play hard to get, he would get her and she would like it. Every time Justin saw her, she had her back to him. It was time for him to make his move. She was wearing a sleeveless, yellow fitted designer dress that stopped just above her knees. The paneling down the front incorporated interweaving straps revealing small diamond shapes of her golden skin beneath it. Simple white high heels with a strap above her ankle displayed her recent pedicure. Her long, dark hair cascaded alluringly over her right shoulder.

Justin ran a knuckle down her exposed back. She spun around. Her face stunned him so much so that he had to pause to take her in. Her big brown eyes devoured him like a hungry wolf. Her full lips moist, a light shade of red—just enough to highlight her natural pout.

"Can I help you?" she asked coldly.

Justin extended his hand. "Hi, I'm Justin," he said with a raised eyebrow.

Montana didn't take his hand, so he slowly dropped it.

"I think we're done," she said in an even colder tone, and turned her back on him. Justin was taken aback. No one ever talked to him like this, let alone a woman he had just met.

"I'm sorry, have I done something to offend you?" Justin touched her elbow. She whipped around to face him.

"You being here offends me. I know who you are, what type of person you are, and you make me sick." The words were spoken with such venom, it caught Justin off guard. His mind raced as he tried to figure out what she was referring to.

Montana continued as if she was reading his mind. "You've never met me, Justin, but you have met my brother. His name is Francisco and he worked with you at Brown & Kessel International. He's told me everything about you—how you would ruin his orders, steal his clients, and make his life a living hell. He had a breakdown once you were finished with him. All so you could be the number-one salesman and sell more than everyone else combined."

Justin instantly clicked. He remembered Francisco. He could see the family resemblance now. It was the first job he'd had after graduating from college. He had done everything in his power to make sure his numbers were higher than everyone else's.

"I remember Francisco," Justin challenged her. "He was a bit of a loser actually. Couldn't do his job without someone holding his hand. He blamed it on everyone other than himself. Let's hope you're an improvement on your brother. Otherwise I guess you'll be heading the same way."

"Don't you threaten me!" Montana hissed. "I don't have to report to you. I don't have to have anything to do with you. I work for Steve. So go fuck yourself!"

Justin glanced around, as some people started to look their way. "I guess we'll have to wait and see. Enjoy the Champagne. It may take some of that sourness out of your mouth."

Montana's eyes were on fire. Not wanting to cause a scene, she sashayed from the room.

Justin pulled Debbie aside.

"Keep an eye on Montana," Justin whispered. "And let me know if she starts to stir up any shit."

Debbie nodded.

CHAPTER SEVENTEEN

IT WAS A WEDNESDAY. The itch Justin sometimes got in the back of his brain was distracting him, and Montana was to blame. He needed a hit. It always helped. It'd been three weeks since his last hit. He thought he could wait until the end of the month. He'd told himself when he started at Soda-Cola he would only do it once a month. It used to be only once every six months. He could wait seven more days, then the hit would be earned.

Justin's fingers started to twitch, and he couldn't hold his pen. He thought about how calm and focused he was after last time. It would be good to go into his afternoon meetings sharper. A hit would help this. Actually a hit would make him better. There was something about the feeling that nothing could touch. He knew he wouldn't be able to do any work until he'd gotten it out of his system. If he wanted the best for Soda-Cola, he needed to be his best, and his best was after a hit.

In the middle of his office was one of the only items he had brought with him from his last job. An antique wooden coffee table that wouldn't look out of place on the Black Pearl. It had a secret, just like Justin. He crouched, and ran his hand down one of its legs, until his thumb was on a knot. He pushed it in, unlocking a hidden drawer. It popped out, revealing its contents. He removed a pair of pig leather gloves, a small leather bag, and a dark green military jacket. His hunting attire.

"Debbie," Justin called as he opened his door. "I'm going out for a walk. If anyone needs me, tell them I'm in a meeting. I am not to be called for any reason."

"Of course, Mr. Truth," Debbie smiled.

"Mark this time down as office training. Just you and me. I would like you to sit inside my office, and do your work from there. Not at my desk obviously."

Debbie smiled and left the room. Justin had her in the palm of his hand. It was obvious to everyone that she loved working for him now. To make sure, he asked her to do some strange things every now and then, to test her. The tasks were always completed without any questions asked. Debbie returned with a bigger smile and her laptop and sat at one of the empty business tables.

Justin left the Soda-Cola building through a side door. The doorway smelled of piss; Justin had been noticing a homeless man around, who'd apparently decided to turn the alcove into a bed-and-breakfast. Justin made a mental note to take care of that problem. He couldn't let some vagrant turn his building into a toilet. He slipped on the jacket, turned up the collar, and stepped out onto the busy street. A warm wind hit his face. He shuffled into the streams of people heading in various directions. Walking as if he were drunk, Justin let the flow of people dictate where he would end up.

At a crowded intersection, Justin pushed to the front. He closed his eyes, breathed in deeply. He filtered out the noise around him. He opened his eyes and she appeared. "She" was a young woman on the other side of the road, about five foot six and in her twenties. She was wearing leopard-skin tights and a white tank top. Pretty, like many girls in New York. She was listening to her iPhone as she strutted down the road without a care in the world.

She was the one. Game on.

Justin pulled an old trucker-style hat out of his pocket. It had a large bulldog embroidered on the front with the word MACK under it. He put it on and pulled it down, obscuring more of his face.

He crossed the road and trailed Ms. Leopard-Skin Tights. He remained back far enough so he could watch her weave her way through the crowded streets, but not close enough for her to know that she was being followed. The way she ambled in and out of stores signaled to Justin that she wasn't on a lunch break, but more likely killing time and making the most of it. She bought a bagel from a street vendor, and sat down on a park bench. Soon, a woman appeared, a friend it seemed, and they started chatting. *Game over*, Justin thought. He was disappointed, he really wanted this girl. He sat on the pavement, his back against a wall, and from beneath his cap angrily watched as the two girls gossiped.

The friend popped to her feet like she realized she was late for something. They kissed each other on the cheek and went their separate ways.

Game back on. Justin grinned.

Ms. Leopard Skin Tights made her way into the Manhattan Mall. It was a hive of activity. Justin knew it well, and he knew how to maneuver in this type of hunt.

Ducking into a narrow alleyway, he inconspicuously pulled out his small leather case. Inside was an assortment of fake beards and prosthetics. He didn't have enough time to put on a prosthetic nose, but attaching a dense black beard and putting on black tinted aviator glasses would only take seconds, and complete his disguise.

Justin walked into the mall through the two sets of glass doors. It was a large, open, circular space with two basement levels, two upper levels, and a glass pitched roof. In the center of each floor was a large hole by which the complex could be viewed from the top to the very bottom. Justin leaned over the railing and looked down toward the basement level. Panasonic had rented out space next to the large water fountain to display flat-screen TVs and home entertainment equipment.

He smiled to himself, as the thrill of the hunt charged through his veins. His eyes darted around the mall. He had to find her, and he had to find her fast. He spotted her. He hung back and watched her float from store to store, though at times he'd get close enough to smell her perfume. At one stage, he deliberately bumped into her so he could look into her eyes, before apologizing and carrying on his way. He was going to do this and he was going to do it today.

Justin left the woman behind and made his way to the top floor. He had been in this building many times and knew what to do. It was now her decision. If she, of her own free will, came to the top floor, he was not responsible for his actions. If she left the department store, she was free to go.

Keeping his head down, Justin ambled to a bench that he knew was a security-camera blind spot. He sat, waited, and played a game on his iPhone. Was she going to be the one today? He wanted her to be. She needed to be the one for him. He nodded as he saw Ms. Leopard Skin Tights on the far escalator approaching the top floor.

CHAPTER EIGHTEEN

IT WAS ALL GO!

Justin sprang off the bench and swiftly made his way down a passage between two stores. At the end of the passage was an alarmed fire-exit door. He didn't need that just yet. What he was interested in was halfway down the passage. He glanced behind him into the mall as Ms. Leopard-Skin Tights entered a bookstore. Good. This was one of twenty scenarios he had for the mall. Each one meticulously thought through.

He took a book of matches and a string coated with a slow-burning wax out of his pocket. He pulled out a line and inserted the rest into a fire sprinkler. It would take about thirty seconds to burn to the sensor. He ignited a match and lit the tail of the string. It sparked into life. A small flame burned its way toward the sprinkler head.

Justin moved quickly to get into position. Ms. Leopard Skin Tights was still in the bookstore. The flame hit the sprinkler, and the fire alarms sounded as water poured from the ceiling. People began to panic, but a lot less than Justin had anticipated. He needed people to be scared for their lives, to shove each other in a mindless stampede to escape. He saw Ms. Leopard Skin Tights leave the bookstore; she joined the other shoppers making their way toward the escalator.

"It's a terrorist attack!" Justin screamed. "Bombs!"

The effect was immediate. Chaos erupted. People started running and screaming. The internal alarm systems had shut off the elevators, so people thundered toward the escalators. Amongst it all, Justin kept his eyes trained on Ms. Leopard-Skin Tights. Like the others, she was panicked and rushed to get out. People pushed and barged their way past each other. Justin saw his opportunity and sprinted toward her. Moving with stealth and strength, he smashed his shoulder into Ms. Leopard-Skin Tights' stomach, picked her up, and flicked her over the safety railing. She tumbled down four floors, screaming. Her back snapped backward over a metal display stand, spinning her sideways. Her head whiplashed into a plasma TV, shattering the screen. She hit the ground hard. Her shoulder fractured on the ceramic tile floor, twisting and snapping her neck.

Justin didn't stop to watch the result of his handiwork. He could clearly picture it in his mind. He ran back along the passage, kicked open the exit door, and leapt down the back stairs where he knew there were no cameras. At the bottom of the stairs was a door that opened to the outside world. His sunglasses shielded him from the bright light.

He slowed his pace; fire engines were approaching, sirens and horns blaring. The closer the engines got, the thicker the crowd of onlookers grew. Justin joined the nosy pedestrians, blending in. He was sweating hard and could feel it trickling down the side of his face. He weaved against the flow of people toward a street vendor and bought a bottle of water.

"What's going on?" Justin asked.

"I heard terrorist attack or something. Fucking ragheads!" the vendor said.

Justin nodded and took a large gulp of water. "Fucking terrorists," he agreed.

The itch was scratched. He was looking forward to his afternoon business meetings.

CHAPTER NINETEEN

ROSS FLASHED HIS BADGE at the officers standing guard in front of the yellow police tape and continued past. A growing crowd of rubberneckers had already gathered, like vultures circling a corpse to pick its bones clean. A few who had seen too many TV crime shows called out advice for the investigating officers.

Ross made his way to the basement level of the Manhattan Mall, broken glass crunching under his shoes. Sergeant Carlos Wagner waved him over. They had worked together on more cases than Ross cared to remember.

"Hey, Carlos, what's the story?" Ross held out his bag of jelly beans.

Over the past twenty years, Ross had given up smoking a few times. One time he substituted his Marlboros with jelly beans. It didn't work, and the Marlboros soon returned, but the jelly beans also decided to stay. Since then, Ross split the world into two camps—those who'd take a jelly bean, and those who wouldn't. It was a simple gesture he'd been making for the past fifteen years, and he found that the people who didn't take a jelly bean normally ended up being an asshole later down the track. Most jelly bean-takers were normally OK. It wasn't foolproof, but the jelly bean test was right on the money 80 percent of the time.

Carlos took a handful of jelly beans as he talked. "Twenty-six-year-old girl, Lydia Young. Fell from the top floor. Happened during a fire alarm. From what I've gathered so far, some people thought it was a terrorist attack. They panicked, and while pushing each other out of the way to escape, this young lady got knocked over the railing."

Ross's knees clicked as he squatted to lift the sheet that was covering her. She was pretty. Her body was twisted and contorted at an unnatural angle from the impact. Crashing through the plasma TVs on display wouldn't have helped.

"Any suspects?" Ross asked Carlos.

"None. From what we can tell she was just in the wrong place at the wrong time."

Ross asked Carlos a few more questions, then went for a look around. He made his way up the stairs to the top floor and peered over the railing and glass wall. It was a long way down. He measured himself against the railing—it was just under his chest. Not something you could easily topple over. A lot of people would struggle to jump or even climb over it. Lydia wasn't tall, maybe five foot six. She would've had to be lifted a few feet off the ground to topple over the rail. Ross closed his eyes, playing it over and over in his mind, but he just couldn't visualize it.

Ross dealt only in logic; if it didn't make sense to him, something was wrong. He would trace back, step by step, until he found a bit of logic and then move forward. He often felt that his fellow detectives were rushed to find the easy solution instead of the logical solution so that they often overlooked what they were really trying to solve.

He scrutinized the area for security cameras, but saw none. A blind spot. The floor was still wet from the sprinklers. As he approached an exit door, his foot slipped, and he nearly ended up on his ass. Something on the ground made him slip; he could see water beading off it. Ross bent for a closer look. There was a waxy residue on the floor. He looked up and saw a fire sprinkler. He glanced back to where Lydia had fallen over the balcony. There was a direct line from where he was to where she got knocked over.

Ross rejoined the crew on the bottom floor and spoke to a few witnesses. They told pretty much the same story. No one saw exactly what had happened, and everyone thought it was a horrible tragedy. Ross stood next to Lydia and looked up to the top floor. Something didn't sit right with him. Ross needed to step back and line up the logic. Until he did, he wasn't going to call this an accident. This was a case that needed to be solved, not written off.

CHAPTER TWENTY

IT WAS A PLEASANT SATURDAY AFTERNOON, just like any other at St. Mary's Care Center, one of the most expensive and exclusive private hospitals in the country. The historical building sat on a grassy hill surrounded by a forest of trimmed trees, small brick units, and a crystal-clear lake.

The expansive, stately home was built in 1812. Originally owned by the Enfield family, it was donated to the St. Mary's foundation after the Great War. The quarter-mile private road was the only way in and out. A cross-section of patients lived here: elderly people who couldn't care for themselves, burned-out CEOs, drug-addicted teenagers. The only thing they had in common: extremely wealthy families.

The clientele at St. Mary's were guaranteed their privacy, and there were at least two security guards in the reception room at all times. To access the hospital, the sliding doors the guards protected needed to be activated by the staff.

Nurse Rose looked up from behind the reception desk as the entrance doors slid open. She smiled as she recognized the visitor, Justin Truth. He grinned at the large security guard by the door as he walked in. The guard didn't smile back. In fact, he had never smiled once in the three years that Justin had seen him working at St. Mary's.

"Morning, Mr. Truth," Nurse Rose said. "Nice to see you, as always."

"Nurse Rose, as beautiful as your namesake." Justin signed in. "How is she doing?"

"Pretty much the same. A lost soul trying to find her way home. With God's love, she will."

"We can but pray," Justin added, playing along.

He listened absently to the middle-aged nurse chatting away about having faith, willing her to push the button to open the sliding doors.

Justin didn't believe in God; he believed in himself. Only the weak believed in things that were intangible. Religion was a powerful tool in the right hands. That's all it was to him, another tool to use.

Finally, the doors beeped, the lock clunked, and the doors automatically opened.

St. Mary's had a large labyrinth of rooms. Each year it got a bit bigger and more modern, while much of the original building was retained simply for appearances. Justin loved the classic look; it spoke of old money. He could have put his mother into a state-funded facility, but in the long run, having her in a place like this had its benefits. The business connections he made from chance meetings in the hallways were more valuable than a dozen golf-course memberships. Today it was quiet, however, and he came across no one of interest.

Justin arrived at his mother's private room and opened the door. The room was more like a high-end hotel suite than a typical hospital abode. Tasteful artwork hung from the walls, well-maintained pot plants bloomed cheerfully, and relaxing music played through hidden speakers. In the late afternoons, sunlight spilled in through the wooden bifold windows.

Sitting by her bed, jotting down notes, was her doctor. His short brown hair was parted to the right, and his face hidden behind large, round glasses. He always reminded Justin of a grown-up Harry Potter.

The doctor glanced up and smiled. All St. Mary's workers were always welcoming. "Justin. It is so good to see you."

"Good to see you too, Doctor David. But it would be better if I didn't." Justin smirked. This was an ongoing joke between them.

"Yes, it would be great if your mother got better and was able to go home."

"How is she?"

"Still the same, I'm afraid, in a state of distance. Every now and then we think we can see a spark in her eyes, but then it fades again. There is no reason she couldn't just wake from it. The brain is a weird and wonderful thing. The death of your father hit her so hard she retreated into her mind. When she wants to join us, she'll come back. Until then, we can only pray for her and make her comfortable."

Dr. David placed his hand on Justin's shoulder.

"You are a loving son to her," he said. "I know we've talked about it, but I want you to know that I've told the board members about you, and they would love to meet you. I'm holding a dinner for my fellow members soon and would love for you to join us."

Justin grinned. The board had some of the biggest names in the business world attached to it, and he'd been working on the good doctor for the last five years to get this invitation.

"Thank you, Dr. David. I am touched that you even thought of me."

The doctor squeezed Justin's shoulder. "I'll leave you to your visit," he said and left the room.

Justin poured a glass of water and sat next to his mother.

"Ohhh, Mom, you look great." Justin grinned. He removed a plate from the kitchen cupboard, placed it in the microwave, and set it on high for twenty seconds. He filled a drinking glass with water. "My job is going great too." He placed the glass on the laptop food tray next to her bed. "I met this lovely girl the other day; she wore these leopard-skin tights. I think you would have liked her. So pretty." The microwave beeped. Justin retrieved the plate, set it next to the glass of water. "She was pretty, really pretty. I threw her over a fourth-floor balcony. The sound she made, crashing to her death, was spectacular, really spectacular. All the chaos and confusion was thrilling as always."

Justin talked as he took a tablet from his pocket, and placed in on the center of the warm plate. With his American Express Centurion Card, he broke the pill in half and then into quarters. Each chalky section was then crushed into a powder. He pushed around his handiwork with the edge of the card, looking for big clumps. Finding some, he broke them down even more. He then pushed it into a single pile and cut it up more with the short edge of the exclusive credit card. The fine powder was scraped back and forward into a fat line.

"There is this woman at work, Montana. Don't you just love how her name rolls off your tongue. *Montana*. There's something about her. A passion. If she plays her cards right, you might get a grandchild. How great would that be? A mini-me running around." Justin scooped up the powder, and added it to the glass of water. He stirred it with his finger to help it dissolve. Wiping his finger dry on her bedsheet.

"Open wide," he grinned as he put the glass to his mother's lips. "Made it specially for you." He gripped her hair tightly, and tilted her head back slightly to pour the liquid into her open mouth. He closed her lips for her, and waited for the water to trickle down the back of her throat. "Now there's a good girl." Justin smiled.

It was this weekly ritual that was keeping his mother in her vegetative state. She could hear and process everything around her. She just couldn't move, talk or react.

"Well, I'd better be going," he said. "I'll see you again next Saturday." He leaned over, gave his mom a kiss on the forehead, and left the room, closing the door behind him.

CHAPTER TWENTY-ONE

IT HAD BEEN ANOTHER FULL-ON start to the week for Justin: eighteen-hour days, every day. The problem that needed the most attention was OrangeFizz. He had to increase the sales of the orange soda fast. At the end of the day, it was all about numbers, and if he could make his go up, he looked good. He had an idea on how to make a big impact fast.

He'd told Debbie a week ago that tomorrow, Thursday, he was going to be working from home. He was not to be interrupted or have any meetings booked in. He had to get the forecast projections optimized if he were to respond rapidly to the iso-trends that came back from the sociodynamic market research. Justin flummoxed Debbie with jargon. What he was going to do needed to be done undercover.

Arriving home, Justin heard Mr. Noodles yapping like usual as he approached his penthouse apartment. He was going to have to do something about that. He didn't want anything that signaled his coming and going.

Once inside, Justin changed into his workout gear and downed a pre-workout shake with a precise collection of his PT's prescribed supplements. As the sups kicked in and spiked his adrenaline, he primed himself with a hundred push-ups, a hundred sit-ups, and a ten-minute prone hold. Then he jumped on his treadmill and ran hard out for twenty minutes listening to Audioslave, building up a mean sweat. He used some free weights to get a pump on before cooling himself down in the shower, and enjoyed the feeling of the water pounding against his hard body. He was ripped and liked to keep it that way. He ran a hand over his abs and down to his cock. He masturbated to make himself come hard.

In the middle of the lounge, on a plastic sheet, he placed all the things he needed for the next day. He'd been planning this before he started at Soda-Cola.

Item 1: A wallet with a false passport, driver's license, plane tickets, and a thousand dollars in assorted clean bills.

Item 2: An iPhone that had the GPS programmed with the required maps.

Item 3: A two-way walkie-talkie, fully charged.

Item 4: Skin-toned latex gloves.

Item 5: Brown-colored contact lenses.

Item 6: A gray beard and a professional make-up kit.

Item 7: Cheap clothes from Target. Gray slacks, gray jacket, blue polo, black loafers, and a light blue flat cap.

Item 8: Twenty bottles of SummerCrush.

SummerCrush was the number-two player in the orange-soda market. The difference in market share between this brand and OrangeFizz was only 4 percent, and the products were basically the same. Orange-Fizz had Soda-Cola's superior distribution to thank for its extra market share. SummerCrush needed crushing. The brand had to be vilified by the media, and the public had to lose trust in it.

Justin picked up a bottle of SummerCrush. Every bottle of Summer-Crush had a code on the bottom. To most people it was just a random series of numbers and letters, but this code gave people in the know a lot of information. It told them when it was made, what production line it came from, and the date it was bottled. Each bottle in Justin's collection had a different code. As he tilted one of the bottles in his hand, Justin broke into a devilish grin.

"God, I'm good."

CHAPTER TWENTY-TWO

THE OLD MAN HELD HIS BREATH as he slipped out the front door of his apartment. He cautiously looked around and quietly closed the door. It was unusually silent without any yapping mutt. Quickly, he made his way down the back stairs toward the Donald Door. The key clicked in the iron lock, squeaked open, and he slithered out the door, locking it behind him.

It was three a.m. and his first flight left in two hours. Justin would normally catch a taxi to the airport, but he was not Justin: he was sixty-eight-year-old Jonathan Smith, one of 680,000 J. Smiths to live in the US. It was a nice, safe name—a name people hear a lot and that drew no attention. And Jonathan would travel by subway.

Justin normally walked upright like he owned the world. If he were to stand next to Jonathan now, he'd look a good four inches taller. The ill-fitting clothes made him look smaller, and he kept his head low, as if the world had beaten him into submission. The flat cap did a good job of aging him and obscuring his face.

The subway was thrilling. Surrounded by people who earned less than what he spent on cocaine per year, he wanted to stare them down. Instead, he remained in character, keeping his head down, ambling across the floor. He was good at acting; he'd had plenty of practice over the years developing his hunting techniques. His fingers tapped the backpack on his lap. The bottles in it were wrapped tight and made no sound when moved. Justin, a.k.a. Jonathan, mentally rehearsed his plan once more.

Maybe it was the early morning that had caught him off guard. A young street kid made a beeline for Justin's backpack and grabbed it. He was fast, and in an instant he was running toward one of the adjoining train doors.

"Fuck!" Justin sprang into action.

The street kid hadn't counted on two things: that the bag was heavy, and that the old man was in fact a super-fit twenty-nine-year-old. Justin made it through the door as it closed and grabbed one of the straps. He was a lot stronger than the street punk and easily yanked the kid backward. The boy turned and pulled at the bag, expecting to be able to rip it out of the old man's grip. He couldn't. Pulling out a blade from his back pocket, he held it to Justin.

"Drop it, fucker! Is your life worth what's in dis bag?" He tried to sound tough. "Cuz I'll cut you, cut you real bad, motherfucker!"

Justin watched the street kid's face. He knew he could take him. The train was empty, with maybe four people in the carriage, but they were all watching.

"You hear me, bitch?" the kid screamed, his voice breaking slightly. Justin knew he had to act fast to retrieve the backpack. He'd spent too many days planning this to walk away defeated. He could see the boy's legs were in striking distance. Using a simple kickboxing move, he kicked his right foot at the kid's knee while leaning back on his left foot. Justin had powerful legs. He heard the kid's kneecap snap on contact with his foot. The kid screamed, dropped the blade, and collapsed onto his good knee. Justin followed up with a left knee to the kid's head. The sharp angular power of his strike instantly splattered the boy's nose. Blood poured from his pummeled nostrils as he crumpled onto the rocking floor of the train.

The four onlookers cheered as the train came to a stop at the next station, and the doors opened. Justin grabbed the kid by his clothes, and threw him out like a rag doll. He landed in a heap on the platform with a slight thud. Justin clocked the station's name; he was only four stops from the airport. Not wanting any more attention, he picked up his backpack, and hurried toward his original carriage, checking behind him to see if anyone was following. He continued from carriage to carriage until he reached the last one. There he sat and waited, his hands tightly gripped around his backpack

CHAPTER TWENTY-THREE

THE TRAIN ARRIVED at the airport on schedule. Justin hopped off and again looked around. The coast seemed clear. At the airport he joined the thousands of people, all so self-absorbed that they wouldn't notice a monkey hanging from the roof with a machine gun shooting a clip full of hot bananas.

Justin joined the check-in line for State-Wide Airlines. The service wasn't great, but the flights usually ran on time and security wasn't the tightest. He detested lining up and would normally walk straight into the first-class lounge so he could relax away from the plebes. Except today he was Jonathan Smith, not Justin Truth.

"Next, please," said the lady behind the counter. This was going to be Justin's first test. He smiled a crooked smile and approached the counter.

"Destination?"

Justin passed her his e-ticket. "Chicago," he said.

Without looking up, the attendant examined the ticket, blindly checked his driver's license, and typed into her computer. They waited.

"Board through Gate 35," she said. "Enjoy your flight, Mr. Smith."

"Thank you," he replied and turned, anticipating that today was going to be a great day. He made a mental note to stay in character and dropped his head.

Gate 35 was only a short walk away. He hobbled, stopped, hobbled some more. He did all the things that traveling old men did that annoyed Justin. Halfway to the gate, he rested in the middle of the walkway so people had to move around him. He turned in a circle like he was confused about where he was going. He knew exactly where he was going. Today he was going to catch seven flights, hire three cars, and catch thirteen taxis. Everything had to go smoothly. To miss just one place would throw everything out.

The next step in the process was the metal detector and random bag searches. Justin knew he'd be able to dodge the metal detector, but the random bag search could be a problem. He'd thought up a few reasons he had so much SummerCrush if searched.

"I'm a photographer, and need to shoot these, they're art directed to be perfect."

"I get thirsty, and they cost a fortune at the vending machines. I got twenty for the price of three."

"I have dementia, I forgot I had bought one and ended up buying again and again. Don't tell my son, he's looking for any reason to put me in a home."

"Did you know that SummerCrush in New York tastes different to the Chicago variety? Must be the water they use or something."

He watched other passengers going through his gate. To avoid using one of his excuses, he thought it would be better to stand next to the right person—a person he thought would get pulled out and checked before a doddery old white male would.

After a few minutes he found the perfect candidates—two young Middle Eastern men. Justin shuffled behind them, bumping into them on purpose to invade their personal space. He listened to their conversation. They were students going home to Chicago for a family wedding. Justin knocked and jostled them a few times, agitating them while they waited.

A plump, white security guard with a handlebar mustache stood behind the metal detector. His eyes scanned each passenger as they walked through. As Justin expected, he stopped the Middle Eastern guys. They called him a racist and a bully. This only compelled the guard to become overly zealous in the execution of his duties. Justin was waved through without so much as a second look. Before he knew it, he was sitting outside Gate 35. He looked at his phone: 5:35 a.m. It was going to be a long day.

CHAPTER TWENTY-FOUR

"I KILLED DAD."

It wasn't the words that had destroyed her; it was their tone, devoid of any empathy. Sarah remembered the look on her son's face as he'd told her with a smile.

At the time, she'd only been bedridden for three months, still in her own bed, in her own house. Like her doctors, she was confused about what was happening to her body. She could barely move; speaking for her was now just a murmur in her chest.

Her condition started shortly after her husband died. At first she was tired all the time. She found it hard to walk. She felt weak until all she could do was stay in bed and watch TV. Even a simple task, like reading a book, became too great an effort. Then she lost her ability to speak. Everyone thought it was the shock of losing Mathew, but they were wrong.

Sarah could clearly recall the day Justin confessed. It was on his sixteenth birthday. He'd come into her room with a big grin on his face, holding a birthday cake. He placed it on the bedside table, before opening the blinds to let more afternoon sun in. Justin had sat on her bed and taken her hand into his, stroking it. She'd lovingly gazed into his face, he'd inherited the best features of both parents and was quite striking.

"I killed Dad," he said.

Paralyzed, Sarah had been unable to react.

"It was the only way things could work out for me, Mom. I know you and Dad have given me everything you could, but that would have only taken me so far. To make it in this world, I need the best—the best! With my grades and athletic achievements, I'm going to get accepted into Harvard. But I would have to live in a crappy dorm and get a shitty job. You see, the friends I want will all have rich parents to pay for their ski trips and European vacations, not to mention money to drop on bottles of wine that cost more than our car. I thought about it and figured that I'd need about a million dollars in disposable income for my stay at Harvard.

"This feels good," Justin stroked her hair and continued. "Two years ago, I put my plan into action. I suggested to Dad that he increase his life-insurance-policy payout. You know, to make sure you were taken care of if anything were to happen. There were caveats though, Mom, and to get the full payout, he'd have to die in a freak accident, something that statistically speaking shouldn't happen. There would be no payout for suicide and only a third for murder committed by a family member, otherwise I would have set you up for it. Insurance companies are very smart about that.

"It required a bit of creative thinking. It had to be a foolproof plan so they wouldn't be able to cancel the policy. Say if Dad were to be killed in a random car accident—a car driven by a stranger. That would get the full payment. Now, on the corner of Westmere and Harold Drive, a tree partially obscures the stop sign. You remember, it's a bit of a blind corner with a slight incline. At sunset, anyone driving around the bend gets hit with sunstrike. So, if a car were to be driving within the speed limit but missed the stop sign at the moment someone just happened to be crossing the road, the result would be a terrible, possibly fatal, accident.

"I used the tree to cover the stop sign completely. By then Dad and I were already taking our evening walks. Remember how you wanted to join us but I'd told you I needed some Dad time? Forty-seven days into our walks, the opportunity presented itself. We came to the corner, the conditions were perfect, and I saw some light reflect off an oncoming car. I suggested we cross. Dad took the lead and I stopped and pretended to retie my shoelaces, asking him to wait. He turned; his attention was on me. The driver ran the stop sign, got blinded by the sun, and didn't see him until it was too late. He slammed on his brakes, but hit Dad. You should've seen it. He flew high and landed in a crumpled mess thirty feet down the road. The car killed him instantly. It was such a rush knowing I'd caused his death. I may not have done it with my own hands, but it was I who killed him."

Justin took a deep breath. Sarah could see on his face how proud he was of himself. Telling her all about it seemed to make him happier.

"Now, you must be wondering why you're feeling the way you are? No energy, tired, can't move? It's all because of these little pills." Justin took a small container from his pocket, opened it, and pulled out a small white tablet. He continued: "I researched many varieties and discovered this one. I could tell you all about it, Mom, but I think it would go over your head. All you need to know is one of these administered once a week, over a course of months, is the cause. Not enough to kill, and not enough to show up on medical reports. With you like this, I can control the estate, which is now worth one-point-five million dollars. This is my money, and you would make it difficult for me to spend it, so I had to make sure I got what I wanted.

"Thanks for this, Mom. I feel so much better. I think we should have these chats more often. I have so much to share."

CHAPTER TWENTY-FIVE

THE PLANE TOUCHED DOWN in Chicago right on time. Justin waited for it to empty before grabbing his heavy backpack from the overhead compartment. He made his way past the zombie-like attendants who were in the process of giving the cabin a quick clean.

Within minutes, Justin was in the back seat of a cab.

"2356 Hill Street, just off West Point," he told the driver. It was a twenty-five-minute ride, which was enough time for him to start covering some tracks.

From one of his backpack pockets, Justin pulled out his two-way radio. It was a military-grade device he had purchased from a backstreet store that dealt in black-ops equipment. Cash only, no questions asked. The handset could transmit over large distances and was specifically developed for the war in Iraq, where there was nothing but sand between targets, and satellites weren't always reliable.

He'd left the other two-way radio back in his apartment in New York, right next to his iPhone. He'd programmed five numbers into the phone's voice-recognition software. Talking into his handset, he was able to communicate directly to his phone. If ever questioned, both his phone record and GPS would show that he'd been in his apartment the entire day.

"Piggy," Justin spoke into his handset. Back in New York, his iPhone picked up his voice and dialed Debbie.

"Hello, Mr. Truth," Debbie answered.

"Hi Debbie, looks like today is going to be intense. Make sure I'm not disturbed. If people do call, I'm putting everything to voice mail."

"OK, you sound a bit faint."

"I must be getting some bad reception. I'm expecting Donna from R and R to send through a reverse brief on the OrangeFizz campaign. Can you follow up with her?"

"I'll do it right away."

"Make sure you talk directly to her, not her account manager or any other retard who works for him," Justin said. "I want that brief tomorrow."

"Even if I get pushed around, I'll get her," Debbie replied proudly. She liked to be bossy and that Justin encouraged this trait.

"Good work, Debbie. Talk soon."

He'd asked for the reverse brief only yesterday. It normally took a week, but he wasn't having any of it. If they couldn't wing it in three days, they were incapable of doing their job.

Again, Justin lifted his handset. "Angus Diaz!" Once again, it worked perfectly. His New York cellphone dialed and he could hear it ringing.

An energetic voice answered. "Hey, hey, J-man!"

"Angus! Hitting the weights, or just hitting on all the girls?"

"Ha ha, just the pretty ones. Not my fault there's only one of me and so many of them! So, we getting you at one p.m. for a workout? Got this killer chest program for you to try."

Angus was one of the top personal trainers in New York. He had a few famous clients and he interviewed everyone before taking them on. Justin didn't pay only for Angus's talents, but also for his hook-ups. He knew all the right people in all the right places. Justin paid him a flat fee each week, whether he trained with him or not.

"My man, I can't make it today. Work is crushing me."

"Dude, that's no good. You always need a bit of gym time."

"I know. Chest tomorrow morning?"

"Hold on for a sec." The phone went muffled and Justin could hear gym equipment clanking in the background. "I can do a ten a.m."

"That's perfect. Let's stack them plates," Justin replied.

"Good one, bro, see you tomorrow. Peace!"

Justin placed the handset back into his backpack. He had four more calls to make over the course of the day. He pulled out his second iPhone and checked the flight schedules. No delays so far.

CHAPTER TWENTY-SIX

THE TAXI STOPPED at the address. Justin thanked the driver, paid him in cash, and surveyed the surroundings. It was still early, and he could hear birds chirping. He was in a well-off, middle-class suburb. The streets were clean, the trees trimmed, and police responded to calls fast. He removed a bottle of SummerCrush from his backpack and slipped it up his jacket sleeve. He'd made a pocket for it so he could move freely without anyone knowing he was hiding anything. He hunched over, and hobbled down to the small 7-Eleven on the corner.

As he entered the shop, Justin checked out the guy behind the counter—Asian, forty-something. There were only two other customers in the store—teenage boys in baggy jeans and heavy metal T-shirts, deciding which Slurpee they wanted.

A Slurpee at this time of the morning? Justin frowned. The teenagers moved slowly and laughed at everything they did. They weren't hiding how wasted they were, and had the full attention of the shopkeeper. There were two security cameras, one overlooking the register, and the other at the shop entrance. The door camera was at a high angle; there was no way it could pick up his Justin's face under his flat cap. Justin made his way to the drinks fridge and opened the door to where the SummerCrush was kept. He moved the bottles around and grabbed one from near the back, replacing it with the one up his sleeve. If they were to do a stock take, the bottle numbers would even out.

"What are you doing?" said a voice behind him. Justin slowly turned to see one of the teens staring at him. Justin wasn't sure what to say and closed the door. He didn't know if the teenager had seen what he'd done.

"What?" Justin clenched the SummerCrush in his fist. If he needed to, he could knock out this stoner and be gone before anyone knew what happened.

"Get a Red Bull, man!" the teen insisted. "It's the shit. That orange shit's for kids."

"I like orange," Justin muttered and hurried to the counter with his SummerCrush. He grabbed a Mars Bar and a pack of gum on the way. This combination would be less likely to stand out in the attendant's memory. The teenager had rejoined his stoner mate and they were laughing about something. The Asian guy didn't bother to make eye contact with Justin as he scanned the items. He was still too focused on the two stoners.

"Five-forty," he demanded, not taking his eyes off the boys.

Justin handed him the exact amount. "Thanks," he said and walked out. The fresh air hit his face.

"One down, nineteen to go," he said to himself.

CHAPTER TWENTY-SEVEN

BRENDON GIBSON WAS FORTY-EIGHT and on his second marriage. The first fell apart when he started sleeping with a colleague. It was not a friendly divorce, and his ex-wife got the house and the kids. When the office fling also went sour, Brendon decided it was time to start afresh. He left his job as marketing manager of Butterkist popcorn and sent his CV to every headhunter he could find.

There were a number of positions available, but the role he decided to snap up was with Uncle Charlie's Beverages in Florida, as national marketing manager for SummerCrush. Moving halfway across the country would mean moving away from his problems. And while he loved his kids, they were now old enough to know what was happening—that Dad wasn't leaving them, just moving to a new place.

Brendon was in charge of the entire marketing department for SummerCrush, with a team of twenty-four. He had to report to a few people, but as long as he made his budget, he could do what he liked. It was a good role. SummerCrush sold itself and was a lucrative money earner for the Uncle Charlie's drinks portfolio. He worked from eight thirty a.m. to six p.m. every day and was home by six thirty p.m., depending on traffic.

Brendon had met his new wife at an industry party, the annual marketing awards of the Florida Marketing Community (FMC). At each table there was a mix of representatives from different companies, as the event was designed for mingling. They were sat at the same table, and her face had melted his heart. Brendon instantly knew he'd gotten lucky, charmed her, and within six months he proposed marriage.

Brendon liked routine. His alarm would go off at six a.m. He'd get up, go downstairs, and jump on his exercise bike while watching the business channel on TV. After thirty minutes, he'd have a protein drink, and go through the emails he'd received overnight. He'd arrange them into three folders: green, blue, and red. Junk to delete went into the green folder, emails he'd reply to after lunch into the blue folder, and the important emails went into the red one. He always answered the emails in the red folder as soon as the sorting was done.

Brendon paid close attention to all the red folder emails until they were cleared. By then his lovely wife would be up and making him breakfast. They'd sit and talk about their plans for the day, a small but important thing he'd stopped doing with his ex-wife. He'd learned from his failed first marriage that communication was key, so now he'd talk with, and listen to, his wife every day.

Following their morning ritual, Brendon would then drive to work and manage his team. He was good at it and treated people with respect. He'd grown older, wiser, and wanted a quiet life.

A phone call at 5:37 a.m. Thursday changed all that. He leaned over to his buzzing BlackBerry.

"Hello?" he said sleepily. The voice at the other end caused him to sit up straight.

"Ahhh fuck!"

CHAPTER TWENTY-EIGHT

MELINDA TAYLOR PICKED UP HER one-and-a-half-year-old son, Jacob, and placed him in his pram.

"Mom! You said we could go!" yelled Jacob's six-year-old brother, Ethan.

"Sweetie, the park isn't going anywhere, OK? Mommy has some things to do." She tried to sound in charge.

"But, Mom!"

"Now, Ethan, a good boy gets a drink on the way. A naughty boy gets…"

"OK, I'm good," Ethan sulked, knowing what his mom was going to say.

A few minutes later they were walking down their street; the park was only five minutes away. It was a great neighborhood with lots of young families. Melinda, who'd chosen to quit work to bring up their boys, passed a few other stay-at-home moms along the way. Allan, her husband, worked some long hours at the restaurant they owned downtown. Their business was doing well. The long hours meant that he was gone for most of the day and got home late, but it wouldn't be forever, and it meant they could live in a lovely home. She enjoyed being a stay-at-home mom; she didn't have much time for herself but she loved her kids and loved to be needed.

Melinda saw the store coming up and knew what it meant. On cue: "Mom, you said I could get a drink!" Ethan yelled.

"I know, honey, and we will." She smiled.

They entered the 7-Eleven and Melinda exchanged pleasantries with Mr. Chan behind the counter. She grabbed a bottle of water for herself and a fruit box for Ethan.

"Mom, I want a drink with bubbles!" Ethan shouted.

Melinda returned the fruit box and grabbed a SummerCrush instead. She paid for it and they headed to the park.

At the small park, there were three other moms with their kids; Melinda knew them and was happy to see them. Ethan ran off to play while Melinda chatted to her friends. They talked about their babies, the hours their husbands worked, the state of the country, the cooking channel, and what they were going to make for dinner that night.

It was a great park. The ground was soft, spongy rubber, and it was fenced off from the road. It wasn't uncommon for local families to have kids' birthday parties here. Ethan came running up.

"Thirsty, Mom, drink," he demanded.

"Sorry, what do we say?"

"Can I have a drink, please?" Ethan said in a friendlier tone.

Melinda opened the bottle of SummerCrush and gave it to Ethan who grabbed it and gulped it down as fast as he could. Melinda didn't like how he gulped everything in front of the other mothers—he only did it when people were watching.

"Nicely," Melinda reminded him.

Ethan stopped and took a smaller sip. His face screwed up and he spat it out.

"Ethan!" Melinda started, but stopped when the next mouthful of liquid he spat up was blood. He looked up at his mom with tears streaming out of his eyes and blood pouring out of his mouth.

"Mommy!" he screamed, and threw up even more SummerCrush and blood. Melinda picked up her son and tried to calm him down. But panic was kicking in. What on earth was happening here? Her own top was now covered in blood. He was screaming. She screamed. Another mother frantically phoned for an ambulance.

CHAPTER TWENTY-NINE

BRENDON CLENCHED HIS JAW as he turned on the TV. He went straight to the news channel and caught the story. It was about five kids from different parts of the country who'd all been admitted to hospital after drinking SummerCrush. He turned up the volume.

"What was one child admitted to the hospital, has now become five," the news anchor said with a stern expression on his face. "At one of the hospitals is our field reporter, Trish Rodriguez. Trish, what's happening?"

"Thanks, Mitch. I'm here with the parents of young Ethan Taylor. Just twelve hours ago, Ethan was a fit and healthy six-and-a-half-year-old boy, who didn't have a care in the world while he played in his local park with friends. Yet his life and that of his family has taken a dark and twisted turn, all because of a soft drink, a soft drink that apparently has nothing soft about it." The reporter held up a half-finished bottle of SummerCrush.

"Ohhh fuck!" Brendon hollered.

The field reporter continued. "When this innocent young boy took a drink of what he believed to be orange soda, he got a nasty surprise. The bottle contained deadly shards of broken glass. They shredded the soft tissue in his throat, and ripped open the lining of his stomach. Now, we advise viewers that the following is actual footage of Ethan throwing up the mixture of SummerCrush, blood, and the deadly glass."

"Ohhh fuck!" Brendon yelled at the TV yet again. "These fucking reporters are going to fucking town on it."

They cut back to Mitch in the studio via split screen.

"Trish, have you spoken to anyone at SummerCrush?" the anchor asked.

"No, Mitch, we haven't. We've made many calls, but no one has returned them."

"Fucking liar!" Brendon exploded. Awoken by the noise, his wife came to see what all the yelling was about.

"Honey, what's up?"

"These fucking reporters are raping us live on national TV, and they're fucking liars! I have to get into work!"

Half an hour later, Brendon was sitting at his desk, his shirt damp with sweat. He had eleven people in his office, twenty-three voice messages on his phone, and his inbox was filling up with emails faster than he could open them.

CHAPTER THIRTY

JUSTIN SAT IN HIS OFFICE with the five LCD TVs on so he could monitor all the chatter about SummerCrush. He switched the volume from one to another and laughed to himself about the viciousness of the media. The story was getting blown way out of proportion, more than he could've hoped for. Justin turned up the volume as National Marketing Manager Brendon Gibson made an official statement to a rowdy group of reporters.

"First thing we would like to say is our prayers are with the families and the young ones who were affected by these horrific accidents." Brendon paused. "At SummerCrush, we pride ourselves on our family of products, and this occurrence has shaken us to our very core. We are investigating how these bottles of SummerCrush came to be contaminated with shards of glass. If it was from one batch, we'd be able to fix this fast and effectively. Unfortunately, we can't find a link between the contaminated products, as they weren't confined to a single area. We've had cases reported in six different states and are conducting a full product recall across the entire country. We are not discarding the possibility that this could be a terrorist attack on us and the American people. We will do everything in our power to make sure nothing like this ever happens again. Thank you and God bless."

The reporters jumped to their feet to fire questions at Brendon, but he'd already left the stage.

Nice move, bringing up the terrorist threat, Justin thought. But for SummerCrush, the damage had been done. Justin had spent days slowly chipping and carving the slivers of glass into each bottle, to make it look like a malfunction at the SummerCrush plant. A lot of people were going to lose their jobs over this.

Justin picked up his phone and called Sandy at Mother's Milk. He answered on the third ring. Good boy.

"Wow, some fucked-up shit," Sandy answered.

"Yeah, terrible. Do you think it was terrorists?" Justin asked.

"Fuck knows in this day and age. The world is becoming a scary place. Now, you wouldn't be calling me just to shoot the shit. How can I help you?"

"Just seeing how you guys are going on that campaign I didn't brief you on."

"It's going good. We have a few directions for you. Just locking everything into place."

"Great, put everything on hold," Justin said.

"What?" Sandy asked with a touch of annoyance.

"I need something else, and I need it fast. Now here's what I want you to do. I need a campaign I can run tomorrow. I want to offer anyone who has a bottle of SummerCrush in their fridge or pantry a free bottle of OrangeFizz. Throw away that unopened SummerCrush, and we'll get a safe OrangeFizz out to you. It's a perfect lead into the other campaign you are developing."

"Great, a fantastic way to get your product into the hands of SummerCrush drinkers."

"You got it. It'll cost us in stock, but the goodwill will be off the chart. And this gives you the 'in' to present that other campaign. Now make this idea so cheap that only an idiot could pass it up. No agency fees, just a free idea. Also get your media partners onto it. Get them to cut their fees, too. I need this to be a bargain. You'll make so much more later on, got it?"

"Got it, give us five hours."

"You've got three!" Justin said as he hung up the phone.

He went back to watching the TVs. By the end of the week, there wasn't going to be anyone in the entire US of A who hadn't heard about the deadly, dangerous SummerCrush.

CHAPTER THIRTY-ONE

DONNA SOUTHLAND WAS HAVING a creative review with her team. They were pitching for Land Rover, a great account to have. They'd spent a long time getting to this place and everything felt pretty good – their idea was great and their presentation was slick. Her assistant interrupted them.

"Donna, Justin Truth is on the phone," she said urgently.

This was an important meeting, and Donna didn't like the idea of putting that jerk first, but she knew Justin's type and they had to be managed a certain way. She had dealt with similar types in the past and always found ways to win them over to R and R's way of thinking. Advertising was as much about ideas as it was about relationships. OrangeFizz was a small part of their billings, but the entire Soda-Cola portfolio was a large part of R and R's business. Being the top-rostered agency meant they got a generous slice of the pie. Justin had the capability to make that slice a lot smaller if he gained more control at Soda-Cola. It was important to keep him happy, so Donna asked everyone if they could regroup in ten minutes.

Once her team had packed up and left her office, Donna heaved a deep sigh before picking up her phone.

"Justin, how are you doing? How can I help you today?"

"Hi, Donna. Have you seen the news today?" Justin got straight to the point.

"I have. The SummerCrush Marketing Department is getting ripped apart. It's a lose-lose situation. No matter what they say, nothing will help. They'll be doing extreme damage control, and hoping something bigger will supersede it in the media. But innocent kids getting hurt by a big corporation never goes down well." Donna said this with certainty.

"It's crazy," Justin replied. "Their bottling depots will be given a going-over with a fine-tooth comb. It's a marketer's nightmare. Glass in a drink?"

"Heads will roll over this," Donna added.

"Now, what do you think we should do?" Justin asked.

"In situations like these, it's best to keep out of the eye of the storm. Don't bring any attention to yourself. Keep it real simple. Don't go out to damn them, but if asked, you guys need a statement. Play the safe card."

"Okaaay. . ."

Silence hung in the air between the two. Donna was unsure of what this meant.

"Why?" Donna finally broke the ice.

"I just got sent an email from Sandy Miller at Mother's Milk."

"Really?" Donna's voice went up a notch.

"Yes, and they've put together a campaign for this situation, and I have to be honest, I think they've nailed it. They even got their media partner to put together a media plan that's ready to go. If I were to approve it, it would be up by the end of the day."

Donna was taken aback. "You thanked them for their initiative, right, and reminded them that they aren't a rostered agency with Soda-Cola?"

"I did tell them they weren't one of Soda-Cola's advertising agencies—a list, by the way, which I didn't select. I was just hoping you guys were thinking about my business as hard as someone who doesn't have it is."

"What are you getting at?" Donna asked, irritated.

"This thing just happened, and we need to move fast. I had to call you to see what you were going to do about it."

"Justin, sorry about that. We will get something over to you first thing in the morning. I'll get our best people onto it."

"Look, Donna, tomorrow is a bit late. Going by what I've seen so far, your best people may not crack it for a few rounds. What I'm going to do is pull the trigger on the Mother's Milk campaign."

"Justin, you can't do that!"

"Yes I can. You dropped the ball. Now make sure you don't do it again. Have a nice day. Bye."

Justin hung up.

"MOTHERFUCKER!" Donna threw her phone against the wall. She didn't lose her cool often, but this guy was seriously pushing her buttons.

CHAPTER THIRTY-TWO

THE TRAIN ROCKED FROM SIDE TO SIDE as Ross ate his cream cheese and ham bagel. There was something about Lydia Young's death that wouldn't leave him alone. People die unexpectedly all the time in the Big Apple, but in this case there was something that just didn't fit.

To distract himself, he picked up a newspaper from the opposite seat. The front-page story covered the SummerCrush disaster from yesterday. Like everyone else, he was disgusted at what had happened. The children affected were going to be scarred for life. Ross flicked through a few pages and stopped on a full-page ad from OrangeFizz. It was a simple message. Anyone who had a bottle of SummerCrush could swap it for a bottle of OrangeFizz. If you couldn't make it to a store, OrangeFizz would send one directly to your home for free. If he had a bottle of SummerCrush, he'd swap it for an OrangeFizz, for sure. He couldn't taste the difference between them anyway.

Ross arrived at work, sat at his desk, and opened the Lydia Young folder. The case had officially been closed, yet every morning he went over all the details.

She had moved from Georgia six months ago to work in New York. She had a boyfriend back home, but the long-distance relationship had fizzled out, and they'd broken up three months ago. Ross had followed up with the boyfriend, who'd been an obvious suspect, but it turned out to be a dead end. Lydia's ex was already in a new relationship and was working the day she'd had her accident. She had dated a few guys since moving to New York, for a bit of fun, but on the whole she'd preferred the single-girl lifestyle. She had lost her job two weeks ago, but had landed a new one and was supposed to start it three days after her death. Everyone he talked to liked her. Going on all accounts, it had been an accident.

Yet there were some things that didn't make sense. First, for Lydia to fall over the railing she had to have been lifted. Given her size and height, she simply wasn't tall enough to just fall over it.

Second, it was the sprinkler on her floor that had set off the alarms. A fire had set it off, yet there was no fire. If the alarm hadn't gone off, people wouldn't have fled the building. That it all happened on the same floor was just too close to be random. And in the third instance, it was reported that someone shouting "Terrorist attack!" had started the stampede. Who shouted? And why would they think it was a terrorist attack? The alarm had gone off just seconds earlier, but there'd been no smoke, fire, or gunshots.

Ross had requested, in writing, to be granted access to all the security footage of Manhattan Mall, but had been turned down twice. On his third attempt, he was finally given the green light, as long as he did it in his own time and not at departmental expense. He didn't mind; he had nothing else to do anyway. Besides, he had perfected the art of lurking around so that people would do stuff for him just to get rid of him. He took a picture of Lydia and taped it up on the wall next to his desk. He smiled at her and touched her cheek.

CHAPTER THIRTY-THREE

JUSTIN RECLINED in the leather chair in Carlton's premium office. Every week they had half an hour scheduled in their diaries to catch up and talk business. The whole company knew and respected Carlton as a formidable, genuine man, but nobody gets to be the CEO of one of the world's biggest companies without having a hidden ruthless side. It was this side of Carlton that ensured Soda-Cola always turned a profit and kept the board off his back.

Carlton poured them both a scotch in large tumblers, neat. It was his drink of choice, which made it everyone's drink of choice. He handed one glass to Justin.

"I have something to ask of you," Justin said, taking a sip.

"You can but ask, my boy," Carlton replied.

"I have been doing the sums, and twisting things here and there on my portfolio. Over all of my brands I have managed to get an extra two-point-five-million-dollar profit forecasted by the end of the financial year." Justin took another sip. "This exceeds the forecasts I was given; forecasts that, until now, have never been reached. I've exceeded them."

"That's a nice way to start a conversation, Justin. Now what is the question?"

"I would like to take some of this extra profit and give each of my team members a bonus at the end of the financial year. Over and above the normal company one."

"That's very generous, but I'm not sure if the other company staff will like it. Half getting money, half not."

"That's up to Steve. Does he want to reward employees who are making money, or those costing money? I want to shine a light on people who go the extra mile. It should make others lift their game. Lift the entire company. I will even forgo my own bonus to add to the pot."

"I will need the board to sign off on this." Carlton smiled. "It's their money you're giving away, Justin. I'd like you to ask them yourself."

"I'd be more than happy to." Justin drank the small amount of liquor he had left. "Now, look at what you've made me do. If you didn't have the world's best scotch stashed away, I wouldn't drink it so fast."

"A top up," Carlton smiled.

"Maybe just one finger this time? I'll get it, you stay there."

Carlton got up, and placed his hand on Justin's shoulder. "I'll get it for you, son." He said, taking Justin's glass. "I got a call from a very put-out Donna from R and R Advertising. She wasn't too happy that you let Mother's Milk run their campaign for OrangeFizz."

Carlton turned his back on Justin to open the double doors of his drinks cabinet. He leaned in and fished out the crystal decanter. Like a magician, Justin waved his hand over Carlton's glass, dropping a tiny fragment of Ziin457 into the light brown liquid. The broken pill instantly started to dissolve.

Carlton turned back to Justin, removing the decanter's stopper. "They are not one of our rostered agencies and doing so has put a strain on the relationship with R and R," he continued. "I hope you had a good reason for actioning this."

"Each month we pay R and R a great deal of money," Justin said, watching Carlton measure out one finger for him. "I know that they were pitching for Land Rover during the SummerCrush debacle, which was more important to them than looking after us. We should be number one in their thoughts. As soon as they wake, at work, at home, and when they dream. It should be how we can sell more products. Mother's Milk was very cheeky bringing their idea to me. They did it all for free. The media was secured with no markups."

Carlton handed Justin back his refreshed glass. "Money is good, but relationships are important, Justin," he said with the echo of experience.

"They are, but the more money we have, the more people want relationships with us," Justin replied smiling, holding up his glass for a toast.

They toasted and he watched closely as Carlton took a sip of his contaminated drink. What Justin had put in was similar to what he used on his mother. Unless someone specifically looked or tested for it, in small doses it was almost impossible to detect. By this time next year, Carlton wasn't going to be in any physical state to lecture Justin on his business decisions. If Carlton was lucky, he could still be alive. Just.

CHAPTER THIRTY-FOUR

AN EMAIL POPPED UP on Steve Barker's computer. It was from Montana Cruz.

> To: Barker, Steve
> From: montana.cruz@sodacola.com
> Subject: Coffee
>
> ---
>
> Hi Steve.
> The regular, 11am?
>
> M

Steve replied:

> To: Cruz, Montana
> From: steve.barker@sodacola.com
> Subject: RE: Coffee
>
> ---
>
> Yes. Talk soon.
> Steve.

Steve knew what she wanted to talk about: Justin Truth.

There was a small coffee shop a few blocks over from the Soda-Cola building. New York was full of coffee shops, but this one attracted Steve in particular. It was crammed with old furniture, and thousands of books lined the walls. Book patrons were welcome to read and borrow without asking. Returning them was not a requirement. It was a trust thing; the books turned over, and the collection grew instead of shrinking. Steve himself had bought books in simply to add to their shelves.

It wasn't the cheapest or the best-tasting coffee in town, but to Steve, the ambience more than made up for it and the place was always full. The seating layout changed regularly so patrons couldn't form a routine and have the same spot, even if they frequented the place.

Steve had asked why they changed the seating so often. "To change your perspective," the owner had told him. Steve liked this approach. He loved a certain brown, bonded-leather chair that was perfectly molded to his body, and he would hunt it out.

Once again he found his chair and claimed it. He was excited to get out of the office; that he would be alone with Montana made it even better. He ordered himself a coffee and a small, sweet tart. He told the server that he was also expecting Montana, and asked if they could make her coffee once she'd joined him. He wanted it hot for her, she liked her drink hot.

He'd sipped half of his coffee and nibbled a quarter of his tart when Montana swept in, grabbing the seat across from Steve.

"He's a bastard!"

"Please." Steve tried to shush her.

"Sorry, it makes me so mad just thinking about him." Montana drew in a few deep breaths to calm herself. "He's poison, Steve."

"Justin rubs some people up the wrong way. That's not to say he's a bad guy."

"Some people? Which people does he not treat like crap?"

"Debbie speaks very highly of him, and he has made amazing increases in productivity and profits. He has even asked for his bonuses to be split among his team."

"Money! That's all he cares about. Sure, he's lining his team's pockets with more money, but he has also retrenched thirty percent of his staff. It's his way or the highway. He puts the fear of God into them, and then props up their pay to make them believe he's looking after them. He's a psychopath!"

"That's a bit strong, don't you think?" Steve sipped his coffee.

"Steve, you're not in a business meeting. You're talking to me." Montana put her hand on top of his. He liked it. "We have been through a lot; you brought me into Soda-Cola, and have helped me so much. I know you put me forward for Justin's role, and I thank you for that. Soda-Cola is a great place, and he's just going to kill it."

Steve looked around and leaned back, the leather cushions squeaked.

Montana continued. "You know, I bet he had something to do with all the shit that went down with SummerCrush!"

"Montana!"

"Well…" She laughed and her eyes sparkled. "Maybe that's pushing it."

"OK, I dislike him a little too." Steve finally said, wanting her to smile. "In fact, I don't trust him as far as I could throw him. He is straining our relationship with R and R Advertising, and I just got a call from a supplier who said he was told that if he didn't accept a ten-percent profit cut for the next eighteen months, the entire Soda-Cola range would be stripped from his stores."

Steve smiled. He felt relieved getting it off his chest. Then a coffee appeared for Montana, hot like she liked it. Hot like her.

* * *

Justin reread the email Montana had sent Steve. Thanks to Guy Chambers, every email that Steve Barker sent or received was blind-copied to Justin. Information was currency. The vast majority of the emails were boring, but then Montana had started sending Steve messages more frequently. At first, they were just simple "let's talk" notifications. This angered Justin, that Steve would be having an affair with a woman who by rights he thought of as his. The more emails Justin read, the more he saw reference to "him." Montana was making waves and that wasn't good. She was forcing his hand. Everything that was going to happen to her was her fault; she had set this in motion, not him.

CHAPTER THIRTY-FIVE

SARAH TRUTH LAY IN HER BED, staring out the window. She was feebly aware of everything that happened to her, and around her, despite the drugs Justin was giving her to keep her in a vegetative state. She wished she could move her head.

In the past after Justin had visited, he'd rolled her slender frame to one side, so that she was stuck facing the wall and was only able to listen to her muted surroundings. The new nurse was a kind woman, and would pop in every hour to make sure she was able to look out the window, or at the TV screen. Today it was raining. She didn't mind, as she liked to watch the water trickle down the windowpane.

Sarah was intrigued by the way the droplets moved. The small ones wouldn't move until another droplet touched it, creating a bigger droplet. Then a lot of smaller droplets would be drawn into this larger one until it became so big, that the weight would drive it down the windowpane, collecting many more until it crashed at the bottom. Over and over the pattern would repeat itself.

The large droplets reminded her of her son. She often wondered if it was her fault, hers and Mathew's. Had they been bad parents? Some signs had manifested when he was young, but she'd explained them away at the time: *Boys will be boys—he'd grow out of it*, she'd thought. Later, when the disturbing behavior decreased, she truly believed that he'd indeed grown out of it. But really, he'd just become better at covering his tracks.

Sarah often wished Justin would just kill her instead of keeping her doped up and bedridden. This was not a life worth living. Stuck in this motionless body. Stuck in this bed. Stuck listening to Justin's weekly sermon of the evil he was inflicting on the world. If he wasn't going to kill her, she was going to kill him. She had to, before he became unstoppable.

She saw that he couldn't help himself; that there was no "off" switch.

She had to find a way to not swallow the water Justin gave her.

Sarah watched another droplet increase in size, and decided it was time to practice again. A few years ago, she'd had an idea, about a way she could fight back. What if she could build the muscles in her throat? What if she learned to control her throat, learned to hold the water, and to spit it out when he left. If she could find a way not to swallow the tainted water, even if it was by a small amount. Then, just maybe, she might regain control of her body. She would then be able to stop him once and for all.

From that day, she practiced, concentrating on her throat when the staff fed her, and her doctor gave her water. She mainly practiced when she was alone, by building up saliva in her mouth, and breathing through her nose to keep her throat closed, trying not to let even a single drop work its way down.

Day after day, month after month, she practiced. She had given up many times, thinking it impossible. Another visit from Justin would make her even more determined to fight. Then finally, three months ago, she had a breakthrough. She was able to hold the saliva for ten seconds while holding her breath, and the next day she was able to hold it a bit longer. She was now able to hold it for a full minute and then push it out through the corner of her mouth, letting it trickle down her neck. If she could have smiled she would have. She was on track to fight back and deal to her evil son.

CHAPTER THIRTY-SIX

IT WAS EARLY SATURDAY MORNING. Jennifer had stayed the night. Justin had awoken restless, bored with her. He'd jumped in the shower as a signal for her to get dressed and pack up. He dried himself, dressed quickly, ignoring her attempts to start a conversation about activities they could do together in New York today. Justin had other plans, plans that did not involve her. He'd given her the best sex of her life. What else could she want from him?

"Are you sure you can't get out of work?" Jennifer asked with a slight smile.

"If I had the choice, what do you think I'd do? The whole day slapping that tight ass of yours, or the mountain of repetitive reports I have to slug through?"

"You always have work," Jennifer replied with a frown. "That's no fun."

"You don't get to live in a place like this and drive the cars I drive without having to put in the hours," Justin winked. "Plus, I need to go out and visit my mother."

Jennifer's eyes softened. He'd told her about his weekly visits, and he knew she hoped he'd invite her along one day.

Justin slowly pushed her toward the door. He was about to tell her to just fuck off already. But she got the hint before he did and opened the door. She spun and gave him a big hug and a kiss. "Miss you already," she said before she sashayed toward the elevator.

Justin watched her hips swing, and her ass bobble. She had a fantastic body. *Maybe I should've fucked her one more time before I sent her on her way.*

Justin's neighbor, Bill Hampton, opened his front door, holding his yappy dog.

"Ohhh, which one was that? You're a busy boy, Jussst-in. Mmm."

Bill smirked.

Justin refrained from rolling his eyes.

"Morning, Bill," Justin replied, as Mr. Noodles yapped at him.

Justin couldn't stand that Bill was keeping tabs on his visitors and his comings and goings, inserting himself into Justin's life.

"Sooo, what are you up to today?" Bill asked.

"Going to spend—"

"I have a date with a man half my age!" Bill cut him off. "I'm meeting him for a day at the beach. No doubt I'm going to get sand stuck in all the wrong placesss." He giggled. "Mr. Noodles here is going to have to stay home all day by his little lonesome. Mmm."

Justin wasn't impressed. After visiting and medicating his mother, he'd planned to spend the day at home watching movies and convincing girls on dating apps to come over to his place. Now he was going to have to put up with this stupid barking mutt all day. Justin rubbed his scar as an idea popped into his brain.

"I'm going to be home all day," Justin said. "Why don't I take Mr. Noodles out for a walk? He'll love it."

Bill looked down at his dog, and it barked enthusiastically back at him. "Oh, Mr. Noodles. I think that is a wonderful idea!"

Later that morning Justin used Bill's keycard to enter his apartment. Mr. Noodles barked, but Justin had come prepared. In his hand was the small beef stick Bill had given him. Mr. Noodles snatched the snack and started to chew it. On the bench were a lead and small plastic bags. If Mr. Noodles had a shit on their walk, Justin had to pick it up and put it in the plastic bag. He hated the idea.

"Fuckin' mutt," Justin growled. He attached the lead to Mr. Noodles, but not to take him for a walk; he had other plans. He tied the dog lead to the table leg, and went back to his apartment. He came back with a mop that had a bright T-shirt tied around the head, and a dog whistle. He blew the whistle, and watched as the dog's ears pricked up. Justin blew the whistle again and whacked the dog in the face with the mop. Mr. Noodles got a fright and started barking. Once more, Justin blew the whistle and whacked Mr. Noodles in the face. He then repeated the process, over and over again. On just hearing the whistle, Mr. Noodles would fly into a vicious rage and attack the mop. Justin put the mop down. He placed a large soft bear (a present from Jennifer) in front of Mr. Noodles, and waited about fifteen minutes for the dog to calm down. As soon as he blew the whistle again, the dog's ears pricked up, and he launched at the soft bear, biting and tearing at it. It was savage.

Perfect, Justin thought.

CHAPTER THIRTY-SEVEN

DETECTIVE ROSS SMITH OPENED the door to the AV depart-ment. He had managed to book some time in one of the editing rooms to go through all the security footage from the Manhattan Mall. He'd had to push to get any time, because as far as the department was con-cerned, Lydia Young was a closed case. The room was dark, and the air was warm from all the machines. He saw a young guy in a chair concen-trating on one of the screens in front of him. The operator wore baggy jeans and a slightly stained T-shirt; one of his hands danced over the keyboard while the other moved a mouse.

"Sup!" the operator said, acknowledging someone had entered the room. He clicked his mouse a few more times before he turned to Ross. The screens reflected off the lenses of his thick-rimmed glasses.

Ross pulled out his packet of jelly beans.

"Hi," Ross replied, as he held out the bag for the young man, who clearly needed a shave. "I'm Ross... jelly bean?"

"Fuck yeah!" The young man eagerly took a few and chucked them back. "The name's Mark and I'm going to help you as much as I can. I have loaded up all the footage, hours and hours of it. I have given them all a name and timecoded them."

"Timecoded them?" Ross asked.

"Yeah, if you see something, just write down the time you see here on the bottom of the screen. That way you can easily find it again. You'll see on the right screen that it's divided into eighteen smaller screens. These are all the security cameras, all linked to play live at the same time. Just imagine you're there in the security room watching in real time. On this screen on the left, any one of the smaller screens can be enlarged, so you can get a better look. Use the mouse to click on the one you want to see. Oh, and just like a DVD, you can fast-forward and rewind. Pretty simple, right?"

"Pretty simple, I guess." Ross hoped that his perplexed face wasn't a dead giveaway about his distain and fear of technology, and that this wasn't going to be simple for him at all.

"Thata boy," Mark said. "I'll be in the next room… have to pull together some files and shit for a case. You know the Beetle Butcher, that's one sick fucker. They ain't got shit so I have to make new tapes of old stuff to make it look like new stuff. When you got something or any questions, come grab me from next door and I'll see what I can do."

Ross offered Mark the bag of jelly beans again.

"My man!" he said, then grabbed another handful and left Ross to it.

After playing around for three hours, Ross understood how the system worked; it was pretty simple after all. Anyone able to work a DVD could work this software. Ross watched the screens and made notes. Writing down the timecode made referencing faster; he was glad Mark had told him to do it. He wrote down the time Lydia entered the shopping mall and every time she'd appeared on any camera. He watched the footage over and over, rewinding, starting again, and cutting between cameras. The footage wasn't of great quality but his eyes got used to the grain. He sipped his coffee, each sip reminding him how great his own coffee machine was. He got good at changing the screens to follow her as she meandered around the building, disappearing into stores and walking back out. She didn't have a care in the world—and no idea that she was going to fall to her death in half an hour. No camera picked up her fall over the balcony, but a few caught her descent and landing.

Ross's eyes were hurting. He wasn't used to staring so hard at monitors. It was getting hot in the small room with all the buzzing equipment. He removed his jacket and unbuttoned the top buttons of his shirt. From the footage, he could tell by the way people were dressed that it was also hot the day Lydia died. She was dressed for the warm weather.

Then something caught his eye: a guy in the background, wearing a heavy jacket and hat. Ross recognized the type of army jacket; he'd seen a few homeless war vets wearing them on the street. The guy wearing it must have been sweltering. Ross sat up. Instead of watching Lydia in the footage he started to focus on the guy in the heavy jacket. He appeared in all the same places as she had. Ross was soon convinced that this guy had actually been following her, and he'd been good at hiding it too. Very rarely did they appear together in the same screen. But wherever she went, he was soon to follow.

Ross flipped over a new page of his yellow legal pad to record the times the man in the heavy jacket appeared on security cameras. He never went in any stores, just drifted about the mall. Ross tracked him to the top floor—the floor Lydia fell from. There was no footage of where he went from there. He just disappeared. Seven minutes later Lydia was dead. Ross couldn't find him in the crowd leaving. Frame by frame he searched the cameras.

Could this man in the heavy jacket have planned this whole thing? To make sure his action wouldn't be caught on camera? Did he know Lydia? He had to have known her. The whole thing smelled of premeditation. She was murdered. Someone wanted her dead. The why eluded Ross. His investigation into Lydia revealed no logical reason why she was thrown to her death. She'd never reported a stalker or getting harassed. Not one of her friends mentioned her feeling scared for her safety. There was no reason for her death. It was all too random. Unless randomness was the whole idea. The fire alarm, the panic, the push. Could that be it? That she just happened to get caught up in this man's sick game? Having no connection could be the connection.

Ross rewound the footage, searching for a screen-grab, and paused the screen on camera seven. "Hello there, Colonel Mustard, I'm going to find you, and when I do, you are going to tell me everything you did," he snarled at the image on the computer screen.

CHAPTER THIRTY-EIGHT

THE KEY NEEDED JIGGLING in order to open the door, which Ross had mastered like a pro after years of practice. He pushed open the door to his apartment and began to carry in all twenty boxes of case files. He made himself coffee, sat at his small kitchen table, and placed one of the boxes in front of him. He could have done this at the station but preferred to be home. His laptop could connect to the police server. He didn't have to talk to anyone about what he was doing, and home had the best coffee.

Each box contained files of all the accidental deaths in New York over the last six months. There were hundreds of them. Each file contained a police write-up, interviews, pictures, and CDs with any available footage relating to the incident. People died in some bizarre ways, and in this day and age there wasn't much that hadn't been filmed, by either security cameras or phones. He had dedicated his entire weekend to going through the files one at a time, and he had ordered five pizzas to tide him over.

One by one, Ross soaked up information about each death. Searching for any mention, sighting or footage of the bearded man in a green army jacket. This was his guy. He didn't believe in coincidence. In fact, he was suspicious of coincidence. The guy had been stalking Lydia. He went to the top floor. She was thrown from that very floor. He never left the floor. Gone, like a puff of smoke. It made too much logical sense to Ross to be anything else. This guy did it. And the way he'd concealed himself spoke of experience. Maybe he was military, maybe he was just methodical; either way he was a killer. A skilled one.

Well after midnight, Ross was feeling tired. The effect of the multiple coffees had worn off. Maybe it was time to call it a night. He knew he'd think more clearly after having a few hours of sleep under his belt. He shook his head, convincing himself to carry on.

He opened the file of an accidental death: a woman in her thirties, Kelly Elliott, who'd fallen in front of a train on the subway. Some believed it was a suicide, some assumed she'd slipped, and family were convinced she'd been pushed. If it was a murder, there were no suspects. Kelly was just a Plain Jane.

Ross watched the security footage of the crowded station as she fell onto the tracks seconds before the train came screaming in. He watched it a few times; it was so crowded he couldn't make out much. He rewound it to her arriving on the platform. He yawned and stretched open his eyelids in an attempt to squeeze out the tired. He watched as she pushed her way to the front of the other commuters. Just before she fell, she'd turned and then stumbled backward. Like she had lost her footing.

Ross's eyeballs hurt. He closed his eyes and rubbed them. His head bobbled. He was done for the night; time for bed. He absently stretched, knocking over his coffee cup.

"Fuck!" he yelled. In the scramble to make sure he hadn't saturated any files with coffee, he bumped his keyboard. The cup, fortunately, was empty. He placed it upright on the table and stared at it, feeling his eyes closing. He couldn't put it off any longer, it was time to go to bed. As he got up, he noticed the video on his monitor scrolling backward.

"Fuck!" he yelled again. He hit the space bar to stop the rewinding. The timecode showed that it was two hours before the train hit Kelly. Ross came wide awake as he spotted a lone figure walking to the place where Kelly fell. A train came and went, yet the lone figure didn't get on or meet anyone. He just stood there and eventually stalked away. His body movements were identical to those of the man on the Manhattan Mall security footage.

"Fuck me!" Ross said out loud. He rewound the footage and paused it. It was dark and grainy, but Ross was sure the guy was wearing the same army jacket as the man he suspected of killing Lydia. Except that he didn't have a beard.

CHAPTER THIRTY-NINE

IT WAS AN AMAZING DAY on the green. Donna Southland hopped out of the cart, placed her ball on the golf tee, and took a few steps back to gauge the distance where she wanted to send the ball. The New York Green Hills Country Club had the best golf course in New York, and the fees alone were enough to feed a third world country. Business wasn't always done around the boardroom table—Donna was a firm believer in that.

"Sure you want me to go first?" Donna asked.

"All yours," Carlton insisted from the driver's seat of the cart.

They'd been playing golf together for a few years now. Donna always made sure Carlton won the majority of the time, but when Donna won, she made sure it was only by the narrowest of margins. Donna lined up her shot and, with a perfect swing, sent the ball over 200 yards down the fairway.

"Ohhh, looks like you're going to be buying today," she joked.

Carlton got out of the golf cart, and placed his ball on his tee. "Not today, my friend, and I'm mighty thirsty, so I hope you brought your credit card."

Carlton lined up his shot and swung. It didn't have nearly its usual power, and the ball only went two hundred yards with a slight hook. Donna noticed that Carlton wasn't looking his best. He seemed tired, and moved sluggishly. Maybe he was coming down with something. Donna was going to have to adjust her game to keep it competitive.

By the fifth hole, Donna thought it was time to broach the subject. As she drove the golf cart she casually brought the conversation around to Justin Truth.

"It's been a few months now. How is Justin going?"

"Justin is a star," Carlton replied. "In the short time he's been with us, he's found ways to increase productivity and profit beyond all expectation. If everything goes according to his plan, all brands in his care will be six months ahead of forecast."

"A bit of a shark?" Donna asked.

"He has a bite. He's a young go-getter. Just the other day he wanted to give up his bonus and spread it amongst his team."

"Wouldn't have taken him for that type of guy," Donna said, surprised.

"I know you may not agree with some of the decisions he is making. He told me about rejecting your OrangeFizz campaign. He liked it, it's just not where he wanted to take the brand."

"That's all good," Donna lied. "We have another cracker of an idea in the pipelines, even better than the original. Talking about new work, what do you think about the swap-OrangeFizz-for-SummerCrush ads?"

"You don't like them?" Carlton asked.

"Not my work."

"But…"

"But, I think they could have been better, less slapped together. I felt the crafting of them let the idea down."

"They could have been done better by you guys," Carlton agreed.

"But we didn't get a chance to help."

"Justin did feel that you guys had dropped the ball on the Summer-Crush incident, which means you left the door open for someone to walk in. And Mother's Milk's idea has generated amazing business. It may not be your cup of tea, but it worked. Not only did we get Orange-Fizz product into SummerCrush consumers' hands, the PR we got out of it has leveraged wonders for us. A large Midwest supermarket chain that for the past ten years didn't want to know us has contacted me directly and committed to stock the entire range of Soda-Cola flavors from now on. That alone will give the Soda-Cola Company an extra 5.6-million profit to the bottom line within the next quarter."

Donna paused. It was going to be hard to argue with figures like that. Justin wasn't messing up within Soda-Cola as she'd hoped. She was going to have to try and win Justin over to R and R's way of thinking. She'd have to find a way to close the door on Mother's Milk. They had a whiff, and no doubt would be going hard to get their hands on more.

"I think it's your shot," Donna said as they pulled up to the sixth hole. Carlton smiled as he got out and placed his ball on his golf tee. He lined up his shot and swung his club back high over his head. His leg wobbled slightly. Then his body shook. He dropped the club. He buckled onto his knees before collapsing on his side. Donna ran over to her companion.

"You OK?" Donna asked, helping Carlton to a sitting position.

"I'm feeling... a bit... dizzy," Carlton said, awkwardly getting back to his feet with Donna's help. "I think we should hit the nineteenth hole, and by my reckoning, it's your shout."

"You were never that good at math," Donna laughed.

Carlton nodded, then ambled with a slight stagger to the cart. He rested his hand on the cart's roof as if he'd just run a marathon. Donna didn't like to see her friend like this. She packed away the golf clubs and made fast work of driving the cart to the clubhouse. If anything happened to Carlton, it wouldn't be good for Soda-Cola, and would be worse for R and R.

CHAPTER FORTY

JUSTIN PARKED HIS brand-new Audi Spyder. Like every Saturday, it was time to visit his mother. There are few places in the world where the truly rich and powerful let down their guard, and St. Mary's was one of them. Having a sick relative in common can bring strangers closer together.

In the late 1950s, a special board had been created at St. Mary's; its purpose was to make sure only the right types of patients were admitted. Each board member had a relative who, at one time or another, was in the hospital's care. As the hospital expanded and became more powerful, so did the board. Membership was by invitation only and had significant benefits. Justin very much wanted to get onto this board, and his mother provided the perfect way in.

He strutted through the imposing entrance doors and glided past reception. He paused and wondered which route he should take to his mother's room. He noticed Eric Smit sitting on one of the day chairs, deeply engaged in conversation with another well-dressed man. Eric's family owned several diamond mines around the world, and the family fortune was counted in the billions. His mother suffered from dementia, a condition Justin had used to form a connection between them. Eric was also on the board, and Justin would have liked to have deepened their friendship with a conversation about their mothers or the upcoming dinner at Dr. David's, but maybe another time. To interrupt would seem too needy, so he smiled with a nod as he walked past the men.

"Justin," Eric called out. Justin turned and approached the two men. Both got up and Eric shook Justin's hand, then introduced him to his companion.

"Justin, good to see you. Here, meet Victor Balenwood."

"Balenwood... not of the Balenwood department stores?" Justin enquired.

"One and the same." Victor Balenwood smiled.

"Victor's father was admitted today," Eric said. "I was just telling him about you, actually."

"All good, I hope," Justin joked. All three men laughed.

"Very good, Justin. I was telling Victor that in today's society, a lot of young people don't believe in the old ways of looking after family. Victor was most impressed when I told him about you and your mother. Such a positive young man with strong moral values."

"The type of person anyone would be lucky to have in their family," Victor added, "be it personal or business."

Justin smiled. It had taken five years of careful manipulation to come to the attention of such influential men.

"I thank you, gentlemen," Justin said. He had to handle these situations with the right amount of tact. He had to be seen putting the needs of his mother first, this would make these types of men want him even more. "I see you were in conversation before, and I don't wish to interrupt any further. If you're still here after I've visited my mother, I would very much like to talk some more with you."

Victor and Eric both nodded. Justin could tell by their expression that it had worked. He'd earned a small amount of respect from these two powerful men. After saying their goodbyes, Justin headed upstairs to his mother's room. He flung open the door.

"Oh, Mother, you look as beautiful as ever," Justin beamed. "What a week I've had. My plan for SummerCrush went perfectly. Just as I told you it would. It was all over the news. Already we have seen our market share jump five percent. By the end of the month, I'm sure it'll be up fifteen, if not twenty percent. I know, you must be so proud of me.

"Soda-Cola needs me more than I thought. There is so much deadwood that needs cleaning out. Lucky I don't mind getting my hands dirty. You wouldn't believe how bad the management team is." Justin was pleased with himself.

He placed the plate in the microwave and went about the ritual of breaking up the tablet to add to her glass of water.

"Montana is like a wild mare," he continued. "She needs to be broken, to be shown who the master is. Once I have broken her, she will be so much happier. She will know her role, then I can make her into the woman that she needs to be. A woman who can be by my side as I make America great once more."

Justin tilted his mother's head back and hurriedly sloshed the water into her mouth. Then discarded the empty glass onto her side table.

"Right, I must be going, I have so much to do today. Two rather important gentlemen are down the hallway that need to be impressed. Well, they already are." Justin stood to admire his reflection in her mirror. "I just need to remind them how amazing I am."

Justin leaned over and kissed his mother on the forehead, and promptly left the room.

* * *

Sarah was alone. Perfect. It was time to fight the bastard. That smug little bastard. She was glad he'd left as quickly as he did; she wasn't sure how much longer she was able to hold her breath. With this amount of water in her mouth she felt like she was drowning; the water felt heavy trying to force its way down her throat. She choked, swallowing half the water. She clamped her throat shut, causing her body to convulse. Her body demanded she swallow the rest. It needed more oxygen. No! She couldn't wait another seven days to try again.

She centered herself, took a deep breath in through her nose, parted her lips slightly and pushed. Then pushed harder. She felt like her brain was going to explode, her eyes pop out of her head, and an alien was going to burst out of her stomach.

Then it happened. A trickle of water escaped her mouth, snaking its way down her neck. She'd done it. She could do it again. It felt like one of her greatest accomplishments ever.

FILE TWO:
KILLER PROFITS

CHAPTER FORTY-ONE

NIGEL YEOWELL WAS RUNNING. No one was chasing him. He wasn't late for an important meeting, a bomb wasn't set to explode, nor was he the only person that could save the president. He was running because that is what he did, what he was born to do, what defined him. He was a runner.

Nigel discovered running after his third child was born; any chance he got now, he'd be into his running gear and onto the streets. Running was life. Life was running.

Nigel's running shoes weren't just running shoes. They tracked how far he ran, his speed, and automatically compared these statistics to his previous runs. He would post the results on his Facebook page so that other runners could track their progress against his. He wore microfiber-weave socks that kept his feet dry no matter how sweaty they were. His pants were tight, they supported his muscle compression and delivered moisture management with an 89 percent reduction in chafing. His multi-colored paneled top was made of the same material and featured an assortment of advertising logos, as he liked people to think that he was being sponsored. He'd paid a lot for it. On his wrist he wore a Nike Fuel band. Everything Nigel wore was designed to help him run with the utmost efficiency and pleasure.

His diet, too, was designed around running. Before he set out, he had three scoops of SuperPump with six ounces of filtered water and a potent protein mix. Each calorie consumed was mapped with exactitude, down to the right number of almonds at the right time. Not one too many, and not one too few. He saw himself as a performance machine that needed performance fuel.

Nigel flew along the dark street. He'd made this run many times. He made sure his breathing was controlled and his form was consistent. His goal was to run the Boston Marathon in six months. He wanted to win, but would be happy to place in the top ten. In his current condition, he'd be lucky to crack the top hundred. Thus, the five a.m. start this morning. It wasn't easy, but that was the life a runner chose. To win in Boston, he had to train hard and on the road. A treadmill wouldn't give him the same physical training as real road. In fact, Nigel was part of a group that looked down on people who ran on treadmills. They weren't runners to them. Hamsters, they called them, running round and round on a wheel. Real runners ran on roads, and only a real runner could understand the difference.

Halfway through his run, Nigel hit an obstacle course of sorts, a construction site. A condemned brick building was in the early stages of being renovated into modern apartments. The old getting pulled down to make way for the new. The route Nigel had planned took him down a side street next to the site, and only authorized people were now permitted access. As he got closer, he knew he could run past the closed-off street, loop around the block, and be able to rejoin his original route. He could do that, but he was a runner, and a runner runs the planned route. A runner lets nothing stop them from running.

He weaved in-between the wooden construction barriers, keeping his speed up. The side street was abandoned at this hour of the morning. Trucks, diggers, and loaders all resembled sleeping dinosaurs. Nigel had to concentrate on where he stepped, zigzagging to miss potholes the heavy machinery had created in order to avoid rolling an ankle. It was like a game to him. He imagined the obstacles were other runners. Each one he passed got him closer to the finish line, closer to winning his first major marathon.

A bright light hit him, followed by a loud horn. Nigel skidded to a stop, inches from the front of a truck that had slammed on its brakes to avoid running him over. The annoyed driver blared his horn more and flipped Nigel the bird, yelling at him to get off the fucking road, can't he fucking read? and detailing a whole number of items Nigel could repeatedly stick up his ass. Nigel backed up to the half-demolished building, returning the savage verbal attack with a condescending smile and a wave, prompting the driver to get even more pissed off and rev his engine at the runner.

Neither Nigel nor the driver noticed the dark figure loitering above them on top of the condemned building watching their interaction. Nor did they see him chip off a large chunk of concrete from the side of the building above Nigel.

The truck driver watched in stunned disbelief as Nigel's skull was caved in by the falling concrete bomb. The running gear did nothing to save his life.

CHAPTER FORTY-TWO

IT WAS CARLTON'S FIRST DAY back at Soda-Cola. Both Justin Truth and Steve Barker waited for him at reception, along with an expected group of Soda-Cola employees. Carlton had been stricken with a nasty virus—or at least that's what everyone thought.

As Carlton walked in the front doors, the group cheered. A broad smile appeared across his face. He'd been away for seven weeks and was looking a lot healthier. Steve was the first to extend a warm welcome.

"Great to see you back in the office, Carlton," he smiled. "The building is still standing —just." The crowd laughed at his joke.

"It's great to be back, people," Carlton responded. "I've missed you all. I think all I needed was a few weeks off, some bed rest, and eighteen holes of golf a day."

Once again, the crowd laughed and gathered around to show their respect. Justin jumped onto the reception desk to look down over the group.

"Now Carlton, we aren't the only ones who've missed you," Justin said as if he were performing on a Broadway stage. "Steve said you'd want your first day back to be a quiet event. But then Steve isn't known as Mr. Excitement, is he? As a founding member of the Watching Paint Dry Club, you can't blame him." His comment elicited a few laughs, especially from the people in Justin's teams, who laughed louder to support their boss.

"So... I've taken it upon myself to make today a little bit special, and what's more special than—Mr. Tony. Bennett!"

On cue, a piano started to play, and people quizzically looked around to see where the music was coming from. Three men slowly wheeled in a bone-white grand piano sitting on a high platform. Tinkling the ivories of the exquisite instrument was a gentleman in a three-piece suit. The group cheered, then swiveled their heads as more instruments became audible. From the other side of the room, hiding behind a partition wall, another platform was rolled into reception. Sitting on it were a saxophone player, double bassist, and guitarist. Like the pianist, each of the men wore a classic three-piece suit and had their hair slicked back in a true sixties style.

The main elevator doors opened, and Tony Bennett made his grand entrance singing "The Best is Yet to Come." Justin watched as a wide grin spread across Carlton's face. He was a massive fan of Tony Bennett.

After the third song had finished, Justin ran up to the legendary crooner and slung an arm around his shoulders.

"Ladies and gentlemen, Tony Bennett!" he shouted to a round of applause.

The crowd in reception had grown considerably since Tony started singing. In fact, it seemed as though everyone in the building had gathered there by now. They all cheered and a few people whistled as Tony left the room.

"Now, I don't want to be the bad guy," Justin said, "but we do have work to do, and I think Carlton has two months' worth of timesheets waiting on his desk to be filled in." The crowd laughed, and started to make their way back to work in a joyous mood. Carlton, still all smiles, shuffled up to Justin with flair, grabbed his hand, and gave it a firm shake.

"Good to see you," Justin said before Carlton could open his mouth. "Everything is ticking along smoothly, and once you've found your feet again, I'll take you through what my team is doing. We have some hot new ideas on the boil."

"From what I've heard, your team is doing very well," Carlton said. "You are making this old man proud."

"Which old man is that?" Justin quipped. He put his arm around Carlton and led him toward the elevators. Justin's aim was to get him away from Steve and create a wall between the two men. They entered the elevator, but to Justin's dismay, Steve slipped in at the last minute just as the doors closed. He stood next to Carlton and smiled.

"I've booked us in for lunch, Carlton," Steve said. "It'll be great to catch up. We've missed you around here."

"Great," Carlton replied. "It'll be good to talk to both of you. You will join us, right, Justin?"

"I'll be there with bells on." Justin said. "Only if it's OK with Steve?"

Steve gritted his teeth and forced a smile. "Even better."

CHAPTER FORTY-THREE

AN EMAIL POPPED UP on Justin's screen, from Montana to Steve.

To: Barker, Steve
From: montana.cruz@sodacola.com
Subject: Need coffee

What a jerk! Can't believe he did that. He just wanted to be the center of attention. He had no right to make fun of you either. Need to vent.
Same place? 2.30pm?
We need to open Carlton's eyes and get Justin out of here. I know we can't prove it, but I'm sure he killed my LemonGreat promo by leaking it to the competition!

M

Justin rested his chin in his hands. He was still getting blind-copied on every email that Steve sent and received. It was proving to be quite a valuable tool. Steve and Montana had built up a rather long conversation about him. He felt pleased with himself, thinking about LemonGreat. Montana had been working for an entire year to get a promo together for the brand using QR Codes and geotagging. Just weeks before the launch, their biggest competitor, 10-Lemon, launched the same idea. As a result, the LemonGreat promo was pulled and it cost the brand hundreds of thousands of dollars. It was an internal disaster.

And Montana was right: Justin *was* the reason it had all turned to piss. He'd pulled the presentation off the Soda-Cola server and sent a simple email from an anonymous address to a 10-Lemon employee who he knew would take advantage of the information. As he'd expected, they'd jumped at the chance to get something to market first and put a dent in LemonGreat sales. This was just one of many things Justin had orchestrated over the last eight weeks to make Steve's team look incompetent and lacking in direction.

After lunch with Carlton and Steve, Justin returned to his desk. As predicted, Steve had spent the entire meal waxing lyrical about the past. Carlton and Steve had a special bond and Justin realized that it would take the very deepest of betrayals to break it. The only good thing to come out of the lunch was that the hot waitress had given Justin her phone number.

Justin's iPhone beeped to remind him of Montana's 2:30 p.m. coffee with Steve. Why was she wasting her time with Steve when she could be with him? She could be The One; she just had to accept it. Justin needed to show her the error of her ways. She would be so much happier on his arm than sleepwalking through her life. What could Steve offer her? Justin pulled out a book from a desk drawer he'd bought a few weeks earlier, rubbing his scar as he thought about all the things they would eventually do together.

Justin made his way to the Soda-Cola underground parking garage. He found Steve's Porsche Cayenne. Justin shook his head. Why would someone buy a vehicle like this? It looked like a minivan had fucked a Porsche to create this awful offspring. He removed a small black box from his pocket. It had magnets on one side and he was able to attach it to the car behind the front wheel, near the engine. It was a simple programmable device that sent vibrations through the whole car. It would set off the car alarm, over and over again.

Justin called Debbie on his iPhone.

"Hello, Mr. Truth?" Debbie chirped.

"Can you inform security to tell Steve that someone may have tried to break into his car? His alarm is going off."

"Will do!" Debbie had taken to her new role well, never questioning anything.

Justin set off the alarm, knowing it was going to keep Steve busy for the next twenty minutes. He exited the building and headed to the coffee shop where Steve and Montana had planned to meet. It was a trendy place a few blocks away that was set up like an old bookstore. He'd followed Steve there once before and had taken photos of him and Montana sitting together. In the wrong hands, the pictures of a married man having secret meet-ups with an attractive woman could do serious damage to his reputation.

When he arrived, Justin ordered an espresso and headed to a chair in the back corner. He scanned the room, observing everyone in the shop. At first glance, he saw no one he wanted to fuck or invest his time in. The girls who worked behind the counter were too alternative for his taste, with an abundance of facial piercings. He couldn't understand why they'd want to make themselves so unattractive.

Justin watched as Montana entered. The air changed the moment she walked in; she had an ability to make an entrance without doing anything. Her natural, dark-haired beauty was like a perfumed wind rushing into the room, and people automatically looked up, drawn to her. Justin felt his cock stiffen. He couldn't take his eyes off her. She paused for a second and her eyes moved around the room looking for Steve, so Justin lifted a newspaper to hide his face from her. She couldn't see Steve, so took a seat at an empty table and waited for a waiter to serve her. Justin folded his newspaper and approached from behind. He softly placed his hand on her shoulder.

"Hi," he said, imitating Steve's voice.

Montana turned around, smiling. Her smile instantly soured when she saw who it was.

"What are you doing here?" she asked coldly.

"I'm returning a book I borrowed a few months ago. I don't know if you've met Jennifer, this girl I'm fucking. And when I say fucking, I mean fucking-her-ass-till-she-bleeds type fucking. Well, she brought me here and told me about how you could borrow books and indulge in bad coffee. I picked this one up. I'm not sure if it's a memoir or fiction?" Justin leaned in closer and whispered, "I think you should read it."

Montana could feel the heat from Justin's breath on her ear, and it made her stomach churn. Justin dropped the hardback book onto the table. It made a loud bang. Montana wasn't sure how to react. She couldn't believe what Justin had just told her.

"I'll see you back at the office then." Justin flashed a sly grin. "Can you pay for my coffee? Thanks, crazy, crazy day ahead." He blew her a kiss, and stepped lightly out the door before she could answer.

Questions were running through Montana's mind. Had he followed her? Did he know what she was planning? Or was it just coincidence?

Montana read the title of the book Justin had left behind: AMERICAN PSYCHO.

A book she had read twice before.

CHAPTER FORTY-FOUR

Ross knocked on the door of his sergeant's office.

"In!" called a gruff-sounding woman. The voice belonged to Sergeant Olive Masterson. She was five foot eight and solid; not overweight, but people often thought she was due to her large round face, E-cup breasts, and short legs. She was also one of only a handful of women to have achieved the rank of sergeant in the New York police department. Every day she battled the bad guys to put them away, and each day she battled the good guys—in their minds—to keep her position. She was razor-sharp and just as cutting when needed.

Olive had inherited this demeanor from her father, a tough-as-nails beat cop. When she was ten, she came home from school one day to find her mother crying. She'd just been diagnosed with breast cancer, and nine days later she was dead. Her father had taken it hard but showed no emotion to the outside world. In his mind, emotions were something men didn't express. He didn't know how to bring up a girl and was hard on Olive, raising her as he would a son. She didn't wear dresses and knew more about hunting and fishing than Barbie dolls and *My Little Pony*.

Olive found school easy and had a natural ability for problem-solving and math. The cool kids, on the other hand, were a bit harder for her to deal with. One day a guy on the football team decided it would be funny to knock her lunch out of her hands, call her an Oompa-Loompa, and sing the famous song from *Willy Wonka & the Chocolate Factory*. In return, she punched out three of his teeth and put him in traction. He never played football again, and no one messed with her again either.

She'd ended up following in her father's footsteps, joining the force. Ross remembered when she'd started at the department a few years ago as an officer. He'd just gone through a bad break-up. His girlfriend at the time was a part-time alcoholic and full-time bitch. They were a perfect match: he was a part-time asshole and full-time alcoholic. He'd upped his drinking to forget her. Forgetting himself was a bonus.

Olive had transferred from Boston to New York and was clearly smart and ambitious. Ross watched as the other guys gave her shit. He didn't go out of his way to befriend her; nor did he go out of his way to make her feel at home. Three months into her new job, Ross stumbled in on Olive crying in a janitor's closet where he stashed a bottle of Jack for emergencies. His first instinct had been to pretend he hadn't seen her and go in search of his other secret stash. Instead he gave her a smile and crouched down so they were eye to eye.

"I guess the vomit in the holding cell can wait another ten minutes." He'd winked. "Life is shitty, but don't let the shit stick."

She smiled back, only slightly. He kept her company for a few minutes, chatted about nothing and everything. On his way out of the closet, he tapped the door handle. "If you twist the handle up, it'll lock the door. Stay in here as long as you need. And there may or may not be a bottle of something in one of those old boots in the corner. Take your time, crime ain't going nowhere." Then he softly closed the door behind him. She locked it.

Seven months later, Olive was on the move again; this time to Washington where she was promoted to detective-investigator and worked some high-profile cases. A few promotions later and she was back in New York, but this time she was in a position of power. The guys who had given her shit the first time around found she was now a brick wall, and if they talked sideways to her, they were gone. She remembered Ross as one of the men who'd treated her well, so she had a soft spot for him. Ross had seen the change in her and respected what she'd achieved.

Ross entered her office, holding a box under one arm and resting it on his hip. "Hi. Is this a good time?"

"What do you want, Ross?" Olive's fingers flew across her keyboard. A fresh cigarette was resting on an ashtray made out of a NO SMOKING sign that used to be screwed to her wall. The small office was immaculate. She would know if something was moved an inch or left behind from a briefing. A whiteboard on the sidewall listed all the priority cases and who was assigned to them.

"I want to reopen a case," Ross said.

"Why the fuck would you want to do that?" she said without looking up. "We're already understaffed, and there are hundreds of new cases coming in every day!" Ross placed the box he was carrying on her desk.

"It's the Lydia Young case. I know it wasn't an accident."

"For fuck's sake, Ross, I thought you would have dropped that," Olive snapped. This was her typical demeanor and he let her words bounce off him.

"It wasn't an accident. It was murder," he said. "Worse, she's not the only one. I've identified the same person at four different crime scenes. He's responsible, I'm sure. He's killing innocent people and making it look like accidental deaths. Real fucking clever."

Olive stopped typing. This meant she was now listening. She stared at Ross, picked up her cigarette, and took a deep drag. "A fucking serial fucking killer or something? You're joking, right? As if we don't have enough on our plates with this fucking Beetle Butcher splashed across the front page every second day. And now you're telling me we have another psycho who throws young women from mall balconies?"

"Yeah, something like that." Ross shrugged. "But he does it in different ways each time. To avoid making a connection between them."

Olive took another drag. Silence held in the air between them as she slowly blew out the smoke.

"You fuck," she finally said. "How much shit is in that box?"

"A lot," Ross smiled, tapping the box.

"Can you wait until seven tonight?"

"I can do that."

"OK, take me through it all then," Olive said, then started to type furiously again.

Ross retrieved the box and turned to leave.

"Oh, Ross—please go solve some of your assigned cases today!"

"Yeah, no worries, boss," he replied with an upbeat smile.

CHAPTER FORTY-FIVE

JUSTIN RELAXED ON the leather couch in his office. Listening to Radiohead, he soaked in the New York afternoon sun. He inhaled two fat lines of Bolivian cocaine as a reward for his productive morning. Everything was going according to plan. All the brands in his portfolio were well above forecast; some better than they'd been in many years.

It was time to work on the transition of power from Carlton to himself. Justin's plan of three years needed to be fast-tracked. He didn't believe that Steve was the man to lead Soda-Cola into the future. It would be safer in Justin's hands. He knew that upping the dosage he was slipping Carlton in their weekly meetings should do the trick of forcing the old man to step down due to ill health. He had other plans for Steve, special plans.

He leaned in and snorted another fat line of coke. He was feeling a little restless. He felt the itch come on, starting at the base of his skull, working its way into his brain. He stared at the antique wooden coffee table, thinking of its hidden contents.

"Let's go and play," a whisper said.

"Not today," Justin replied.

"Why not, you deserve it, buddy."

"I know."

"So, let's go and play."

"Not today, I'm going to wait. The deal was once a month."

"New deal, buddy, once a week. You can swing that. You're the man. You always work harder after a hunt. It's good for you, good for the company, it's good for America."

Justin liked that idea. Jennifer slipped into his mind. He'd kept her around longer than he thought he would.

"What about you fuck her, slice her throat? That would be fun," the wicked

whisper said.

"She's too close to me. They always suspect the boyfriend."

"Fine, break up with her, then in twelve months do it. You drive a hard bargain, buddy."

There was a knock on his door, Justin knew it had to be Debbie. No one else was allowed to interrupt him.

"In!" he yelled.

Debbie opened the door, beamed at Justin, then closed the door behind her. He made no attempt to hide the small pile of cocaine in front of him. He snorted another line as she sat in the single chair to his right, and he didn't offer her any.

"Sir, here is the latest collection of information I have gathered about the people on your list," she said, holding up a file. "Must say, Guy has been doing wonders helping me. I think he may have a bit of a man–crush on you." Debbie giggled. "At the top of your list was getting rid of Peter Weller on NiceTea. I think you'll find he has visited some websites on the Soda-Cola banned list. Instant dismissal," she said matter-of-factly.

Justin nodded, and let a small grin form on his lips.

She smiled back. "I also have a friend who works at the tennis club where Steve Barker's wife, Trisha, is a member. I have never been there myself, but a few girls here go. Sounds pretty nice, if you like tennis. Um, I was talking to my friend, and she was talking about how Trisha and her stuck-up friends—"

Justin interrupted her, "Debbie, It's me here. Call them what they are. Unworthy rich bitches who haven't worked a day in their lives. Not like you have."

"Yes," Debbie's smile broadened even more. Her heart fluttered. Her eyelashes flicked. Her stomach flipped. She continued, "These rich bitches all have a group lesson with one of the young South African tennis pros. My friend said it's disgusting how these middle-aged women fawn over this man half their age. After the lesson she has to listen to them gossip about how hard their lives are over a few summer cocktails. How their husbands don't deserve them, blah blah blah. I thought this would be helpful for you, I'm always thinking about you. Um, and how great you are doing here, and what I can do for you. I gave this friend of mine a few hundred dollars to eavesdrop on them, and she went one step further and recorded them." Debbie handed Justin a flash drive.

"Good work, Debbie. Each day you impress me."

Debbie beamed, blushing a little. "Thank you." She felt a little giddy, stood, and went to leave.

"Debbie," Justin called after her. She stopped and turned to face him.

"Come back," Justin beckoned. He opened his desk drawer and pulled out a small envelope.

"Here," he said, offering her the gift. "You amaze me, Debbie."

She eagerly reached out to take the envelope. Justin held it for a second, as well as holding her eyes. "I just had an idea," Justin said, letting go of the envelope. "I want your friend to start a rumor. I want her to spread it around that Steve's wife was seen giving the tennis instructor a blow job after one too many cocktails at the bar."

"I can do that," Debbie replied, staring at the envelope.

"Those are front-row tickets to *The Lion King* on Broadway," Justin smiled knowingly. "I know how much you love Disney films. Take someone special. There are also dinner reservations in there too. They charge it back to me."

"I don't have someone special," Debbie looked longingly at Justin.

"You should. Someone like you deserves to be treated special every day."

He nodded to let her know she could now leave. Once the door closed, Justin cut up a long line of coke, then wolfed it. He looked forward to listening to what Steve's wife flapped her gums about. Something he could use later would be helpful.

Jennifer slid back into his mind. Beautifully simple Jennifer. A naive girl trapped in the body of a goddess. She woke up as beautiful as she went to bed. No, he couldn't kill her, but he could educate her before flicking her like a discarded takeaway coffee cup. Justin knew he was a skilled lover; he'd been told many times by many ladies. He did like fucking her, but found that she was a bit restricted in the bedroom. He needed to show her what she had been missing her whole life, expand her sexual knowledge. She would thank him in years to come.

He wanted her tonight, but also wanted to test her. To see how far she would go to please him. Thus, pleasing herself in the end. He grabbed his laptop, accessed his own private server—so no one could trace his online activities—and logged onto a porn site that didn't come up on any Google search. MrHardcoreX.com. You name it, they had it. He entered his password, which allowed him access to the clips that weren't on public display, and began to search. Justin scanned through a few until he found something that appealed to his mood. He watched the seven-minute video three times. Yes, that is what he wanted to do to Jennifer tonight. He was going to require a few items on his way home; a stop at The Pink Kink Sex Shop was called for.

CHAPTER FORTY-SIX

OLIVE FLICKED THROUGH the last page of the Lydia Young file, having read it twice.

"You sure you want this?"

"You know I do," Ross replied.

"There's some good stuff here, some solid police work."

"That's my job."

"You'll be surprised with some of the bullshit that comes across my desk." Olive pulled out a cigarette and lit it.

"Can I have one?" Ross asked.

"This is a smoke-free building, so no, you can't." Olive smiled, throwing Ross the pack. "Say I reopen this for you. What's in it for the department?"

"Catching the bad guy," Ross said, taking a puff on his bummed cigarette.

"What I need is the Beetle Butcher caught. You haven't put your hand up for that case."

"My hand gets slapped a lot."

"Tell you what, you work the Beetle Butcher for me, and every hour you log on it, you can log ten minutes of department time onto Lydia's case." Olive stared at Ross intently.

"Can I negotiate?"

"No."

"Then it's a deal," Ross smiled. "I'll start tomorrow morning."

"Nice try." Olive took a thick folder off her desk and threw it to Ross. "Something I had prepared earlier for you. Now don't let the door hit your ass on the way out. We have bad guys to catch."

Ross left Olive's office in good spirits. He got what he needed, even if it meant eighteen-hour days for the foreseeable future.

Back at his desk, he smiled at Lydia's photograph taped to the wall.

"We're one step closer," Ross addressed the photo. He glanced around the office to see who was still there. He was one of only a handful still working at this late hour. It made him happy that people were with their families—he hoped—and not at a bar. He wished he had spent more time with his and not at his desk at this time of night.

Ross had to remember how to log an online request form to ask for time with the departmental sketch artist. A few failed search attempts later, and he was on the right webpage. He hated all this online form-filling; a conversation would be so much easier. Once upon a time he would have gone straight to the artist and asked for help, but now he had to fill out four different online forms, and wait for each one to be approved, then be issued a job number before he was allotted a set amount of time. It was as if they didn't want police doing their job, by putting obstacles in the way of simple procedure.

He persisted. He had enough grainy footage of the guy in the green army jacket, but a well-drawn picture would help his cause when asking people if they had seen him. He got an instant email informing him that his request had been logged, and if successful, he could see the artist at an assigned time. If he missed the time, he would need to re-apply.

Now that was done, he took a deep breath, and stared at the fat folder Olive had given him. On the cover, it read: Case HGF232. Written under it: THE BEETLE BUTCHER. The case folder was about two hundred pages thick. Everything was also archived on the internal data system these days, but Ross liked having a folder. He liked reading off paper, moving pieces around to make logic, and holding photos in his hand. Olive knew this, and made sure he got what he needed. Ross respected her for that. She actually thought about people, and how she could get the best out of them. He opened the folder, but before he read one word all he could think of was coffee, *his* coffee.

The cool air brushed his face. Ross put a smoke in his mouth, sparked his lighter, and welcomed the taste. He didn't know what extra skills he'd be bringing to the Beetle Butcher case; after all, well over a hundred pairs of eyeballs were already trawling the clues. It was high-profile, and the person who cracked it would be smartly promoted.

Ross had avoided cases like these. Promotion wasn't his game. He'd rather go after the cases that fell through the cracks, the ones that weren't likely to advance his career. He actually believed in making a difference in the real world, that solving any crime was reward enough. Stopping bad guys shouldn't be about glory and pictures in the paper. It was about doing what was right for the victims.

During the train ride home, Ross flicked open the case folder to a random page and quickly shut it. The page contained graphic photos of a victim, among the most disturbing he'd ever seen.

CHAPTER FORTY-SEVEN

DONNA SOUTHLAND TOSSED A baseball from one hand to the other, then tossed it back. She spun the ball on his desk, watched it blur, then as it slowed, snatched it up. She bounced it off the wall a few times, then tossed it again from one hand to the other while pacing. She was thinking. When she did this type of thinking, she liked to play with a baseball.

She had worked in the advertising industry for the past eighteen years. She loved what she did, and for the most part, she liked her clients. She had started her career at a small shop in Orlando, McMillian Partners. From there, she'd made a big move to Portland and one of the world's best agencies, Wieden+Kennedy, where she learned how important the creative solution was and how to sell it.

Donna had started at R and R eight years ago. From the beginning, it had been one of the places to be, and in her opinion, it still was. They were winning plenty of international creative awards and were talked about in all the right magazines. True, sometimes they pushed their clients hard to be cutting-edge in order to win awards, but most of the time it also resulted in sales. Any idiot could make an ad with a large pack shot, and a buy-now message, but only special pieces of work made people fall in love with brands and form an ongoing relationship with them.

Donna was a fan of this style of promotion, creating consumer love through advertising. Many of her clients bought into her way of thinking, but Justin Truth wasn't one of them.

Justin was something entirely different; Donna had to figure him out. She had to get Justin to appreciate what R and R could do for him. From what she'd heard, Justin was gaining influence within Soda-Cola, and over the spending of advertising dollars. If it were up to Donna, she'd tell Justin where to go and have nothing else to do with him. But if she did that, she would lose a large chunk of the Soda-Cola business. Besides, she'd have to retrench a number of good people, and that was far worse than having to deal with Justin.

Donna picked up a classic wooden baseball bat and bounced the ball on its well-worn surface. Moving the bat ever so slightly on each hit to juggle the ball. All the small techniques she'd tried on Justin hadn't worked; Justin managed to keep her at arm's length. Donna thought a bit harder. She always found a way in. In her heart, Donna was a nice person who liked people, although she sometimes had to do things that weren't nice. She had seen tears, breakdowns, screaming, rage, and anger from all types. She didn't like it, but she didn't loathe it either. If someone had to drop an axe, it was her.

Donna leaned back in her chair, throwing the ball at the ceiling, catching it, and throwing it again. Maybe she found cracking Justin hard, as she didn't really like him. Most of the time she found something to like about the people she worked with. She was always able to keep it at a professional level. Justin had a habit of blurring that line. He'd pressured their receptionist, Sophie, to go out with him a few times. Justin wasn't one to take no for an answer. Donna couldn't see it going anywhere, as Sophie was lovely, and Justin was a prick. Also, Donna was sure that Dusty and Sophie had a "thing" they were keeping quiet.

Donna wondered if Justin saw himself as a bit of an action hero, that he wanted people to look up to him and, in particular, for women to fawn all over him. Donna had treated Justin as a reasonable person and not a giant walking penis. Maybe if she threw some pussy at him, easy-to-fuck pussy, Justin would respond. Maybe she could create a day out for people from both Soda-Cola and R and R. After all, team-building sessions were very common at both companies. She could find some activities to make Justin shine, and maybe hire a bunch of promo girls with the brief of stroking his ego and anything else he wanted stroked. It would have to be done in a way that made it impossible for Justin not to enjoy it.

CHAPTER FORTY-EIGHT

CARLTON WELCOMED JUSTIN into his office for their weekly meeting. "Justin! I still can't believe you got Tony Bennett in for me." He had repeated this several times since his first day back.

In the eight months since he hired Justin, Carlton had visibly changed. His face was gaunt, his cheekbones more prominent, and his eyes hollow. The medication Justin had been slipping him was slowly destroying him. Doctors had sent Carlton for multiple tests to find out why he was deteriorating like this, but the drug wouldn't turn up on those broad tests. It had to be tested for specifically.

"Tony Bennett," Carlton repeated.

"I did it for me," Justin responded. "I was just looking for an excuse." Both men laughed. But then Carlton took on a more serious tone.

"I realize I have only known you for a short time," he said. "But I have seen the qualities of a natural leader. I have been with this company for over thirty years; I've had to fight hard to get to where I am, and to stay. The older I get, the harder I find it to take up that battle, and sometimes I forget what all the hard work is for. But then I look at where Soda-Cola is now, and how it dominates the other brands. I know I've done well. I used to worry about what would happen if anything were to happen to me. While I was off work, I didn't think about it. Do you know why? Because I've never felt as confident that it is in safe hands as I do now. Justin, I don't want people to know this, but I'm thinking of stepping down."

"What?" Justin said, the picture of concern.

"It's not going to be for some time—I've still got a few years left, but I want to make the process smooth. So, I've decided to hand more of the running of the company over to you and Steve. Steve will take over the bulk of it."

Justin didn't like the sound of that.

"So, Steve will be my boss?"

"Not right now, but eventually he will take my place and be every-one's boss." Carlton was watching Justin very closely; he knew Justin had big plans, and he had to handle this situation with care. He didn't want to lose Justin.

"Justin, you're a man after my own heart," Carlton said. "You will grow this business like no one else. You'll crush those who need to be crushed. Soda-Cola needs you, but they also need Steve. People love him and he's in the right place in his life to take over control."

Justin could feel Carlton's eyes on him, looking for something to give away how Justin was feeling. Justin's goal was to take the CEO position; it didn't matter to him what Carlton planned, as long as he didn't do anything before Justin could execute his own plans.

"You will, of course, take over his role," Carlton continued. "If you want, you can look over the entire Soda-Cola portfolio. It will be up to you to run them how you like, to promote someone into your old role or not, and to create some new positions. You will effectively run So-da-Cola."

"That's sounds like a great idea!" Justin smiled. "I am only a young man; I have so many things I want to do before I get all of your wrin-kles," he added with comic timing that widened Carlton's responding smile. "Now how about that drink you haven't promised me?"

Carlton smiled and slowly stood to fetch them both a scotch from his drinks cabinet.

"What do you think you're doing?" Justin said motioning for him to sit. "I know how to pour a drink, and you shouldn't be running around after me."

Carlton eased himself back into his chair.

As Justin made his way to the drinks cabinet, he palmed a pill from his pocket. Carlton was going to be stepping down, a lot sooner than he thought.

CHAPTER FORTY-NINE

BILL HAMPTON CAME from a wealthy family and was partial to his creature comforts. He loved to be himself and to be fabulous. From a young age, he'd known he liked his male friends more than he should have. He liked hanging with the girls, but he couldn't stop looking at the boys, and wanting to touch them. As he entered his teenage years, he tried to be with women to please his openly homophobic father.

"Fucking poofters, goddamn cocksuckers are killing the country. Should be drowned at birth." Such were the words of wisdom passed down from father to gay son.

Bill would have stayed in the closet a lot longer if his father hadn't died of a major heart attack when Bill was twenty-two. When his inheritance kicked in on his twenty-fifth birthday, Bill made the move to New York to live the ultimate gay lifestyle. He had money and wanted to play. The one thing he loved more than anything was to suck balls, especially when they were sweaty. He'd take one into his mouth, at a time, and rotate it. He would fuck other men, but didn't enjoy the reverse—he was a pitcher, not a catcher. He would suck balls and play with cocks all night, but very rarely did he let them fuck him. As the rich one, he usually called the shots, but sometimes he'd do special favors for men with the features of an angel and the abs of a god.

Bill had experienced only a few long-term partners. With his large bank account, there were always younger men who wanted him. He knew, as he got older, that they were only with him for the money. But, as long as they did whatever he wanted them to, a few expensive gifts here and there didn't go amiss.

Mr. Noodles was Bill's fifth dog and the most loved of all. Mr. Noodles could do no wrong. It was a fantastic day out, so Bill decided to take Mr. Noodles for a walk. This mainly involved Bill carrying him. Right across the road from the Luxor Apartments was a well-maintained park within Central Park. It had a kids' playground, and was fully fenced, so Bill would let Mr. Noodles off his lead and let him run around without the risk of him running onto the road.

As per usual, the park was full of young children and their parents. Bill ignored the DOGS ARE PROHIBITED TO BE OFF LEAD IN THIS AREA signs. Everybody loved Mr. Noodles. He was a good dog, and Bill knew those signs were for naughty dogs. It was a fabulous day.

Across the road, Dan the Cab-Man pulled up outside the Luxor Apartments. Justin was in the back of the cab scrolling through Steve's emails on his iPhone.

"You be fucking Jennifer tonight?" Dan asked with a devious smile. "Need me to pick her up, my good, good friend? I will remind her how lucky she is to have special time with you."

"Not tonight. I'm taking Sophie from R and R out tonight. Might fuck her in the restroom at Milestones," Justin boasted.

"Oh, you bad motherfucker. Milestones is super expensive."

"Yep, sure is. She's pissing me off a bit. This could be her last chance."

"I will park near Jennifer's place all night, mister sir. In case she is needed. Like a dessert for you."

Justin was using Dan to drive him around more often these days; in fact, he was at his call 24/7. He liked how important money was to Dan and that he knew his place. Justin checked his messages, no reply from Sophie about dinner. She was still playing hard to get, and this was starting to annoy him. He liked the chase, but he liked the chase to be quick, so the fucking could begin.

As he got out of the cab, Justin caught Bill Hampton's horrible shrieking laugh in the wind. Normally he'd have gone in the opposite direction, but today he changed tack and followed the laugh to the nearby park. He found him, it wasn't hard in his loud yellow shirt. Justin leaned against a lamppost, watching Bill talk to a group of young mothers. Mr. Noodles was at his feet enjoying the attention of their small children. Justin grinned. Leaving work early today had just paid dividends. He pulled out a small silver dog whistle. The same one he'd used to taunt and tease Mr. Noodles with.

Justin wet his lips in anticipation, watching for the right moment. A three-year-old boy dressed in a bright blue jumpsuit bounded up to Mr. Noodles and patted his head. Mr. Noodles got up on his hind legs and knocked the boy on his butt. The boy giggled as the dog eagerly licked his face. The boy's mother chatted with Bill, amused at her son's giggles.

Justin took a deep breath, and blew long and hard on the small silver whistle. The silent sound flew across the park. Within nanoseconds all the Pavlovian conditioning Justin had inflicted on the small dog kicked in; Mr. Noodles reacted fast and viciously. Saliva dripped from his mouth as he flung open his jaws, and sunk them into the nearest thing available—the boy's face. With his incisors clamped onto the boy's soft flesh, he snarled and shook the boy like a rag doll; unclenching his mouth only to get a better, deeper bite hold. The toddler's screams shattered the familiar sounds of the park. At first no one moved; people were in complete shock. The boy's mother started screaming like her son. A father standing a few feet away pushing his daughter on the swings, ran toward Mr. Noodles and booted him in the ribs. The dog's small body lifted, but his jaws stayed locked on the boy's bloody face. A second harder kick sent Mr. Noodles flying.

The man scooped up the screaming boy, who blindly thrashed in pain, blood pouring from the bite wounds. Someone yelled out about calling an ambulance, another shouted that the dog should be shot.

Bill was motionless, his head twitched in shock, everything had happened so fast. Mr. Noodles slowly limped back toward Bill, who grabbed the dog, tucked him under his arm and ran like a man who hadn't run in decades.

Justin placed the whistle back in his pocket, and strolled the other way. He felt like devouring a donut, knowing it was going to taste super good. It wasn't part of his usual diet, but everyone deserves a treat sometimes.

CHAPTER FIFTY

SARAH TRUTH WAS MAKING good progress with her efforts to control the muscles in her throat. Each time Justin visited she was able to retain more tainted water in her mouth and expel it after he'd gone. She wasn't able to spit out all of it, but she was swallowing less each week. She could feel the change. The less she drank, the stronger she got.

It was a hot day, and Sarah was lying on her bed, dressed in a cotton slip. Today she could see her toes at the far end. She stared at them and all ten stared back at her. She had a good grasp on how her brain controlled her body. That it was electrical impulses in the brain that fire movement and thought. At high school, her science teacher had been fixated with the workings of the human brain and would often play documentaries about them in class, trying to encourage his students to use their brains. Sarah's body had not responded to her brain for a long time. She hoped her brain still worked. It had to work. She stared at her toes again, willing them to move.

She wondered if her brain had forgotten how to get the relevant signals across. The drugs Justin gave her did something that had caused her brain to stop talking to all the other parts. Her eyelids gave her hope. She could still blink most of the time. On occasions, they would also stop working. Without blinking, her eyes would dry out, and a nurse would have to administer drops every half hour. It was painful when that happened, as if her eyes were on fire. It hadn't happened for a while now, and she noticed her blinking was becoming more frequent since she had begun to fight back.

Sarah looked at her toes again and commanded them to dance for her, to move back and forward, to do anything. Then the big toe on her right foot moved. She was sure of it! She went to move it again, nothing.

Maybe her mind was playing tricks on her? Maybe she had wanted it to move so badly that she believed it had. She was starting to feel tired. The huge concentration it took was draining her energy.

Sarah stopped concentrating on her toes and rolled her head so she could look out the window. Was she actually getting stronger, or did she just wish it? She thought about her Mathew. She missed him; he had been the love of her life. But it hadn't been love at first sight when they'd met at college. They'd moved in different circles without anything in common. Their conversations didn't go any deeper than "hey" when passing in the corridor. He was on the football team, hung around other jocks, and always seemed to have a new girl on his arm. She had thought if you removed his good looks, all you would have left would be an empty shell.

One stormy night, Sarah ditched her friends at a drunken party, deciding it was better to walk home than get groped by wasted guys who wouldn't remember her name the next day. Five houses down from her apartment, she saw someone passed out in the gutter. It was a student town, and not uncommon to see drunken students crashed out in strange places. She was living with four other students at the time and thought it might be one of them, or a friend of theirs. She rolled the drunk over and saw that it was Mathew Truth. He was so drunk he couldn't speak and just lay on his back making goofy sounds. Sarah had stood up to leave. The lightning, thunder, and heavy rain changed her mind. He seemed so helpless that she couldn't bring herself to just leave him in the rain.

Mathew had been too big for Sarah to lift, but the icy storm water managed to bring him around slightly, and he'd stumbled to his feet. She helped him stagger back to her place and onto the couch. There he stayed for the next two weeks, showing a side of himself she had never seen. He wasn't full of himself and always treated everyone kindly, never bullying the smaller guys, unlike some of the other jocks at the school. The reason he was so drunk the night she found him was that a friend of his was planning to drive home drunk after the party. Mathew's answer to that had been to shotgun his friend's beers in quick succession, one after another, until they handed their car keys over to a campus security guard.

Six months after she'd found him, a devastating knee injury put Mathew on the bench, marking the end of his promising football career. Sarah suggested they find a place together so she could help look after him, and he jumped at the idea. He'd often say that his injury was one of the best things to happen to him, as it showed him what his life was really about: it was about her. They graduated together and moved back to Sarah's hometown where they married and started a family.

Sarah looked back at her toes at the end of the bed. She had to try again. Justin had taken everything from her and she was going to fight. She had come so far, pushing through the pain to make her body hers again. She focused once more. This time, instead of trying to move all her toes, she just stared at the big toe on her right foot. It was a Mexican standoff; no matter how hard she stared, there was no movement. She felt as if her eyeballs were going to explode with the strain. Then she felt something running from her nose. She couldn't see it, but sensed that it was a small trail of blood.

Sarah relaxed, closed her eyes, took in a deep breath, and this time—instead of pushing as hard as she could—she made a mental picture of her big toe, imagining it moving back and forward. She held onto this image for a few minutes while controlling her breathing. Then she opened her eyes, focused on her toe, and took another deep breath. It moved! It was only a slight twitch, but a controlled twitch. This was really happening. She tried again and it twitched again. A tear rolled down Sarah's cheek. She was going to do this. Not just for her. For Mathew.

CHAPTER FIFTY-ONE

JUSTIN WAS DRINKING a power shake at his breakfast table when Jennifer joined him. She was naked but for a thin see-through silk slip. Justin insisted that she wear it when staying over. He checked out her flawless body as she floated about the kitchen, making her own breakfast, and he got a semi hard-on. Not enough to act on, but enough to have to adjust himself.

There was a loud commotion in the hallway. Justin sprung to his feet, telling Jennifer to go to the bedroom while he went to see what was going on. Outside Bill's door were two uniformed police officers and a dog control officer. The largest of the police officers was banging on Bill's door. "Open this door now, sir!" he yelled. His monobrow forehead crinkled with anger. Justin recognized the roided-up type from his gym. Anything could set them off. His police partner was more chilled, tall, and lanky.

Justin was pleased to see them. He'd been waiting for them to turn up for the dog. The small boy Mr. Noodles had attacked had spent three days in the hospital and would be scarred for life.

"Can I help you?" Justin asked.

The lanky officer turned to him. "Morning sir, everything is fine. Please return to your apartment."

"Sorry, but everything is not fine if three men are banging on my neighbor's door," Justin persisted. "What's this all about?"

The dog control officer stepped forward. "Your neighbor's dog attacked a young boy last week. He has refused to return our calls or take any responsibility for its actions. The boy's parents are not very happy, as you would expect. We have a court order to remove the dog and have it destroyed."

"This piece of shit has to pay," the roided-up officer stated. "I'm a goddamn dog owner myself. And it's pieces of shit like him"—he banged on the door again—"that give all dogs a bad name. If he doesn't open this door, I'll break it down!"

"You'll need a tank to get through that door," Justin informed the officer. "On this floor, the doors are built to withstand unwanted entry and there are eight bolts holding it closed. But hold on, I have a key that will open it." Justin returned to his apartment and came back with the security swiper that Bill had given him.

"Bill! It's Justin," he yelled. "I'm coming in." Justin nodded at the officers, and used the swiper to unlock the door. He asked the officers politely to wait outside and told them he would get the dog without any drama. They agreed he could try. But, with any sign of danger, they would act swiftly.

Justin cautiously entered the apartment for show, like he was afraid of the dog. "Bill, look, I want to help you. Some people think Mr. Noodles was a bad, bad dog," Justin said in a firm but friendly voice. "We both know that's not true."

"I don't understand," Bill trembled from his bedroom. "It must have been that kid. He must have done something. Mr. Noodles has never bitten anyone. I'll sue them!"

"That's a good idea, Bill. I bet he was a brat. Once the judge sees Mr. Noodles, he'll know what's right. Who couldn't love Mr. Noodles?"

Justin glanced around the apartment, smirking. Bill had been hiding out in here ever since the day at the park. The curtains were drawn and the apartment was a mess. The couches were overturned and chairs stacked on them, as if Bill had made a fort out of his furniture. Half-eaten boxes of takeout food were stacked on the kitchen bench. Copious empty wine bottles littered the floor.

As Justin crept closer to where Bill's voice was coming from, the smell of dog shit hit him, causing him to block his nose. It was coming from the spare room. To avoid going out, Bill was letting Mr. Noodles use it as a toilet. Justin felt like throwing up.

"How about he stays with me until you win the court case?" Justin asked as he approached Bill's room. Justin pushed opened the door and saw Bill in the middle of his bed cradling Mr. Noodles like a baby.

"We'll clear this mess up, and he can come home again." Justin reached out his hands.

Bill hesitated. "You'll take good care of him?"

"Like he was my own little doggy woggy."

"He's a good boy."

"I know."

Bill kissed Mr. Noodles, then reluctantly handed him to Justin.

"Thank you, Bill. How about you find his favorite rubber bone and bring it out. I'll tell the officers to go away. He's with me now."

Justin backed out of the room, and as he reached the front door, Justin pretended to be scared. "He's gone weird, weirder than normal. He said he was going to kill himself."

"What?!" the roided officer roared. "Like fuck he is. He's going to face his crimes like a man."

Bill appeared in the lounge holding a rubber bone. The cop jumped as if he saw a gun and bolted past Justin. He flew at Bill. Smashed him with a spear tackle. They hit the ground with a heavy thud. Bill screamed.

"Drop the gun!" the cop yelled, hitting Bill's face with a heavy punch. Bill went limp, the rubber bone fell from his hand and made a quiet squeak as it hit the floor.

The officer grinned up at his comrades. "This fucker wasn't going to take the easy way out. He's going to pay for his crimes. He's lucky I didn't bring my dog up here to chew his fucking face off!"

CHAPTER FIFTY-TWO

ROSS HELD A SKETCH the departmental artist had composed from the grainy CCTV footage. He'd asked him to not draw a beard, and put the suspect into a shirt and tie. The drawing showed a typical office worker from New York. Generic at best. As they didn't have any other solid pictures, this would have to do. This was Lydia Young's killer.

Ross made his way to the street where he had finished up yesterday and started the laborious process of stopping people and asking them to look at the picture. The hardest thing about New York was that he could cover the same section every day for a year and see someone new each time.

Ross had a search plan and was sticking to it. On a map of New York, he had marked all the locations where he suspected so-called accidental deaths had happened. He then drew lines intersecting the locations and worked out a grid of where the killer could work or live. It wasn't a small area, but it was a place to start. He began in the middle, and worked his way out in an ever-expanding spiral. Each day he'd highlight the area he had hit and worked out where he would go the following day.

For the past fifteen days, every lunch hour, Ross searched a different section of the grid, talking to anyone who might have seen something. He wasn't getting far. As a lone ranger, he could only talk to a limited number of people in a week. If he had the team that was working on the Beetle Butcher case to support him, he'd have the grid covered in half a day.

He didn't want to be in Olive's shoes. She was under growing pressure to get results on the Beetle Butcher case. Their lieutenant had foolishly guaranteed results, three victims ago. Each day that went by, more and more blame was landing on Olive's shoulders for the unsuccessful ongoing investigation. The Beetle Butcher was very smart; the only clue left behind was his calling card. Every victim had been beaten and tortured over the course of five days. Then on the fifth day, he'd sedate them to operate. He'd surgically cut a hole in their stomachs so he could insert a small funnel pipe to release hundreds of juvenile beetles inside of them. He would then sew their stomachs back up, bury them in a shallow grave, and leave them to die as the beetles slowly ate their way out.

Ross hated it and hated all the politics surrounding it; the less time he spent working on that case the better. Those sorts of sick freaks were better kept out of his head.

It was nearly one p.m.; he had to finish up and head back to the office. He sighed. Another day of nothingness. A young businessman scrolling through his Facebook feed and not looking where he was going bumped into Ross. When he gave Ross a dirty look, Ross opened his coat, and glanced down at his police badge clipped onto his belt. The guy instantly lost his hostile attitude.

"Sorry, man, wasn't watching where I was going," the businessman said.

"I'll let it slide if you can have a look at this picture," Ross asked in a way that was more a demand than a question. He held up the drawing. The guy looked at it and shook his head.

"Sorry, man," he said, and carried on walking. After a few steps, he stopped and turned back to Ross. "Can I have another look?"

This time, he looked at the picture more intently. "That looks like the jerk who stole my cab one night," he said, with a hint of snark. "I was two blocks over, waiting for like fifteen goddamn minutes for a cab in the pouring rain. Finally, one pulled over, and out of nowhere this cun... this idiot shouldered me out of the way, and jumped in. He gave me this shit-eating grin, then flipped me off as the cab drove off. Smug piece of shit!"

"Have you seen him since?"

"Nah, I'd have punched him right on the nose if I had." The businessman suddenly remembered that he was talking to a cop. "You know I wouldn't really, but I would like to!"

Ross waved it off. "Where did this happen?" he asked.

"It was just outside that building, shit, the cola one. Massive logo on the side of it. Soda-Cola I think," the man replied.

CHAPTER FIFTY-THREE

JUSTIN SAT IN HIS OFFICE, going over his upcoming speech. In twenty-four hours, he would be delivering it in Las Vegas. Every year, Soda-Cola held a week-long sales conference for its marketing department and a host of its top sales people. It was traditionally an exciting affair: a time to share ideas, plan for the future, and bring everyone together. Plus, there was usually a lot of drinking involved, not to mention the odd interdepartmental hook-up.

It was a privilege to be invited to this event, and those who weren't were always hugely disappointed. While PAs weren't usually invited, Justin had made sure that Debbie was going; she was very excited, as this was her first time. The IT department was never on the list either, but once again, Justin had used his position so that Guy Chambers was booked in. There were a few jobs Justin needed him to do, and it would be easier to take Guy than trust someone new. When Guy found out he was going to Vegas, he was over the moon.

Rehearsing his presentation again, Justin imagined himself standing in front of the large crowd with everyone's eyes focused on him. Both he and Steve would give the opening presentations on the brands in their portfolios. They had sixty minutes each to talk to the group and excite them. Then, over the next few days, their teams would go into greater detail on the vision and mission of each brand.

Justin wanted to blow Steve's presentation out of the water. It was important for him to be seen as the rising star, and for people to engage with him as their leader. The conference was a great place to shine. And while Steve would be writing his own presentation, Justin had hired two comedy writers and a motivational speaker to write his, with him tweaking and guiding the process. Reading over it, he smiled. The speech was tight. To add a bit more excitement he had also arranged some pyrotechnics.

Mother's Milk was based in Las Vegas, so he would see how they were progressing on the tasks Justin had assigned them. They had still not been paid a single cent for all the work they'd done. When the subject of money cropped up, he would remind Sandy that this was a small investment to get millions and millions of dollars in future revenue, and the future was just around the corner. He was eventually going to have to give them something, but the more he got for free, the better his bottom line was going to be.

His iPhone beeped with a text from Jennifer:

```
HI J WE STILL ON 4 2NITE?
I CN BRNG OVR SOME STUFF.
LKING 4WRD TO HOUSE SITTING
4 U. XXX
```

Justin hated how Jennifer cut out most of the vowels when she texted him. He'd told her to use all the letters in the alphabet. Now he was going to have to think up a suitable punishment for her.

She had been very excited when he'd asked her to stay at his place while he was in Vegas. He knew she saw it as a sign of affection and a growing intimacy between them. He just wanted to make sure he knew where she was every minute he was away. He'd written out a list of rules she had to follow. He texted her back.

```
Jennifer. Come over at 8pm
and we'll go get some dinner.
Dress sexy and don't wear any
underwear.
```

Justin put his iPhone back in his pocket and closed his laptop. He was happy with his presentation. Vegas was going to be a whole load of fun. The main thing he was looking forward to was fucking with Steve.

CHAPTER FIFTY-FOUR

THE FIRST-CLASS DEPARTURE lounge was too busy for Justin. They needed to make it more exclusive. It felt like they were just giving passes away these days. He'd arranged to meet Steve and Carlton there, so that they could compare notes for the week ahead and travel together. Carlton had pulled out at the last minute. His excuse was to work on the hundred and tenth birthday celebrations for Soda-Cola. The real reason was that his health was again in serious decline. Justin could think of a thousand things he'd rather do than hang out with Steve, yet he couldn't ditch him.

Justin spotted Steve sitting in a curved cushion chair, with a spare one across from him. A small, round table sat in no-man's land between the chairs. If he was going to have to talk to Steve, he should reward himself first. A trip to the bathroom was called for.

Justin joined Steve five minutes later, the cocaine he'd inhaled already making his front teeth numb. Steve lowered his newspaper as Justin sat. With his game face on, Justin asked him about his family and what he'd been up to recently. Telling him that he was looking forward to hearing one of his famous presentations. And how disappointed he was that Carlton couldn't make it.

After a few minutes of idle banter, Steve excused himself and pulled a folder from his bag. Justin could see that Steve was going to use this flight as a chance to add the finishing touches to his presentation. Steve's ritual for writing presentations hadn't changed much in the last decade. He liked to write everything out with a pen first, then when he was happy, he would type the final version.

Justin watched Steve scribble down his notes. They really were two very different people. He was the future, Steve was the past. Justin imagined a broken-down shack in the middle of nowhere, like Texas. The sun high in the sky, the ground dry, the air quiet. Lying on the ramshackle deck was an old Labrador: Steve. A good old Texan man walked out of the shack wearing a ten-gallon hat, a big gray mustache, and a rifle cradled in his arms. He told his old dog to get up and follow him around to the back of the house. Of course, the dog did, stumbling along the way. The man told him to sit, cocked his rifle, and placed the barrel at the back of the dog's head. The man grinned. The man was now Justin. His finger tightened on the trigger.

"This is the final boarding call for fight BTA45 to Las Vegas," a voice announced to the awaiting travelers, interrupting Justin's daydream.

"That's us." Steve smiled, closing his folder.

Justin nodded. He stood wishing he had one more line of coke left, or a rifle to put Steve out of his misery. Justin glanced down at Steve as he packed up his folder. He stood over him, the way the Texan had done to the old dog. Steve stood, not noticing Justin was so close, and bumped into him. He quickly apologized. Justin deftly removed the presentation folder from Steve's bag and dropped it back onto the chair.

As they boarded the flight, Justin checked out the flight attendants. He didn't like what he saw. Justin believed that only young, sexy women should be hired as attendants, and he despised the number of middle-aged gay men now aboard most flights. Justin's mood lightened when he saw who was serving in first class. *This could be a lot more fun.* He put on his most charming smile for the long-legged blonde attendant. As the plane started to taxi backward, one single word, yelled very loudly, emanated through the first-class cabin.

"FUCK!"

Steve had just discovered that his folder was missing. Justin chuckled to himself and signaled for the glamorous blonde to serve him another glass of champagne.

CHAPTER FIFTY-FIVE

FOUR HOURS INTO the flight, Meri, the blonde attendant, was in the first-class toilets, bent over, with Justin's cock deep inside her. Justin had promised her the lead in an upcoming Soda-Cola television commercial. She wouldn't be cast, but as long as she thought she would, she was game. As he was sliding in and out of her, listening to her moan, the thought that she should get a boob job crossed his mind. She had amazing legs, but was a bit flat in the chest department. He felt himself about to cum, and held her tight. He slowly pulled out, removed the condom and flushed it, before putting his cock back in his pants. Meri pulled up her panties and straightened her skirt.

"Tell your agent to phone this lady," Justin said as he handed her Debbie's card. "She'll take care of everything. You're going to be a star."

Justin returned to his seat and opened his laptop. He scrolled through his presentation once more. It was great. He looked over at Steve, who was still fuming at himself. Being as connected as he was, Steve was able to get a call put through to the departure lounge staff to see if his folder had been left behind. A lady checked and found it. They were going to put it on another flight, but it wouldn't reach him until eleven p.m. He knew it was going to be a late night with an early start tomorrow.

An hour and a half later the plane touched down in Las Vegas. Justin gave Meri a kiss on the cheek, certain he'd never see her again, and made his way to baggage claim. Steve was still in a bad mood.

They grabbed their bags and headed out to their hired limo. Their driver was holding a sign with Justin and Steve's names written on it. He smiled at the two men. Justin smiled, as the driver had written his name first. On the drive to the Palms, Steve remained quiet, scribbling down notes he could remember.

Justin strutted through the doors to the Palms, soaking in the sights and sounds. He was booked into the penthouse, only the best for him. Steve walked in behind him, folding up his notes, and placing them in his inside jacket pocket.

"Welcome, gentlemen," the immaculately dressed receptionist smiled. "Checking in?"

"We are, mainly because we were told you worked here," Justin smoothly grinned. He turned to Steve. "After you. The sooner you are checked in, the sooner you can relax and finish your speech."

"Thanks, Justin," Steve replied with a sigh. "Steve Barker," he told the receptionist, "part of the Soda-Cola conference."

The receptionist typed into her keyboard. Stopped. Typed again. Crinkled her nose. "It's Barker, right? B A R K E R," she spelled it out.

"That's it."

"I'm sorry sir, you don't seem to have a room."

"That's impossible."

"I'm sorry, it's not in the system."

"Then just give me another room, I'll charge it back."

"I'm sorry, sir, the whole hotel is fully booked. Maybe you booked at another hotel?"

Steve's face went slightly red. "I suggest you type my name in once more. If you can't find it, then you will find me another goddamn room. We are spending a fortune with this hotel, and you fucked up. You will fix it. If you can't do your damn job, get me your manager!"

Passing people in the lobby stopped to watch Steve get angrier and angrier. Justin placed a hand on Steve's shoulder.

"Steve, it's all good," Justin assured him. "Look, get some fresh air, and I'll sort it out."

Steve agreed, storming outside in a huff. Justin returned to the receptionist. "Forgive him, how's your day going? Have you ever modeled? Would you like to be on TV?"

A few minutes later, Justin joined Steve outside, Steve's head was down, his back resting on one of the hotel walls. "It's all sorted," Justin announced. "I've got you a room."

"She found my booking?"

"No. Must have been a glitch in the booking. I managed to find a way."

"How?"

"Just say, I'm going to have to take that young lady out for an expensive meal." Justin grinned. He handed Steve his new room's keycard. "Also, someone else is going to turn up later and not have a room, but that's their problem."

"Thanks, Justin, I feel so bad I lost it at her like that."

"Don't think twice about it."

"Thanks. I…" Steve paused. "I appreciate you doing this."

"We're family, Steve. Got to make sure you have a roof over your head. Now go and hit your room and relax. You have a lot to do once your presentation arrives."

"Yes, that's true," Steve said in a low, disappointed tone.

"I wish I had spotted that you left it behind," Justin said, putting his hands in his pockets.

"It was my own fault. Thanks again for organizing the room."

Justin watched Steve head toward the hotel elevator. They hadn't lost Steve's booking. Justin had canceled it weeks ago. He'd then booked the smallest room in the hotel with the longest walk to the auditorium for the conference.

On his way to the penthouse, Justin gave Sandy Miller at Mother's Milk a call. He answered immediately. "You're here!"

"Yes, how's everything going?" Justin asked.

"Great, can't wait to take you through it."

"I know it's going to be great. Now have you organized the other thing?" Justin inquired. He was more interested in this than seeing the work.

"Yeah, it took a bit of doing, but in two nights it's all on. Are you sure you want to do this?" Sandy asked in a slightly raised tone. He was nervous.

"Have you followed my requirements to the letter?"

"Yes. Of course."

"Then yes, this is what I want to do. It won't be forgotten, Sandy. This is just the beginning of a very profitable friendship." And with that Justin hung up. He was pushing Sandy, and in two nights he was going to see how far the man would go.

Justin opened the doors to his penthouse suite. It was incredible; the spacious living area and gourmet kitchen rivaled his own back in New York. The main reason he wanted this room was the floor-to-ceiling windows that overlooked the glittering cityscape below. Sliding the glass doors open, Justin stepped out onto the deck and dropped to one knee to scoop up some warm water from his own private pool. He was definitely going to make sure he fucked a different girl in every room of the suite over the next five days.

CHAPTER FIFTY-SIX

JUSTIN ENTERED THE CONFERENCE HALL at seven thirty a.m. It was a hive of activity with all the final preparations for the day ahead. A thousand chairs were set out to face the impressive curved stage. At the front of the stage was a LED lectern featuring an animated Soda-Cola logo. The back of the stage was a giant digital screen that was going through its final tests. Spotlights were spinning and roaming about the room, working out where they would be needed for certain presentations during the day. The rest of the room was decked out in Soda-Cola colors, along with branded balloons, T-shirts, and merchandise bags for the attendees. It was an impressive sight.

Justin walked onto the stage and took his place behind the lectern, resting his palms firmly on top of it. He gazed out into the auditorium. He visualized the reaction he was going to get, the standing ovation. He could hear it clearly. He imagined himself standing like this in front of the country, as the new president of the United States—cameras flashing, music playing, and people chanting his name.

"Justin Truth," a voice called. "Justin Truth!" Justin raised a hand to block out the glare from the stage lights. The voice belonged to a technician in his early twenties. He was wearing overalls, holding a clipboard, and there were three other young men with him. Justin knew who he was, and he was on time. He beckoned him over.

This young man was responsible for the 3D holographic machine Justin had hired for his presentation. No one had used one before, another first Justin would bring to Soda-Cola. Halfway through his presentation, Justin would stand in the middle of the stage and a 3D world would appear around him. It would slowly rotate, and as he talked about different countries, they would be projected out, and float in front of him. He couldn't wait to give it a test run.

By ten thirty a.m. the room was crowded with regulars who knew how important it was to be seen displaying the Soda-Cola spirit, and to appear excited about it. Attendance was mandatory, and if anyone missed it, it was noted, and they could expect to have a very serious conversation with their department manager.

The plan for the first day was simple:

11 a.m. – Celebrity host, to entertain and welcome everyone.

11:15 a.m. – Steve Barker's presentation.

12:15 p.m. – Lunch break.

1:45 p.m. – Celebrity host to welcome everyone back.

2 p.m. – Justin's presentation.

3 p.m. – Head of Human Resources: Steph Gallows to give an overview of what to expect from the five-day event—where people needed to be, timetables for guest speakers.

5:30 p.m. – Celebrity host to wrap it up for the day.

Justin worked the room, shaking hands and dishing out smiles. He noticed Steve near the front of the stage, and it was obvious that he hadn't had much sleep. His normally sharp blue eyes were bloodshot. He hadn't shaved, and his hair was sticking up at the back. The normally calm and collected man seemed slightly wired and frazzled.

"All good, Steve?" Justin asked.

"Tough night. By the time, I got to bed it was close to two a.m. I think? It was late, I know that, two a.m.," Steve repeated, his tiredness creeping into his speech. "I had just gone to sleep, I'm sure, when I was woken at three by a constant tapping on my door. Tapping, tapping, tap tap tap. Wouldn't stop. It was a lost Asian tourist thinking my room was his friend's room, so I sent him on his way. And then. And then, just as I'd fallen asleep again, the same thing happened! Not tapping, banging. More banging on my door, this time by a drunk man in an elephant onesie."

"That's awful," Justin said, hiding his mirth. He'd hired those two men.

Steve continued. "I just need to give Guy, where is he? The presentation for him to load into the system. You know so it can . . . display on the... shit... those things to read while on stage? Anyway, it's all good. I'm sure it's fine. Right? Yeah. A few coffees and I'll be fine." Steve let out a deep sigh and put on a brave smile.

"I, for one, am looking forward to it, Steve," Justin said. "I can't think of a better way to start. I just hope my presentation can live up to yours, and people don't fall asleep on me."

"You'll do fine, Justin. Please excuse me now, I've got... a few things. Last-minute things to go over and then it's showtime."

Both men exchanged smiles but for very different reasons. Justin knew it was going to be a show, just not the show Steve was hoping for.

CHAPTER FIFTY-SEVEN

MONTANA CRUZ PUSHED OPEN the front door of her family home in Las Pasco, New Mexico. It was a small place, in a simple neighborhood, but her parents loved their house and were never going to move. Montana had offered to buy a new place for them in a much safer area, but her dad was a stubborn man who refused to stray from his friends, his work, and the life they had built for themselves. This wasn't a house to him. It was their home.

She dropped her bag in the lounge and called out. It was just ritual to yell out whenever you walked in the front door. But it was quiet, a sad quiet. Noise and the hubbub of activity were part of life at home, and it was unusual for it to be empty.

Montana stood in the doorway to her parents' room. It hadn't changed much since she was a little girl. One of the walls in the bedroom featured a collection of family photos. She loved this wall, it was a history of their family's life. The pictures came in different shapes and sizes, and no two frames were alike. Montana looked at a photo of her parents when her mother was heavily pregnant with her. She had always been told this was the day they had arrived in America to start their new life. It wasn't. They had entered America months before the picture was taken.

For years Montana never knew the truth. She believed what her parents had told her, that they had applied and received a work visa through the green-card lottery. One night when she was sixteen and was molten angry at her mother for not buying her a new dress for a school dance, her father sat her down and told her the real story about how they came to America.

Montana looked at a faded picture of the village in Mexico where her parents had met. They'd been young and in love when her mother fell pregnant. One night, staring at the stars, they decided they wanted to raise their child in America. They found a local coyote who said he could get them over the border if they were willing to leave immediately. They'd rushed home and each packed a bag. Her father told Montana how he'd laughed at the weight of her mother's bag. As if she'd packed it with rocks to build a house once they arrived in America.

Together with twelve other people, they squashed into the coyote's small, battered van. On the drive, the coyote told them what to expect and bragged about how successful he was at making this run. How he'd dug a tunnel under the fence, and a cousin of his would be on the American side to drive them to their new lives. If they wanted jobs, it was taken care of. The coyote was the only one talking; everyone else remained quiet, knowing the risks. The drive went on for hours, longer than her father was expecting. He'd held his wife's hand. She'd gripped her bag tightly.

As they reached the fence, the van stopped. Armed with a rusted AK-47, the coyote pulled open the back doors, and yelled to force everyone out. His cousin was there, but on the Mexican side of the fence, also holding an automatic rifle. The coyote wasn't planning to take them to America at all: instead he was going to sell them to a local drug lord. He laughed at them, pointing to the other side of the fortified fence. His cruel joke to show them that America was the last place they would ever go now. As he sorted out the people for delivery, one of the men decided that he didn't want to be a slave, and in a spontaneous move, knocked the coyote to the ground. The automatic rifle went off, sending bullets flying in all directions. One cluster of bullets ripped into his cousin's van parked in front of the fence. It must have had C4 in it, as the van exploded, blowing a gaping hole in the wire-mesh fence. Everyone had made a run for it, each person going their own way. Her mother was the slowest to escape, her father yelling at her to drop the bag and run. She refused.

When they could run no more, they hid in cavern under an enormous boulder. A perfect hiding spot from the weather and the Border Patrol. It was here that her father discovered why the bag was so heavy. It contained two large bottles of water.

Her father couldn't remember how long they had spent in the desert, only walking at night, hiding during daylight from the police and the harsh sun. They slowly sipped from the water bottles and conserved energy as much as they could.

Then one night they could see lights in the distance. They hugged each other and danced in joy. Once they reached the town, they were able to find locals who helped them. They never found out whether any of the other escapees had made it to freedom. If not for the water, her father was sure they wouldn't have survived.

When he finished his story, he had a tear in his eye. He kissed Montana on the forehead, reminding her if not for her mother, none of them would have this life, this better life in America.

Among the collection of pictures, there was one of Montana and her two brothers, Francisco and Arizona. She was five, and her brothers were three and two, respectively. They were all sitting in the backyard, in clothes made by their mother. They had big smiles, each holding a half-melted Popsicle.

Montana smiled at the memory, then felt sad. A few years ago, Francisco had reached out to her for help. She was too caught up in her own life at the time to really listen to his stories about the new guy at his work, Justin Truth. A guy who was making his life hell. By the time she did make an effort to see him, it was too late. His confidence was shattered. He'd lost his job and gained a drug habit. He was currently driving trucks from one end of the country to another, and didn't keep in contact with the family unless he needed fast money.

Montana opened her mother's wardrobe. it was full. Her mother never threw anything out.

Last week her mother had collapsed while shopping and had been rushed to the hospital. Tests revealed the cause of her sickness was a blood clot. Seven hours ago she'd gone into the operating room to have it removed. The operation was successful. She needed rest and would need to stay in the hospital until she was well enough to go home. Montana decided to take some of her mother's belongings to her to make her hospital stay feel more friendly and homely. She selected a few items and placed them in a suitcase along with pictures, ornaments, and plastic flowers. Her mom loved plastic flowers. Anything to make the hospital room feel less like a hospital room.

She was just about to head out the door when her cellphone buzzed with an incoming email. It was from Martin Goodby, a guy she knew from college. They had stayed in touch, mainly because he had a crush on her and wanted to hang in there, just in case. She liked him, but not in that way. He was a computer whiz who held a lucrative position at Microsoft.

When Montana's LemonGreat files were leaked to the competition, she knew it had to be an inside job, to make her look bad. She had contacted Martin to see if he could find out how it had happened–it was a long shot, but worth a try.

The subject header of the email read: LEMONGREAT. I'VE CRACKED IT!!

CHAPTER FIFTY-EIGHT

SITTING IN THE FRONT ROW, Justin clapped with the entire crowd as the celebrity guest was unveiled—Jimmy Fallon. Jimmy dazzled the crowd with his wit and charm.

To the left of the stage was Guy Chambers. He was behind a desk of monitors controlling the audio and visual elements. Justin caught his eye, he nodded back; he was all set up and ready to go. Justin smirked. Earlier that morning Steve had taken Guy through his presentation. As soon as Steve went, Justin slipped in and changed it all.

Jimmy Fallon finished his set with a retelling of Goldilocks and the Three Bears, inserting Soda-Cola into it instead of porridge and turning the whole fairy tale on its head. The comic timing was pitch-perfect. The crowd was enthralled. It was going to be hard to follow. Jimmy exited the stage. Now it was time for Steve Barker.

The lights slowly faded. Through the loudspeakers, the intro of "We Will Rock You" boomed.

Dum Dum... Clash!

Dum Dum... Clash!

Everything was running smoothly, so far. Then the song started to skip, jumping between the intro and the chorus. People started to whisper. Steve, standing in the wings, glared at Guy, who shrugged. He hit stop, and started again, to the same result. Steve was confused. He had given Guy the tracks, and they worked perfectly on his computer. Steve gave the international signal for "cut it," running a finger across his throat. Guy responded and started the next part of the presentation on the large screen.

As the video started, the house lights that were meant to stay off, came on, making it hard to see the screen. Panicking, Steve looked for someone to turn off the lights. He signaled wildly to a hotel worker standing near the stage to summon help, and the young guy sped off to do the requested damage control.

The man who controlled the lights had two hundred dollars in his back pocket, courtesy of Justin, and he knew exactly what he was doing. He turned off half the lights first, then the other half, fading back and forward between them. A few people were laughing openly now. The inspiration was nil, but by the time the video finished, the lights were perfect.

Steve took to the stage to enthusiastic applause, waving to everyone. Most people in the audience liked Steve and were happy to see him. He'd downed a few energy drinks and looked like he was feeling good. All he needed to do now was appear upbeat and read his speech through the autocue.

"Soda-Cola!" Steve yelled. "Thank you for coming all the way to Las Vegas!"

The crowd clapped, cheered, and stomped their feet.

Steve stood behind the lectern and continued, "I can't wait to show you what's bubbling under the surface for the next year. I'm excited, and I know you all will be too."

Steve relaxed and read the autocue for the rest of his introduction. It all went smoothly until he started to talk about a brand-new Soda-Cola flavor, then he started to trip over his words.

"—the bubbles in Soda-Cola Sweet are magical, magical like sweet cola soda in bubbles. When you open the bottle, bubble, bottle magical sweet when you open the bubbles bottle." Steve stopped. He was sure that made no sense. He continued reading. "In a world first, the bubbles in the sweet bottle of bubble are magical when the bubble bottle is sweet opened."

He glanced at the screen behind him. On it was the graphic for another product. He realized that he must be sounding like a blithering idiot. After the highly entertaining Jimmy Fallon, the crowd was losing interest. Steve stopped reading the autocue and used his memory to talk his way through the rest of the graphics on the screen, throwing in a few jokes and winning back some people's attention.

The advertising section ran smoothly, and Steve was looking forward to the grand finale, where he would present a lucky Soda-Cola employee with a giant check worth ten thousand dollars. The check always got a huge response.

Steve took position in the center of the stage. "Who wants money?" he taunted the crowd. A Vegas showgirl in fishnet stockings and a sequenced bikini with large purple feathers peacocking out of her headgear sashayed onto the stage. She glittered under the lights as her long legs took graceful steps in nine-inch heels. In her hands was the novelty check covered by a silver cloth. The crowd cheered, with a few whistles pitching in.

Steve cleared his throat. "And the winner of the ten thousand dollars is..." Steve pointed to the showgirl who removed the silver cloth and in a squeaky helium voice announced: "Sally Murray!"

Half the attendees clapped, while the other half whispered to the person next to them. Something wasn't right here—Sally Murray had been fired recently and she was in the process of suing the company. Her name would have been at the bottom of the list.

Steve looked as if he wanted the ground to open up and swallow him whole, but fortunately, Guy hit the outro song. This time, the Queen track played perfectly. Steve got into position and waited for his cue. The music cut and Steve said his line: "You are the champion!" Unfortunately, his microphone cut out just at that second, and only a few people sitting close enough could hear it. The pyros went off. Well, one of them did—the other just made a small pop. But a spark flew out and hit an overhead banner, causing a small fire. Three attendants were onto it and within seconds they had sprayed the whole stage with industrial fire extinguishers.

Covered in foam, Steve didn't know what to do. He stood baffled amidst the chaos. As people fled the room, Justin remained seated, clapping.

CHAPTER FIFTY-NINE

STEVE SLUMPED ON A CHAIR outside the events room. A small bit of foam was still stuck to his head. His presentation had been the worst Soda-Cola presentation in the history of their conferences, and that was saying a lot. In 2003, a very drunk Dennis Raynes had slurred his way through an hour-long presentation for LemonGreat, which ended with him falling face-first off the stage. But the presentation itself had been highly entertaining.

He wished Montana had come to Las Vegas with him. Having her with him would have made life that much easier in times like these. Steve had never felt so alone as he watched people walking by trying to avoid his gaze and not laugh.

He thought about calling his wife and getting her to come out, but bringing partners to these events was frowned upon. The main reason was cost—it would mean Soda-Cola would have to accommodate at least twice as many people, and then add on the requests for children, and the budget would explode. To hell with the conference rules! He was top of the food chain, and if he wanted his wife here, he'd have her here. They were having a few marital problems and this could be a way to bring them closer. He pulled out his BlackBerry, and scrolled to his wife's number.

"Steve!" someone called. He looked up and saw a grinning Justin. He braced himself for the ribbing Justin was going to dish out. He would take it, then call his wife and spend the rest of the week treating her like she deserved.

"Don't be so hard on yourself," Justin said. "Technology isn't always reliable at the best of times. I was just talking to Jimmy Fallon, and he asked if he could steal your presentation to recreate on his show. You're a star. He loved it." Justin pulled Steve to his feet. "Our job is done for the day. I'll do my presentation tomorrow. There is no way I could top yours." Justin winked.

Steve was surprised by Justin's response, but it did get a smile out of him. He nodded. All they really needed to do was launch the conference—unlike the rest of the Soda-Cola employees who had to attend all the presentations and mixes. It was going to be an easy five days for both of them.

"Steve, I want you to have a fantastic time. Lead by example. With Carlton absent, you are the top dog here. Sitting around feeling sorry for yourself isn't going to cut it. Are you ready to be the top dog?"

Steve was taken aback. Justin was really trying to help him pick his confidence up off the conference floor.

"Yes, I'm ready!" Steve said, puffing out his chest.

"That's my man. I'm not letting you out of my sight. Tonight, you will own this town," Justin said, grabbing Steve by the shoulders. Steve suddenly felt a lot better.

Justin took control and whisked Steve around the venue, supporting him as they chatted with people. Steve was slowly forgetting about his embarrassing ordeal. Thinking about it now made him laugh, a little. Justin had arranged dinner for the two of them and four of the top sales reps from around the country at the highly sought-after Hallberg restaurant. The place had a six-month waiting list, yet Justin had managed to book a prime table for them when they rocked up. Steve was impressed. He'd never seen Justin in action and even found himself admiring the man's devil-may-care attitude.

As they talked about all things Soda—and a few things not—Justin always brought the conversation back to how well Steve was doing. Steve was starting to think that maybe he'd misjudged Justin. Didn't he just want to be his best, just like everyone else? Maybe Montana's hatred for Justin had inappropriately rubbed off on him? He thought about it. Justin was arrogant but he sure did him a lot of favors. Maybe he wasn't the spawn of the devil sent to bring down Soda-Cola. Maybe Carlton was right about him. He'd told Steve that Justin was very enthusiastic when he told him his plan for transitioning into retirement and promoting Steve into his position.

Every time Steve thought about calling it a night, Justin would deliver a fresh drink to his hand, bring along another interesting person for him to talk to, or whip him off to another club. The worst day in his life was soon becoming the best night ever. The alcohol was kicking in big time. Steve felt increasingly energized, strong, and powerful. Then he spotted someone out of the corner of his eye.

"Montana!" Steve yelled out. "Montana!" he called again. She didn't turn around. He was so happy that she'd been able to make it after all. He bounded over to her, admiring her stunning red designer dress. He gave her a hug from behind, she spun around to face him. Steve was confused. It wasn't Montana after all.

"I'm sorry," Steve mumbled, letting the stranger go.

The girl in the stunning red dress smiled at him. "Don't be. What's your name?" she asked.

"'tis Steve," he replied with a big smile and a drunken wobble.

"Hi, I'm Natalia. Would you like a drink?" she said with an inviting smile.

"Why yes, I would." Steve placed his hand on hers. "But you won't be spending any of your money. This drink is on Soda-Cola." He smiled.

Steve ordered a bottle of Bollinger, and they retired to a secluded booth in a corner of the club. As they talked, Steve was blown away by how much they had in common. After the second bottle was empty, they somehow ended up in Steve's room, both drunk and extremely turned on. The mini bar raided, music on.

She kissed Steve passionately, then pushed him backward onto a chair, her eyes telling him to stay put. "You are so cute," she said. "So cute and funny." She undid the zip of her dress, and let it cascade to the floor. Steve couldn't take his eyes off her. She had a beautifully tanned body with voluptuous breasts, twice the size of his wife's.

"Do you like my body?" she asked Steve.

"Very much so," he managed to reply.

She turned her back on him, unhooking her bra. "Do you think I look better with it on, or off?" she asked. "I like it off myself." The bra landed on the floor. She slowly rotated her body, exposing her naked breasts to him, playing with her nipples, making them hard. "You like me like this?"

Steve nodded.

She seductively moved to the music, getting closer and closer to him. She was intoxicating. All Steve could think about was making love to her, pleasing her. She placed her hands on his shoulders, leaned in, and kissed him intensely. He grabbed her around the waist, pulling her toward him. She arched her back, drawing away from his lips. She dropped her head back and let out a little moan. Steve opened his mouth and ran his tongue up her breast. Flicking her erect nipple with the tip of his tongue. She slipped onto the chair, straddling him, grinding against him. Pulling his head harder into her cleavage.

"I can feel your cock against me," she purred licking her lips. "I think I'll have to let it out to play." She slowly slid her way down his body, releasing his hard cock out of his pants. She wrapped her mouth around it and moaned. Steve moaned louder.

Steve was about to experience the best sex of his life.

CHAPTER SIXTY

JUSTIN FOUND A COMFORTABLE CHAIR, moved it into the hotel hallway, and sat on it exchanging dirty texts with a few girls he knew. Every now and then he'd hear a sound and look up—false alarm—so he'd go back to his texts.

He was happy with how things were going in Vegas. Over the last twelve hours, he'd made Steve's life complete misery and then lifted him back up into the clouds. The Ecstasy he'd slipped into Steve's drink had helped. Everyone likes to have their ego stroked, and going out of his way to make a colleague feel better about his horrible presentation was a good look. People liked that he was putting Steve first; it made him seem more human.

Justin heard the sound of a door opening. When he glanced up, he saw Natalia quietly slipping out of Steve's room. Her dress was creased, her hair was wild, her makeup was smudged. She dangled her stilettos from her fingers.

"You did good," Justin said.

"Oh. Thank you," she replied, appearing startled. She wouldn't have been expecting to see Justin this quickly. He stood, opened his jacket, and pulled out a small envelope containing five thousand dollars. He handed it to her.

"All that stuff you got me to learn paid off," she said. "He was putty in my hands. It's the most research I've ever done for a job. He had the night of his life, as promised."

"I bet he did."

"He seems like a nice guy, too. A bit confused, but nice." She nervously smiled. When she turned to walk away, Justin grabbed her arm.

"Haven't you forgotten something?" he asked.

Natalia acted tired and nodded. She was a professional and hadn't had any champagne. Her drunkenness had just been for show. She handed over her small handbag.

"It's all there," she said

Justin opened it, pulling out a smartphone. He reviewed the footage she'd shot. He gave Natalia an approving nod, dropped the phone into the bag, double-checked its contents and slotted it under his arm.

"Like I said, he's a nice guy," Natalia said, looking Justin straight in the eyes.

Justin grinned. She looked so much like Montana. It was the reason he'd picked her for this night. He ran a hand through her hair, imagining for a second that she actually was the real thing.

"How would you like to earn another thousand?" he asked.

CHAPTER SIXTY-ONE

SARAH TRUTH WAS GAINING more control of her body with every passing day. She wasn't imagining it. She felt sharper, stronger, and more alert than ever before. The hard part was making sure that Justin didn't notice. Now that he was on the board of St. Mary's, he had less use for her, and he could easily end her life. She wondered if the only reason he kept her alive now was so he had someone to brag to about his evil deeds. He was so proud of what he was doing, and it pained him that other people didn't know how truly clever he was.

The door to her room opened, and Nurse Rose peeked in.

"Hello Mrs. Truth," she smiled. "I thought I would just pop in and keep you company for a little while. Your wonderful son appreciates all the special attention I give you. He is such a good boy. You wouldn't believe how many others never get a visit from their children. He is so handsome, too!" The nurse ambled around the room, tidying up, just moving things to keep her hands busy.

"Silly me, I nearly forgot why I popped in, you got a letter from Justin. An actual letter, very rare. Such a good boy." The nurse rested in the visitor's chair, adjusted her glasses and unfolded the paper. She read:

> Dear Mother,
> You are the only one who truly knows me. I am away for business and I want you to know I'm thinking of you.
> I'll be back as soon as I can. I know you enjoy my visits as much as I do. No doubt, I will have so much to share.
>
> Love, Justin.

Nurse Rose lowered the letter and looked at Sarah. "I wish I had a son like this."

You can have him. Sarah was able to read between the lines. He wanted her to know he was always watching.

"It's all the talk of the hospital you know—your son being asked to join the board. Everyone is so excited for him." Nurse Rose continued her monologue for a good thirty minutes, mainly gossiping about her family and who wasn't doing what they should.

Sarah drifted off into thoughts about her own family. She and her husband had wanted three children. After Justin was born, it took two years for her to become pregnant again. They had been so excited to have another baby—also a boy, born with jet-black hair. Sarah's mother had been dark, and she was thrilled that he had her hair.

They had called their new son Michael; he was such a good baby. He liked to eat, sleep, smile, and rarely cried. Justin had been distant toward his younger brother. He had just turned four and didn't like sharing the attention of his parents. She'd been told this was normal, and that he would soon grow to love being a big brother. They had to make sure Justin knew that there was enough love to go around and that he wasn't getting replaced.

Sarah woke one morning feeling a slight chill in the air. Her husband had already left for work. Once a week he had to go into work at five a.m. to have conference calls with some other bankers from around the country. She felt something in the bed—it was Justin snuggled into her side. She'd stroked his hair and closed her eyes. Then she'd opened them again. Something was wrong: the air felt too still.

She got up to check Michael's cot, to see if he was all right. He wasn't. He was a light shade of blue and was lying motionless. In a panic, Sarah pulled Michael from the cot, rocking him in her arms to wake him. She tried CPR to resuscitate him. Nothing worked. She screamed to God to fix this.

"Mommy? Mommy? What's wrong?" Justin had asked. Sarah couldn't reply. Her heart was ripping apart.

The doctors told Sarah and her husband at the hospital that it was a case of crib death. There was nothing they could have done. Sometimes babies just stop breathing. No one was to blame. Justin had sat with them quietly, not asking what had happened to his baby brother.

Sarah hadn't thought about her baby Michael for a long time. Only now did she remember Justin in bed with her on the morning that it happened. He'd always been an independent child, and had never crawled into their bed before. She started to think the unthinkable. Had Justin killed his baby brother?

Suddenly Sarah felt an itch on her nose, and without thinking she went to scratch it. Her arm moved slightly. She froze. She'd been so caught up in her daydream that she'd forgotten about Nurse Rose. Her mind started to race. Had Nurse Rose seen her move? If she did, she'd alert the doctors, who would inform Justin about her improved condition.

Nurse Rose stopped talking, removed her glasses, and cleaned them with a corner of her shirt while staring intently at Sarah. She replaced them and sat forward.

"Sarah?" she asked gently.

Sarah could feel her breathing increase, her chest rising and falling a bit faster than normal. Nurse Rose got out of her chair.

"Sarah?" she asked again.

Sarah could feel Nurse Rose getting closer and closer. The smell of her Red Door perfume overwhelmed her nostrils and made it hard to breathe. She forced her eyes to defocus. Make the world blurry. Stop her pupils from reacting, her eyeballs from twitching.

"Sarah," Rose finally spoke again. "Would you like a blanket, dear?"

Sarah felt relieved. Maybe she hadn't seen her hand move. But she did continue to stare at Sarah without saying anything for a long minute. Sarah began to panic.

"I think I'll get a blanket for you. Your skin is covered in goosebumps."

The nurse fetched a blanket from the cupboard and draped it over Sarah. "Enjoy the rest of your day, Mrs. Truth, and God bless you," Nurse Rose said finally and turned on the TV before she left the room.

CHAPTER SIXTY-TWO

JENNIFER WAS IN HEAVEN.

She had Justin's apartment all to herself. No rules. No worries. Maybe a few rules, but she could handle those. She stretched out on the luxurious bed watching the E! channel on the wall-mounted big screen TV. The blinds were pulled open, allowing the glorious sun to warm the room naturally.

She loved this apartment.

No way could she afford a place like this. With Justin away in Las Vegas, she pretended it was hers. She loaded the fridge with the food she liked, chocolate milk, buffalo wings, sour cream for bagels—stuff Justin never bought. He was particular about what he ate, and when he ate it. After all, no one got a body like his by eating all the foods she loved. She loved his body, but she needed to have some naughty, yummy food as well.

Jennifer slowly rolled out of bed; it was eleven a.m. She'd decided to take the week off work while Justin was away, to take total advantage of the apartment. She was wearing full-length pink flannel PJs with little love-hearts all over them. They felt so good to sleep in and helped her wake up happy. Justin always insisted that she sleep naked when she stayed over, but he wasn't here this morning.

She took a large container of fruit yogurt from the fridge and meandered around the apartment while eating it with a silver spoon. She had to send Justin another nude of her tonight. Every night she had to send him one. It was one of his rules while he was away. Each one had to be taken it in a different place in his apartment. She wanted to make him happy, so she played along.

She liked sex but had never seen herself as sexy. To her, sex was more about getting close to someone, the closest way two people could become one. Justin's view on sex was different. Some of the things she'd gotten up to with Justin, the things she'd consented to, were things she'd never tell anyone, ever. Every now and then a turgid memory would haunt her and make her feel slightly nauseous.

Jennifer finished her yogurt, slipped into jeans and a T-shirt, and went out for a walk. It was such a beautiful area, and often she would see a celebrity passing by. She headed to a corner store for a paper and grab a coffee. The old man behind the counter smiled and gave her a free donut. She often had that effect on people. She strolled the long way back to the apartment, taking in the sights of Central Park.

When she got back, she heard Bill sobbing next door, and her heart went out to him. She liked Bill and thought he was funny. More than once after leaving Justin's apartment, Bill would pull her into his place to chat. After Mr. Noodles had attacked the small boy, everything changed. Grieving over his furry companion, Bill had lost weight and wasn't looking after himself. Justin had told her the boy's parents were suing Bill for a lot of money. She wanted to help get him back to being the person that would tell her about his fabulous adventures. She knocked on his door. Waited. Knocked again. Maybe not today.

Back in Justin's apartment, she turned up her favorite music and looked at the clock. It was still too early for wine. Then she remembered when you are on vacation, anytime is wine time. She opened a bottle of Chardonnay and poured herself a healthy measure.

The large oil painting on the wall drew Jennifer's attention once again. It was so massive compared to paintings she had seen before. She'd asked Justin about it, and he said it was a piece he'd bought ten years ago from some obscure artist. Jennifer stood in front of it and tried to envision what the artist might have been feeling when he created it. The red handprints seemed so primal, screaming out against the slate-gray background. She cocked her head to one side. Something was different. She took a few steps back and looked again. Then it clicked. There was an extra handprint on the bottom left corner, she was sure of it. Why would another handprint appear on it, she wondered?

Jennifer laughed at herself for being silly. She flopped down on the couch and told herself she was just imagining things. But just in case she wasn't, she picked up her mobile phone, and took a photograph of it. She counted the handprints. Forty-three in total.

CHAPTER SIXTY-THREE

JUSTIN FLUNG OPEN the doors to Mother's Milk like he owned the place. He tapped a tune on the reception desk and announced loudly: "Hi, Justin Truth, national marketing manager for Soda-Cola North America, here to see Sandy Miller."

"Yes, Mr. Truth," the receptionist answered, bewildered. She was told to expect him, but for a secret meeting. She called Sandy and told him Justin was fifteen minutes early. Sandy got up from his desk, excusing himself from the group working on the OrangeFizz campaign, and rushed to reception.

"Justin," Sandy warmly greeted him. "So good to see you. Come with me. I have a meeting room already prepared. You're a little early, but we're ready."

"No rush," Justin replied. "I came early in the hopes you could give me a tour of this place I have heard so much about."

"Sure," Sandy said, a little taken aback. Maybe he'd judged this meeting all wrong; maybe it wasn't as secret as he'd expected after all. For the next twenty minutes, Sandy showed Justin around the office. Justin greeted everyone he met warmly, introducing himself, and asking them about their role at Mother's Milk. This was a side of Justin that Sandy hadn't seen. One of the young creative teams he introduced Justin to were working on a charity campaign for The American Deaf Foundation. Justin told them how much he loved their campaign, flipped out some large notes, and added them to the donation bucket.

On the way to the meeting room, Justin turned to Sandy, dropping his tone. "Is everything sorted for tonight?"

"It is," Sandy replied. "Are you sure you want to do this?"

"I can't come to the home of the Ultimate Fighting Championship and not get into a cage, Sandy," Justin said. "Just make sure everything is how I asked it to be. This is something I will greatly appreciate, and that's a good thing."

Sandy responded with his best salesman's smile. "Nothing is ever too much for our clients at Mother's Milk, Justin."

"Good, because I like you, Sandy. I like Mother's Milk. Now make me love you too."

* * *

Back in New York, Donna Southland was enjoying lunch with one of her senior account members when her phone rang. This was the first of many calls she'd receive today, all with the same news. Justin Truth was spotted at Mother's Milk, and this wasn't good. Donna was going to have to implement her strategy to win Justin over faster than she'd planned to. She wasn't going to lose any R and R business on her watch, and especially not to an agency like Mother's Milk.

CHAPTER SIXTY-FOUR

JUSTIN'S TAXI ARRIVED AT the address Sandy had texted to him. It was a good thirty-minute drive from the heart of the city. He was wired, high, and pumped. This was a place not many people got to see; this was where fighters really made a name for themselves. Justin watched as the taxi's back lights disappeared into the darkness; this wasn't an area the driver wanted to hang around in, especially this late at night.

Justin dropped his gym bag on the ground and stared at the foreboding warehouse, flexing his fingers. Punch Club was famous for the talent that came through its ranks. Its name was proudly spray-painted in thick block letters on the heavy dented roller door.

He knocked on the fortified door and was let in by a well-built Italian man. He was one of Punch Club's head trainers. He didn't smile. The gym stank of dirty sweat from dirty men who trained hard. It was darkly lit, but Justin could make out the posters covering the walls of famous fighters who had trained there. The space was divided into three areas: one for weights, one for cardio, and the other for jiu-jitsu and wrestling.

The trainer led him to a side door that opened into the adjoining warehouse, the cage room. Justin had seen pictures, but it was even more awesome in real life. In the center of the room, highlighted by four spotlights, was an octagon cage, surrounded by folding chairs. Small MMA shows were held in here for upcoming fighters.

Sandy stood next to it with a worried look on his face.

"Justin!" Sandy said. "You're right on time. Are you a hundred percent sure you want to do this? You really don't have to. What do you say we just get some coke and bang some pole dancers?"

"Sandy, I want this," Justin said. "If you give me what I want, you will get what you want, and I know what you want." Justin grinned knowingly, dropping his bag and taking off his sweatshirt. Back at the hotel he had wrapped his fists and put on fighter's gloves. He was already covered in a light sweat from the anticipation. He strutted into the awaiting cage with confidence, soaking it all in. He warmed up by moving around the caged area, ducking, dodging, rolling, and throwing different attacking combinations.

"Bring him out, bring this fucker to fight me!" Justin yelled. Sandy nodded to the trainer, who banged on the changing-room door, not taking his eyes off Sandy. The door opened, and out walked a skinny man with a big bushy beard. He wore Tapout shorts and full MMA gear that was too big for him. His eyes darted about the room as he was led into the cage.

Sandy had found Bob a few streets off the main strip, where all the hobos hung out. He'd shown him a wad of cash and said they just needed to give some white-collar playboy a thrill in a ring, nothing sexual. All he had to do was put up a fight, take a few punches, and he'd make more money than he would in a year on the streets. It was as Justin had specifically requested. He didn't want a fighter, he just wanted to beat the living hell out of someone in a cage. Justin stared him up and down. He had a good hundred pounds on the guy.

Bob wandered around the cage, looking dubious. He didn't look like much, and Sandy hadn't asked him any questions. If he had, he would have discovered that Bob was an ex-Marine who had fought in Desert Storm. His first day in, his unit was caught in a heavy firefight. He'd been scared and had hidden in the truck, watching as his entire unit was cut down, blown up, and ripped apart. When he finally tried to help, he was hit by a mortar explosion, knocking him out with a severe concussion. He was the only survivor, yet the memory of his unit never left him, and their screams haunted his every waking moment. During his hospital stay, he turned to any narcotics he could find to numb his brain; the more he took, the more he needed. Bob managed to see out his tour and then opted to leave the army and go home. Home was different after that; he hated to be inside, and he was always angry. Before long, he gave up on himself and so had his family. Moving from one fix to another, he found his way to Vegas, killing himself with anything he could get his hands on to block out the painful memories.

Justin looked at Sandy and yelled, "You've done good, Sandy. Now ring the bell!" Sandy picked up a small hammer and hit a bell screwed onto wood. Justin took the center of the cage and signaled for Bob to fight. Slowly, Bob shuffled forward in a defensive stance, his shorts hanging off his malnourished body.

Justin toyed with him at first, throwing some gentle jabs. He wasn't intent on doing any real damage at this stage. Ducking and weaving, finding his distance, he showed off his technique. Bob relaxed a little, and threw a few jabs of his own, which Justin easily defended.

Justin saw an opening and threw a heavy body shot to his kidneys. Bob crumpled.

"Fuck yeah!" Justin yelled. He stared at his downed opponent. "Get the fuck up. I'm not paying you to sit around." Bob glanced at Sandy, who nodded for him to get up.

Slowly, he got to his feet and raised his guard. Now Justin swooped in; he wasn't playing anymore. He connected with a hard jab. Bob's right eyelid split open. Three more quick jabs hit the same spot. Blood poured from the wound. Bob stumbled back, blinking to get blood out of his eye. Justin stepped in and hit him with another heavy body shot, followed by a right hook. Once again, Bob hit the ground.

"And you're a winner!" Sandy yelled out in his best announcer voice.

"Shut the fuck up, Sandy! I'm not finished yet." Justin glared at Bob. "Get the fuck up!"

Bob shook his head. With lighting speed, Justin pulled the homeless guy to his feet.

"Come on, cocksucker! What you got? What you going to do?" Justin cracked Bob on the jaw with a straight right hand.

Bob heard an explosion in his head: he was back in the army, back in the truck. His unit was pinned down, it was up to him to save them this time. He snapped. He popped up. Faked left. Then with all his strength, he swung a wild overhead right and clocked Justin's scar on the side of the head, just below the temple. The weakened skin split, and blood seeped out. Justin staggered back, his head ringing from the well-placed strike. Bob started throwing body shots. Justin dropped his guard to cover his ribs, exposing his head. Bob leapt in and connected with a

Superman punch to Justin's jaw. Justin fell onto his back. Bob went to finish him, jumping on Justin with wild punches. Justin got his arms up to deflect most of the shots. He could feel each punch getting weaker and weaker. Bob's body just wasn't up for this sort of physical activity anymore; he was gassed.

Justin felt the pins and needles up the back of his neck. The hunter took over. He pushed Bob off him and scrambled to his feet. Bob was confused, standing awkwardly. Justin dropped his shoulder and spear-tackled Bob to the ground. He instantly went into full mount and rained down hammer fist after hammer fist. After the first five, Bob went limp, but Justin continued breaking Bob's face, caving it in.

Finally, Justin stopped. He was breathing heavily, covered in specks of blood. He got up, and glanced down at his handiwork. He wouldn't be surprised if the guy died from the damage he'd inflicted. Justin calmly opened the cage door.

"Sandy, make this go away. I was never here."

CHAPTER SIXTY-FIVE

THE CABIN CREW went about their final tasks, preparing the plane for landing. Justin looked out his first-class window at the sprawling metropolis that was New York. It was good to be back, Las Vegas had gone perfectly. He had wowed everyone with his presentation and made Steve look like a babbling fool. Mother's Milk was cranking away on the OrangeFizz campaign, and he still hadn't paid them a single cent. He knew that Donna at R and R Advertising would have heard about his appearance at Mother's Milk; he wanted people to know he'd been there so the grapevine would send a clear message to Donna that she was going to have to do something very special to close it. Justin's long-term plan was to play them off against each other, slashing their fees as they did it.

As the plane landed, Justin screened his iPhone for emails and texts. There were a few from Jennifer, telling him how much she missed him, and how she was making them a special dinner. He was pretty tired. He had fucked his way through Vegas, and his cock was feeling it. He replied that he was looking forward to it.

One of his emails was forwarded on from Debbie concerning the air hostess he'd fucked on the flight to Vegas. He'd hoped she would be on the flight back; alas she wasn't. He was about to delete the email, but then decided to reply to Debbie, instructing her to forward it to Donna with a note saying that she needed to help out on this. Justin saw this as a test. Would Donna cast this girl just to make him happy?

Justin departed the plane first, collected his bag from the baggage carousel, and headed to the passenger pick-up zone. For this trip, he'd instructed Debbie to organize a Soda-Cola vehicle to transport him home. After a long flight, he needed a luxurious car with leg room, and the smell of fresh leather. Instead, he was surprised by a sexy female chauffeur in a revealing outfit standing in front of a stretch limo. She looked more like a stripper playing dress-up than an actual chauffeur. Her short black skirt was split up the side and held together with safety pins. A tight white shirt was pulled into a knot at the front, pushing up her cleavage, and showing off her flat stomach. A chauffeur's hat sat atop of her teased black hair. Her sign read: WELCOME BACK, JUSTIN TRUTH.

Justin liked what he saw. He approached her and smiled. "That would be me you're looking for."

"Well, they said you were good-looking," Ms. Sexy Chauffeur said, biting her bottom lip, as she looked Justin up and down. "We've been asked to give you a ride home."

"We?" Justin asked, intrigued. The door to the limo opened, and two equally hot-looking girls got out, dressed just as alluring.

"Donna Southland sends her regards," one of the girls said in a husky voice.

"And you may want to take the long way home," the other smiled.

Justin liked this. Finally, Donna was joining the game.

"Sandy, I want this," Justin said. "If you give me what I want, you will get what you want, and I know what you want." Justin grinned knowing

CHAPTER SIXTY-SIX

OLIVE MASTERSON PUT HER phone down gently. The mayor was six months away from his next election and wanted to go into his final run with good news to share with the voters of New York City. His demand got passed down the chain, getting heavier and heavier: results were needed on the Beetle Butcher.

In her head, she slowly started to count to ten. She only made it to three before she started swearing like a salty sailor. They wanted the impossible. They knew it. She knew she didn't have a lot of fans in the force, but she had worked hard for everything she'd accomplished. At least twenty times a day she fantasized about walking out the door and not coming back. Yet she didn't want to give all her haters the satisfaction that she was leaving.

There were many who coveted Olive's job. They wouldn't be better at it, but that didn't stop them from thinking they could and being very vocal about it. The Beetle Butcher was a clever fucker and slippery as hell. They were doing everything they could to nail him down, but nothing was sticking, and no one had any worthwhile clues to go by. There was no common element that connected all the victims. It was like he didn't have a type, which made it random, which made it near impossible to predict what he would do next.

Olive composed herself, left her office, and headed to the Briefing Room. She could hear the rabble of voices before she opened the door. No one was happy about this case. The room was at capacity; she had called everyone in. Every chair was filled, and those who missed out on chairs crowded at the back. Olive took her position at the front of the room, resting her notes on the wooden lectern. All eyes were on her. She had to be strong and show no sign of weakness. She saw Ross among the crowd, which made her feel a little better. Not everyone here wanted her to fail.

"Listen up!" she started. "We have nine dead bodies, a thousand bugs, and not one step closer to solving this case. I just got off the phone with people who had some very colorful words to describe us all. Everyone is watching us—the FBI, the CIA, every TV network you can imagine. And we have nothing. I've been told we have to double our efforts, but we won't be doubling our team."

The group let out a collective groan. "That means overtime and it's unpaid."

"You have to be joking!" someone called out.

"The joke is we have nothing," she replied without blinking. "And I have been told no one working here will get paid overtime for having nothing. This sick fuck has to have slipped up somewhere. We have to start from the beginning, and go through everything again. If you don't like it, you can always leave your resignation on my desk, and I'll wish you the best finding another job. I'm told Christmas is a great time of year for hiring mall-cop security."

The room went silent, a metal chair scrapped the floor. Everyone knew she was telling the truth. Times were tough, and losing a job wasn't ideal for any of them.

"Now, do we have anything new?" Olive posed the group.

A voice piped up. "Five of the victims had gym memberships. Maybe the Beetle Butcher stalks gyms?"

"Did they go to the same gym?" Olive asked.

"No, it's a bit of a stretch but we're looking into it," the detective said.

"Good luck on that! Any word on why he uses these types of beetles?"

"We have spoken to leading entomologists," a voice piped up. "We thought we may be onto something, but they are so common anyone with a mound of dirt can breed them. If they are symbolic for something, we have no idea what."

"Great. A whole load of nothing." She wasn't getting anywhere. She had no idea what she should do next. Silence hung in the air.

"I have a question." The voice belonged to Ross. "I've recently dropped into this case, and I've read most of the reports. It might be nothing, but it's been niggling in my mind ever since I looked over the photos."

"What is it?" Olive asked. All eyes in the room were on Ross.

"Everything he does is the same. Every victim is treated the same. He doesn't change his method of killing. It's step by step. There is no variation on what he does, but there is on who he does, who he kills. We have a mixture of females: a tall blonde with long hair, a bottle-blonde with cropped hair, a pixie-face brunette, a dark-hair Italian, and an Asian of Korean descent."

"The randomness is what makes it so hard to get ahead of him," Olive stated.

"But he's far from random. His method betrays a logic that leaves nothing to chance. Each of these women were selected for a reason. What if he's not randomly picking one?"

"Elaborate, please."

"What if he's group-selecting?"

"There is no link between them."

Ross approached the whiteboard on the wall behind Olive. In his hand were headshots of all the victims. On the left side of the board he placed five pictures, on the right, four.

"What about this connection?" he asked. "He's selecting a group based on looks."

The two groups of women looked identical. The only difference was the group on the right didn't have an Asian member.

"What if his next victim is going to be Asian? Korean, to be certain," Ross offered up.

Olive began to feel hope. The first real break in the Beetle Butcher case had just happened.

CHAPTER SIXTY-SEVEN

CARLTON ENTERED THE reception area as Justin and some of his team were preparing to leave for their day's adventure. They were dressed in sports gear, as the email invitation had suggested.

"Justin, are you guys ready?" Carlton asked.

"As ready as we'll ever be. It should be fun. Are you sure you can't come?"

"I'd love to, but I have work to do here. Enjoy your team-building exercises with R and R, though—they're a wonderful group of people, and we've achieved great things together."

"I don't just want great, Carlton, I want epic!" Justin sported a winning grin. He shook Carlton's hands firmly and noticed how much weaker the other man was getting. This made him happy. He had more work to do and hoped Carlton would hang in a bit longer to experience it.

Four well-toned women and two men, all dressed in combat gear, strutted into the reception area. One of the women was holding a metallic megaphone. She jumped onto the reception desk.

"Ladies and maggots," she announced. "Are you ready to get your butts kicked, whipped, and maybe smacked? Do you have the cannonballs to shoot down the competition? Will you rise to the challenge, or go limp like a wet piece of spaghetti?

"My name is Jane, and I'm going to be your worst nightmare or your wettest dream. And they can both be the same thing."

For the next five minutes, she yelled instructions, using as many sexual innuendos as she could, while looking at Justin like she wanted to take him right there on the spot. Once the briefing was done, she ordered them outside into waiting Hummers.

An hour's drive out of the city was a corporate retreat park used for days like these. The sprawling forest had areas designed for outdoor team-building activities. There were also conference rooms and cabins that could be used for talks, brainstorming, and presentations. Today had one purpose: Donna wanted to crack Justin, to bring the two of them closer. If putting Justin up on a giant egotistical pedestal was going to do that, then she would budget that into the account. She'd briefed the combat girls to fuss over Justin as much as possible. They could go as far as they wanted and would be paid accordingly.

The doors of the Hummers opened at their destination and people piled out. Donna's team members were already at the park, and the two groups mingled. Donna made a beeline to Justin.

"It's going to be a great day, Justin," Donna said.

"It's started that way," Justin grinned. "Let's hope it ends the right way."

Donna smiled. "You think you will win today?"

"If it comes down to you and me? Call your husband now, and tell him you love him. Because you're not going home, unless it's in a body bag."

CHAPTER SIXTY-EIGHT

THE TEAMS OF Soda-Cola and R and R gathered around a collection of camouflage-painted oil drums draped in netting. Jane jumped onto it, making it a stage. She was stunning, wearing a low-cut shirt that exposed her large, tanned cleavage. The tight camo shorts highlighted her legs perfectly.

"Listen up. We have arrived! Remember, you will do as I tell you all day. I will push you, hard. You don't want me to punish you. But looking at some of you, I guess you do." The group laughed. "And you would pay a lot of money for it, too." She had them in the palm of her hand.

"We have a few adventures in store for you today," Jane continued. "Each team will build up points at every station. At the end of the day there will be a winning team. And as winners, you will be treated as such. You will receive golden dog tags with your combat name on it, and your entire team will enjoy a very fancy meal at a very fancy place. And I mean very fancy. And for the special one of you who is so much better than everyone else, you'll be awarded Action Hero of the Day and receive a large phallic trophy. Who knows, we could maybe even throw in a night partying with me and some of my better-looking friends." She looked directly at Justin and blew him a kiss. "Go forth and dominate." She pulled a starter pistol from her waist band and fired it into the air.

Next, each group was assigned their own combat guide who went over the rules and activities with them in greater detail. Justin looked over his group. It wasn't the worst. He was going to inspire them to win and make sure he took out the individual trophy. The day course was structured into ten activities. They were simple, fun tasks that everyone could do: rolling tires down a hill, making a fire to boil water, and, as a group, carrying a log across a stream. Then there were slightly more challenging activities that required a bit of strength and hand-eye coordination such as archery, rifle shooting, and an impressive assault course.

After the first three activities of the day, Justin found another member in his group who was rather good at everything and could actually come close to beating him. His name was Davis, and he was new to Soda-Cola. He was of average height with a blond mop of hair and an athletic build. He was quick-witted, with a surfer's flowing attitude.

Justin had hired him a month ago, and at the time liked his drive and attention to detail. That like soon disappeared as Davis openly challenged Justin in front of other Soda-Cola employees. This annoyed Justin. He was the boss. Everyone did what Justin said, no questions asked. Davis had dared to try and show him up. He was on thin ice, and if he didn't play his cards right, he was going to find himself drowning in icy water.

CHAPTER SIXTY-NINE

DETECTIVE ROSS SMITH HOVERED outside the Soda-Cola International building. From the outside, it looked like a high-end art gallery to him. People half his age constantly came and went through the front doors. Maybe his guy worked in here and he would casually bump into him on his way to commit another murder. But in the real world, he was going to have to search for the bastard.

He followed two young men in suits through the revolving doors into the building. On the walls, large TV screens played various Soda-Cola commercials from over the years. In the middle of the floor was a circular reception desk proudly displaying the Soda-Cola logo.

Ross approached the reception area where two women in their early twenties operated the desk. Ross made sure he had the attention of both women before showing them the identi-kit picture. At first, they said nothing and waved him on, but Ross asked them with a slightly sterner tone to look again. New Yorkers gave nothing away, but this time they inspected the picture more closely.

"It kind of looks like Justin," one of them said.

"Maybe," the other added. "Why are you looking for this person?"

"We think he may have seen something that could help us," Ross said. He'd learned many moons ago to never tell concerned citizens he was asking them about suspects in a crime. If they knew them, they wouldn't want to get the suspect in trouble. But if they thought the suspect was helping the police, that was a different story.

"Is he around?" Ross asked.

"No, he's out of the office all day. I could see if his PA is around."

"His PA?"

"Yeah, Justin Truth basically runs the whole company."

"He's kinda important," the other receptionist added.

"If I could talk to his PA, that would be great. They are?"

"That's Debbie. If you take a seat, I'll see what I can do."

Ross thanked each with an offer of jelly beans, then took a seat and watched the big screens sell him soda. The doors to one of the executive elevators opened, and out stepped a short well-dressed lady with what looked like a permanent scowl. One of the receptionists pointed her in Ross's direction.

"Good afternoon, Debbie," Ross said politely as he got up. "My name is Detective Ross Smith. I'm so glad you could take a few minutes out of your day to talk to me." Ross shook her hand, and produced his bag of jelly beans. "Jelly bean?"

Debbie thought about it, and took one with a naughty smile.

"How can I help you, Detective?" she said.

"I was hoping I could arrange a meeting with Justin Truth."

"He is a very busy man, Detective."

"I understand. I've been told he is one of the top dogs here."

"Justin is amazing. He is one of the kindest people I've ever met. What would you like to talk to him about?"

"I'm working on a case, and I was hoping he might have seen something that could help with the investigation."

"Why do you think that?"

"Just walking and talking. I have a lot of people to talk to and am just crossing the t's and dotting the i's," Ross said, trying to appeal to a fellow paper-pusher. "You know all about paperwork. It has to be done."

Ross decided to underplay why he needed to talk to Justin. He got the feeling that Debbie was protective of him.

"I just need five minutes, so I can tidy up a few things. When could I come back? I really want to move onto another case I have concerning a stolen car."

"He can't do it on the phone?" Debbie asked.

"I wish, but rules are rules. If someone follows up, I'll get in trouble." Ross gave Debbie his best I'm-a-loser-and-not-a threat look.

"I'll make time in his calendar for tomorrow, to get it out of the way," Debbie said.

"You've made my day," Ross replied with a big smile.

CHAPTER SEVENTY

"WHY HAVE YOU been avoiding me?" Montana asked, standing in the doorway of Steve's office. One of her hands planted on her hip, the other folding some files.

"I haven't," Steve replied, suddenly finding that he needed to check his tie.

"Really? I got back on Monday and today's Wednesday. I've left you messages, but you didn't respond. Not like you at all."

"Don't look at me like that," Steve looked back up at her. "I've had a hard time since Vegas—you would have heard it didn't go so well. And with the Soda-Cola birthday this Friday, I have a lot on my plate."

"That was just a stupid conference, Steve. People only go to get drunk and fuck." Montana closed the door behind her. "So Justin spent a truckload of his own money on his presentation to stroke his own ego. You don't need that. People respect you for all the hard work you've done."

"Justin's not that bad."

"What? Did you guys become best friends in Vegas?"

"No, he was... he was good. He helped a lot. I understand that your brother didn't like him. I can see why people can get that impression of him."

"He fucked him over, just like he will fuck you, and fuck us both over!" Montana slammed her files on his desk.

"Montana, we have gone through this so many times. Can't we just move on?"

"No!"

A tense silence hung in the air between them. Montana's face softened. She knew Steve was a good man, and yelling at him for trying to see the best in people wasn't going to help. She changed tack.

"Look, he's a clever guy. He is controlling and manipulative in the way he treats others. But he isn't a genius, and he slipped up."

"What do you mean?"

"I have proof that he was the one who gave our competitors the plans for the LemonGreat campaign."

"He leaked it?" Steve asked, surprised, catching a whiff of her perfume.

"Fuck yeah, he did. He was very good at covering his tracks, but I found a guy who knows how to find the unfindable. He has spent weeks doing stuff that I barely understand, but the crux is he was able to track an outgoing email address. He set up some spiders, and waited for the email to go active again. This morning it did, and he was able to piggyback to an IP address. He could then log on to scan the computer that had sent the email. One name popped up that we both know only too well…"

"Justin?"

"Justin Dickhead Truth!" Montana gave Steve a high-five. "How are we going to bring this asshole down? Do you want to take it to Carlton? Or should we call Justin out and get him to quit? Or send it straight to *Market Trends* magazine, and get it on the cover?"

"I need to think," Steve replied.

"Think? We have him."

"This is big, and we have to handle it right. We can't just go running blind. If it's not done right, it'll backfire on us. Whatever we do to remove him, has to be bulletproof."

"Can't I just shoot him?"

Steve laughed. "No."

"We've done good, Steve." Montana smiled. "We did good!"

CHAPTER SEVENTY-ONE

MORE THAN HALFWAY through the day at the team-building experience, people were having a great time. Points were being awarded left, right, and center to much applause and laughter. To make it more fun, mystery bonus points were also handed out, which kept the scores near even. Justin was leading the individual race by three points. Davis was getting close, and if it weren't for the bonus points that had been awarded to Justin, Davis would be in the lead by eleven.

Donna had subtly been controlling the proceedings so Justin would be in the lead. The assault course was its own beast; the person with the fastest time in each team would score fifteen points. The second place would get ten. If Davis were to win, he would be the Action Hero, and that wasn't something Donna wanted to happen. It was out of her hands now, however. She couldn't manipulate the scoring anymore without people noticing.

All the teams were called together at the lunch area to announce the points. Jane, the combat girl with the megaphone, jumped onto a table and worked it like a catwalk.

"I love it when people look up to me!" she said with a smirk that elicited a few laughs. "Right now, some of you are good and may make my squad, but most of you aren't fit to lick my boots." She squatted in front of a slightly overweight man from Soda-Cola. He blushed as she gave him her full attention with her long, tanned legs on either side of his head. "Or any other part of me for that matter." She grinned as she patted his head and stood back up.

"Now for the points. Starting in last place, The Dog Heads!" She quickly rattled through the six other teams that didn't make the top two. There were two teams left: The Honky Tonk Blues, led by Donna; and Atomic Boom, led by Justin.

"So now we come down to the final two teams," Jane announced. "The day is over for the rest of you and you can drink away your failures at the mess. The race for the Action Hero of the day isn't over just yet. There are two of you who have been trading the lead back and forth all day. Let's hear it for Justin Truth and Davis Redding!"

The members from all the squads clapped and cheered. A few people chanted for Davis. No one did the same for Justin. Justin's dislike was turning to loathing. Davis was going to be gone by the end of the month. Debbie would find something to action a dismissal.

"There is a lot on the line," Jane said. "The first prize of that fancy dinner at that fancy restaurant is valued at well over a thousand dollars."

Davis borrowed the megaphone to address the groups. "What's up, my people? How great is this day? Big shout out to R and R." Everyone clapped. "As some of you know, my daughter, Chloe, has MS. If I win today, I want to donate the prize to MSAA and let them auction it off. All proceeds going to MS research."

The group cheered even louder. Justin was seething. He couldn't believe that Davis would take the spotlight like that.

Jane took control of the megaphone again. "Thank you, Davis. Cute and generous." She turned her attention to the group. "My question is to you all. Are. You. Ready? It's time for the final test, the main event, winner takes all!

"To our left is the Assault Course. It has a few challenges in store for Justin and Davis. First up, there are three walls to scramble over, each one higher than the last. Make it over them and you'll need good upper-body strength to rope swing yourself over a dirty, stinky pond. Then onto the zigzag beams—fall off and you have to start again. Scramble up the cargo net and down the other side. No time to rest, as you'll need to shimmy along the Burma bridge between the platforms. Your arms will be burning; get those legs pumping through rows of tires, and keep your knees high so you don't trip up. Tired? Well, there are more tires to go, so navigate your way through the hanging tires. Then scale the rock-climbing wall all the way to the top and, after taking in the view, zip line the 250 yards back down. Think you are finished? Close. If you have anything left in the tank, a hundred-yard dash to the finish line! I'm exhausted just talking about it." Jane took in a few exaggerated breaths, making her large breasts rise and fall. She approached Justin and Davis, placing a hand on each of their chests. "Impress me, boys, and I'll make it worth your while." She bit her bottom lip.

Jane lifted her starter pistol and pulled the trigger. At the sound of the crack, Justin and Davis were off. Each man hit the course with gusto, flying over the walls and swinging across the pond. Davis started to pull ahead. He moved with the agility of a cat. Justin hit the cargo net at full speed, jumping halfway up it, and with his strong arms he was soon over the top and rolling down to the bottom. As Davis worked his way along the ropes, Justin was able to catch up. Neck and neck, both men pumped their legs through the tires. Davis glanced at Justin and gave him a big smile. He was loving this.

They both reached the rock-climbing wall together, and had to be strapped in with carabiners before climbing. Justin yelled at the attendant to go faster. He started to climb first, with Davis a mere five seconds behind him. Those five seconds were soon lost, and halfway up they were neck and neck. Justin sensed that Davis was going to overtake him, and it would be hard to take back the lead. He faked a slip that sent his body flying into Davis, knocking them both off the wall. Hanging from the safety ropes, they both scrambled to get a footing; in the mayhem, Justin poked Davis in the eye. Davis cried out and clapped a hand over his injured eye. Justin regained his footing and started to scale the wall, again smiling to himself, but as his hands reached the top, he looked down and saw that Davis was right behind him.

"Fuck!" Justin mumbled under his heavy breathing. He didn't believe this little upstart should win. He didn't show his superiors enough respect. A Davis win would be another sign of disrespect. Justin then got an idea how to put Davis in his place, to teach him a lesson for openly challenging him.

As Justin pulled himself onto the creaky platform, he faked a cramp in his calf, allowing Davis to overtake him, and get to the nearest zip line. One of the attendants standing on the platform grabbed Davis's carabiner and clicked it onto the safety line. Justin hopped past and patted Davis on the shoulder. To the onlookers, it seemed as if he was wishing him the best, as it was obvious that Davis was going to win now. What they didn't see was Justin unhooking Davis's carabiner from the safety line. Davis leapt off the platform, holding onto the handlebars, yelling at the top on his lungs. Justin grabbed his bars as his carabiner got clicked in. He again faked his calf injury, hopping up and down, causing the zip lines to ripple. The waves shot down all the cables, throwing Davis around with a vengeance. His hands slipped and he fell. Without the carabiner in place there was nothing to catch him, and he hit the ground hard. Justin jumped and flew down the line, passing over Davis, whose body was contorted into a terrible shape. People ran toward the fallen man.

Justin arrived at the bottom of the zip line and landed perfectly. He turned to the commotion and smiled to himself.

"You should be recovered by the time you're fired," he whispered under his breath.

CHAPTER SEVENTY-TWO

JUSTIN STOPPED IN AT Soda-Cola on his way home. He was in a good mood. It had been a most pleasant day. He strutted past Debbie, grinning broadly, and dropped his trophy for winning Action Hero of the day on her desk. Debbie admired its size, then quickly followed him into his office.

"Mr. Truth, I heard about Davis. Terrible."

"It was. I was right there when he fell. If only I could have caught him," Justin dropped onto his chair, his legs were sore from the assault course.

"You're not Superman, Mr. Truth."

Justin leaned back in his chair, and thought about that for a second. *I could play Superman in a film*, he thought, staring off into space.

Debbie continued talking. "You are the closest thing to a real Superman, or a Captain America I know. The way people look up to you. That could be why a detective stopped in today to see you."

Justin snapped his head toward Debbie, and slowly sat upright. "A police detective?"

"He had a badge, a Detective Ross Smith."

"I don't know him. What did he want?"

"Wasn't hugely important. He's investigating something and is tying up some loose ends before he moves on. Someone told him you may have seen something."

"Did you tell him I was too busy?"

"I did. I even suggested you could do it by phone."

"And he was fine with that?"

"No, he said it had to be face-to-face to comply with the departmental rules. He looked like the sort of old timer that people palmed their unwanted work onto. I've cleared five minutes in your calendar for him to see you tomorrow at three p.m., if that's OK?"

"Sure," Justin said, as his mind ran through a thousand possibilities. "Anything to help our boys in blue in their work protecting our city streets."

"Anything else you need from me?" Debbie asked.

"No, you can go home if you want," Justin said, craving some space.

"Thanks, Mr. Truth," Debbie smiled. She smiled a lot more these days, and she had lost some weight.

As soon as his office door closed, Justin's mood took a more serious tone. He didn't know who this detective was, but that was about to change. Justin opened his laptop, and began searching online and sending inquiring emails. In a few hours, Justin would know everything about this Ross Smith.

CHAPTER SEVENTY-THREE

DETECTIVE ROSS SMITH ARRIVED at Soda-Cola at 2:50 p.m. His meeting with Justin was at 3 p.m., and no way did he want to miss a minute of it. He signed in at reception and took a seat. The Soda-Cola ads on the big screens hadn't changed from his last visit.

At 3:30 p.m. he was still waiting. He approached reception a few times and got the same response, that Justin wasn't too far away. The seats next to him were filled and emptied by other visitors, while Ross continued to wait. By 4:54 p.m. Ross saw a ray of hope as Debbie appeared.

"I'm so sorry to keep you waiting," she said. "Justin is a very busy man, and you wouldn't believe the amount of work he has to deal with every day. Tomorrow night is a very big night for Soda-Cola. Would you believe the company has been around for over a hundred years?"

Ross nodded, he did know, having seen the ad repeated on the reception screens for the last two hours. "A hundred years. That's a long time. Lucky I didn't have to *wait* that long."

"Sorry again about keeping you, but if you want to follow me, we can get this done and dusted for you."

Ross followed, keeping up his meandering appearance for Debbie. Asking questions about Soda-Cola and Justin. He found all her responses about Justin were too sugarcoated for his liking.

She stopped outside Justin's office, knocked, then opened the door for Ross. She didn't follow him in, gently closing the door behind him. Ross was impressed by the lavish office, doing a little whistle as he looked around. He assumed it was Justin talking on the phone, for the man did look a little bit like the sketch.

"Tell the mayor I can't wait to see him. Look, I've got to go, talk soon, and thanks again for getting me onto the board. Bye."

Ross picked up that the whole name-dropping of the mayor was for him, a subtle show of power. He wouldn't be surprised if Justin's suit cost more than his yearly salary.

"Good to meet you, Detective Smith," Justin said, getting up and extending his hand.

"Thanks for making time to see me," Ross said. He noticed the firm handshake. Justin was a strong man.

"Jelly bean?" Ross asked, offering him the bag.

"No thanks. No protein in those," Justin said with a smile.

Ross put the bag back in his pocket and took a seat.

"How can I help you, Detective Smith?"

"Ross, you can call me Ross. This won't take too long. Just trying to tie up a few loose ends."

"Loose ends? I have no idea what ends I could help you with." Justin stared hard at Ross, asserting dominance.

Ross dropped his eyes. He didn't need to out-macho this guy. He just needed him to slip up. "Do you know Lydia Young?"

"No, who is she?"

"A dead girl."

"That's a shame."

"Yes, and for no reason." Ross shifted his weight in his chair. "Do you like trains, Justin?"

"Trains? I'm not sure what you're getting at, Detective." Justin raised an eyebrow.

"I like trains and travel by them a lot," Ross continued. "Did you hear about the poor girl who fell to her death at Manhattan Mall?"

"Yes, I did. It was the talk of the office."

"Do you know her name?"

"No." Justin's voice gave away no emotion.

"It was Lydia Young," Ross said slowly.

"The girl you mentioned before?"

"So I did," Ross said, as if he couldn't remember mentioning her name. "And you didn't know her? Do you know what she looked like?"

"No, is this going anywhere?"

"No, well, maybe. Where were you when Lydia was killed?" Ross leaned forward, resting his elbows on his knees.

"Killed? I thought she fell?"

"Some people think we landed on the moon," Ross remarked. "So where were you when it happened?" He looked Justin directly in the eye.

Justin picked up his phone, not breaking the staredown. "Debbie, can you bring in my calendar, please?"

She joined the men, holding an iPad.

"We need to help the good detective here. What was the date, Detective Smith? My life is an open book."

"July twenty-six, twelve-forty-seven p.m."

"Where was I on the that day, and at that exact time, Debbie?"

"You were in your office working on a NiceTea market trends analysis from twelve thirty p.m. to two p.m. You then went to a late lunch at Ralph's."

"Was anyone here with you?" Ross asked.

"Debbie?" Justin barked, his eyes still on Ross.

"No, you were here alone. Going by my records, I was outside the door the entire time to stop people from interrupting." Debbie looked at Ross. "Justin's time is very important."

"My time is very important," Justin reiterated.

"It is, and I'm sorry for taking more of it than I should have. It's—" Justin quickly cut him off.

"Look, Ross. I know you are just doing your job by interrupting mine. I want to help you as much as I can, but in this situation, I have nothing to add. There must be more pressing jobs waiting for you back at the station. Jobs that are better suited to your time, jobs that will make a difference. What ever happened to this Lydia Young sounds like a terrible accident. Such things happen all the time. We live in New York. There must be a million other things the mayor would rather you do than look into a closed case."

Ross nodded. "You are right."

"And I think that's our five minutes," Justin added.

Ross maintained his underwhelming demeanor. "Look, sorry for wasting your time," he smiled. "You have no idea how much paperwork and red tape we have to go through. To be honest, I have no idea why I'm actually here."

Justin got up and shook Ross's hand.

"I know about paperwork. Move on, Ross," Justin said, as if it were an order.

Outside, Ross stared back at the Soda-Cola building. Justin was just as he thought a corporate shark would be, aggressively arrogant. There was no direct link from him to Lydia; the calendar was a nice touch, but that could have been easily manipulated to cover his whereabouts. No one was actually with him to collaborate his story. There was something else that didn't make logical sense: if Justin didn't know about Lydia, how would he have known her case had been closed as an accidental death? He would have only known if he had looked into it. Justin knew more than he let on. Ross was certain of it.

CHAPTER SEVENTY-FOUR

IT WAS LATE FRIDAY AFTERNOON, and the Soda-Cola building was mostly empty. Most of the staff were off getting ready for the 110th birthday celebration. For a lot of the employees, this was going to be the biggest night of their lives.

Justin, in his office, went through reports he'd had compiled about Detective Ross Smith. After yesterday's meeting, Justin had dug deeper to find out more about the man. He felt uneasy that Ross had linked him to Lydia Young. He needed dirt, some leverage to push him in another direction. Being on the board of St. Mary's gave him everything he'd hoped for. He was able to put in a call to a friend of a friend, and within minutes he had the entire work history of Detective Smith sitting in his email. Ross had reopened the case and was gnawing at it like a dog with a bone. Justin was going to have to take the bone off him.

The last week had been a roller coaster for Justin. He was looking forward to tonight. He saw this as another opportunity to be the star of the show. It was going to be a massive party. Soda-Cola had invited a number of business partners: advertising agencies, bottlers, designers, and media. All Soda-Cola employees were invited.

The theme was: *After 110 years, the toys have come out to play.* These kinds of parties always had a dress-up theme, which helped people get out of their nine-to-five personas and have some fun.

A large loft in Soho had been turned into a giant toy box for the occasion. Three bands and two DJs would help guests party into the early hours of Saturday morning.

Justin spent a part of his day at the venue, doing last-minute touches. He had big plans for tonight. It was going to be a night people would remember for a mighty long time.

CHAPTER SEVENTY-FIVE

MONTANA WAS IMPRESSED at how magical the entire party scene appeared. Everything was oversized. A giant child's hand hung from the roof so guests could be photographed looking like toys in its grasp. When she'd read about the theme, she had no idea what she wanted to go dressed as. A friend of hers talked her into going as "old school" Lara Croft from *Tomb Raider*. "It's easy," she'd said. "And you have the assets to pull it off," she'd teased. Montana had her hair braided, and two massive guns were strapped to her thighs. She was worried that her tank top was a bit tight, and going by the looks she was getting from guys, it was.

There were pop-up minibars everywhere, stocked with standard and exotic mixers. One bar caught her attention: it was serving jelly vodka shots.

"We have twenty different flavors," the young man behind the bar told Montana.

"Give me a pineapple one." She smiled.

He placed a shot on the bar, his eyes never leaving hers as she swallowed the shot. She was impressed he didn't check out her cleavage.

"Be careful," he said as she placed the empty plastic container on the bar. "They're stronger than they taste. You work for Soda-Cola, right?"

"I do, like most people here."

He laughed. "Funny. I mean, you're one of the influential people. Up the ladder. My name's Oscar, and if you need anything, just ask for me by name. It's my way of sucking up, in case you are hiring in the future and I'm in the mix."

Montana smiled. She was used to people coming on to her for sex; seeking a job was a refreshing change. She liked his openness about working the room for a position.

"I'll keep that in mind. Do you know Steve Barker?"

"Of course."

"Do you know where he is?"

Oscar pointed to the far corner behind her. "See those hanging teddy bears? You'll find him there."

"Thanks, Oscar," she said. "Keep up the good work."

Ever since Steve had returned from Vegas, he'd been acting distant. She wanted to talk to him about the dirt they had on Justin and how to use it. Steve was a cautious guy by nature, and a part of her understood that this TNT of information she had on Justin had to be handled right. They only had one shot, but they should have dealt with it by now. She wanted to expose him to the entire company and the wider industry. He'd never get a job again once people found out what he'd done to his own work colleagues.

Montana headed toward the floating bears. Oscar was right, and she caught a glimpse of Steve. He was dressed as Captain America and was talking to Donald Duck. Under Donald's bill was an exposed face she recognized: Donna Southland.

Montana approached them with a greeting and kissed them both on the cheek. "Donna, you look fantastic. Would you mind if I stole Captain America here for a second?"

"He's all yours," Donna said, then waddled toward a dancing bear.

Once Donna was out of earshot, Montana cut to the chase. "Have you decided what we are going to do about Justin?" she asked.

"Straight to that?" Steve replied, through gritted teeth.

"The sooner we deal with it, the sooner we can get him out of our hair and our lives." Montana shot back.

"In the wake of the buildup to tonight, I haven't thought about it as much as I should have. Give me a few more days."

"What?" Montana raised her voice, causing a few people to turn toward them. "If you don't want to do anything, I will!" She turned, about to storm off.

Steve grabbed her by the arm, harder than intended. He released his grip as soon as he saw the pained look on her face.

"I'm sorry," Steve said, giving the onlookers a friendly wave. "We can't just go off half-cocked. What if your guy is wrong? We would both have to resign. We have to do this one hundred percent. If it's ninety-nine percent, I have no doubt that Justin will find a way to turn it back around on us. I'm talking to a lawyer friend of mine. She's going through his contract, making sure he's broken it. Once she's happy, I'm happy to pull the trigger."

"You're right," Montana said, letting go of her anger a little. "What if we also got another digital specialist to go over what Martin found? We would be twice as prepared. Two hundred percent." she smiled

"That sounds like the smarter option. If we are going to do this, it needs to be bulletproof."

"For a second I thought you were going to back out. Does Justin have something over you, Steve? You haven't been yourself since Las Vegas. I know your presentation didn't go to plan, but it shouldn't have shaken you like this."

"It's nothing." Steve waved her off. He really didn't want to talk about Vegas, and he especially didn't want to talk about cheating on his wife with Natalia, nor how the stunning lady had ignored all his efforts to connect with her again. "It's my wife. We're going through some problems. There's a rumor going around the tennis club that she's cheating on me with her tennis coach. I asked her about it, and she yelled at me and stormed off." Steve dropped his head. It was good to tell someone. Montana gently placed her hand on his cheek.

"Steve, you're a wonderful man. She wouldn't cheat on you. Just like I know that you wouldn't cheat on her."

Right at that moment, what Steve wanted to do is take Montana into his arms and kiss her passionately. He wanted to please her more than anything, and exposing Justin would achieve just that. He had been dragging his feet; it was time to be the man Montana believed him to be. Then, he may have a chance to be with her.

Standing just a few feet away from them was a giant bumblebee. Justin was inside it, and was watching them closely.

CHAPTER SEVENTY-SIX

DISGUISED AS THE BUMBLEBEE, Justin followed Montana around for about an hour. He was happy when Steve begrudgingly left her side. Most people were here to party, and Steve had to make sure all the important guests were looked after. Justin hadn't heard what Montana and Steve had been talking about, but thought he could see his name mouthed more than once. He watched Montana mingle from a safe distance. She was like a butterfly. People wanted to talk to her. She smiled and moved with grace.

Justin's iPhone vibrated, reminding him he had to be elsewhere. He needed to make his move now. He swooped in on Montana, placing a flower in her hair and buzzing around her as if he was trying to pollinate it. She found it rather amusing, and didn't notice the small pill dropping into her champagne glass. When Justin was sure it had dissolved, he moved on to another woman, repeating the same routine. He observed Montana inconspicuously, waiting for her to taste the drink. She took a small sip. Justin had a win.

He swiftly disappeared into a small room and dispatched the bumblebee costume. It was no longer needed. It was time for him to make his grand entrance, in his real costume. Using the stairs, he made his way to the rafters in the roof where his costume—a fully animatronic Buzz Lightyear outfit—was waiting.

His prep team helped him into the custom-built suit, and attached the cables. They had tested it three times during the party set-up to make sure it was fail-safe. Down below, the music stopped, and the partygoers wondered what was happening. A spotlight beamed down on a girl dressed as Jessie the Cowgirl, and a group of acrobatic ninjas grabbed her.

"To infinity and beyond!" a voice thundered through the loudspeakers. Another spotlight beamed up at Justin, standing in all his glory. He jumped and the cables moved him through the air as his jetpack roared into life. The crowd gasped at the awesome sight of Buzz Lightyear swooping down to rescue Jessie. As he landed, the ninjas were choreographed to help unhook Justin while they performed a fight routine. Justin beat up all ten of them and saved Jessie to roaring applause. He had, once again, blown everyone out of the water.

Justin was instantly surrounded by people, all excited to talk to him. He basked in the attention. He watched Steve and Montana, both of whom kept their distance from him. After chatting with some bystanders, Justin made his way to a room near the back that had a large Staff only sign on the door. Inside he found two men waiting, both dressed as Buzz. He instructed them to mingle with the partygoers, but not to talk to people, just to create a presence. The venue was massive, and he'd instructed the guys not to be seen together. From a distance, it was hard to see who was under the large visor, and any of them could be Justin.

Justin changed into a third costume, a black skintight latex suit, and put on a large yellow plastic smiley mask that looked like a giant novelty badge. He headed back to the party. Within ten minutes he'd found Montana. She was leaning against a wall, talking to another girl. The pill Justin had slipped her was a slow-burn variety, so she wouldn't feel the effect until it was way too late. He now just needed to wait and pick his spot.

Montana stumbled from one conversation to another. Most people were a few drinks in and didn't think too much about her slurred words. They thought she'd just had too much to drink, but she'd only had two glasses of champagne. When she dropped her glass, the shattering sound told Justin he had to make his move. First, he needed a diversion. A man dressed in a Hawaiian costume was it. Justin pulled out his lighter and set alight a patch of his grass skirt. Smoke streamed from the smoldering dry material. A passing girl dressed as Barbie screamed as she noticed the growing flames. The guy dropped to the ground, rolling from side to side trying to extinguish the fire, while a group gathered around him.

Justin made his move. He grabbed Montana from behind, and placed her arm around his shoulders. She was dazed and didn't take her arm away, smiling at the giant smiley face.

Justin kicked open a door that led down a corridor and scooped her up into his arms to move faster. He knew where he was going, as he'd scouted it while they did test runs for his entrance. He carried her through three more doors and entered a dark, windowless room used to store the ride-on floor-polishing machines. It smelled of oil and chemicals. Justin put Montana down on her feet. She stumbled around in a half circle, confused.

"Where am I?" she asked, as she wiped her fingers across one of the walls. She turned to the smiley face, her vision blurry. She could only make out warping, rough patterns. She felt happy, and the large yellow smiley face made her smile, too. The smile was soon gone as she felt a hard slap across the face, sending her crashing to the cold concrete floor.

"Baby girl, what's the matter?" Justin asked.

Her right eye instantly started to swell up. "Ohhh, you got a boo-boo on your eye?"

Montana scrambled around on the ground trying to get away, yelling for help. Justin grabbed her by the hair, yanking her back on her feet. He let her go and cracked her with a heavy backhand to the other side of her face. Montana flew backward, her back hitting the wall before she crumpled to the floor once again.

"Baby, why do you keep falling down, too much to drink? You bad, bad girl."

Montana was in a state of shock; she had no idea what was happening to her. She started to cry and pleaded with the man to stop hurting her. Her eyes couldn't focus and were puffing up.

Justin squatted next to Montana. He ran his hand tenderly through her hair; she pulled away, swinging her fists at him. He easily blocked the punches then gripped her hair tight, dragging her into the center of the room.

"I didn't want to do this. You brought it all onto yourself. You could have been the one. There is still hope for you. I do believe in a happy-ever-after for us."

He tore the fabric of her tank top, ripping it down the center. She went to scratch him, her fingernails unable to penetrate his thick latex suit. He kicked her in the floating ribs, the pain a reminder to stay still.

"Oh, Montana. You won't remember any of this. It's a shame, as I think you are going to enjoy it. A lot."

Montana felt dizzy, her head dropped back on the hard floor. Her eyes flickered as the world slowed around her, then went black.

CHAPTER SEVENTY-SEVEN

JEFF PILLION WAS WORKING as a waiter at the Soda-Cola birthday party. He didn't want to be a waiter; he wanted to be a famous actor. He hadn't taken any acting lessons, but felt his natural charisma would be enough to secure his big break. Everywhere he went, people told him how much he looked like a taller, better-looking version of Tom Cruise.

Jeff was pushing a trolley of empty bottles out to the back dumpster, a job that should have taken five minutes but was taking a lot longer as every time his phone beeped, he checked the notification. While looking at some Instagram pictures, he heard a low moan. It sounded like someone was hurt. He cautiously followed the sound to a janitor's room and pushed open the thick door. There he saw a naked woman, badly beaten, crying on the floor. Jeff ran to her, asking if she needed help. She just moaned. He took off his jacket to cover her. He yelled out for help. No one responded. He phoned his manager, who phoned his boss, who phoned for an ambulance and the police. The small room was soon busier than a train station in rush hour.

News of the attack spread like wildfire back at the party. Justin, now back in his Buzz Lightyear outfit, heard it through a number of people. No one knew what had happened, but the general vibe was something terrible had happened to Montana. Justin tracked down Debbie, who was among a large group of Soda-Cola employees.

"What happened to Montana?" Justin asked.

"Oh my God." Debbie seemed shocked. "Sounds like she was attacked."

"Attacked, by who?"

"No one knows. She was found with her clothes ripped off."

"Do you know where Steve is?" Justin asked the group.

"Steve?" Debbie asked, confused.

"I heard they had a heated argument earlier in the evening," Justin replied.

"They did, I saw it," piped up a young girl. "He grabbed her hard."

"He wouldn't have done it," a second voice added, jumping to Steve's defense.

That was all it took for Steve's name to be pulled into the vicious circle of gossip. Justin pulled Debbie aside.

"I'm going to go to the hospital," he said. "You stay here, make sure everyone knows where I'm going. Do what needs doing, Debbie. Make me proud."

Debbie nodded.

Justin rushed to the hospital. People had to see him as a person who cared about a member of Soda-Cola getting hurt. Steve was already there sitting in the waiting room.

"Steve!" Justin called out.

Steve turned; he was distraught. Justin sensed that Steve really didn't want to see him. Justin softened his expression, faking concern.

"What are you doing here?" Steve snarled.

"Look, I know Montana doesn't like me," Justin started. "But I have done nothing to warrant her hatred. Have you met her brother? He has a drug problem and blamed everything on everyone else but himself." Steve looked unconvinced. "It makes me sick to my stomach that something like this has happened to her. Just last week I put in a good word for her with Carlton, about getting her a position on the management team. You can ask him, I have nothing against Montana. Hell, I like her fire. I respect that." Steve sat, frustrated, and Justin sat next to him.

"This is just horrible," Steve whimpered, as tears filled his eyes. "She's like family to me. I hired her, and brought her up through the ranks. And now I can't even go and see her!"

Justin placed his hand on Steve's shoulder.

"If you want to see her, go see her," Justin said, aware that this was the worst thing a person in Steve's position could do. "You're one of her best friends. Her boss. She loves you and would want you by her side. Time to man up, Steve. Go to her."

Steve didn't need further convincing. He got to his feet and marched toward Montana's room where two security guards stopped him as he placed his hand on the door handle.

"Family only, sir," one of the guards said.

"Do you know who I am?" Steve said.

"I don't, sir."

"If you did, you would know better. Now get out of my way. I need to see her." Steve tried to push past the guard. The guard wrestled Steve to the ground, much to Justin's amusement.

CHAPTER SEVENTY-EIGHT

A SMALL PLUME OF FOG left Debbie's mouth as she breathed out. She pulled her jacket tighter around her body to keep warm. Her princess costume wasn't built for warmth. Justin had paid for it to be tailored to her shape, as he wanted her to have a great night. He'd also arranged for a makeup artist to give her a makeover. It made a huge difference. She was asked for her phone number by two different men. That never happened to her before.

When Justin left, she spread the rumors about Steve that he asked her to do. People were shocked about what had happened to Montana, that she was so pretty and didn't deserve what happened. Debbie didn't like what happened to Montana, but it annoyed her that it was because she was *pretty* that people didn't think it should have happened. She wondered if she had been attacked, whether these same people would care as much.

The party was winding down. People weren't in the mood to carry on after what happened to Montana. Debbie watched people drift off in groups. She wasn't invited to join them. There were still people in Soda-Cola that didn't like Justin; as his PA, she felt they projected their dislike for him onto her. She was ostracized from the gatherings the "cool" people had outside of work. Justin was tough on people; he did things that she didn't always understand. She helped him do them. They weren't friends; she worked for him. She really wanted friends. She didn't like it that at the end of a long day, she often opened a bottle of wine by herself and finished it by herself.

She squinted as she saw Justin leave the hospital and get into a cab. If she went through with this, it would change everything. She was sure she would get what she really wanted, and to do that, she was going to have to cross the road and enter the hospital.

Debbie approached the information desk. "Hi, how may I help you?" the nurse said pleasantly.

"I'm here to see Montana Cruz. She was admitted a few hours ago."

"I'm sorry. She's requested no visitors."

"I understand," Debbie bit her bottom lip. "Could you please just ask? I work with her at Soda-Cola. I was at the party. She—she needs to know something. It's important."

The nurse nodded sympathetically and left the desk. She returned a few minutes later with the news that Montana would see her after all.

Debbie pushed open the white door. There was just one bed in the small hotel-like room. Montana's position at Soda-Cola gave her the best health care plan available. Debbie's own plan was basic. She doubted hers would cover a room like this or the care Montana was receiving. There were already flowers and gifts next to Montana's bed.

Montana was propped up on pillows, breathing heavily through her broken nose. Debbie was shocked by Montana's face. To hear what had happened was different from seeing it. But even in her battered, cut, and bruised state, she still was beautiful.

"I'm surprised to see you," Montana said with a slight lisp through her puffy lips. "Why would you of all people be here?"

Debbie knew what she meant. Because of Justin they had had a few run-ins at work. Just last week she had told Montana to go fuck herself or to stop being a poisonous cunt—something along those regrettable lines. Debbie knew what she had to say, but found it hard to get the words out.

The silence irritated Montana. "What?" she grumbled.

"I... I want to be friends."

"You what?"

"I don't have any, not like you."

"This is not the time for this shit. What are you thinking?"

Debbie turned her back on Montana, dropped her head and started shaking. "Ju... Justin," she stuttered, before giving up and heading back to the door.

"Justin? What?" Montana hissed. "What do you know?"

Debbie froze on the spot. Without looking back, she replied, "If I were you, I would get a rape test. People who've been sexually assaulted have to ask for it. They won't do it unless you give them permission."

"Who told you I was raped?" Montana fumed.

Debbie didn't reply. With a sense of relief, she left Montana to do what she needed to do.

CHAPTER SEVENTY-NINE

EARLY MONDAY MORNING, Detective Ross Smith rocked up to the Soda-Cola building. He didn't have an appointment to see Justin. He hadn't made one on purpose; he wanted to surprise Justin. The more he looked into Justin's background, the less he liked him. On the outside, he was the perfect all-American male. But once he delved deeper and removed all the layers, Justin emerged as a nasty piece of work.

The reception area of Soda-Cola was awash with people. There were groups of people gossiping about what happened on Friday night, comparing perspectives. Ross listened in. At the Friday night party, an employee had been viciously attacked. It sounded like she was lovely, and people were shocked that it had happened to her.

Ross waited for his man to arrive. Over the weekend, Ross had managed to persuade Mark, the video technician, to help him with the city video cameras. The two men had spent hours trawling security footage around the Soda-Cola building, looking for any sign of Justin sneaking out around the time of Lydia's death. They didn't find Justin leaving, but they did find a man in a heavy green army jacket slipping out a Soda-Cola side door. The man's face had been obscured. Ross knew it had to have been Justin.

Ross clocked Justin through the crowd of gossips. Ross waved at him and weaved between people to get to him. Justin wasn't happy to see Ross.

"You have to make an appointment," were his first words.

"I only need a minute," Ross shot back, trailing after Justin.

"Then book in a minute," Justin said firmly.

"I'll take it under advisement," Ross said. "Now, do you own a green jacket?"

"No," Justin said flatly.

"That was fast, I don't know if I do myself. So, you know every piece of clothing you own?"

"Yes."

"I just thought I'd seen you in a green jacket. Kind of like an army jacket. Have you ever been in the army?"

"I told you, I don't own a green jacket. You're starting to rub me up the wrong way, Detective Smith."

"I get that a lot." Ross smiled. "Can I come over to your place and snoop through your drawers? You know, in case you have one, and have just forgotten about it. Maybe under some free T-shirts, or hidden under some dirty magazines."

The elevator doors opened and Justin entered alone. Ross didn't follow; he knew this was as far as he could go without a warrant or an invitation. Justin stood in the middle of the elevator, his head tilted back, looking down his nose at Ross.

The doors started to close. Ross waved his hand between them, forcing them to re-open.

"You sure I can't pop up for a minute?" he asked. "Let's hang out, please?"

"Detective Smith, you couldn't hang with me on your best day." Justin removed a folded paper from a jacket pocket and handed it over. "You want to fuck with me? Be careful, you have a lot more to lose than I do. And when I fuck with someone, I go all the way."

Ross let the elevator doors close this time. He opened the embossed, letterheaded paper, knowing it wasn't good. It was from Justin's lawyers, with a whole load of words that only made sense to other lawyers. He got the gist of it. Justin was trying to bully him. All that said to Ross was that Justin needed to be smacked around the head.

Ross had never let anyone bully him before, and there was no way he was going to let this pompous prick be the first.

CHAPTER EIGHTY

STEVE BARKER WAS AT WORK, but work was far from his mind. He was devastated by what happened to Montana, and his feelings for her were overwhelming. He did wonder if his wife had suspicions about his feelings for his coworker. Maybe that was why she fucked her tennis coach, to rub his nose in it. They'd had a big argument over nothing on the weekend, and he'd brought up the rumor about her again. She'd slapped him, packed a bag, and moved out. She needed her space, she'd said, and couldn't believe that he'd give any credence to ridiculous gossip. He wanted her to come home, but another part of him wondered if this was a sign for him to pursue Montana. He felt ill.

The phone on his desk started ringing. He ignored it. Steve didn't want to talk to anyone. A second later his cellphone started ringing as well. His eyes widened when he saw that it was Montana. Steve hit the answer button.

"Montana?"

"Steve?" The voice at the other end sounded like Montana, but without her strength and confidence.

"It's been three days. I've called, left messages, tried to see you."

"I know," Montana replied. "I needed space. It's hard to talk about what happened. I was in so much pain and I couldn't have you close by. What you did at the hospital got a lot of people talking."

"I know," Steve said meekly.

"What were you thinking? I wasn't in a good state and there you were getting into a fight with security guards right outside my door. I'd just been beaten and raped, for God's sake."

"Raped?"

"Yes, that fucker raped me."

"I didn't know."

"No one does. I didn't want that getting out, people don't need to know that."

"What can you remember?"

"Nothing really, it's a blur. They tested my blood and found that I was drugged. I have no idea how, or when."

"Oh, Montana, I'm so sorry. Is there any way I can help?"

"Debbie visited," Montana said, ignoring Steve's offer.

"Justin's PA?" Steve asked.

"Yes."

"What did she say?" Steve was on full alert.

"She didn't say much. She wants friends, and I think she was trying to tell me that Justin did it."

"She said that?"

"Not in so many words, but I was able to read between the lines. The doctors took some swabs. If it was Justin, he tried to cover his tracks. He used a condom, but was too rough, it must have split. They were able to find some traces of semen left behind."

"Oh my God!"

"We have his DNA now! Steve, he has to pay."

"I'll grab him right now, and drag him to the police station." Steve jumped up, phone in hand, ready to pounce.

"Wait… wait!" Montana screamed. "I've already spoken to a lawyer, and they said he can't be forced to do a DNA test. He has to do it voluntarily, and I don't see that happening. If we get a sample illegally, the case will be thrown out down the line, and he'll walk free."

Steve sat back down. "So, what do you want me to do?"

"I've been thinking about it. We need to fool him into taking a test."

"How? He knows he'll be caught."

"Not if he thinks he got away with it, that he didn't leave any DNA behind."

"Can't we just ask him?"

"We can, if we make it part of something his ego will talk him into." Montana took a breath, then continued. "I'll tell people that it was just a physical attack, no CSI-type leads to follow. Justin will think he did it perfectly and lower his guard. You convince Carlton that after the attack,

Soda-Cola is taking a drop in consumer confidence, and that he has to do something to generate some positive PR."

"A marketing stunt?"

"That's the one. You get Carlton and Justin together to brainstorm some ideas, then suggest something bold, like getting in a medical team to take DNA samples from all the males. This would prove that Soda-Cola takes this kind of thing seriously. Then you take leadership of it, push Justin to one side."

"The more I don't want him involved, the more he'll want in."

"Yes. His ego will go nuts. Next thing you know, Justin's taking control and standing next to you getting swabbed. Then we'll have him, and he won't be able to worm his way out of it. Next stop, fucking jail!" Montana had been thinking about this plan all weekend. "What do you think? Can you do that for me, make this prick pay for what he did to me?"

Steve didn't have to think about his response. "I'll email Carlton right now and get the ball rolling."

FILE THREE:
BOARDROOM COLLATERAL

CHAPTER EIGHTY-ONE

HELEN LEWIS HAD TOLD HER husband that she was on her way to the mall to pick up a few essentials. She needed to stop at Walmart, Kmart, Marshalls, and might need to pop into Costco. She'd lost his interest at the mention of Walmart, just as she expected. Her husband hated shopping. In fact, it seemed the only thing he disliked more than shopping was spending time with her.

She waited on him hand and foot, and all he could do was complain about waiting. Where her lover, Ian, found anything she did fascinating and couldn't get enough of her. A man who was in touch with his emotions. A man who made her feel like a woman. He was a man who was married—but she was married too. Their romance had blossomed over chats while waiting for the school bell to ring so they could collect their children. Ian was mesmerized with her, she was his rose. Ian was a real man.

There was a place, a motel chain, they had adopted for their private times together. They'd both agreed it was more than sex, it was something on a higher level. Their bodies needed to be together, like people needed oxygen. It was deeper than love, it was all their past lives getting what they finally needed: To be together in their own world of worship. Soul mates. Forever.

She'd been excited leaving the house. She had about three hours; Ian could do a lot to her in that time. Inside her car, she tapped her handbag while waiting at the traffic lights. Something special she wanted to try was hidden inside one of the zipped pockets.

The light turned green, the other light was red, the drunk driver plowed straight into the side of her car. The door crumpled around Helen. Her head smashed against the steering wheel. Her brain ricocheted around in her skull, causing major trauma. She was rushed to the nearest hospital, and her family was informed that she'd be lucky to make it through the night. No one informed Ian.

Helen survived through to the next day, and every extra day she hung in was a miracle. Two months later, she was still in a coma, but was getting stronger, and her chances of coming out of it were improving. The stand next to her bed held cards, small gifts, and keepsakes. The one constant thing was a single rose in a basic glass flute. It was changed regularly, never shedding a dead petal. Only one person knew what it meant; that person prayed every day that she would wake, see the rose, and know it was from him.

The door to her room opened slowly, and a dark figure entered. He was in the hospital for all the wrong reasons, checking up on a friend for all the wrong reasons, and had slipped away to roam the hallways in a surgical smock for all the wrong reasons. He walked in with such confidence that anyone would have thought he was a doctor.

The man picked up the chart that was hanging from the edge of Helen's bed and inspected it. He placed it back, then inspected the red-headed woman. Reading her pale face, imagining her sad life until this moment. A sad life, compared to his own spectacular life. He inspected her side table, a scattering of useless junk. A single rose stood out. He laughed at how pathetic it was, a single rose, a whole two bucks of cheap love.

He pulled a syringe from his pocket, grabbed her drip and without a second thought, inserted the syringe into the tube. There was no liquid in the syringe, just air. All he wanted was a simple air bubble to enter the woman's bloodstream. He steadied his hand, and with a gentle push, a small bubble headed into the tube. The man watched as it surged down toward her body. There was no struggle as it entered, and soon Helen's heart monitor machine started beeping to signal danger. The sound got louder, faster, and more urgent by the second.

He snatched the rose and waved it under her nostrils. Her cheap life could take in the aroma of the cheap rose with her last breaths. From outside the door, he could hear a pair of feet running toward Helen's room. The noise of the wailing machine attracting nurses like nectar attracted bees.

The dark figure disappeared from the side of the bed, resting his back on the wall, near the door. The door swung, and a nurse ran in. He slipped out. Strutting down the hallway, he spun the rose between his fingers like a skilled drummer waiting for the beat. He heard Helen's heart monitor flatline and slammed the rose's head on a trash bin, sending the petals flying in all directions. He stopped. Did he have time today for an encore? He scanned the adjoining rooms. Maybe.

CHAPTER EIGHTY-TWO

JUSTIN STRUTTED INTO Steve's office sporting a winning grin. Steve had scheduled this meeting just for Carlton to attend. The plan was to not invite Justin because that would guarantee he would turn up. And here he was, chest puffed out, just as Montana had predicted he would be. The more Justin thought he was manipulating Steve, the less he would notice he was the one getting played. Steve returned Justin a smile, an actual smile.

Steve started the meeting, and all three men were soon exchanging ideas on ways they could leverage some positive PR for Soda-Cola. Carlton and Justin were seated at a round table while Steve stood, using a whiteboard to highlight ideas that had merit, gauging a time he could add the DNA test into the mix. He wanted to find a way to leapfrog off ideas the other two men offered up and segue it into what he and Montana had planned. It had to feel like a group solution, that way it would be harder for Justin to kill it.

"We have some good ideas here," Steve said, looking at the whiteboard, tapping the back of his thumb on his chin. "What can we do to tell the world that what happened at the Soda-Cola birthday had nothing to do with anyone at Soda-Cola?"

"We know it wasn't," Carlton answered.

"What if we took out a full-page national newspaper ad, have everyone here sign it," Justin offered up. "Publicly shaming that sort of atrocious action."

"That's really personal," Carlton added.

"Personal is good. Could we make it even more personal?" Steve enquired.

"Like how?" Carlton asked.

"I don't know," Steve mused "Soda-Cola is love. That's the DNA of

Soda-Cola as a product and a company. It's the core of everything we do, even the people. We need something big, something people wouldn't expect to show that."

"You're right," Carlton added. "The DNA of Soda-Cola is love. And love is the furthest thing from what happened at the birthday party. We've been around over a hundred years, and in that time, nothing like this has happened before. Never."

Steve looked at Justin, willing him to contribute. He was feeling close to getting what he needed.

"What happened tests us all," Justin finally said. "Thinking about Montana for a minute, do we really want to drag out what happened to her? Should we think about something else to gain some PR traction? Find a positive story to shine a light on? The OrangeFizz community work is gaining local support, that's a good story. The Orange Walls project is perfect to throw PR money behind."

Steve glanced at Carlton, who was nodding at Justin; this wasn't good. One: Justin was hijacking the meeting to push his own brands. Two: it had to be about what happened to Montana. Steve quickly wrote SODA-COLA DNA on the whiteboard, then TEST US ALL. He turned back to the table.

"I haven't spoken to Montana since the night," Steve lied. "How about you, Carlton?"

"I've talked to her a few times, She's a strong lady. From what the police have told her, they don't think they'll catch the perpetrator. She doesn't want to play the victim, she wants to send a clear message that what happened to her is not acceptable, and people in her situation should not be ashamed. Her attacker should be ashamed."

"Wow," Steve said, impressed. He slowly walked around his office, like he was thinking. Making his way behind the other two men, he slumped into a chair as if he was giving up. "We have to do something for her!"

"We will, Steve," Carlton said in a comforting tone.

"Does she know what happened? On the night?" Justin asked.

"She told me she was drugged, beaten. She said the attacker must have been disturbed, as she wasn't... violated. It could have been worse."

All three men dropped their heads in silence.

"Wait," Steve said as he jumped to his feet and stared intensely at the whiteboard. "What if we take Justin's '*signature*' idea, but add '*Soda-Cola DNA*', and '*test us all*' to it. Instead of signatures, we give DNA signatures? It's a statement that every man in the building can make, a personal one."

"It's big," Carlton said.

"It's your idea really," Steve encouraged.

"That isn't going to happen," Justin added. "It's an invasion of privacy."

"Let's think about it a little more," Steve said.

"I think it's a bad idea," Justin replied sternly.

Steve placed his hands on Carlton's shoulders, making them a visual team. Justin still had to respect Carlton; his word was final. "Carlton tweaked your idea, you were the one to say make it personal and test us all. Are you saying Carlton's idea is bad?"

"That's not what I'm saying," Justin backtracked. "This sort of thing should be left to the police."

"As Carlton pointed out, the police have nothing. It's not about helping the police, we're not *CSI* or *Criminal Minds*. What I like about the DNA pledge idea you guys came up with, is it's a stunt. It will get people talking."

"Don't see it happening, Steve. We should drop it and move on. What about Carlton's idea about the balloons over the building?"

"No, this is great!" Steve shouted, getting excited. It was time to hit a home run. "What I like about it, it's bold. Out of the box. It's a leadership move. It shows a man who knows right from wrong. A man who people will look up to and say, 'That man is a true leader. He is the future of Soda-Cola.' Just thinking about it makes me want to do it even more. It says, I am the type of man who has nothing to hide, and who people follow because he walks his talk and leads by example. I will do my test in front of the entire company. I will stand in front of everyone, and show them what a real leader does in times like these." Steve hoped he'd remembered it right and hit the points with enough punch.

Carlton stood. "I'll do it with you, Steve," he said with determination.

Justin sat in his chair, unmoved.

"Thanks, Carlton. We'll be the leaders Soda-Cola needs."

Steve peered at Justin. He could see the wheels turning in his head. It would kill him that Steve would be standing alongside Carlton in front of the entire company.

"Justin," Steve said. "I know some people won't volunteer, that's their choice. What about you represent those employees, tell them it's OK. Stand with them while Carlton and I do the rest."

Carlton rubbed his hands. "Start the ball rolling, I'll get the board to sign it off tonight," he said. "You've made me very proud, Steve. This is ballsy thinking."

"Wait!" Justin interrupted. "If we're going to do this, we need to do it right."

"And how is that?" Carlton asked.

"It has to look unanimous. If you love it, Carlton, then I love it. I'll be standing right next to you both."

Steve gave Justin a disappointed look, while inside he was beaming.

CHAPTER EIGHTY-THREE

JUSTIN STOPPED IN at a pet store on his way home. He wasn't happy with the way Steve had tried to force him out of a leadership opportunity. Maybe Steve was finally getting a backbone. Not inviting him to such an important meeting was classic gameplay. It was obvious to Justin that Steve was using this as a way to gain back some leadership within Soda-Cola. Justin hated the whole PR idea. It was not right for Soda-Cola. He knew more than ever that the only way for Soda-Cola to thrive was under his direction.

Justin wandered around the glass cages with puppies on display. He wasn't entirely sure what he was looking for, but trusted that he'd know it when he saw it. His mind flicked to Montana. Even hearing her name in the meeting had made him aroused. He'd dropped by the hospital a few times to keep tabs on her, as she would be there for a few more weeks. The beating he'd given her was severe; he'd played it over in his mind and even jerked off to it a few times. A part of him wished that he'd filmed it. What she had told Carlton was all talk. She was hurting. She knew she had been raped. She must be blocking it out, pretending that she didn't deserve what she got.

A caramel Havanese pawed the glass as it tried to get his attention. Its eyes slightly obscured by fluff.

"Hello, little one. I think I know someone who will love you very much," Justin said, with a twinkle in his eye.

Back at the Luxor, Justin knocked on Bill's apartment door.

"Bill!" Justin yelled. "It's Justin. I have something very special for you—you will love it. And I do mean looooove it!" Justin pulled the puppy out of its cage and hid him under his jacket. Slowly, Bill opened the door. He looked at Justin with hollow eyes.

"I need help," Justin said as he pulled out the Havanese and rubbed his face against it. "You see my caramel friend here? He has no home. I told him I know of a man who would love him more than anything in the world—a rich man, who's a bit fruity."

Bill smiled at Justin's attempt at humor. Justin held out the pup and he could see Bill's eyes glow. It was love at first sight and the first smile to pass Bill's lips since the park incident. He took the ball of fluff into his arms, smelled it, and held it close.

Justin pushed the cage into Bill's apartment with his foot. It had everything a puppy needed.

"I'll leave you two to get acquainted." Justin grinned. With that, he went into his own apartment, took off his coat, and put on some Chris Cornell unplugged. He checked his online dating apps for new matches and messages. Sent out a few hooks to see who was up for a visit later. Made himself a whiskey sour and let it sit for ten minutes, allowing the ice to chill the frothy liquid before taking a sip. Perfect. He stretched out on the couch and dialed a number from the Luxor body corporate folder.

"Hello?" a voice answered down the line.

"Lillian, it's Justin. How's the firm going?"

"Going well, thank you. Always up for a chat about representing Soda-Cola."

"We always need good counsel. Anyway, the reason I'm calling is, I saw Bill with a new puppy."

"What?" Lillian shot back.

"Yeah, I know."

"What does he think he's doing?"

"It looked harmless, I don't think he'll turn it into another attack dog. Should be fine, don't you think?"

"I've had enough with that man! No, I don't think it's fine at all. I'm sorry, Justin, I have to make some calls about this outrageous behavior. Bye."

Lillian would easily get the votes she needed to kick Bill out and take his place as president of the Luxor's Homeowner's association. Justin would give her his vote, of course. He was sick of seeing Bill's sad-ass face around the building. It was time he was gone.

CHAPTER EIGHTY-FOUR

DETECTIVE ROSS SMITH had made it his mission to get under Justin Truth's skin. He started by turning up in places where Justin wouldn't expect to see him—at his gym, at the bars Justin liked, outside his apartment building. He knew Justin was his guy, but getting solid evidence was proving difficult. Ross thought if he rattled Justin enough, something would crack.

Ross delved deeper into Justin's history. He called past work colleagues, old girlfriends, and Justin's old Harvard professors. For all the glowing articles about him in magazines, and his rise up through the ranks in the world of marketing, there were twice as many unpublished stories about backstabbing and fearmongering. More than once, Ross was told that those who went up against Justin never won, that they ended up crashing and burning.

During his research, Ross stumbled upon the case of Justin's father's death. It had been a freak accident, apparently. He'd been killed by a car running a stop sign. Justin was with his father when it happened. There wasn't much on it, it had been an open-and-shut case. There was a substantial insurance payout and this money, it seemed, had set Justin up for a rather comfortable life.

Ross decided to pay a visit to Justin's hometown. He knew he'd never get the time off work for this so, for the first time in his career, he called in sick when he wasn't. He bought a cheap flight online, caught a cab, and was soon standing outside the house in which Justin had grown up.

It was a beautiful two-story house with a pitched roof. The wooden exterior was painted a crisp white, with double-hung, multi-pane windows placed symmetrically on both sides of the central front door. The grass was thick, dark green, and freshly cut. The small white picket fence that ran along the footpath was more for decoration than to stop intruders getting into the property. It looked like all the other houses on the street, yet he could feel it was empty. It was too perfectly presented for anyone to be living inside it. Justin still owned the property. Ross guessed that a local handyman made sure the gardens were taken care of and that the house looked immaculate from the outside.

"Can I help you?" a gruff voice called out.

Ross turned and spotted a guy who looked to be in his late seventies marching toward him. He was in good shape for his age, probably ex-service. His plaid shirt was tucked firmly into his jeans, and his belt was tight, making sure it didn't slip out. Ross held his bag of jelly beans out to him.

"Hi. The name's Ross, would you like a jelly bean?"

The old guy smiled and took a few. "You can call me Allen. You looking for someone?"

"This is Justin Truth's old house, isn't it?" Ross asked.

"That little prick!" Allen sneered. "The day he moved out was the happiest day of my life."

"Not a fan?"

"His parents were great, such a lovely couple. They moved in when Justin was a baby. Even then he was a bit odd. The older he got, the more odd he got. A bit of discipline would have sorted that out."

"Justin needs more than a clip around the ears," Ross said.

"A boot in the ass would have done him good." Allen smiled. "I used to have chickens," he continued. "Kept them in the backyard. One day they all died. Every time I got more, they'd die, for no rhyme or reason. Then I decided to watch them, you know, sitting inside just watching. For eight days I waited. My wife thought I was crazy, but it's a man thing, and I had to see this through. One morning my wife got ready for church. She loved going to church, which meant I also loved going to church, if you know what I mean. Every Sunday we went. But as I said, I had a mission, and nothing was going to divert my attention from it. So, I sat inside near the back door, hidden-like, listening to the radio, watching my chickens through the screen door. Then a football from the Truth's place flew over the fence. A minute later six-year-old Justin jumped over to retrieve it. I sat quietly and watched him. He picked up the ball, looked around, and took a few steps toward my chicken coop. The chickens were going crazy, as if a fox was in there. Then he stopped, turned, and looked directly at where I was sitting. I was sure he couldn't see me, but it was like he could feel me watching. Everyone knew we went to church on Sundays, so the little rat would have known that too. I bet he thought the house was empty. Maybe he was looking for movement, that I was home.

"He turned his head toward the chicken coop and then back at the house. He didn't move, just stood there staring. I froze myself to the chair too, not wanting to move a muscle, in case ... hell, in case he was killing my chickens. I wanted to catch that little bastard in the act and give him a right walloping. Eventually he kicked his ball back over the fence and scrambled back after it.

"A couple days later, I got home from the supermarket and my chickens were all dead. Sitting on my chair in plain sight was Justin's football. The same one he'd kicked over on Sunday. I told his father about it, but there was no proof that he'd done anything. His father took what I said seriously. Came back to me the next day that he'd had a chat with Justin. Justin had pleaded black and blue he hadn't touched the chickens, ever."

"That little shit."

"Couldn't prove anything, smug little bastard."

"It's a shame what happened to his father," Ross added.

"A real shame, all right. He was a fine man. He'd always ask if I needed a hand with anything. The biggest shame is what happened to his wife."

"And what is that?" Ross inquired.

"Just days after her husband died, she breaks down, bedridden, and then is gone too."

"Dead?"

"Not dead, just gone from the house. Justin had her hospitalized. I think he did it so he could get all the insurance money. They were good people, they were. Sometimes bad shit happens to good people, and the bad ones have the luck of the devil."

Ross joined Allen for lunch and listened to many stories about strange happenings around the neighborhood and Justin Truth. Anything bad that happened, Allen blamed Justin.

Ross wanted to stay and listen to more stories, yet he also wanted to visit the intersection where Justin's father had been killed. Logic told him that the best time to visit the site would be the same time of day it originally happened. Ross walked the same route Justin and his father would have taken on the fateful day that he died. He paused at the stop sign. In the report, the driver said he never saw the sign. Ross looked at the large tree behind the sign. He grabbed some low-hanging branches and found they were easy enough to place in front of the sign, hiding it completely. Next, Ross worked out the spot where Justin's father had been run over. A car drove past him and made him jump back. He hadn't seen it coming. The slight hill leading to this spot hid oncoming cars. He glanced at the car driving away. The sun was low in the sky, prompting Ross to squint. He ran back to the stop sign and looked back toward the accident site. The sun was blinding, and Ross had to lift a hand to block it. He removed his hand and the sunstrike now made it impossible to see anything. There was no way a driver would see someone standing in the road.

Ross shook his head. Another accidental death that had Justin's name written all over it.

CHAPTER EIGHTY-FIVE

ON HIS "SICK DAY," Ross received a message from Sergeant Olive Masterson. She'd asked to see him ASAP, but he ignored her and decided to see her the next day. That's what a real sick person would do. The following morning Ross went into work early, at seven a.m., so he could get a head start on the information he'd collected about Justin. He hadn't been able to source much info on Justin's mother, other than that she was in a fancy hospital for the rich and famous. Ross really wanted to pay her a visit. Looking online, it wasn't going to be easy—it was a private establishment.

Ross had only been at his desk for a few minutes when Olive yelled at him to come to her office. He hadn't expected her to be at work so early. He hastily joined her in her office, and going by the fresh cigarette butts still smoldering, she'd been there a while.

"Ross!" She took a deep breath. "You're giving me dark headaches on one hand, and offering the only bright light I have on the other." Before Ross could answer, Olive continued. "Whoever this fuck Justin Truth is, leave him alone. If his name pops into your head, slap yourself. I've had the word that he is to be left alone. And they weren't nice words, believe you me."

"He's a prick, and a guilty one at that," Ross sneered.

"Do you have any proof? No, you don't." Olive picked up a piece of paper. "You see this? This is a letter telling me to fire you. To cut you loose."

Ross looked at the paper.

"Why?" he asked.

"Because this Justin, this prick as you call him, has friends in some very high places—places that would give people like us nosebleeds. And these people don't like it when you 'harass' one of their good friends."

"So, I'm fired?"

"No, you're not. I can't cut the only person who has made a break-through on the Beetle Butcher case. Do you understand me, Ross? This thing you have for Justin Truth, it's gone. Put him in a box, and leave it the fuck alone."

"I don't think I can do that." Ross gave Olive a hard, honest stare.

"You will do that!" Olive fired back, twice as mean. "You've had one get-the-fuck-out-of-jail card; there won't be any more. All your other cases are being reassigned, and you'll be full time on the Beetle Butcher case from this moment on. You will eat, sleep, and drink this until it's over. And if we manage to get this sick fuck, I'll put in a good word, and you can transfer anywhere you want and maybe have a job until you retire. If you get kicked out now, you can say goodbye to your pension, and to the money that you've squirreled away for your daughter."

Ross sat in his chair, fuming. He loved his daughter. She may have given up on him, but he still wanted to look after her, and he knew his savings would soon disappear if he were to lose his job. If that happened, he wouldn't be able to leave her anything. He stood with a heavy sigh, nodding.

"Please, Ross, you are one of the only people here I count as a friend. Don't fuck up your life over this."

Ross dropped his head in defeat. As he reached the door, Olive spoke up again.

"Give me everything you have on the Beetle Butcher, Ross. I'll make sure you get at least one prick in this lifetime."

Ross looked at Olive and nodded before returning to his desk. He was feeling so good ten minutes ago. Now, not so good. He pulled the picture of Lydia Young off his wall and dropped it into a file box along with everything else he had. He carried the box back into Olive's office, placing it by her desk with a weary smile.

That little show should give him more time, he thought. Back at his desk he removed a flash drive from his computer. Over some very late nights, Ross had scanned and backed up everything he had on Justin, no matter how obscure it was. Justin wasn't untouchable. Once he was ar-rested, none of his high-powered friends would go to jail for him. Justin would be discarded like a piece of trash.

Ross looked at his computer screen. On it was the address of the hospital where Justin's mother was staying. If he could arrange to see her and talk to her about her son, he could perhaps put the pieces of the puzzle together. No one had talked to Justin's mother or heard from her in years. The only way he could get into the hospital would be if he were on official business relating to the Beetle Butcher. He opened the case folder. Someone in there must have a connection to this hospital somewhere. Line by line, person by person, he started searching.

CHAPTER EIGHTY-SIX

JUSTIN LOCKED THE DOOR to his office. He needed to be alone. The DNA test was happening the next day, and he had to be all over it. The test was going to be performed by Dylon Corporate, an independent workplace drug-testing specialist that had no ties to Soda-Cola or the police force. They were considered to be one of the best in the country, discreet, and very professional.

Justin looked into the test procedure a bit more closely. Everyone would have a swab placed inside their mouth to collect their DNA, and each person would have two swabs taken to rule out mistakes.

Justin hated the idea his DNA signature would be held somewhere on permanent record. He had worked too hard covering his tracks to have a stupid marketing stunt ruin everything. No DNA test could ever be linked back to him, ever. In twenty-four hours, he was going to be swabbed in front of colleagues. He had to figure out a way to get around it while doing it. No one could have his DNA on file, no one. As he wracked his brain about how to achieve this, his phone rang.

"Hello. Justin speaking."

"Hi, Justin, it's Eric."

"Mr. Smit! How is the diamond trade treating you? I may be in the market for a rock if my relationship gets any more serious."

Both men laughed. Eric was one of the people who had sponsored Justin to join the board at St. Mary's. He was rich and powerful. And men like him also had powerful friends who could use a mere phone call to make the impossible possible.

"Good to hear, Justin," Eric said. "I just wanted to let you know that Detective Smith shouldn't be bothering you any longer. I had a chat with a dear friend of mine, the chief of police, and he said he'd put a stop to him and his little vendetta."

"Thank you, Eric. I was thinking I might have to take out a restraining order against him. He's infatuated with me. I did wonder if he was gay. He turned up at my gym's changing room once, I'm sure to see me naked. I'm sorry for bringing you into this sordid affair."

"You did the right thing telling me," Eric said. "Consider this problem resolved."

"Once again, thank you, Eric. I'll see you soon. Please give my love to your family." Justin hung up and leaned back in his chair. Now that Ross was taken care of, he could concentrate fully on the test tomorrow.

CHAPTER EIGHTY-SEVEN

DONNA SOUTHLAND PACED the reception area of Soda-Cola. It took one minute to do a circuit from the seats, around the reception desk, past the elevator, along the big screens, across the glass windows, and back to her seat. Justin had called her earlier to drop everything and come see him, even though he knew that today was her daughter's birthday and that she'd scheduled this special day off months ago. Donna considered blowing him off, but the relationship was strained enough as it was. Instead, she left the party and drove the fifty-five minutes in heavy traffic. She arrived on time just to pace the reception area twenty-seven times.

Debbie eventually appeared and led her to Justin's office. Justin was sitting behind his desk and didn't stand up as Donna walked in.

"Take a seat," he instructed Donna coldly. Then, just as Donna obliged, he announced, "If you excuse me for a minute, I need to get something. Can Debbie get you a drink?"

"I'm fine," Donna replied. She really wanted to get back to her daughter's birthday party as soon as possible. Forty-five minutes later, she wished she'd ordered that drink, as she still sat waiting for Justin to return. She had asked Debbie a few times where Justin had gone, but she wasn't able to tell her.

Finally, Justin arrived back. He gave Donna a warm smile as if they were best friends, leaving Donna feeling confused.

"I have something to show you," Justin said as he sat down at his desk. "I know your team has been working on a new campaign for OrangeFizz, but I have some bad news for you." He swiveled his computer screen so Donna could see it.

"I'm going to go with this brand campaign Mother's Milk has come up with."

Donna stared at Justin coldly. "I thought you and I were working on this together?"

"I work with people who do what I want them to do, and the work you've shown me isn't doing it for me. This campaign talks directly to mothers and shows OrangeFizz as the brand that loves their family as much as they do."

Donna watched an animatic of the proposed television commercial and all the print that went with it.

"Are you sure you want work like this?" Donna asked. "It's a bit basic."

"Yes, I do. It may be basic in your view, but it will do what you guys haven't been able to do, and that's increase sales. I wonder what the creatives at Mother's Milk could do on the LemonGreat campaign that just got pulled? Your agency created that campaign at enormous expense..."

"Justin. Look. . ."

"No, Donna, you look. I want to know how much you want our business. I know how much Mother's Milk wants it. You would have heard through the grapevine that Carlton is looking at stepping down. My new role will be across the entire portfolio of Soda-Cola. I will be able to move any account to any advertising agency I want. If I pulled the entire Soda-Cola business from your agency, how many people would you have to fire, Donna? Thirty percent? We make you a lot of money. Would you lose your job? How would it look on your CV if you lost your agency's biggest client? A giant global client! No doubt I will be interviewed by all the marketing and advertising magazines as to why I pulled the business away from R and R. It would be because of you, Donna, and that is what I would say. Your name would be mud. Who would want the chick who personally lost half of her agency's billings?"

"What do you want, Justin?"

"First, I want to see you in action. Call your reception right now and fire Sophie. And I mean don't just move her to another part of the agency—I want her gone now!"

"But why?" Donna asked in disbelief.

Justin had tried to fuck Sophie, but she never let him get close enough, even after he'd dropped thousands of dollars on an expensive night out. All he got was a kiss on the cheek. He wasn't going to tell Donna that was the real reason.

"The OrangeFizz account has now gone to Mother's Milk," Justin replied. "You never question me. Do it now."

Donna felt her stomach tie in a knot. Sophie was a wonderful girl. But she would find another job easily enough, and Donna would help her. She would call in some favors once she left Justin's office. She called her agency from her cellphone.

"Hi, Donna. How can I help you?" Sophie asked.

"Hi, Sophie, I'm sorry but you are fired. Please clean out your things and leave. If you are not gone within the hour you will be escorted out of the building."

"Is this a joke?"

"No joke. Your services are no longer required and I wish you the best with your future endeavors." Donna hung up and looked at Justin, who now sported a victorious grin.

CHAPTER EIGHTY-EIGHT

SANDY MILLER FROM MOTHER'S MILk was in a cab heading down the Las Vegas strip when his phone rang. He pulled it out to see who was calling.

"Justin," Sandy answered.

"Sandy. First off, you are awesome, and I love what you have done for me. Secondly, how would you like to have the entire OrangeFizz account?"

Sandy was speechless. "We'd be over the moon!"

"Great. There is just a small obstacle I have to overcome. I have a lot of heat on me to keep it with R and R. When I told them, they went to Carlton and dropped their price. If you guys can match it, it's yours."

"I'm sure we can do that. What did they come back with?"

"They said they'd halve their fee."

"Half? We would just break even to service the account for that much. I think we would actually lose money."

"Sandy, this is what you have been working so hard for. It's in your hands. Trust me, once the heat goes, and people see how amazing you are, I'll make sure it is increased back to the full amount over time. So, do we have a deal?"

"I should talk to my partners first..."

"Sandy, I have gone into battle for you, and this is just the first of many accounts that will come your way. There is talk about me soon taking over all the Soda-Cola brands. And with you on the roster, it makes it that much easier to send more work your way. I need to know right this minute: are you in for earning shitloads of cash over the next few years, or are you out?"

"OK." Sandy paused. "We're in."

"Good man. Let's get this all drawn up. Welcome to the family. I'll come out and visit you soon. Oh, and I think I could go another round in the cage, too!"

After saying goodbye, Sandy put the phone back in his pocket. He had pulled in a multinational account, but for a fee that could cripple the agency if not handled properly. The amount they'd already spent was going to cost some people their jobs. On top of that, the bum he'd set up to fight Justin in the cage had died from his injuries, and they'd dumped his body back at the spot Sandy had picked him up from. The local cops had chalked it up to one homeless person attacking another over some alcohol.

Sandy rubbed his face. He was having second thoughts about jumping into bed with Justin. The risks of getting fucked over were sky-high.

CHAPTER EIGHTY-NINE

DETECTIVE ROSS SMITH GOT OUT of a cab in the parking lot of St. Mary's. He'd trawled through all the Beetle Butcher files looking for any valid reason to visit the place. He felt bad that he wasn't helping catch the Beetle Butcher, but there was a whole department on the case, and no one was investigating Justin Truth.

Late the night before, after endless digging, he finally found a lead to St. Mary's. A dog had bitten the Beetle Butcher's second victim a few weeks before she was killed. It wasn't a nasty bite, just a small nip on her ankle. The dog's owner, Nathan Clements, had been interviewed and provided alibis about where he was when the first two victims were taken.

Nathan bred Cavalier King Charles Spaniels. He told the interviewing officer that he'd often visit different parks, as his dogs were the best form of advertising. That when people saw them, they had to have one. He remembered the lady and was terribly sorry for what his dog had done. When Ross cross-referenced him with names at St. Mary's he got a hit: one of the doctors there had bought a dog from Nathan a few years ago. With all the dead-end leads on the case, no one would care if this one led nowhere. But for Ross, it led to Sarah Truth.

Ross walked into reception, asked for Dr. Frank Brownstone, and within minutes he was cleared and told where to go. He took his time walking along the corridors. He knew he'd have only one chance to see Sarah. His plan was to meet Dr. Brownstone, ask him enough questions to fill out the paperwork, and find a way to get to Sarah's room.

Ross knocked on Dr. Brownstone's door.

"In," a very English voice responded. As Ross entered, he found a thin man with gray hair sitting behind an old Victorian desk. He was birdlike in appearance, with a hooknose, long neck, and prominent

Adam's apple. He got up with great enthusiasm and charged across the room to shake hands with Ross.

"Do sit down, Detective," he exclaimed, smiling from ear to ear. "This is all a bit exciting—I've never had a detective come out to talk to me about anything. I've seen it on TV and films a lot—always love watching those cop shows. Must say, I often solve it before the TV cops do. Ha-ha. How can I help you?"

Ross was so thrown by the man's friendliness that he forgot to get out his jelly beans.

"It's about your... dog," Ross remembered.

"My dog? Really?" Frank sounded surprised. "I don't think Charlie would hurt anyone."

"Your dog is fine. It's the man you bought him from; one of his dogs bit someone who could provide a lead, and I'm just following up. We can't have a dog running around biting people," he added with a smile. "Tell me about Nathan, and how you found him?"

"The bug man, you say," Frank replied.

Ross stopped, and a shiver ran down his spine.

"The bug man?" Ross asked.

"Yes, that's what my daughter—Poppy—called him. When we picked Charlie up from his place, I was talking to him about how we should look after Charlie, and what food he should and shouldn't eat. Dogs are funny things; some can eat anything, but dogs like Charlie need a special diet. Anyway, while we chatted, Poppy disappeared and went for a bit of a wander around his house. She can be a nosy girl—gets it from her mother, you know. On the drive home, she told me about the bugs she saw. She said there were lots of them, and they were kept in large glass cases, like the ones you'd normally keep fish in. That's why we called him the bug man; it was our little joke."

"He had bugs? Like as pets." Ross sat forward.

"From what Poppy said, yes."

Ross stood, sat, then stood again. His mind was racing. What had he stumbled onto? "Would you please excuse me for a moment?"

"You're excused." Frank chuckled.

Once in the hallway, Ross phoned Olive. He'd never wanted her to answer her phone as much as he did now. Often, she just let it go to voicemail.

"What!" she yelled to Ross's relief.

"Sergeant Olive, Olive… Um shit… Fuck," he stumbled, his mouth not keeping up with his brain.

"Ross, you have five seconds before you're working the weekend."

"Olive, the Beetle Butcher. I think his name is Nathan Clements."

CHAPTER NINETY

ROSS HUNG UP. He composed himself and walked back into Dr. Brownstone's office. The doctor was holding a picture of his daughter and Charlie.

"Here's a photo of Charlie and Poppy," Frank gestured. "Do you need it?"

"No thank you, Dr. Brownstone. You've been incredibly helpful, and thank you for your time."

"It's nice to be helpful, and to be helpful is nice." Frank cracked up at his own joke.

"More than anyone would have hoped," Ross smiled. "Now if you could excuse me, I need to be off to follow up on this."

"Let me see you out." Frank got up. Ross had to think quickly. He needed to be able to wander the hospital looking for Sarah's room. To talk to her about Justin.

"I have troubled you more than enough," Ross said. "I think your daughter may even receive a merit from the department for her sharp eyes. I have to make a few more calls—do you mind if I make them in the corridor?"

"That's fine. Just go back the way you came in. Good to talk to you, Detective Smith. My Poppy helped out the police—she will be so impressed with herself."

"Thank you very much." Ross pretended to dial a number on his phone as he left.

He hovered outside Dr. Brownstone's office, thinking of ways to find Sarah's room. The converted mansion felt like a labyrinth to him. Armed with his trusty pack of jelly beans, he saw a nurse heading toward him. Minutes later he was standing outside Sarah's room.

He composed himself and knocked, but there was no answer. He knocked again. Still no answer. Dread gradually set in. Had she gone out? There was only one way to know, so he slowly opened the door. Inside the room, a woman, presumably in her late fifties, lay in a bed, gazing out the window.

"Sarah? Sarah Truth?" Ross asked, but she didn't react. "Sarah, my name is Detective Ross Smith. Is it OK if I come in?"

She could hear him; she couldn't actually believe that there was a policeman in her room. Concentrating hard, she managed to turn her head so she could look him in the eyes. What a long way she'd come.

"I'd like to talk to you about your son," he said.

Finally, someone knows, she thought.

"Sarah, can you hear me?"

I can hear you.

"Sarah?"

Ross touched her shoulder, but there was no response. Ross felt his heart drop. There was a reason no one had talked to her; she was in a catatonic state. He kept looking at her; he had heard that people in states like this could hear and process information. He had come all this way, it was worth having a chat, even if it was one-sided. Maybe she was able to talk—maybe.

"I'm here to talk about Justin."

Her eyes flickered slightly. He was encouraged by this reaction.

"Would you say he's a good son?"

Are you kidding, he's done this to me! He's a murderer!

"I have reason to believe that he may be involved in some illegal activities. Even hurt some people."

Involved! He's killed dozens of times! Sarah wanted to shout.

"I can't prove it, though, so if there's anything you know, or if you're able to help me out... I know he is your son, but you wouldn't want him to hurt anyone else, would you?" Ross held her hand, his eyes holding her eyes. She was awake in there; he was sure of it. "I also think... Justin was responsible for your husband's death."

Sarah's nostrils flared. *I know, I want him to pay for it. I want Justin dead!*

Ross searched Sarah's eyes. "I need help to stop him. Can you help me?"

Sarah didn't respond. He wondered if Justin was responsible for his mother's condition. After talking to Allen, her former neighbor, he wouldn't put it past him.

Ross gently patted her hand, placing it back on the bed. He took a business card from his wallet, looked around the room, and picked up a book by her bed. He showed Sarah the book, hid his card inside, and placed it under the bedside table. He didn't want it in plain view in case Justin came to visit anytime soon. He turned back to Sarah.

"You're in there, I know. If you ever need me, call. I'll be here in a flash to protect you. I need you. Hell, the world needs you."

Help me! Please stay, and stop my son from poisoning me, Sarah begged silently.

Ross turned the handle of the door to leave. He paused; it was as if he could hear Sarah yelling inside her head for him to stop. But when he saw no movement, he opened the door and left. He was going to have to find another way to bring Justin to justice.

CHAPTER NINETY-ONE

IT WAS THE DAY OF the DNA test. An email had been sent around the building three days earlier to let staff know it was happening. No one could be forced to take the test, but 90 percent of the men in the company voluntarily stepped forward. The 10 percent who didn't were looked down upon, and the topic made for heated conversation around the water cooler. The majority argued that if the men had nothing to hide, they would do it. The minority objected on the grounds that it was an invasion of privacy and one step closer to a police state.

Justin joined Carlton and Steve in the social room. He was the last to arrive. Dylon Corporate had taken over the room for the testing. A station had been set up at one end of the room where the swabs would be collected. To the right was a poster made for the PR component featuring a bold headline: TOGETHER WE STAND. The plan was that the top three men would go first, followed by the other consenting men.

"Friends, looking at you all fills my heart with pride," Carlton addressed the men. "What we do today sends a clear message to those around us, not just for today, but for the years ahead. To stand together, for the love of one another. We are all here for Montana, and I know that she would be here for each and every one of you. She thanks you. I thank you too."

Moved by his speech, the group nodded in solemn agreement.

"That's enough of me prattling on." Carlton smiled. "Once your swab has been taken, please sign your name on the poster."

Carlton went first. A young lab technician in a white coat asked him to open his mouth, then wiped a sterilized swab around the inside of Carlton's cheeks and sealed it inside a self-contained lid. He then numbered the lid and placed it into a unit before taking another swab and placing that one in a second unit.

Justin eagerly watched each step. What he was about to do made him want to throw up. In his pocket was a small container of saliva he'd purchased off the dark web. Before he was to be swabbed, he was going to rinse his mouth with it, and thus contaminate his sample. He'd done a few tests in the bathroom, to control his gag reflex. It had taken a few goes, causing him to be late. He knew Steve would go after Carlton, and while all eyes were on Steve, he'd rinse and swallow the rest of the saliva.

Everyone clapped as Carlton signed the poster. Steve took a step forward, then turned to Justin. "I'm so proud of you. Together we will run this whole place. Come, let's do this together, side by side."

Justin didn't like that idea at all. It wouldn't give him a chance to take one more mouthful of the saliva. "No, I can go after you," he insisted.

"Justin, remember Vegas?" Steve beamed. "Me dying on stage? Because of you, I won back a lot of people's respect."

The entire group was now watching. There was no way he could sneak another mouthful now. His only choice was to get the test done faster, hoping what he did in the bathroom minutes earlier would be enough.

"Can I go first?" Justin asked.

Steve smiled. "By all means."

CHAPTER NINETY-TWO

STEVE FIDGETED IN THE visitor's chair, trying to find a comfortable position. The nurse had told him Montana would join him in a minute. It had been fifteen. It was driving him crazy that he couldn't see Montana every day. His wife had taken their kids and gone to stay with her parents for a few weeks. She had told Steve that she needed to get away; that she still loved him, but felt he no longer loved her, and that it wasn't fair for her. He could have fought for her to stay, but he didn't.

Steve sipped his coffee, then remembered it had tasted bad for the last eight sips as well. He took another sip. The door to the visitor's room opened, and Montana entered in a wheelchair. Steve got up to help her but the look on her face told him to sit back down. His heart broke when he saw the damage that monster had done to her face. It was now five days since the attack and her face was still puffy.

"Montana…" Steve really wasn't sure what to say.

"It's OK, Steve, we have mirrors here. I know how I look—and what that bastard did to me."

"He will never take your inner fire, and that is what draws people to you."

Montana lifted a hand to her face, and ran her fingers over the bruised and battered skin. Even in this state, Steve found her as beautiful as ever.

"You did it, you got him to take the DNA test. That's amazing."

"I was worried for a moment, he was late. I thought he'd invented a reason to skip it. But he turned up just on time. He looked so arrogant, but I could see he was as nervous as hell too. To make sure he didn't run, I played to his ego, even got him to go before me so I could watch."

"You got him." Montana smiled.

"We got him, your plan. I bet he has no idea that Debbie stabbed him in the back."

"You can't tell anyone that, Steve!"

"Why?" he asked.

"If Justin finds out, what do you think he'd do to her?"

"Bastard," Steve gritted through his teeth.

"Enough about Justin," Montana said. "How are you? How's the family?"

Steve went quiet. What he wanted to say was something like, *My wife has left me and that's a good thing because I'm in love with you, and I think you're in love with me. Let's run away together and make babies.* He wasn't sure if this was the right time to come clean though and besides, he didn't want to talk to the woman he loved about his wife.

"Carlton is going to step down, maybe next year," Steve said. "He told me I'd get his job. I think I can swing it so you'll get my old job. With Justin out of the way, it'll be you and me running the show."

"I only want the job if I'm right for it, and at the moment I'm not sure I'm right for anything." Montana squeezed his hands.

"I love you!" Steve blurted out.

"What?" Montana abruptly pulled away her hand. Steve couldn't believe what he'd just said, especially since she was still in recovery.

"I'd love you to take the job," Steve quickly said. "What do you think I said?"

Montana dropped her shoulders, looked at Steve caringly, and placed her hand back on his. "I'm sorry, of course I'll think about it. I'll have a better idea once Justin is gone, and life is back to normal."

CHAPTER NINETY-THREE

JUSTIN HATED THAT HE wasn't in control of the DNA test. He made some calls and didn't like what he heard. Dylon Corporate ran a tight ship; their state-of-the-art security left nothing to chance. Two independent labs, GenLab and MediLink, were contracted to collect the data from the swabs. The information would then be correlated back at Dylon and stored on their private server, and a hard copy locked in their security vault. He needed to know if his plan had worked. Information was king, and he saw himself as the king of kings.

His iPhone bleeped, alerting him that he had a new email. He grinned—it was from a friend with a unique talent for getting the things he needed done without asking questions.

To: Truth, Justin
From: thebw316@gmail.com
Subject: Old Friend

Justin,
My good friend, I hope this finds you well. My generous sister is sick. She is waiting on her meds to come back from the lab. She is hoping everything will be fine. How is work going?
It's my 38th birthday soon and our friend Williamson from just down the road wants to catch up. How does 11:05 suit you? I played the lottery last weekend. I didn't win, but a guy at work won $50,000. Can you believe it? Great to get that type of money in the hand. That's about all, talk to you soon, same bat time, same bat channel.

Justin decoded the message. Black Wolf would never write an email exhibiting explicit information. What the 'real' message revealed was:

GenLab – 38 Williamson Road
11:05 p.m.
$50,000 in cash to the contact.
Drop my fee into the account.

Black Wolf had sourced an insider who was willing to give Justin a copy of the results. It was a lot of money, but if that person was found out, it would mean serious jail time. Once Justin had a copy, he would know what he needed to do next.

Justin transferred Black Wolf's fee into his Bitcoin account. He looked at his watch: two thirty p.m. Things were looking up.

CHAPTER NINETY-FOUR

NATHAN CLEMENTS VISITED THE supermarket every day at the same time: seven thirty p.m. Maximum number of cashiers, minimum number of shoppers. He wrote out a short list of what he needed for the next twelve hours, then went over it again and made a tick next to every item. He never ran out of what he needed. That was what the list was for.

He said goodbye to the pet restrained in his basement. Made sure all his dogs were accounted for, and in their caged room. He counted them. Closed the bedroom door. Opened it, and counted them again. He stepped out onto his porch and shut the door behind him. He locked the door, and then tested it to make sure it was fastened. He unlocked it and locked it again. His keys went in the right front pocket of his jeans. He tapped them three times through his denim. Then he counted the twenty steps to his station wagon, avoiding the cracks in the pavement. At his car, he tapped the keys in his pocket three times again and then retrieved them. He unlocked the car, sat down, put the key into the ignition, clicked his seatbelt in. Unclicked it, clicked it again. Turned on the car and waited. The engine warmed. The supermarket was an eight-minute drive. When the car's clock read 7:22 p.m., he checked the mirrors for people, bikes, and cars. He turned on his headlights, placed his foot on the brake, put the car into reverse, and slowly began backing down his driveway.

Such routines made the Beetle Butcher so hard to catch.

Nathan didn't have the greatest start in life. Both his parents were addicted to meth before he was conceived. They were addicted during his birth. And after he was born, their addiction remained. They saw no reason to change. When meth becomes your world, the next score is far more important than a child. Nathan was kept more as a pet than as an infant. When he was six years old, a child welfare officer turned up on their doorstep. His parents were happy to see Nathan go, and they didn't hide their glee.

Nathan stopped at the end of his street. He glanced left and right for oncoming cars. Tapped his steering wheel three times. Waited. Once more he glanced left and right and tapped the wheel. There were no cars. The station wagon remained at the yield sign. The dash clock changed to 7:25 p.m. He put the car in drive to turn right. He passed through seven intersections, then at the eighth, he turned left, then a right turn. Two more intersections, and a final right into the parking garage.

Placing Nathan in a foster home wasn't easy. He was aggressive and lacked discipline. His only forms of communication were to growl, bite, hit, kick, and scream. A staunch Christian couple welcomed Nathan into their home and enrolled him in a local Catholic school. The nuns that ran the school were strict. Nathan quickly adapted to the place. It was at this school that Nathan found a friend. The older boy took Nathan under his wing. He taught him swear words and encouraged him to be more of a disruption than he already was. One of his favorite tricks was getting Nathan to eat bugs in front of the other children.

One afternoon, Nathan ate a handful of bugs in front of a group of girls and made them scream. He liked it when they screamed. It was funny. Normally they'd run away, this group didn't. They hit him with their shoes. Over and over the shoes rained down on him. A nun passing by asked the girls what the commotion was about, and they just screamed, "Bugs!" As if on cue, Nathan opened his mouth, and out fell dozens of half-chewed slimy critters. The nun grabbed Nathan by the scruff of his shirt and repeatedly struck him with a leather strap, admonishing him for being a dirty beast. Nathan pushed the nun to escape her grasp. She stumbled backward, tripped, and fell, cracking her head open on a concrete step.

His foster parents were mortified by what had happened. They blamed him, and were so embarrassed by his actions that they pulled him from the school and sent him back to child welfare. He didn't miss his foster parents. He did miss his friend. He missed doing things for him. He missed his attention. He blamed the girls. It was their fault.

They had taken away his only happiness with their stupid screaming.

Inside the supermarket, Nathan picked up the top basket from the stack with his right hand. Placed it back. Picked it up again with his left hand, and switched it to his right. Tonight was ribs night. He checked his list. He needed ribs, coleslaw, bacon bits. Not on the list were a large potato and sour cream; he already had those at home.

After his first failed foster family, Nathan bounced around a few more families, not connecting with any of them. He became more withdrawn, distant, and antisocial. When he was in his teenage years, one of his school counselors helped him get a part-time job at a local vet. The counselor thought that being around animals would help pull Nathan out of his shell. It worked. He liked the job. He smiled more. He loved how much the animals needed him, especially the wounded dogs. He spent any free minute at the vet clinic. It became his life. When a full-time assistant job became available, he jumped at it, ditching school.

Year after year, Nathan dedicated himself to the vet. He was planning on going to summer school to get the qualifications needed to apply for veterinary school. Then out of nowhere, Nathan's birth mother contacted him. She told him what he needed to hear, that she loved him so much, and that they all could be a family again. Nathan fell for her lies, and when she asked for help getting narcotics, he hooked her up with an assortment of prescription veterinary medicines. Things were good until his manager discovered his pilferage and fired him. Once his access to drugs dried up, his mother had little use for him and again abandoned him. Feeling alone and hurt, he started to breed dogs. It was an easy way for him to earn money, and he didn't have to deal with people too much. He was good at it, and gradually built up a profitable business.

Nathan walked down the pet-food aisle. Looking at all the brands he would never purchase for his dogs. No. Only the best would do for his champions. But for the pet in the basement, they were perfect. He picked up a can that said ASIAN BEEF on the label. He thought his pet would appreciate him thinking about her needs.

Breeding dogs had become his life until he discovered dark areas of the internet. To delve deeper into the dark web, he upgraded his home computer and bought his own IP address and server. It was mandatory, a security measure that allowed him into some very special chat groups. It was in one of these chat rooms that Nathan met someone who became his role model. His online name was Caesar. He was smart and able to articulate and understand Nathan's complex feelings.

With everything in his basket, Nathan headed straight to the empty express lane. He paid for it with a credit card. The cashier placed all his items in a paper bag. Nathan removed them, and placed them in again himself. He didn't smile. He wanted to. He wanted to rush home. He needed to get home. It was going to be a big night.

After a few years of chat, Caesar invited Nathan on a trip overseas to India. On a squalid back street, his new friend introduced him to the pleasure of murder. By demonstration, Caesar taught Nathan how to enjoy the misfortune of others, and he encouraged him to continue when he returned home. Caesar tutored him online, sharing techniques on how to kill without getting caught. Nathan got hooked. From that day on, Nathan's life belonged to Caesar; he was his willing and obedient student. Anything he was told to do, he did. He loved Caesar so much that he had the symbol of the Civic Crown tattooed over his heart. When Caesar thought he was ready, he gave Nathan permission to kill on his own.

The rush Nathan got from his first abduction was everything he'd hoped it would be. It went exactly to plan, and his dogs played their part to perfection. He contacted Caesar on video so he could be visually guided through the next part. Caesar liked to watch. The play. The torture. The operation. The screams. And where to bury them alive. The body had to be discovered. It was all part of the way of Caesar.

Nathan parked his car in the same spot in his driveway. He got out with his bag of groceries, locked his car, unlocked it and locked it again. Placed the keys in his front right pocket and tapped them three times. With a slight spring in his step, he hurried toward his front door, avoiding the cracks in the path. Tonight he was going to take his time with his new pet before he operated on her. Caesar had told him she would be the last for six months, that he was going to have to move to another part of the country before he could start again. He always did what Caesar said.

Nathan paused outside his front door. The dogs barked as they always did when he got home. He looked around the neighborhood. Something felt different, but he couldn't isolate what it was. His dogs sounded a little more hoarse than normal, as if they had been barking before he arrived home. He took a few steps away from his front door, and sniffed the air. He stood still for a few moments as his eyes scanned the surrounding area. Searching for something out of place. When he was satisfied, he entered his house and closed the door behind him, locking it, then unlocking it and locking it once more.

What he didn't see were the three sniper rifles pointed directly at him for a kill shot.

CHAPTER NINETY-FIVE

DETECTIVE ROSS SMITH SAT in the front of one of the unmarked lead police cars, a few houses down from Nathan Clements. The last forty-eight hours had been hyperintense. He'd had about three hours' sleep, and that was being generous.

He watched as Nathan ambled up the pathway to his house. He held a collective breath with his comrades as Nathan opened his front door. A few officers got nervous when he stopped and looked around. As if he'd noticed them.

Ross listened to the chatter on his radio. An order was given: if Nathan made a run for it, take him out. They were all sure this man was the Beetle Butcher. For the last five years, he'd done an amazing job of hiding his past. He lived a clean life; all his bills were paid on time, and he never got on anyone's radar. But once they started to pull threads, his alibis fell apart, and everyone began to realize this could be the Beetle Butcher.

They all breathed a sigh of relief when Nathan entered his house.

Olive was sitting in the command bus one street over, directly behind Nathan's house. This was her operation. From the moment she'd gotten the call from Ross, she played it by the book, making sure she had every warrant needed for the operation.

When Nathan's front door closed, she made the call.

"Bravo, Tango. Positions Echo. Wait for my call on Alpha."

The Special Operations Response Team maneuvered into position. They had an extraction plan that would take forty-five seconds to blitz the house and remove Nathan alive. This is what they did, and they did it well.

Ross watched as the SORT team members scrambled into position. Olive had quizzed him on how he made the connection between Nathan and the Beetle Butcher. Nathan had already been interviewed twice and both times cleared. He couldn't tell her the truth, that he was still investigating Justin. He just told her he was following up on a lead and he tripped over it. He'd gotten lucky. She hadn't pushed any harder. She was just thrilled they had him.

Ross's cellphone started to ring. Only a few people ever called him, and he was going to let it go to voicemail but when he recognized the number—St. Mary's—he answered straight away.

"Hello?" he asked.

Silence came down the phone line.

"Hello?" Ross could hear breathing. Finally, a very frail female voice crackled down the phone. She had his full attention. It was Sarah Truth, he was sure of it. She was clearly struggling to get the words out.

"Ross... Justin... help..."

Then the phone went dead. She knew something about Justin. Ross was sure of it. If Justin discovered that she had broken out of her catatonic state, he'd make sure she would never talk to Ross, ever. Justin might even make her disappear like all the others.

Ross knew that he was her only hope. Yet he couldn't leave the biggest bust of his career. He couldn't just turn up at the hospital at this time of night without a court order. He had to stay and see this through. Once they had Nathan locked up, Olive would do him this favor. She owed him. She'd swing it so he could get into St. Mary's and pull Sarah out. He'd have her out by morning, afternoon at the latest. She'd be safe.

"FUCK IT!" he yelled as he started his car's engine and U-turned, speeding toward St. Mary's as fast as he could. This was the wrong decision. It was also the right one, to him.

CHAPTER NINETY-SIX

NURSE ROSE WAS WORKING night shift on reception for her second week running. It meant she'd earn a little bit more money for a lot less work. Very rarely did anything happen on the night shift. Most of her time was spent playing game apps on Facebook.

She loved being a nurse at St. Mary's. Not only was she able to help people, but the people she helped were very generous. If you showed certain clients a little more attention, above and beyond the great care they already received, their family would slip you a little extra. At first, she said no to the money. Now it was expected. Once a month, Justin Truth would slip her an envelope with five hundred dollars in it, just to keep an extra special eye on his mother, and to call him if anything out of the ordinary happened. He was such a loving son.

All the phones in the hospital went through a digital switchboard. One of the screens at reception displayed when the phones were in use. Nurse Rose got a bit confused when a message popped up on the screen indicating that the phone in Sarah Truth's room had become active. It was a call to an outside number—and it lasted thirty seconds.

Nurse Rose opened her purse and pulled out Justin Truth's business card. Maybe he would like to know this? She looked at it; then went to put it away. She was being silly. One of the cleaners could have stopped in the room and used the phone, or one of the on-call doctors. But if she did let him know, it would show that she was doing a good job, and maybe he'd slip her an extra something. She was saving up for a holiday in Rome, after all.

She dialed his number.

CHAPTER NINETY-SEVEN

JUSTIN TRUTH DROVE TOWARD GenLab as Black Wolf had instructed. The results of the DNA tests had been processed and were about to be sent to Dylon Corporate for collation. Justin would arrive early but knew he couldn't miss this small window to get his hands on them first.

His iPhone started ringing.

"Answer!" Justin bellowed into his hands-free kit.

"Hello, Mr. Truth. It's Nurse Rose. How are you tonight?"

"I'm good, Rose. On my way to a very important meeting. How may I help?"

"Look, it may be nothing but you always tell me to let you know if anything happens concerning your mother. And I want you to know, when I'm here I keep a very close eye on her."

"Thank you for that. I appreciate it very much. Was there something concerning my mother, Rose?"

"It might be nothing. A few minutes ago, the phone in your mother's room was used. We know it couldn't have been her, right? But I thought you'd like to know anyway. It could have just been a cleaner or a nurse."

Rose had Justin's full attention. "You wouldn't happen to know the number that was called?"

"Why yes, the numbers are displayed on the screen. I wrote it down. Now, where did I put it?"

Justin bit his tongue and stopped himself from screaming abuse at the middle-aged nurse.

"Oh yes, here it is…"

Justin listened to the number, thanked her, and hung up. He knew whose number it was, and it wasn't good. He had seen it on the card Detective Smith left with Debbie. Justin slammed on his brakes, fishtailed into a U-turn, and sped back the way he'd come.

St. Mary's was twenty-five minutes away. He had to get there fast.

Justin's mind flicked back over the last couple of weeks of visits with his mother. Things had felt different, but he hadn't been able to put his finger on it. He'd asked Nurse Rose to pay her more attention. The only thing Justin could guess was that his mother had found a way to fight the drugs. He smiled to himself—he was proud of her, but he was now going to have to do something about it. He turned up the stereo and changed it to fight music: *"Cleanin' Out My Closet"* by Eminem.

The Audi hugged the road as he thundered into the St. Mary's parking lot at speed. He came to a quick stop and was momentarily stunned by what he saw. Leaping out of a car and running to the front doors was Detective Ross Smith.

CHAPTER NINETY-EIGHT

ROSS STORMED THROUGH THE doors at St. Mary's and slammed his hands on the counter. The nurse on the other side looked at him in horror. This was not the normal way people enter St. Mary's, especially at this time of night.

"Sarah Truth!" he yelled. "I must see her!"

The woman quivered, unable to get out a word as her eyes scanned the empty room. Ross took a deep breath. He must have looked like a crazy man running in the way he did. He read her name badge.

"Look, Rose. I need to see Sarah Truth. It's very important."

"Are you on the list?" she squeaked.

"No."

"Then I'm sorry. No one can see a patient if they're not on the approved list."

"You don't understand," Ross growled.

"Those are the rules. If you want to see her you can always apply for a visitor's pass tomorrow when the hospital manager gets here."

"Look!" Ross paused, and composed himself. "I'm a police detective. I was just here the other day to see Dr. Brownstone. This is important police business. I think you can understand that."

"I think you can understand that we have rules to follow," Rose replied. The hospital security doors opened, and a stoic-looking guard entered

"Excuse me, sir!" the guard said in a gravelly voice. "I think you better leave before someone gets hurt, and that someone being you!"

Ross turned around. The guard looked ex-military, judging by his body language and stance. His simple white uniform didn't hide his massive build, and his thick biceps stretched his white T-shirt as he rubbed his hands together. Ross put his arm inside his jacket to pull out his police ID. Thinking he might be going for a weapon, the security guard shot out a jab, connecting with Ross's jaw, and knocked him to the floor.

"I'm a cop, goddamn it!" Ross shouted, pulling out his badge, but lying on his back, it didn't have the effect he was hoping for.

"Unless you have a warrant in that jacket too, you have to leave."

Ross knew that if he left now, there was no way Justin would ever let him back. He had to do this now. Sarah wouldn't survive the night if he didn't.

"OK, you got me, son. I was just trying to do my job like you're doing yours. Now help an old man up." Ross extended his hand. The security guard towering over him decided that the man on the floor wasn't a threat anymore, so he grabbed his hand and helped him up.

"Thank you, and sorry," Ross said.

"Sorry?" the guard replied as Ross kicked him as hard as he could in the testicles. The guard dropped to his knees. Ross followed up with a heavy overhand right and connected square, knocking the guard out, and breaking his own hand in the process.

He turned back to reception.

"Move, please!" He ran toward the desk, jumped onto it and slid off the other side, landing on his feet. He knew there would be more guards, but he had a head start and once he had Sarah, he didn't care what they did as long as he got her into protective custody.

Ross kicked open the back door and ran out of the office and into the hospital area. He looked behind him and heard a commotion. A few more security guards had arrived at the front door—no doubt they'd be going after him shortly, as Nurse Rose would have told them where he was heading. His lungs were burning and his body screamed for him to stop, but his brain yelled for him to get Sarah to safety.

Ross stopped himself. He was heading the wrong way, or was he? He had to keep moving. He could hear the sound of more security guards sweeping the corridors, searching for him. He recognized the corridor that led to Dr. Brownstone's office, ran toward it, then up the flight of stairs the young nurse had pointed to. Out of nowhere a young security guard appeared in front of him. Ross dropped a shoulder and slammed into him. He was surprised that the guard took the hit and was able to hold on. They both crashed onto the ground, and his bag of jelly beans popped open, sending them flying.

Ross threw a right hook. His hand throbbed. He had done more damage to himself than the security guard, which gave the guard a chance to scramble to his feet.

Ross was in no condition to fight a man half his age. The guard smiled and shot in for a takedown, but his foot slipped on the jelly beans. He stumbled. Ross saw an opening. As the guard's head went down, Ross was able to bring up a knee. The force of knee-on-chin knocked the guard out. He hit the ground face-first.

Ross steadied himself. He was only two floors away. As he pumped his legs up the stairs, he could feel his knee starting to give way, but he sucked it up and ignored his aching body. He got to the top and turned left. He could see Sarah's room just up ahead and charged toward it, flinging open the door.

CHAPTER NINETY-NINE

JUSTIN RAN TOWARD THE East Wing of the building. If his mother was communicative, he was going to have to fix that. She really had brought this whole thing on herself. Justin had made sure she had the best of everything. The best care. The best doctors. He knew he was the best son a mother could ever want. That's why it made him so mad that she would go behind his back like this. It was time to take care of his mother, forever.

Unlike Ross, he knew every access point in and out of the hospital. This would help him get to his mother's room on the third floor before the detective did. Ross shouldn't get past reception, but you never know what throwing a police badge around could get him.

Justin scaled a drainpipe on the side of the brick building and shimmied over to a bathroom window on the second story. A small chain held the window in place, and with a well-placed kick, he ripped it away from the wood. Seconds later, Justin was inside the small cubicle.

At this time of night, most of the residents would be sleeping, dosed up on a hundred different types of sleeping pills. He listened at the cubicle door. It was dead quiet, so he opened it and looked around. The communal bathroom was empty, so he made his way to the door leading to the corridor, pushing it open just far enough for him to peer through the gap. Suddenly he heard footsteps thundering toward him, but managed to pull the door shut again before a security guard hurried past, yelling into a radio. Sounded like Ross was causing a scene in reception. As soon as the guard was gone, Justin slipped into the deserted corridor.

The East Wing of St. Mary's was a large atrium. Justin peered over the balcony and searched the ground floor for movement. He then leaned his head back, looking in the direction of his mother's room. It was up one flight of stairs to his right and down a corridor just above him. The area was open, not many places to hide. He heard a loud crash from the ground floor. Ross was up to something. Justin had to move fast, faster than Ross.

Justin ran to the staircase and jogged up the stairs, his back hugging the wall. His eyes scanning for danger. Halfway up, he heard footsteps approaching from above. He had to act. He had no choice but to jump over the side of the balcony. He flung himself over, holding onto the banister with his fingers gripping the polished wood. Justin felt his shoulder muscles burning as he dangled three stories above ground. Hoping whoever was coming down the stairs wouldn't see his exposed fingers.

The light footsteps whipped past him. Not stopping. His fingers were screaming. He couldn't hold much longer. He engaged his biceps and chest muscles to lift him into a chin-up. The figure of a nurse reached the second-floor landing and scurried out of sight.

Justin swiftly pulled himself over the banister, landing back on the stairs with catlike stealth before running up the remaining stairwell to his mother's floor. He stopped near the top to make sure the coast was clear, but it wasn't. Just ahead, two nurses stood chatting in the main corridor. Another obstacle in his way. His mother's room was down an adjoining corridor to the right of the stairs. They were engrossed in their conversation, and weren't going anywhere in a hurry. There was no cover for him, but he had to make his move and hope they didn't look in his direction.

He cautiously crawled along the ground until he reached the corridor opening. Once he was out of the nurses' sight, he slowly got up. He could hear a commotion and peered back around the corner. The gossiping nurses were now running to where he'd been just a minute ago. He'd made the right decision just in time.

Justin turned and sprinted to his mother's room. As he reached her door he saw it was ajar.

CHAPTER ONE HUNDRED

SARAH LAY ON HER bed, breathing heavily, vocal cords burning. Her head was spinning from the effort it had taken to reach the book, pull out the card, get to the phone, and dial the number. The muscles in her body had atrophied from lack of use over a decade of being bedridden. It had taken her two hours to make the call, and now she needed to rest.

She was sure Detective Ross Smith was on his way over to protect her. Once she was safe, she could tell him everything her son had told her. But for now, she needed to relax and regain her strength.

Suddenly the door to her room slammed open. She turned her head to greet Ross, but was horrified to see Justin's face instead.

"Ohhh, Mother!" Justin cried. "I thought I had noticed a difference in you."

Sarah tried to scream, but all she managed was a gargle. Justin was on her like a flash, pushing her down hard.

"I think I've outgrown you, Mother. Now that I'm on the board, I no longer need you here with all you know about me. It's just a bit dangerous."

Justin grabbed a pillow and held it over her face. Sarah's body convulsed weakly as she struggled to breathe. Justin pressed down even harder, suffocating her. It only took a few moments for her body to become still and go limp. Justin lifted the pillow. "Thank you. Without you, I wouldn't be the man I am today," he said, placing it back over her face.

ROSS CRASHED THROUGH the door into Sarah Truth's room.

"No!" he yelled as he saw the pillow. He ran over to Sarah, pulled the pillow away from her face, revealing her mouth open in a silent scream. Her eyes were wide and bloodshot. He quickly placed his fingers on her neck to check her pulse. He couldn't find one so he started performing CPR, pushing down on her chest to get her heart moving. He tilted her head back and blew four breaths into her lungs. Again, he took her pulse, and again he got nothing. At that moment, Ross felt a cool breeze on his face. The window to Sarah's room was open, the curtain swaying gently. Below on the grass, staring back at him, was Justin. He looked pleased with himself and gave Ross a friendly wave.

"Fuck you!" Ross roared. He would save her; he would bring her back. But before he could inflate her lungs again, he was crash-tackled by two security guards, who proceeded to kick and punch him with all their might. Ross didn't fight back. He was spent.

The guard he had kicked in the testicles earlier entered the room and picked Ross up by his jacket. "No, I'm sorry," he said, and kneed Ross so hard in the balls that the pain caused him to black out.

CHAPTER ONE HUNDRED-TWO

JUSTIN HAD HIS FOOT FIRMLY planted on the accelerator, screaming his way back to GenLab, when he received the call from the hospital
that his mother had passed away. They didn't give him any details over
the phone, and he didn't ask for them either. In a choking voice, he told
them he'd come over as quickly as he could. His Rolex told him he wasn't
going to get to GenLab in time. It was fast approaching 11 p.m. His
window was 11:05 p.m. He needed to drive faster.

Other cars, buildings, lamp posts, all whipped past him at light speed.
Red lights meant nothing. He barreled through every intersection, beeping his horn, warning those who were obeying the laws of the road to
watch out. Screeching around a corner, he narrowly avoided sliding into
a group of parked cars before the Audi straightened out. His performance car was getting pushed to its limit. Justin was smiling. He wasn't
looking at the clock anymore, just the obstacles coming at him at over a
hundred miles an hour.

Finally, he reached the side entrance of GenLab and gunned it for
the delivery door. It was 11:28 p.m. and his only hope was that the technician had stuck around. Justin leapt out of his car and saw that the place
was dark and empty.

"Fuck!" he yelled as he kicked his car tire. He stood seething. Blam-
ing Ross. He was going to kill him for making him miss this pickup. He
would find a way to slit open that fucker's throat and rip out his tongue.
He would—

A single headlight beamed at him from across the parking lot. Next
thing, a small scooter pulled up in front of him.

"You the Wolf's man?" the rider asked through his tinted bike hel-
met.

"Indeed, and who are you?" Justin lifted a hand to block the light.

"I'm nobody. You got the money?"

Justin reached into his coat pocket and pulled out a thick envelope containing fifty thousand dollars.

"You're lucky, man," the rider continued. "I was just about to go. If you'd arrived at 11:31 p.m., you would have been all alone. Throw me the money."

"Do you have what I need?"

"I have the results of that test done out at Soda-Cola, if that's what you're after?" The rider pulled a black satchel from between his knees.

"Here!" Justin threw the envelope over to him. It bounced off the rider's chest, and he caught it.

"I should count it but I trust you, man." The rider put the satchel on the ground, gunned the scooter, pulled a donut, and sped off like a wasp. As the scooter disappeared, Justin got a look at the license plate.

"PZY 678," he said out loud, committing the number to memory.

Justin collected the satchel and returned to his car. He balanced the case on his knees, popped it open, and smiled. The front page read SO-DA-COLA: DNA TEST RESULTS. Justin turned the first page and quickly flicked through the rest.

"Fuck!" he yelled and whacked the steering wheel. He had the results, all right, but they weren't in a form that he could decipher. It listed all the samples, just none of the names. They were barcoded. He couldn't see whose DNA was which. Dylon must have the names at their end to add to the final report. He got what he'd asked for, but not what he wanted. The rider's voice was young; he was probably an intern at GenLab. No doubt he'd been shitting himself as he printed out the results from an internal station. Not knowing what he was printing. He had Justin's money, and Justin had nothing.

CHAPTER ONE HUNDRED-THREE

SERGEANT OLIVE MASTERSON STOOD OUTSIDE the holding cell, staring daggers at the lump hiding under the blankets from the fluorescent lights.

"Ross!" she barked.

Ross stirred on his cot and rolled toward her, swinging his feet over the side.

"Sergeant," he mumbled, looking at his feet. His broken nose made his voice sound like a limpet pierced by a seagull.

"You dumb fucking fuck!" she yelled.

"It sounds so nice when you say it," Ross joked.

"What were you thinking? Jesus, where do I start?" Olive massaged her temples to relieve the headache.

"Was it him? Was I right about Nathan?"

Olive rested her head on the jail bars. "You were right. Nathan was the Beetle Butcher. That bastard had already abducted his next victim. She was sedated and tied up in his basement. By the look of things, he was going to kill her that night. Because of you, she's alive, Ross. You saved her.

"His place was crammed with evidence, and he documented every single murder he committed. He knew he'd been caught so he made a full confession on the spot. What is fucked up is that he didn't want to call a lawyer—he wanted to call an agent and sell his story. He wants everyone to know that he did it. He's even asked to talk to the person who pieced the puzzle together."

"I'm pretty busy," Ross wheezed.

"Ross, I'm not asking for you to talk to this piece of shit. His ego just wants to know how he slipped up. Once he started talking, he wouldn't shut the fuck up. You were spot-on about the grouping of women. They were based on a schoolyard incident that had traumatized him as a child.

"He'd been fantasizing about killing these girls for a long time, but never did anything about it until he met someone, a friend, who changed everything. He taught him to tap into his inner anger, and use it to take revenge against the girls. A twisted mentor of sorts. He even helped him track down his original tormentors. He knew where they lived, what they looked like now. He knew everything about them."

"A friend?" Ross asked.

"Yeah, this friend of his also helped him act out his urges, showed him and how to hide under the radar and to create alibis. He advised him not to touch the original girls, as that would link back to him. The women he murdered had done nothing to him; fucking innocent. The only reason they were killed was because they looked like the ones he wanted to kill."

"Someone was helping him? Who?"

"That's all he calls him—a friend. To protect him, I guess. He was the one who planned it all out for Nathan so he wouldn't get caught. Making sure there were no links back to him."

"He had help?" Ross asked, trying to see the connective logic in it all.

"Whoever it was, they were the mastermind behind everything, a total evil fucker. There is nothing that leads us to him, though. The moment we took Nathan down, his computer and files were stripped of any contact between them; all that was left were files relating to Nathan's murders. This friend was definitely well-prepared for Nathan getting caught..."

"What are we going to do about this accomplice?"

"Nothing right now. We'll look into it, but first we're going to nail Nathan to the wall. His story is a damning one. This is what the mayor wants to champion as part of his reelection campaign." Olive unlocked the cell. Ross didn't move. She entered, sat next to him on his hard cell bed. Close enough so their legs were touching. "You know that's not why I'm here."

"I was kinda thinking you weren't here to let me out with a smack on the ass. They think I killed her right? That I killed Sarah Truth."

"I don't."

"But, 'they' do."

"I warned you, Ross. Justin Truth has his hooks into some powerful people. I've been told to step aside. The lieutenant is personally coming for you. Word is the mayor wants to make an example out of you and show everyone that cops aren't above the law. It's going to be a circus." Olive stopped and her face took on a sad, quizzical expression. "Why did you ignore me, Ross?"

"I had a chance and I took it," Ross said without blinking.

"I warned you to stay away from Justin Truth. Now his mother is dead, and you were the one in the room when it happened. Your fingerprints all over the murder weapon."

"He killed her!"

"He wasn't there, Ross. You're the only suspect in the murder of Sarah Truth."

"It's all Justin, Olive. He's evil. Give me five minutes alone with him in a room, and I'll get a confession out of him."

"The only place you'll see Justin is in court. Between his lawyers and the mayor, you're fucked."

Olive got up and placed her hand on Ross's shoulder.

"I'm going to fight for you, but you have to know there's only so much I can do. This hole you've dug for yourself goes all the way to fuckin' China."

Ross placed a hand on hers and looked her in the eye.

"Do what you can. We can't let Justin get away with this. He's worse than the Beetle Butcher. Read my files—it's all him."

Olive nodded and left the cell, locking it.

"Take this fuck down, Olive. Please!" Ross called out after her. "He'll kill again and again and again."

CHAPTER ONE HUNDRED-FOUR

STEVE BARKER PACED HIS office like a caged tiger. The scam of the Soda-Cola market stunt worked perfectly. All of the DNA collected on the day had been processed, and the analysis forwarded onto the police that morning. The large poster everyone signed had small print that gave the police permission to check the collected, donated DNA against the DNA of Montana's attacker. Justin's DNA.

They would find out today. Steve was so obsessed with the whole scenario that he started stalking Justin through the Soda-Cola building, making sure he was around for when the police came for him. Justin walked around so smug, unaware of what was going to happen to him today.

Steve's phone rang. He had asked reception to inform him at once if anyone from the police turned up.

"Hello?"

It was Montana. "Steve, they got a positive reading!"

"Oh, my God. Then it was him!" Steve collapsed into his chair. "When did you find out?"

"Just now. The protocol is to inform the victim first." Montana paused. "They're on their way now. Did he come into work today?"

"He's in today."

"Get to him before they arrive. Don't let him get away! Once he hears the police are in the building, he'll make a run for it."

"On it!" Steve hung up. He got out of his chair, smoothed out his suit, picked up some folders, and walked briskly to Justin's office. As he passed Debbie's desk, she told Steve that Justin was not to be disturbed. Steve ignored the warning, telling her he'd never be too busy for him. Steve opened the door and felt a sense of calm when he saw Justin sitting behind his desk writing an email.

"Can I help you, Steve? I'm in the middle of something."

"Carlton wants me to take him through my forecast for the Soda-Cola brand and, as you may be running it all soon, I thought it would be a good idea to get your unique perspective and essential input."

Steve's words flattered Justin. "Sure." He smiled. "Can it be done later?"

"Unfortunately not. Carlton wants it now, and I thought it would be best for you to see it first, in case you spot something you think is off-track. You have such foresight. I really need your help. I've been distracted lately."

"Since you asked so nicely." Justin got up and sat at his meeting table, inviting Steve to join him.

Ten minutes into it, Steve received a text from the receptionist saying that a team of police officers had just stormed the building and were traveling up the elevator. Steve got nervous. It was about to happen, and he was going to see it go down. He beamed at Justin, who grinned back.

Seconds later, five police officers burst into Justin's office.

"Don't move!" one of the officers yelled. Steve turned to Justin with a smug look.

"You're going away for what you did," Steve barked as the officers approached them. Two of them grabbed Steve, slammed him face first onto the floor, and slapped cuffs on his wrists.

"Wait. That's Justin over there!"

"We know who you are, Steve Barker, and now the world will know you're a rapist," one of the cops sneered.

"What?" Steve yelled. "I didn't do it, he did! It was Justin Truth!"

The officers yanked Steve to his feet and the man in charge eyeballed Steve. "That's not what the DNA evidence says."

"Someone must have swapped the results. It was Justin, you hear me! He's just standing there, for fuck's sake."

"Sir, you have the right to remain silent," the officer continued, reading Steve his Miranda rights as he led him out of Justin's office. Steve twisted to look at Justin, who was sporting a massive grin as he mouthed the words: *I fucked her good.*

This had the desired outcome. Steve lost it, broke free from the officers, and charged toward Justin. A quick-thinking officer drew his Taser and stunned Steve with ten thousand volts. His body jolted as he crumpled onto the floor, pissing his pants.

Justin bent down so that only Steve could hear him. "And I'm going to fuck her again, cocksucker."

He stood up and implored the officers. "Please take care of him. This is not the Steve we know and love."

Two officers helped Steve up. A large crowd had assembled outside the office, and a wall of whispers followed him as he was manhandled out of the building with piss dripping from his pants.

CHAPTER ONE HUNDRED-FIVE

MONTANA COULDN'T BELIEVE what she'd just heard. Steve Barker had been arrested for her rape? Surely, they must have made a mistake—Justin must have swapped their DNA samples!

Montana discharged herself from the hospital instantly. On the way to the hospital taxi queue, she tried to phone Steve, but his mobile went straight to voicemail. She also tried the jail where he was being held, but was told that Steve wasn't allowed any outside calls except from his lawyer and wife. She had no choice but to sort this out herself and prove to the authorities that Steve was innocent. When she called her own lawyer for help, he advised her to listen to the doctors and go through the correct channels.

Montana stormed past reception, ignoring the smiles from the receptionists, and straight into the elevator, thumping the close button. Outside Justin's office she found Debbie packing some of her belongings into a box.

"Debbie!" Debbie looked up, startled.

"Montana? What are you doing here?"

"Did he fire you because of me?" she asked, pointing to the box.

"What?" Debbie seemed baffled.

"Did he find out that you told me about what he did to me? You have to tell the police what you know."

"I don't know what you're talking about!"

"You told me it was Justin who beat and raped me." Montana was surprised at Debbie's denial.

"No, I didn't. Why would I do that? There is no way Justin would have done that."

"You said he did."

"I think you have your facts wrong. I just suggested that you get a rape test, that's all."

"Why are you packing, then?" Now Montana was confused.

"Justin has ordered me in a new desk. I asked for one of those electric ones that can rise up and down. So excited." Debbie smiled. "Should be arriving any minute now."

"But you…?"

"But nothing. If you'll excuse me, I have things to do."

Montana saw red. She heard a noise inside Justin's office and, brushing Debbie off, charged in.

Justin looked up from behind his desk. "Ah, Montana. I didn't know you were back at work already?" He flashed her a winning smile.

Montana walked over to him and slapped him hard across the face. Justin placed a hand on his cheek and his smile broadened.

"That was a free one. I'll let you have that."

Montana prepared to strike again, but Justin caught her wrist and spun her around, twisting her arm behind her back. He pushed her against the wall, pinning his body against hers with his mouth right by her ear.

"That all you got, baby girl? Did you come here to go another round? I bet you liked what I did to you in that dirty backroom, didn't you? You like to be slapped around."

"I'll get you!" she growled.

"No. No, you won't. Who's going to believe you? You've caught your attacker. Steve's had multiple DNA tests, and each one proves his guilt even more. Steve is such a bad boy! Cheated on his wife and raped you."

"No, he didn't, you sick fuck!"

"OK. One out of two is true. Poor Steve, he really missed you in Vegas. So much he fucked a prostitute who looked just like you. Don't worry, he was safe. He used a condom, which happened to end up in my possession with a video of what they got up to. I'll send it to you. Rather a bit of a letdown; he didn't last long. Anyway, maybe that's how Steve's precious swimmers were found inside you. Maybe? Maybe he raped you. Maybe I left them behind for you to find?"

"You—!" Montana gasped.

"And don't even think about the LemonGreat dirt you think you have on me. I left that trail for your friend to find. You think I'd be so care-less? It's gone now, and so is he. Would you believe his work computer was discovered to have child pornography on it? Microsoft doesn't look too kindly on that."

Montana struggled to break free but Justin's grip was like coiled steel.

"I can do whatever I want, whenever I want, to whoever I want. I could kill you, and no one would know."

"You're a fucking psycho!"

"Who, me? No. People will think you're just crazy. But I want to help you and your family, Montana. Save them from being kicked out of the country and losing everything they have. Making them start all over again in Mexico with no money. It would be so easy for me to have your parents deported. You know as well as I do that they're still illegal immigrants."

"Don't you dare!"

"That's up to you. We could be so good together; you'd have the world at your feet. So, what you're going to do now is walk out of here. You will never contact Steve Barker ever again—I'll know if you do. You will hand in your notice, and take a fantastic new role with our compe-tition over at Phizz. They'll love to have you and your experience. But you'll still be working for me, too. What you know, I'll know. You will tell me everything. And you'll do this or bad things will happen to you and your family. The video I have of Steve could pop up, hurting his case even more."

Justin licked her neck and released her. Montana spun around and looked him in the eye. She knew he meant every word of what he'd said, and for the first time in her life she was petrified. She didn't know what to do; her head was spinning. No matter what she thought about, Justin had her. He had so many ways to hurt her and those she loved.

"Please, stop it. Don't touch my family. You've done enough."

"That's up to you!" Justin repeated with a devious smile, grabbing her arms. "We are going to be together, baby girl. Give yourself to me. You know it's what you want, to be the one."

As Justin's eyes burned into hers, Montana felt the fire inside her die. She could try and fight, but he would hurt everyone she ever cared for.

This was just some sick game to him. She dropped her head in defeat and let her body go limp. He released her, his fingers leaving marks behind on her skin.

She stumbled out of the office, not sure where she was going, or who she was anymore. Her brain was swirling. Her heart beating like a tribal drum, the primal sound deafening her ears. The rhythmic sound carried her out of the building. She closed her eyes, letting the drums guide her forward.

CHAPTER ONE HUNDRED-SIX

ONE WEEK LATER, Justin strode into the decadent Soda-Cola board-room on the top floor. He was the last to arrive. Carlton sat at the head of the table, surrounded by seven of the nine board members.

"Thanks for making it," Carlton said weakly. The last few weeks had hit him hard, as Justin had recently increased his dosage.

"Anytime the board needs me, I'm there," Justin said with an air of improvised integrity.

The chairman of the board spoke up. "There's no need to waste any-one's time here. Carlton has informed us that he will be stepping down as CEO. His health isn't what it used to be, and he wants to spend more time with his family while he can."

Justin looked at Carlton, who nodded back. The chairman continued. "Now we could search the world for a replacement, but we all know we won't find anyone as good as you, Justin."

Justin smiled, flattered, and pretended to be humbled. "Everyone's impressed with the results that you've achieved and the leadership you've demonstrated," the chairman added. "We all agree that we have every-thing we are looking for right here, so we put it to a vote, and you got the job with a one hundred percent vote of confidence."

Justin's smile broadened. "I don't know what to say."

"It's easy—say you will accept the job and lead Soda-Cola into the future."

"Very well, gentlemen, I graciously accept your invitation. You have found your new CEO. And I think I can start straight away."

CHAPTER ONE HUNDRED-SEVEN

JUSTIN STUDIED HIS RED-STAINED HAND. He stepped forward and placed his right palm hard against the large canvas in his apartment. Holding it in place, he lowered his fingers so his entire hand was touching the gray. He held it in place, letting the red paint soak in.

He thought it was tacky for serial killers to collect mementoes from the people they killed. But he understood why they did it. It gave them a rush to relive the scenario all over again. He considered himself above these basic killers. He didn't need bits of hair, jewelry, or Polaroids. He had his artwork. To the outside world, the canvas looked like a magnificent piece of professional fine art. But to Justin, each hand symbolized a unique reality; it represented how much smarter he was than the person he'd killed. He looked at it objectively for a moment. It was beginning to look rather crowded, and he considered if it was time to start another masterpiece.

This new handprint was a special one. It was for the young intern at GenLab who had sold Justin the useless DNA results. He'd wanted to know the semen he had planted had done its job. A day later, when the police hauled Steve Barker out of his office, he found out it had. His own swab had been contaminated, as he'd planned. He didn't need to do a retest, as they had their man. Justin's DNA was still not on any register.

Justin easily tracked the intern down via his scooter registration. The intern had a nasty accident on his bike leaving work, taking the knowledge of his late-night meeting with Justin to an early grave.

Justin pulled his hand from the canvas, stood back, and admired his masterpiece. He thought it would be a great idea to add a handprint for Detective Ross Smith. It wouldn't be hard to pay someone on the inside to stick him like a pig; there'd be many people who'd jump at the opportunity to kill a dirty cop for a few hundred dollars. Would that count?

Could he add a handprint for paying someone to kill him? No.

Justin resisted. He liked that Ross was serving life for a crime he didn't commit. The detective hadn't stood a chance in court; the state prosecutors had a strong case. A case Justin had orchestrated to make Ross look highly guilty. Unknown to Ross, Justin had hired a private detective to trail him. Ross thought he was rattling Justin, he wasn't. All he was doing was giving Justin visual evidence of a vindictive cop who was trying to extort money. Justin had spun a convincing story about Ross.

Justin washed his hands and poured himself a drink. Jennifer was on her way over. He was going to break up with her tonight. He'd fuck her first, and then tell her she was getting too fat for him or something equally as horrible. She was getting too close, too clingy. Justin had to think about his future, a future that didn't have someone as simple as her by his side.

After Bill had been kicked out of his apartment a few weeks ago, Justin played a large part in helping shortlist the applications. He wanted someone fuckable; his vote went to an international supermodel who liked to party. She got the apartment, much to his delight. The line of models dropping by to party was a great improvement over Bill. Justin made sure that the new neighbor felt very welcome.

Life was good. After all, he was Justin fuckin' Truth!

EPILOGUE

BRENDON GIBSON DIDN'T WANT to go to the BBQ. In fact, he didn't want to do anything but binge watch Netflix at home. The black cloud of SummerCrush followed him everywhere he went, and it would eventually rear its ugly head. When meeting new people, he feared that common question, 'What do you do for a job?' The slight mention of SummerCrush would make the person's face screw up, as if they were sucking on a lemon.

The stress of the contaminated bottles had taken its toll on Brendon: he'd lost fifteen pounds, his hair was thinner, and he had a few more bags under his eyes. Each day he took a handful of pills to help him sleep, relax, and control his stomach ulcer.

He'd kept his job through the media tirade on SummerCrush; most days he would pull out his resignation letter ready to hand it over. Only pride, and knowing it wasn't his fault, stopped him from quitting.

Brendon stood in a corner of the garden under a large tree, drinking a beer. There were about thirty people at the gathering. His wife had disappeared into the kitchen to help; she was the only reason he'd come. She'd been his rock through everything. He knew she wanted to get out of the house and catch up with her friends, so he sucked it up and put her first.

"Brendon," a deep voice called out. "Brendon Gibson. Gibbo!"

Brendon recognized the voice from his past and looked around for its owner, Harry Anderson.

"Brendon, me old mate," Harry said, materializing in front of Brendon with a big grin on his face and his arms open wide for a hug. For a large man in his fifties, Harry moved like a shadow, his years of service in the Australian Special Forces still ingrained into him.

"It's been way too long, mate," Harry continued in his strong

Australian accent. "Would it be over ten years, you think?"

"Harry, good to see you. It's—"

"Been way too long," Harry interrupted. "What are you doing here, mate?"

"My wife works with the birthday boy. So I'm here—"

"Because she won't root yah tonight if yah stayed home watching the footy. Happy wife, happy life, right?"

Brendon laughed, a genuine laugh that he hadn't done for a while. He'd first met Harry twenty years ago while Harry was running security for a large building Brendon worked in.

One night on the way to his car, three street kids stopped Brendon for money, waving knives to encourage him to hand over his wallet. Harry appeared out of nowhere and beat the living hell out of the punks without breaking a sweat. From that day on the two men often had a drink every Thursday night. Even though Harry was on duty, it never stopped him from having a beer.

"What are you doing here?" Brendon asked.

"Mate, see that beautiful lady over there. I'm doing my best to trick her into thinking I'm the man of her dreams."

"How's it going so far?"

"Not as fast as I would hope." He smiled. "What are you doing for a job out here?"

It was the question Brendon feared, but he knew Harry wouldn't judge him, so didn't mind dropping the S word.

"I'm the marketing manager for SummerCrush, it's been pretty tough this year."

"Why's that?"

"It was all over the news, it was awful. Somehow bottles of Summer-Crush had glass inside them. No one knew until they drank them."

"Fuck me."

"Yeah, I wouldn't wish that on anyone, they got pretty sick." Brendon took a sip of beer. "It hurt us pretty bad, we've had to lay off half our staff. It wasn't a manufacturing fault. Someone did it on purpose," Brendon said with conviction.

"Shit, they catch the person?"

"The police came up with nothing."

"Those guys couldn't find their assholes with their elbows."

"Nice!" Brendon laughed. "I hired a few investigators, no luck. It's like a ghost did it."

"Right," Harry said and lifted two cold beers from a box at his feet. "Now finish that drink. You are drinking with me until we have no beers left, mate. It may take a while but it's got to be done." Harry placed an open bottle in Brendon's free hand. His eyes told Brendon to quickly finish the other beer, which he did.

"I may be able to help you," Harry continued. "In my travels I've heard about a bloke, what's his name? Shit… Nick, Nick Harvey, that's it. Nick Harvey is like this ghost hunter, that's what people call him, as he finds people no one else can. It's like Nick has this bloodhound gene or something. If anyone can find this ghost who did this shit to you and those people, it's him."

"Nick Harvey?" Brendon asked.

"The ghost hunter!" Harry smiled. "He'll get this bastard, no two ways about it."

REVIEWS

IF YOU ENJOYED CORPORATE TRUTH, I need your help.

I write because I like creating stories, characters, and twisting plots that make my readers need to read just one...more...page...

If you crave more twisted tales from the world of Justin Truth, please consider leaving a review for Corporate Truth on my Amazon website. Your review, which need only take a few minutes, will help other readers discover the world of Justin Truth, which, in turn, will help me be able to create more twisted stories for your reading pleasure.

Help more readers discover the Truth, write a review today.

Thanks!

CRIMINAL TRUTH

BY
KARL WILLIAM FLEET

CHAPTER ONE

MARK BENOIT WAS STILL DRUNK—not uncommon for his Saturday mornings. He had no desire to be awake as he faded in and out of a conscious state. His toxic slumber seemed like a far more attractive option than the inevitable heavy hangover.

A distant, muffled beeping reminded him of a popular Taylor Swift remix. The repetitive sound echoed around his skull like broken stilettos on a cold concrete floor. He imagined for a second that he might have passed out in one of the dingy clubs he frequented at the end of a drunken night out, hidden in a dark little corner all by himself.

He tilted his head upward and discovered his tongue welded to the roof of his mouth, his throat a Sahara. He worked his jaw up and down to encourage saliva. Half-heartedly he tried to open his eyes; full-heartedly they remained closed.

The beeping got louder as fragments of the previous night filtered back into his murky memory. Mark worked for a broker on Wall Street; he made money, just not the big money. Still, he liked to suit up and talk the talk as if he were a big fish, but in reality, he was just lucky to be in the water. Yet his lack of funds didn't limit his fun.

Mark had a tried-and-true method of impressing party girls. He knew they were more impressed by certain branded bottles of champagne than the actual champagne. After a few drinks, their taste buds weren't that refined. One night, while removing the wet label of a bottle he regretted buying with his rent money, Mark realized that once it was "naked," it could be any bottle. If he stuck another label on it, an even more expensive label, one downloaded from the internet onto the right paper, would half-drunk girls notice?

The beeping that threatened to wake him got closer and grew louder, so Mark rolled to one side, squeezed his eyes tighter, and gritted his teeth.

He summoned all his willpower to descend back into the darkness of sleep. It worked; the annoying sound faded from his consciousness.

Mark's method of switching bottle labels worked like magic the first time he'd tried it, so it became a regular late-Friday-night thing. He'd wait until the timing was right, go to the bar and order three of the cheapest bottles of champagne, a bucket of ice, a bottle of water, and a double shot of house whiskey on the rocks. He'd then pour the water into the bucket and leave the bottles to soak at his feet, taking his time sipping his whiskey.

The cold water made it easy for him to remove the labels from the cheap champagne bottles—which he would do while pretending to tighten his shoelaces. The "naked" bottles were then dried with a napkin, and the five-hundred-dollar sticky labels perfectly attached. Mark had it down to a fine art, and like a magician, nobody would see him do the switch.

Back at the table, he'd bang the bucket down and pop open a bottle. "Who wants to get fucked up?" he'd yell to a raucous applause.

He'd pulled this stunt twice last night to impress his latest dream girl, Elizabeth. She was playing hard to get, so he tried to get her more drunk. It had worked with plenty of other girls. But maybe he drank too much himself because the night turned into a blur. He lost Elizabeth at some stage; he recalled cold air hitting his face as he left the club in search of her. He had a vague memory of vomiting against an alley wall, spinning lights, and then nothing. Until now.

A terrible odor entered Mark's nostrils and forced his eyes open. He hoped he hadn't shit the bed. But he wasn't in bed, he was surrounded by darkness, and the air smelled sickeningly rancid. The beeping was even louder now, and it was right by his head. He could barely move, and strangely shaped objects dug into him.

Suddenly, his dark, suffocating world shook. Mark yelled as he realized that the beeping belonged to a garbage truck lifting the dumpster he was in. He reached for the opening to pull himself out, but he slipped on the moving trash and fell further into the vile garbage. The higher the bin went, the steeper the angle became, and the harder it was for him to find his balance.

The dumpster shook violently, and Mark tumbled out with the rest of the trash into the compactor below. His screams for help were in vain, as no one could hear him above the sound of the truck's engine and hydraulics. The only person who knew to help him was the dark-suited man responsible for Mark's current predicament. The man had found Mark passed out hours earlier, gently picked him up, and put him inside the dumpster, knowing the garbage truck would pass by to empty it early in the morning.

The compressor hissed into a second gear, and with a low, metallic screech, the walls slowly began closing in on Mark. He kicked and clawed at his surroundings, trying to get leverage to escape the shrinking tomb. As the surrounding trash compacted tighter and tighter, he shoved his back hard against one wall of trash and slammed his feet on the opposite wall to halt its movement. He let out a high-pitched scream as the closing walls blew out his kneecaps, tearing skin and snapping bone. His skull cracked and contorted beyond recognition as metal crushed every part of him.

The dark-suited man watched as the truck returned the empty dumpster to its original position with a thunderous clank and continued on its way. Happy with his morning's work, he stepped out of the dark alley into the first rays of the morning sun.

CHAPTER TWO

JUSTIN TRUTH STOOD and stretched his muscular legs. He spent way too many hours sitting behind his desk. For the last ten months, he had been the CEO of American icon Soda-Cola. With its vast empire of products, there wasn't one country in the world that didn't sell Soda-Cola products, and he controlled all of it.

He walked over to the large windows that overlooked Manhattan. Justin checked himself out in the reflective glass and flexed his biceps. He was more interested in looking at himself than at the panoramic view. He liked how his tailored shirt wound tightly around his toned upper body, and how his vest emphasized his powerful, broad shoulders. He stroked his perfectly groomed stubble-beard and ran his hand through his wavy, dusty-blond hair.

For the last three months, Justin had been modeling himself after Ryan Gosling: from the suits, to the physique, to the Botox injections that gave him Gosling's famous "bedroom eyes." His charcoal three-piece Gucci suit was of the same cut as the one Gosling wore to the *Gangster Squad* movie premiere. To complete the look, Justin wore a bright orange, handmade, Italian silk tie with a matching pocket square and his initials stylishly embroidered into them.

After taking over from Carlton, the former CEO, Justin had sliced through the hierarchy of Soda-Cola, firing anyone who he didn't believe was on his side, a time the survivors now infamously referred to as "Tornado Tuesday" during their watercooler chats. A few threatened legal action, but Justin had obtained some form of dirt on everyone. He used the smallest of reasons—visiting inappropriate websites during work hours, arriving late, or even taking stationery home—as grounds for dismissal.

When Justin first joined Soda-Cola, Carlton was a healthy sixty-four-year-old silver fox. But to edge him more quickly into retirement, Justin slowly and regularly poisoned his daily glass of Scotch until Carlton was too sick to work. Once he was out of the way, Justin let the former CEO return to his former healthy self. He would stay healthy as long as he limited his time to board meetings and left the running of Soda-Cola to Justin.

Steve Barker had been Justin's rival for the CEO position until his reputation was ruined. Justin still smiled at how easy it had been to set up Steve so everyone thought it was he who'd raped Montana Cruz, destroying the man mentally and financially. Steve ultimately avoided jail time, but that was the least of his problems; Justin heard that Steve had taken up heroin, killing himself one injection at a time.

Montana, who'd been so desperate to bring Justin down and have him fired from Soda-Cola, was now his broken plaything. He'd made her apply for a job at Soda-Cola's fiercest competitor, Phizz. How quickly they had snatched her up, thinking she would bring all of her Soda-Cola knowledge with her. They were wrong. She still worked for Justin and kept him up-to-date about everything Phizz was doing and planning. He'd give her tasks to perform to help keep Soda-Cola one step ahead.

Justin's office phone beeped.

"Debbie," Justin said, hitting the speaker button. Debbie was his personal assistant. Nothing happened in the building without her knowing about it. After proving her loyalty to him again and again, Justin promoted her to office manager, which gave her a little power and a few people to manage. Debbie's main job was to take care of Justin's calendar, and she protected it with a venomous zeal.

"Hello, Mr. Truth," Debbie chirped. "Just a reminder that you have drinks with Mr. Rip Gordon tonight. And on Saturday afternoon, I've booked the Soda-Cola chopper to take you to Bell Island to visit that awful Ross Smith. God, after what that man did to your poor mother! How can you even look at him?"

"It actually helps me focus on the good things in life. He wanted to hurt me, but all he did was hurt himself. My visits show him how strong he has made me."

"You have such strength, Mr. Truth," Debbie fawned. "I've set up the Number Two boardroom for your management meeting—they're all there waiting for you."

"Great, tell them I'll be there soon." Justin ended the call.

Detective Ross Smith was serving a life sentence for the murder of Justin's mother—a murder Justin had committed himself. He'd thought about having Ross killed; it would be easy enough to have some gang member stab a dirty cop without anyone batting an eyelid. But he liked the irony of Ross being in the exact place he'd tried so hard to put Justin into. He found his monthly visits therapeutic, as he could rub it in Ross's face that he was in prison while Justin was free to do as he pleased.

Justin checked his much-loved reflection one more time, running through a few favorite poses and looks. He grinned, happy with himself. It was time to feed his Young Lions, throw them some raw meat and watch them fight over it.

CHAPTER THREE

EIGHT MINUTES LATER Justin's The Number Two boardroom was surrounded entirely by glass walls that frosted over during meetings, obscuring the interior from passersby. It was white, bright, and featured wireless equipment that could be controlled remotely. A plateglass table ran down the middle of the room, surrounded by rippled, white leather office chairs. Justin had designed it himself.

When he took over as CEO, he also restructured the management team, whom he named "Young Lions." He split the accounts amongst them to create fierce competition. In meetings, Justin cranked up the testosterone; he wanted warriors fighting for him, men who would do whatever it took to impress him.

All conversations stopped as Justin entered the room with gusto.

"My Lions!" Justin roared.

The entire room roared back at him. The energy was primal, almost savage.

"When I took over, I knew it would be a fight to revive this dying dinosaur. As a company, we were slipping, growing old, and fast becoming irrelevant. Today, because of me, Soda-Cola is transformed. This company is now a flesh-eating monster of magnificent proportions." The group applauded enthusiastically.

"And as each of you know, I have big plans—new products, smarter marketing, and tighter, more focused advertising to take Soda-Cola to new heights of global domination. We have heard the weak-minded idiots say it's too hard, that we expect too much, that we should roll over and embrace mediocrity. But those fuckers are weak, pathetic, and quitters They are the cancer eating away at this great country of ours!"

The group roared again, banging on the table with their fists. Justin glared at his warriors, his eyes encouraging them to be louder. When he wanted them to listen, he prowled the room slowly, and the group went silent.

"Caleb," Justin said. "Caleb-Motherfucking-King. Please stand up."

Caleb looked at everyone and stood boldly.

"Caleb is crushing it on NiceTea, fighting to make it the number one iced tea in the market. It's the best tasting iced tea in the world, goddammit!" Again, the Lions banged their fists on the table just as Justin had trained them to do each time he made a point.

"Our competition, Tea-Sip"—the Lions responded with well-trained boos and more fist-banging—"got the drop on us and secured a tight sponsorship deal for the college football championship game. They shut us out. Those assholes at Phizz thought they were so damn clever, right? So, what did Caleb do? Did he say, 'Good one! We'll get you next year.' No he didn't, because he's a Young Fucking Lion! He hired ten of the sexiest bitches that ever walked this earth. He had them wear the tiniest-of-tiny denim shorts and the tightest-of-tight white T-shirts, with NiceTea emblazoned on them, big and in your face, just like their enhanced cleavages. They set themselves up outside the main beverage stand and each time a teenager emerged with a Tea-Sip, they gave him an option. They could keep their disgusting pitiful choice of a drink and sit in the stands like the losers they are. Or if they poured that shit into the gutter, where it belongs, we'd give them a bottle of water to pour over our sexy-as-hell NiceTea girls' tight white T-shirts.

"Did they pour it out? Goddamn right they did. Each guy who did then had their picture taken, and that shit got Instagrammed, hashtagged, and Facebooked. Splashed all over social media! Tea-Sip paid for sponsorship, but we owned that event. That's what it means to get business done!"

The Lions got louder and more boisterous. Caleb raised his arms like Rocky Balboa as the men close to him slapped him on the back.

"Now, what did we learn from this?" Justin scanned the room. "If the competition tries to out-think us, we out-fuck them.

"Michael. Please stand up." Michael got up from his chair, his eyes darting around the room. "Michael, Michael, Michael… Can everyone look at the big screen, please," Justin said, lowering his tone. He pushed a button on his iPhone. The lights dimmed as the screen came to life and played a ninety-second commercial for Diet Soda-Cola. Everyone in the room watched silently.

Once the ad finished, the lights came back on, and Justin turned back to Michael.

"Michael, how did this ad get made?"

"I saw an opportunity to get one over the competition and went for it," Michael stated.

"Tell me more," Justin replied, tapping his iPhone against his chin.

"Um, yeah, so four weeks ago, R and R Advertising came to me with this idea. They discovered this artist who has no arms, right? It was incredible—she dances and paints at the same time. The floor is one giant white canvas, and she spreads glue onto it with her feet while moving around the room to music. You can't tell what she's painting because the glue is white, you know? Toward the end of the dance, she kicks over containers of colored glitter, a giant fan blows the glitter around, it sticks to the glue, and the picture appears like magic. It all ties into the music and dance. R and R pulled it together and presented me with a finished ad to play during the final of *American Idol*. The media company pulled some strings and got us the spot for next to nothing. They got a sixty at first, but I pushed them for a ninety. It was truly inspirational."

Justin prowled the room again. "I don't remember signing it off?"

"I had to move fast to seize the opportunity," Michael answered gingerly. "I tried to show it to you, but you were in meetings, or out of the office. I couldn't see you."

"So, it's my fault?"

"No, you... It's my fault, sir."

"Damn right, it's your fault. What makes me mad is that we had a spot during the final of *American* fucking *Idol*, with millions of eyeballs, and that shit is what went to air. Could anyone read the branding at the end? Was there a range shot? Our end sting? I did not see one person in the ad drinking Diet Soda-Cola, not one person holding an actual bottle. Not one Diet Soda-Cola, the product we are selling."

"I researched it..." Michael mumbled.

"You did what?"

"I researched it, I asked a few girls in the target audience and around the office. Sally on reception said it was the most emotional TV ad she'd ever seen. It talks to the target audience in a way we haven't before— it reached them on a new level. Helping them see the unachievable is achievable."

"So Sally on reception thinks it's great?"

"Yeah…"

Justin used his iPhone. "Hello, Sally… can you join me in the Number Two boardroom please. Yes, now. Right now."

The Lions sat in silence as they waited for Sally. No one dared to say a word.

The doors opened and a slim blonde meekly entered. Each Lion stared at her with lustful grins as she tentatively took a few steps toward Justin.

"Hi, Sally," Justin said gently. "A question. What is your job description?"

"I work… I work at reception," she stammered, shyly dropping her head as her cheeks turned bright red.

"Have you ever been the CEO of this company?"

"Umm, no."

"Thanks Sally, glad you could clear that up." Justin flicked his fingers to tell her to leave. With the poise of a ballet dancer, she turned on her toes and left the room.

"There you go, Michael. Sally confirmed it. She is the receptionist. Now I ask you again: How did this ad, that I never signed off, with fuck-all branding, and featuring a bitch who can't even hold the product, get to air?"

"I thought—"

"Well, you thought wrong," Justin stated. "Nothing, and I mean nothing, ever goes to air without me saying so. Do you see me now?"

"What?" Michael asked.

"Do you fucking see me now?"

"Yes, yes I do."

"Good. You have twenty minutes to gather your shit and get your fired ass the fuck out of my building."

Michael looked around his colleagues' faces for support. Finding none, he exited the room. As soon as the door closed, Justin addressed the remaining Young Lions.

"Now I have an option for you all. I can hire someone to replace that worthless bag of shit, or you can divide his workload among yourselves along with his salary. Make a group decision and email me your collective answer by noon. We are here to get rich, not to get fucked. And that pussy just got fucked!"

CHAPTER FOUR

THE AIR CONDITIONING INSIDE the Phizz International Building had been malfunctioning for weeks. Montana Cruz could hear technicians slowly working on the air ducts, their tools echoing above her desk.

Bang, bang, clank. Bang, bang, clank.

She sat staring at the wall behind her computer, zoned out. Every now and then she ran her hand through her black hair, catching herself surprised at its new length. It used to be a lot longer—about halfway down her back—but now it stopped short of her shoulders.

Bang, bang, clank.

Montana often stared at the wall and spaced out these days, wishing to be anywhere other than where she was. She felt like Justin had sliced open her skull and used an industrial blender to turn her brain into liquid mince.

Bang, bang, clank.

A shiver ran down her spine. She was glad she had an office to herself so when her body reacted violently to thoughts of Justin, she didn't have to explain why she suddenly banged her fists on her desk in fits of anger or threw up in her wastebasket.

Bang, bang, clank.

Her job at Phizz was basically the same job she'd had at Soda-Cola. A little easier, in fact. She was good at what she did and was shining in her new role, despite her trauma. In fact, she was killing it—so much so that she'd already received a pay rise and an all-expenses paid trip to Rome.

Bang, bang, clank.

There was a courtesy knock at Montana's door as Kenny Longwater walked in. He was the general manager for Phizz and in charge of the marketing team. He had headhunted Montana personally and was eager to make sure she got what she needed. Even after five months, he still dropped by frequently to check up on her. Kenny seemed to always wear a broad smile beneath his large, hawk-like nose, which made his eyes, already naturally close together, look even smaller. The whole look accentuated his curly mop of blond hair.

"Hi, Montana." Kenny smiled. "I have the case studies you asked for. You really do put in the hard yards. I knew you were good, but you're better than good. You're knock-it-out-of-the-park good!"

Montana returned the smile. She knew Kenny didn't have to drop the files off in person. His dark gray suit and white shirt were too big for his small frame. He'd lost a lot of weight recently, due to his increased interest in long-distance cycling.

"When I said I'd come here," Montana said, "it was to make you guys number one, and to do that, I need to know your strengths and weaknesses—what you have tried, what you are planning, and what's been successful. As my mom says, 'Every little crumb makes the cake.'"

"You're amazing, you know that?" Kenny asked genuinely.

"Thank you, Kenny." She smiled again. She didn't find him at all attractive, but if his liking her made life easier, she'd smile as much as he seemed to need her to.

Kenny licked his dry lips. "We all love having you here."

His eyes scanned the front of her blouse. Montana's hand twitched, her throat tightened up, and she could hear her own heart beating like a tribal drum. She closed her eyes to stop the world from spinning. She needed to get him out of her office. She centered herself and opened her eyes to gaze at him. Then, she picked up a gold-plated letter opener and played with it while she seductively stood up, exhibiting her curves.

"I think about you," she whispered, as she placed her hand on Kenny's chest, feeling his heart beat faster beneath her hot palm. She moved her body in close, sliding up against him as she flicked the inside of his ear with the tip of her tongue. He got hard and pushed against her. She moved her hand from his chest to caress his face and hair, her fingers toying with the curls. Slowly her hand tightened its grip on his hair until he let out a little whimper of pain.

"I want you…" she gasped longingly. "I want you… to fucking die!"

She stabbed the letter opener again and again into Kenny's exposed neck. His eyes widened in fear and confusion as blood exploded out of his gaping mouth. Montana released his hair. He fell back against the wall, blood gushing from his neck. His hands desperately tried to stop the torrent of crimson liquid flowing out of him. He slid down the wall and onto the floor into a pool of blood, his beady eyes wide and terrified. Montana stood over his body, his blood dripping off her hands.

"Montana," Kenny said.

She couldn't understand how he could talk with such a gash in his neck.

"Montana? Hello? Earth to Montana...?"

Her eyes opened. She snapped back. Kenny stood in the doorway, very much alive. She gazed at her bloodless hands. Her vivid daydreams about killing were getting stronger. She dropped the letter opener onto her desk and stood, desperately wanting him out of her office. She put a hand on his shoulder, pulled the files from his hands, and leaned in, speaking softly.

"Thanks, Kenny. This will be a massive help. Can't wait to compare the forecasts and write up a course-of-action report on the changing market trends for you." She subtly turned him around and motioned him to leave. "You're the one that's amazing, Kenny."

"Thanks, here whenever you need me," he said hopefully, playing with his wedding ring as he shuffled out.

Montana closed the door and slumped her back against it. Slowly she lowered herself to the floor, clenching her eyes shut to hold back tears as she wrapped her arms around her knees. She had to pull herself together. She was meeting Justin for lunch in under two hours.

She hit her head against the door to the incessant rhythm of the echoing air conditioner.

Bang, bang, clank. Bang, bang, clank.

CHAPTER FIVE

A SMALL BROWN PAPER BAG bounced up and down on Nick Harvey's knees as he sat in an upscale dental waiting room. He fidgeted a lot, but it had nothing to do with the five cups of coffee he'd consumed. He got bored easily and needed constant stimulation. He stood five-foot-nine and was twenty-eight, but looking at him, anyone would think he was twenty-one. He tried to grow stubble to help age him, but it didn't do much.

Nick played with his tie and smoothed out his white shirt. He wore a slim-fitting suit with a shirt and tie. They were far from designer—he'd purchased his entire attire for under a hundred dollars at Walmart—but they fit his small frame well and he liked how he looked. He never had to think of what to wear, it was always a suit and tie.

"Mr. Harvey," the receptionist called out.

"That's me!" Nick said, raising his hand in the air.

"Dr. Wagner will see you now."

"That's the best news I've heard all morning." Nick sprang to his feet and did a slight tap dance. The receptionist smiled behind her rectangular glasses as she watched him skip down the corridor to the awaiting white room.

"Take a seat," Dr. Wagner said. The dentist was in his fifties, his white hair swept to one side. His face was well tanned, and his extra chin revealed a man who fancied a second helping of dessert. He sat on a small swivel chair at his desk, peering at a computer screen.

Nick leapt onto the dentist's chair, clutching the paper bag in his lap.

"How can I help you?" Dr. Wagner smiled, pushing his chair away from the computer and gliding over to Nick.

"Doc, can I call you 'Doc'? Man, I love this room." Nick looked around the room with an animated expression as if he were in Disneyland.

"It's so white and clean. And that smell—so good. I love a clean-smelling room."

Before Dr. Wagner could reply, Nick continued. "Now Doc, I have this problem. How is the best way to say this? I like to piss people off. And sometimes they don't like it and will punch me right in the mouth. Would you believe that? In this day and age?"

"Did you lose a tooth?" Dr. Wagner asked with a half-raised eyebrow.

"Not yet, knock on wood." Nick tapped his knuckles on his head. "But Doc, I guess it's the people I piss off, they kinda deserve it, you know? I don't just walk up to strangers and go, 'Hey you, you suck!' or 'Oi you! Fatty boom sticks! Eat less donuts, porky.' Or 'Hey ugly! Stop scaring small children, it's not Halloween.' It's mainly people I meet in my job. I bet you meet some crazy people in your line of work, too… people with some weird, fucked-up teeth, right?"

"I meet a large selection of people, Mr. Harvey."

"I bet you do. In my job, I deal with all kinds of creeps and weirdos," Nick chirped on. "It's my job to uncover them, expose their dirty little secrets."

"Okay," Dr. Wagner replied quizzically, looking toward the door. Nick picked up on the subtle change in attitude from the good doctor and opened the paper bag. He pulled out a soft toy, a Lopsy Lulu doll with large button eyes and floppy pink hair.

"This is for you, by the way," Nick smirked, throwing it toward the dentist.

"I'm a bit old for this." Dr. Wagner laughed.

"Yeah, you are," Nick laughed back. "I just thought you'd like to have it as the little girl who used to own it no longer needs it. Her name was Emma, cute as a button she was." Nick removed a photo from his paper bag and showed it to Dr. Wagner. It was a picture of Emma on a swing sporting an infectious smile. "You see, she got hit by a car in a small vacation town about eight months ago. The car was speeding, lost control, and hit her as she played in her front yard. The driver didn't stop. He must have seen her, as her body smacked across the windshield." Dr. Wagner moved uneasily in his chair. "The local police looked into it, but found nothing. It was as if a ghost had done it. Do you believe in ghosts?

I get called 'the ghost hunter' because you know what, Doc? I find these ghosts. I sat in that front yard, in the exact spot her body landed. For six hours, I lay there watching the clouds roll overhead, holding this very photo. Waiting for her to trust me enough to tell me what happened. What type of car it was… a sleek black convertible driven by a guy with shiny white hair."

"I don't understand why you're telling me this." Dr. Wagner moved his chair away from Nick.

"I'm sorry. I just thought you might like to know that you killed Emma. I would like to know if I'd killed someone, seems only right. Wouldn't you? Did you know she was dead? Maybe it didn't cross your mind as you sped away. Or maybe you did know and just didn't give a fuck. Yeah, that could be it. You just don't give a fuck."

Dr. Wagner's voice became agitated. "You can leave now. I have no idea what you're talking about!"

"Good one, Doc. You tried really hard to cover your tracks, even booking your car in for a detail. That was one clean car, no scuff marks from Emma's body. Lucky for me they don't clean the ventilation intake at the base of the windshield. That little vent collects everything."

"Get the hell out!" Dr. Wagner grabbed Nick by the collar of his white shirt, dragging him out of the chair and throwing him onto the ground.

"Ease up, Doc." Nick got to his feet and produced a Ziploc bag. "You see this little hair in there? This little hair puts you at the scene, and this little hair will make sure that you're held accountable for what you did. And you know what I said about getting punched a lot? I wouldn't try."

Dr. Wagner swung a wild right at Nick's head. Nick pivoted, easily blocking the punch, and returned his own with interest, striking the sweet spot on the dentist's jaw. He dropped instantly, falling face-first into the spit basin, smashing out his front teeth before crumpling onto the floor.

"Thanks, Doc, that felt good! You can now add 'attempted assault' to your long list of charges. And I'm thinking you have about two minutes to clean yourself up before the cops get here and haul your ass out in front of everyone. No need to rush."

Nick leapt back into the dentist chair and listened for the distant sound of police sirens to drown out the groaning Dr. Wagner.

MORE...

JUST NEED ONE MORE HIT? A little more of the Truth sounding good about now? Don't worry, you're not alone. Go where others have discovered even more of the Truth: karlwilliamfleet.com.

Sign up to be a Truth Seeker today and receive ongoing bonus short stories, behind-the-scenes snippets, audiobook chapters (with author's commentary), plus loads more exciting stuff—all exclusive to Truth Seekers.

And, as a special collector's edition extra for Truth Seekers, I'll send you an exclusive Blood Red Hand Print Cover of 01: Corporate Truth eBook, signed by myself.

We do need your email address to send you all this awesome stuff. Don't worry, I guard email addresses from people like Justin—I'll never sell or give them away. And of course, you will have the option to unsubscribe whenever you wish.

And... you never know, one day you might find your own name within the pages of the Truth Files. Passionate Truth Seekers have been known to make appearances...

THANK YOU

THANKS TO EVERYONE who read the antics of Justin Truth when it was just a jumbled mess.

Thanks for your time.

Thanks for your advice.

Thanks for asking, "what happens next?"

Thanks for fixing typos, pointing out plot holes, and challenging every word.

Thanks for letting me go slightly insane and then welcoming me back.

Thanks for believing.

Thank-you.

My foundation of help, support, and encouragement:
Andrew Robett, Emma Wright, Nick Worthington, Kate Salvin, Julie Hersum, Steph Sharp, Kirsten Leach, Darick Robertson, Lachlan McPherson, Barbara Hill, Delia Sang, Ant Sang, Anya Kussler, Mike Johnson, Simon Veksner, Joel Sanders, Aaron Henry, Kirsten Dundas, Jim Thomsen, Steve McCleary, Heather Gioia, Angela Whitehead, James Shaw, Lincoln Jaques, Odette Singleton-Wards, Gary Fleet, Sharon Scott, Marilyn McArthur, Tina Fleet, Tracy Fleet, Rebecca Fleet, Caleb Just, Dion McCracken, Sasha McCracken, T-boon, Vinny Dunn, Alf Vorderman, Karina Seabra Guimaraes, Pam Martin, Foodtown, Levi Salvin, Billy 'owl' McQueen, Hannah McQueen, Chris Hocquard, Mark Raynes, Mackenzie Fleet, and Catherine McGregor.

KARL WILLIAM FLEET has been fascinated by story and the act of storytelling since childhood.

Born in NaeNae, Wellington, he moved to Auckland in his teenage years, where he later attended college and discovered advertising as a career option. Intrigued by the creative process, he completed a bachelor's degree in business marketing, with a major in advertising.

During his advertising career, Karl tapped into his love of storytelling and quickly discovered success. In his first year within the industry, Karl won an opportunity to represent New Zealand at Cannes in the Young Lion's competition. In his second year, he won a rare and highly coveted Gold Pencil award at the One Show. The publication, Campaign Brief, soon named Karl their "Number One Australasian Advertising Creative" for his accomplishment of winning the largest number of international advertising awards between the period of 2008-2009.

While writing ads, Karl also dabbled in writing scripts for short films. One of them, "Signs," found a special place in people's hearts and has been viewed over 10 million times on YouTube.

Karl's love for storytelling even led him down the most unlikely of paths: professional wrestling. As his alter ego, Curt Chaos, he defied the odds and became the New Zealand Heavyweight Champion. He held this prestigious belt for one year and thirteen days—the third longest title run in New Zealand's history.

Karl then had a crazy idea to write about an ultimate "negative protagonist,"

Justin Truth. As the negative protagonist genre is one of the hardest to write, Karl went back to university and earned a master's in creative writing to help build Justin Truth's world. Karl spent the next three years writing, crafting, and editing Corporate Truth, Criminal Truth, and Fractured Truth.

Everything Karl's learned from advertising, wrestling, and earning his master's degree comes together as a creative and unique form of written prose that he calls "binge reading."

He released the first three volumes of the Truth Files at once so readers can binge read to their heart's content.

He hopes you'll enjoy his stories as much as he enjoys creating them.

Lightning Source UK Ltd.
Milton Keynes UK
UKHW040707141118
332315UK00002B/609/P